Anonymous

Proceedings of the Tenth Anniversary of the University Convocation of the State of New York

Anonymous

Proceedings of the Tenth Anniversary of the University Convocation of the State of New York

Reprint of the original, first published in 1874.

1st Edition 2024 | ISBN: 978-3-36885-113-2

Verlag (Publisher): Outlook Verlag GmbH, Zeilweg 44, 60439 Frankfurt, Deutschland
Vertretungsberechtigt (Authorized to represent): E. Roepke, Zeilweg 44, 60439 Frankfurt, Deutschland
Druck (Print): Books on Demand GmbH, In de Tarpen 42, 22848 Norderstedt, Deutschland

PROCEEDINGS

OF THE

TENTH ANNIVERSARY

OF THE

UNIVERSITY CONVOCATION

OF THE

STATE OF NEW YORK,

Held July 29th, 30th and 31st, 1873.

———————

ALBANY:

THE ARGUS COMPANY, PRINTERS.

1874.

CONTENTS.

THE UNIVERSITY CONVOCATION

OF THE

STATE OF NEW YORK.

I. Sketch of its Origin, Objects and Plan.

[Reprinted from the Proceedings of former years, by direction of the Convocation.]

At a meeting of the Regents of the University, held on the 9th day of January, 1863, the reports of colleges and academies, and their mutual relations, being under consideration, the following resolution was unanimously adopted :

Resolved, That it is expedient to hold annually, under the direction of this Board, a meeting of officers of colleges and academies, and that a committee be appointed to draft a programme of business for the proposed meeting, to fix the time and place, and to make such other arrangements as they may deem necessary.

The committee of arrangements on the part of the Regents were Chancellor Pruyn, Governor Seymour, Mr. Benedict, Mr. Hawley, Mr. Clinton, Mr. Perkins and Secretary Woolworth.

The meeting was held according to appointment, on the 4th and 5th days of August, 1863. Chancellor Pruyn briefly stated the objects entertained by the Regents, which were mainly " to consider the mutual relations of colleges and academies, and to promote, as largely as possible, the cause of liberal education in our State. While it is a part of the duty of the Regents of the University to visit the fourteen* literary colleges and more than two hundred academies subject to their supervision, it is obvious that this cannot be done as frequently as desirable, and that some such method as is now proposed, whereby teachers may compare views with each other and with the Regents, and discuss methods of instruction and general modes of procedure, is alike practicable and necessary.

"A law enacted more than three-fourths of a century ago was cited, by which the University was organized and clothed with powers similar to those held by the Universities of Cambridge and Oxford, in England. The University of the State of New York, though gene-

---

* Now twenty-three (1878).

rally regarded as a legal fiction, is, in truth, a grand reality. The numerous institutions of which it is composed are not, indeed, as in England, crowded into a single city, but are scattered, for popular convenience, over the entire State. It is hoped that the present meeting will more fully develop this fact, in accordance with which the officers of colleges and academies now convened are cordially welcomed as members of a great State University. It is also confidently expected that the deliberations now inaugurated will result in the more intimate alliance and coöperation of the various institutions holding chartered rights under the Regents of the University."

The Chancellor and Secretary of the Regents were, on motion, duly elected presiding and recording officers of the meeting. A committee, subsequently made permanent for the year and designated as the executive committee, was appointed by the Chancellor to prepare and report an order of proceedings. Among other recommendations of the committee, the following were submitted and unanimously adopted :

The Regents of the University of this State have called the present meeting of the officers of the colleges and academies subject to their visitation, for the purpose of mutual consultation respecting the cause of education, especially in the higher departments. It becomes a question of interest whether this convention shall assume a permanent form and meet at stated intervals, either annually, biennially or triennially. In the opinion of the committee it seems eminently desirable that the Regents and the instructors in the colleges and academies should thus meet, with reference to the attainment of the following objects :

1st. To secure a better acquaintance, among those engaged in these departments of instruction, with each other and with the Regents.

2d. To secure an interchange of opinions on the best methods of instruction in both colleges and academies ; and, as a consequence,

3d. To advance the standard of education throughout the State.

4th. To adopt such common rules as may seem best fitted to promote the harmonious workings of the State system of education.

5th. To consult and coöperate with the Regents in devising and executing such plans of education as the advanced state of the population may demand.

6th. To exert a direct influence upon the people and the Legislature of the State, personally and through the press, so as to secure such an appreciation of a thorough system of education, together with such pecuniary aid and legislative enactments, as will place the institutions here represented in a position worthy of the population and resources of the State.

And for the attainment of these objects the committee recommend the adoption of the following resolutions :

Resolved, That this meeting of officers of colleges and academies be hereafter known and designated as " The University Convocation of the State of New York."

Resolved, That the members of this Convocation shall embrace,

1. The members of the Board of Regents.

2. All instructors in colleges, normal schools, academies and higher departments of public schools that are subject to the visitation of the Regents, and (by amendment of 1868) the trustees of all such institutions.

3. The president, first vice-president and the recording and corresponding secretaries of the New York State Teachers' Association.

Resolved, That the Chancellor and Secretary of the Board of Regents shall act severally as the presiding officer and permanent secretary of the Convocation.

Resolved, That the meeting of this Convocation shall be held annually, in the city of Albany, on the first Tuesday of August [see *amendment*], at ten o'clock A. M., unless otherwise appointed by the Board of Regents. [*Amended*, in 1873, as to the time of meeting, by making it the first Tuesday after the Fourth of July, except when the Fourth occurs on Monday, in which case it shall be the second Tuesday thereafter.]

Resolved, That at each annual Convocation the Chancellor shall announce the appointment, by the Regents, of an executive committee of seven members, who shall meet during the recess of the Convocation at such time and place as the Regents may direct, with authority to transact business connected with its general object.

At the fourth anniversary, held August 6th, 7th and 8th, 1867, it was

Resolved, That the Regents be requested to invite the attendance of representatives of colleges of other States at future anniversaries of the Convocation.

At the fifth anniversary, held August 4th, 5th and 6th, 1868, the following resolutions were unanimously adopted :

Resolved, That there be appointed by the Chancellor, at each annual meeting, a committee of necrology, to consist of three persons.

Resolved, That it shall be the duty of each member of the Convocation to notify the chairman of the committee of necrology of the decease of members occurring in their immediate neighborhood or circle of acquaintance, as an assistance to the preparation of their report.

Resolved, That the secretary publish, with the report of each year's proceedings, the original resolutions of 1863, as they are or may be from time to time amended, together with the two foregoing, as a means of better informing the members of the Convocation in regard to its nature, and the purposes of its organization.

II. Minutes of the Tenth Anniversary, July 29, 30, and 31, 1873.

The sessions of the tenth anniversary of the University Convocation of the State of New York were held at the Capitol, in the city of Albany, beginning on Tuesday, July 29th, 1873, at 10 o'clock A. M., and ending on Thursday, July 31st, at 1:30 P. M.

Chancellor Pruyn, as President *ex officio*, called the Convocation to order, and the Rev. Dr. Wilson, of Cornell University, said the Lord's Prayer, after which the Chancellor addressed the Convocation as follows:

Gentlemen of the Convocation.—Every year brings its matters of interest, and in that which has passed since we last met, several events of importance have occurred in our educational history, to some of which your attention may be directed during our session.

Death too has been busy, and friends who belonged to our number are no longer here. The Great Teacher has called them, and they have gone to their reward.

The brief duration of our session, the papers announced to be read and discussed, and, I may add, the usage of the past, admonish me to say but little beyond those words of welcome which the occasion appropriately calls for as introductory to our labors. Those labors in the past, presented to a great extent in the annual publication of our proceedings for ten years, have given to the world many papers of great interest and importance, some of which, I am sure you will justify me in saying, rank among the ablest contributions to the educational annals of our country. If nothing more has been accomplished by our organization, these will carry its history to the future with the grateful acknowledgments of many thoughtful minds.

The world is full of duty and labor, and much as we have already done, very much more remains before us. That our meeting may witness duty well discharged is, I am sure, our earnest wish.

In the name of the Regents of the University, I heartily welcome your presence, and trust that the result of this session may advance the cause of sound learning in our State.

The Executive Committee appointed at the last Convocation, and having in charge, in connection with the officers of the Board of Regents, the arrangements for this anniversary, consisted of the following persons:

Professor William D. Wilson, D. D., LL. D., L. H. D., Cornell University.

Professor Cornelius M. O'Leary, A. M., M. D., Ph. D., Manhattan College.

Professor Henry L. Harter, A. M., Potsdam Normal and Training School.

Principal Erastus F. Bullard, A. M., Keeseville Union School.

Principal John C. Gallup, A. M., Clinton Grammar School, Female Department (Houghton Seminary).

Principal Abraham Mattice, A. M., Hudson Academy.

Principal Alexander J. Robb, A. M., Waterford Union School.

The Chairman of the Executive Committee, Dr. Wilson, reported the following order of exercises for the first day, which was approved by the Convocation:

ORDER OF EXERCISES.

Sessions (except the first), 9 A. M. to 1:30 P. M.; 3 to 5:30 P. M.; 7:30 P. M.

Tuesday, July 29.

10:00 A. M.—Opening of the Convocation, and Report of the Executive Committee.

11:00 A. M.—The Relations of Christian Educators to the Scientific Problems of the present day—Professor Daniel S. Martin, A. M., Rutgers Female College.

12:00 M.—A Duty of Academies—Principal Elisha Curtiss, A. M., Sodus Academy.

1:00 P. M.—Miscellaneous Business.

1:30 P. M.—Recess.

3:30 P. M.—Differentials and the method of finding them—Professor William D. Wilson, D. D., LL. D., L. H. D., Cornell University.

4:15 P. M.—Influence of John Stuart Mill on Modern Education—Professor Cornelius M. O'Leary, A. M., M. D., Ph. D., Manhattan College.

5:15 P. M.—Miscellaneous Business.

5:30 P. M.—Recess.

8:00 P. M.—Principles and Methods of Education—Professor (elect) Joseph R. Buchanan, M. D., Eclectic Medical College.

8:45 P. M.—The Science of International Law, with reference to Peace Arbitration—Rev. James B. Miles, D. D., Secretary of International Code Committee and of American Peace Society, Boston, Mass.

Members are requested to register their names on the Secretary's book as early as practicable.

The rule limiting all papers to thirty minutes will be strictly enforced, except when more time is allowed on the recommendation of the Executive Committee, the same to be announced before the reading of the paper. Remarks on any paper will be limited to five minutes for each speaker.

Each paper presented is to be considered as belonging to the Proceedings of the Convocation, and should be left with the Secretary, together with a brief abstract thereof for insertion in the newspaper reports. Each person taking part in the discussion of any subject is also expected to furnish, at the earliest practicable moment, a copy or abstract of his own remarks.*

---

* The abstracts furnished under this rule are entered upon these minutes, to which most of the papers in full are appended.

In accordance with the foregoing order of exercises, Professor Daniel S. Martin, A. M., of the Department of Geology and Natural History in Rutgers Female College, read a paper on " The Relations of Christian Educators to the Scientific Problems of the present day " (Regent Goodwin in the chair).

Professor Martin began by referring to the twofold character of the development of the modern age, which we are wont to express by the term Christian civilization, the material and intellectual progress of mankind, guided by the principles of the Gospel. But, instead of the mutual harmony and sympathy between those two great agencies of human improvement which we would naturally expect, there has been and still is a great deal of suspicion, jealousy and even conflict.

This evil he proposed to trace to some of its causes, and then to suggest some ways in which Christian educators in particular may help to remedy it in the future. In the first place, he based the whole discussion on the fundamental position of faith in the Christian Scriptures, as the divine revelation of God and His Son. He had no wish to discuss this or any other question from any different stand-point. Here, of course, we encounter the first ground of contest, in the atheistic position assumed by some scientific men, and in the unfriendly attitude of many others who do not avow distinctly atheistic views. Then, too, there is a large class of men, with no skill or repute at all in science, who use its name for the purpose merely of opposing religious and Christian truths, and who, as lecturers, periodical and newspaper writers, etc., make a great deal of the irreligious hue and cry for which scientific men are unjustly held responsible.

But the object of this paper is rather to show the position that should be held by Christian men who have influence over the minds of youth ; and therefore it would consider rather the grounds of difficulty that are due to the action of religious writers toward science. Referring first to some minor causes, the paper then spoke strongly of the want of sympathy and interest toward the methods and principles of scientific study, and the want of intercourse with scientific men, that are so frequently seen among religious thinkers. To this kind of non-intercourse much of the trouble is due.

As a result of this, and closely connected with it, is the ignorance, on both sides, of each other's familiar facts and real position. Many scientific writers, absorbed in their own subjects, reason loosely and unphilosophically for want of familiarity with logical principles; and many religious writers display a mournful ignorance on questions of recent scientific discovery. After treating of this subject at some length, Prof. Martin traced it partly to two points in our educational training,—the system of elective studies, and the defective character of our text-books in science.

The elective system tends to cut short general culture in the interest of professional specialties, and thus to make one-sided men in all departments, who will not be able to sympathize with each other's labors and harmonize each other's results. Our text-books in science, too, are all defective, partly through excess of details and scantiness of principles, and partly through the fact that they go for some years unrevised, and so fail to keep up with the rapid advance of science. This fact is largely due to their being stereotyped, which makes it the interest of publishers to keep them in use as long as possible unaltered. He suggested the appointment of a committee of scientific professors to consider this whole subject, in connection with the Board of Regents.

Prof. Martin closed by urging the absolute necessity of separating our physical ideas about creation, gained from Paradise Lost, from the divine and spiritual truths of the Scripture. The image of God in man is in the soul-character, not in the outward frame. These distinctions are fundamental, and Christian educators must labor to impress them on the minds of youth. Religion has lost nothing from the advances of science in the past—Copernican astronomy, the nebular hypothesis, the ages of geology, have only expanded our ideas of the Divine power and wisdom. Why fear now from the Correlation of Forces, or the Development of Species? Let us trust the future of humanity fearlessly to Him who has guided and directed all its past.

Chancellor Pruyn referred in complimentary terms to this paper, and expressed the hope that it would lead clergymen and educators to study more closely their relations to science. He was not able to follow the line of thought as closely as he could have wished, but some of the points struck him as very forcible. He hoped the paper would enjoy a wide circulation, and lead to more enlarged views upon the subject.

Prof. Buchanan remarked that the paper just read suggests to his mind the principal cause of the error among scientists, which had been alluded to. First, the arrogant, defiant, domineering spirit so strong in our Anglo-Saxon race, which we inherit from our barbarian ancestors, through some thousands of years of battle and strife. For this there is no remedy but in a higher moral education. Secondly, and in consequence of this trait of character, the rigid adherence of science to the field of physics, in which man is the dominant master, to the exclusion of the spiritual, in which man must occupy a more humble and docile position.

When the constitution of man, in which the psychic and the physical work together in so intimate connection and co-operation that the study of each is necessary to the comprehension of the other, is studied as a purely physical science; when the scientist in this sphere of investigation approaches the most magnificent sphere of Divine wisdom and power in the operations of the human soul,—a sphere of knowledge fully co-extensive with that of physical science, higher in its sphere and even more important in practical utility,—and as he approaches turns his back upon it, confining himself to physical considerations, he, in so doing, ignores all beyond matter. And thus the leading physiologists of to-day speak of a man as a purely physical being, regarding all the phenomena of the soul as mere *phenomena* of organized matter.

Moreover, we see men as eminent as Prof. Carpenter, president of the British Scientific Association, saying distinctly, that if there is any existence beyond the physiological life of man, science cannot recognize it,—which evidently implies that no such thing exists; for if it exists we must *know* it and it must be a subject of science.

So Prof. Henry, Secretary of the Smithsonian Institution, suggested at the Tyndall banquet, that when we get beyond the sphere of physical science into that of moral nature, we are in a region of Egyptian darkness, where we can but expose our ignorance.

If science thus rigidly fixes itself upon the ground, and refuses to look up, its life must be groveling, downward in its tendencies, saurian, rather than human. Let it steady man's whole nature, soul and body combined,—enlarge and elevate its scope, and cease to adhere to the purely physical.

Principal Wiggin, of Nassau Academy, thought it obvious that there is some opposition existing between the positions of the advanced scientists of the present day and the mass of religious teachings which we receive from the pulpit; but the cause of that opposition has not been pointed out.   The difficulty is not so much that the scientific attainments of the ministers of the Gospel were not respectable when they left the seminary; not that there is any just charge lying against the instruction of theological seminaries in regard to the bearings of science upon revealed religion; but rather in the fact that science advances while many who are in the ministry do not keep up with the times.

The ministry is divided into two classes, the one, men who study from day to day and increase their knowledge by general reading, while others, and this is perhaps much the larger class, allow the condition of scientific knowledge to advance and leave the minister far behind.   This latter class must often be heard alluding to settled principles of science as science " falsely so called."   A similar state of things exists in the medical profession.   Some continue their practice and study, thus keeping up with the advance of medical knowledge; others enter upon the practice, and begin to forget all not brought into frequent practice.

Principal Gallup, of Clinton Grammar School (Houghton Seminary), said that, with relation to this subject, one fact is suggested which is perhaps worthy of a moment's consideration.   In the present condition of very many of the institutions represented here, not a few of the instructors themselves have neither the needed time nor taste for impressing this class of truths upon the minds and characters of their pupils.   But we find great encouragement in the fact that the office of the instructor is every year becoming more highly appreciated, compensation of his labor is increased, and more time is allowed for the prosecution of the higher range of thought.   Under the influence of these truths, the spirit of antagonism between the teachers of science and the advocates of religion is becoming less and less apparent, and we hope will soon cease to be the serious hindrance to the progress of truth that it heretofore has been.

Principal Mattice thought there was a good deal of antagonism among clergymen against science, falsely so called, but that they are not opposed to established facts in science, and, as he believes, are often misrepresented in this matter. They are, it is true, a little chary in accepting all the alleged discoveries in science, but they tell the scientists, establish your facts, and we will accept them. The ministry, as a profession, are not opposed to *true* science. It is with science falsely so called that they find fault. True science they are sure harmonizes with, and is a supporter of, the principles of the Christian religion. Take the science of geology. The Christian ministry are not prepared to receive as truth to-day what the investigators of science will reject to-morrow. Prof. Martin, in his valuable paper, alluded to the principle involved, when he said, in effect, that the text-books on geology of ten years ago are worthless now. When the assertions of scientific men are demonstrated to be truth, the Christian ministry, as a class, are prepared to receive them. As to theological seminaries teaching scientific subjects, he thought these institutions very properly expect the academies and colleges to do this work.

Rev. Mr. James, of Albany, being present as a listener, asked leave to thank the last speaker for his defense of the clergymen. He knew of no clergymen of the present day who assail science as such. They regret that they have not more time to study the truths of science. They are, however, opposed to the pretenders in science, who send forth their crude dogmas broadcast. He expressed his pleasure at hearing the sentiments advanced in Prof. Martin's paper.

A communication was read from Prof. Hough, inviting the members of the Convocation to visit the Dudley Observatory, which was accepted with thanks.

Principal Elisha Curtiss, of Sodus Academy, read a paper entitled "A Duty of Academies" (Regent Rankin in the chair). He made a number of suggestions in reference to the proper course of study to be followed in the academies, and urged that the influence and mission of these institutions can be materially extended. It should be their aim to educate common-school teachers, fit young men for business life, and prepare others for college.

He thought common-school teachers could be as well prepared at academies as at any other class of schools, and he argued that it is the interest of the State to encourage the education of teachers at these institutions. It is the duty of the academies, therefore, to display a greater interest in the common schools. The appropriation made by the last Legislature places the principals of the academies under renewed obligations, and it should be their aim to keep up a teachers' class during the entire year. He suggested that the State Superintendent ought to aid the teachers' classes in academies. They now educate three-fourths of the common-school teachers, and will continue to educate about this number. If the academies educate a class gratis, the Superintendent ought to encourage the class by giving a certificate to at least the best one. Every branch taught in common schools can be taught in a model manner to the teachers' class, and the instruction will be cheaper than can be obtained elsewhere.

Secretary Woolworth thought it not possible for the normal schools to furnish the education required by the common-school teachers in the rural districts of the State, in the majority of which only small salaries are paid. It is natural that such teachers seek their education in institutions near them, where the expense is less. It is incumbent upon the academies, therefore, to keep the peculiar needs of this class in view. He trusted, however, to hear a full expression of opinion upon this subject.

Principal Flack said he had been accused of magnifying the academy interests, but he believed he was warranted in so doing. The great need of the State is teachers, and all the normal schools and academies are wanted for this work. He insisted, however, that the academies must educate the teachers and raise the standard of education. Too much cannot be said upon the subject, and he thought a committee ought to be appointed to ascertain how many of the 28,654 teachers of the State have been educated in the academies. It is stated that 500 of them have been educated in the normal schools. He wanted to ascertain how many of the remaining 28,000 have been educated in the academies. He thought the result would be creditable to the academies, and would have a good effect upon the next Legislature.

Principal Smyth, of the Central New York Conference Seminary, made a few remarks on the same subject. He held that we need not only to instruct the teachers in the ordinary branches taught in the common schools, but that it is necessary to give them a thorough normal training. He believed that the academies were really doing the bulk of the work in turning out teachers for this great State, and he did not believe the money set apart for the aid of the academies would be misappropriated. The normal schools are plainly unequal to the work of providing teachers for this commonwealth, and while he did not underrate their usefulness, he felt that the claims of the academies in this connection should secure at least an equal hearing.

Regent Goodwin thought that if there was to be a comparison instituted between the academies and normal schools, the advantage would be greatly on the side of the academies. If it be true that over 27,000 (or even 7,000) teachers are educated in the academies and institutions other than common schools, a great responsibility rests upon the academies. The question is one of great magnitude, and places the position of these schools in a new light. He was glad the question had come up for discussion to-day, and he hoped it would not be laid aside.

Principal Snook, of Monticello, also dwelt upon the special efficiency of the academies as the educators of common-school teachers. He was willing to start a teachers' class in his academy for one year. He thought we could all do it for the sum appropriated.

Superintendent Beattie, of the Troy High School, said his experience had shown that the best teachers come from the rural districts and the academies. Those who grow up under the special courses—the high-toned courses—grow up as two men, as it were, the wise man and the fool, and very frequently the fool will predominate. There are serious defects in these special schools. He wanted something more comprehensive, something which will call forth the full powers of the man.

He hoped the statistics to be called forth would also show how many men there are on the school boards whose prejudices are bounded by the narrow domain of the church to which they belong; men who have no idea of the great work of education, and who constitute the great discouragement to the progress of our work.

Under the head of Miscellaneous Business, the following resolution, offered by Professor Wilson, was adopted:

Resolved, That a committee of fifteen, five of whom shall be a quorum, and of which Principal Alonzo Flack shall be chairman, be appointed to collect facts and statistics with regard to the relative number of pupils of the Normal Schools, Graded Schools and Academies, and that are not educated in other than common schools, who are engaged in the work of public education in this State.

On the recommendation of the Executive Committee, the time of holding the Convocation in future years was changed from the first Tuesday of August to the first Tuesday after the Fourth of July, except when the Fourth occurs on Monday, in which case the time shall be the second Tuesday thereafter.

Afternoon Session—Three and One-half o'clock.

The Convocation met in the Senate Chamber (on account of the disturbance caused by the delivery of a large amount of coal at the Capitol, outside the Assembly Chamber).

Professor Wm. D. Wilson, D. D., LL. D., L. H. D., submitted a paper entitled "Differentials, and the methods of finding them."

Dr. Wilson began by alluding to some of the metaphysical questions involved in the ordinary explanations of the Calculus.

He defined a differential as a rate of change, and as such necessarily a fraction, with an amount of change for its numerator and some amount of time for its denominator, as, *e. g.*, six miles an hour. A differential, therefore, is not a number; it has, however, either expressed or implied, a co-efficient, which is a number, as $1dx$, $2dx$, xdx, etc.

He then proceeded to show how one may find the differentials of
the various forms and combinations of variables, by reference to
series. In this consists the peculiarity of his theory.

He then discussed the signification of 2x, when used as the differential co-efficient of x square.

He next stated the character of the cases in which it is necessary
to make the unit of rate of increase very small, and closed with some
remarks as to the value of the Calculus as a means of education.

Professor Charles Davies discussed the subject at some length,
complimenting Professor Wilson on the ability of his paper, and
enlarging upon the definition of a differential. He also expressed
the opinion that this theory of differentials applies only to continuous
quantities.

Professor Cornelius M. O'Leary, A. M., M. D., Ph. D., of Manhattan College, read a paper on the "Influence of John Stuart Mill on
Modern Education," which was characterized as in various respects
unfavorable to the cause of sound learning.

Dr. Martin approved the paper of Professor O'Leary as for the
most part both just and discriminating; and yet there were some
points to which exception might be taken. If he heard correctly, the
paper had spoken of Mr. Mill as deriving his habits of speculation
from the study of the Scotch philosophy. To this he could hardly
subscribe. Mr. Mill came forward as an exponent of the positive
philosophy of M. Comte, which he was the first to interpret and even
to introduce to the English mind. A great distinction is to be made
in regard to Mr. Mill's influence. As a logician he has accomplished
some most valuable and beautiful work; but as a metaphysician he
must take a much lower rank. The two departments are indeed so
closely related that it is difficult to discriminate them strongly from
each other. Yet, practically, they are distinct. Mill's merit lies
wholly in the department of logic, and that, not the philosophical
foundation and reason of the science, but the simple coördination of
facts and phenomena. His systematic organization of the different
methods of scientific inquiry is the most complete, comprehensive
and elegant account of scientific processes which science possesses;
but when there is a question of any purely philosophical achievement,
our estimate of Mill must be a very different one. He has systema-
tized nothing, and established nothing. He holds, ever, a weak and
uncertain tone, and falls into inconsistencies and contradiction.

Dr. Martin referred to Professor O'Leary's account of Mill's doctrine of the infinite, and differed in his view of it. The term is itself
ambiguous. It is with us a Germanism not properly naturalized, and
therefore of uncertain meaning and use. It may denote either an
abstraction,—in which case the infinite is truly, as Hamilton called it,
negative,—or it is a concrete term, when viewed in connection with
some content of meaning, and it then becomes a true and positive
element of our knowledge. This distinction is constantly overlooked,

and all discussion of the philosophy of the infinite which disregards it is fallacious and useless.

Recess until eight o'clock P. M.

Professor (elect) Joseph R. Buchanan, M. D., of the Eclectic Medical College, read a paper on "Principles and Methods of Education" (Regent Warner in the chair).

Professor Buchanan's leading idea was that the three great elements of human nature, the intellectual, moral and animal, are equally susceptible of culture and development, and that a complete system of education would make its pupils intelligently wise, refined and virtuous, and not only efficient in business life, but as great as their inherited capacities would permit. The system of moral education, in which he proposes a new system, was not included in his address, nor did he explain his system of practical education. The time allotted was barely sufficient to sketch the mere outline of his system of intellectual education, which is controlled by four fundamental principles:

1. To impart everything, so far as possible, by ocular observation ; to let the pupil see everything that he is to learn, if not in reality, at least in representation, by models, drawings, pictures, etc.

2. To use books as little as possible, and impart all that is not visible, by the voice of the living teacher.

3. To require the pupil to comprehend and reproduce in his own language everything he learns, not only by answering questions, but by giving the substance of each lesson at its close, and by giving at the end of the week a sketch of all he has learned in the week, and when he is familiar with any subject, to lecture upon it, no matter how briefly at first, until he can do so with fluency.

4. To compel him, by the Socratic method of teaching, to understand everything thoroughly and to reason independently, and at length give him subjects of investigation, and require him to prosecute original inquiries.

This method of teaching science is similar to that so successfully followed by Professor Henslow, of England, as described in the Popular Science Monthly for June, 1873, and, in some respects, also to that of the Kindergarten.

Geography and history, orally taught, with maps, drawings, models, engravings, busts, and stereoptic illustrations, he thought could be made as fascinating as novel reading, and his whole scheme of instruction was designed to be so attractive that children could be kept away only by compulsion.

He dwelt very fully upon the superiority of living oral instruction over the dead knowledge of the book, referring to the experience of medical schools, and showed the superior development of character in the pupil when taught orally, and under the influence of harmonious personal relations between pupil and teacher.

Principal L. D. Miller thought the paper ignored the fact of strength derived from hard study, and the duty of learning obedience, instead of following the dictate of mere inclination. Again, the paper suggests that a boy of ten years should know altogether too much for his years. The paper also seems to ignore the distinction between culture and knowledge.

Professor Buchanan explained that his views were really in accordance with those of Principal Miller, and that the seeming omission of the points referred to in the criticism was due only to his fragmentary treatment of the subject as presented.

Rev. James B. Miles, D. D., Secretary of the International Code Committee and of the American Peace Society, addressed the Convocation on the proposed scheme of an International Code for the peaceful settlement of national disputes. A conference for framing such a code is to be held in a few months at Brussels, commencing October 28th, next. This body, for want of a better name, may be called a Congress of Publicists, meeting unofficially, yet composed mainly of such persons as would, by common consent, worthily represent their respective nations. The Geneva Arbitration has exerted a very powerful influence upon European diplomatists, and Dr. Miles, on a recent mission to the leading courts of Europe, found them very favorably disposed to the plan suggested. Dr. Miles further stated that he has strenuously urged the distinguished presiding officer of the Convocation, Chancellor Pruyn, who is a member of the International Code Committee, to consent to act as a member of the "Congress of Publicists," and that he has received some encouragement in this direction. Dr. Miles briefly remarked upon the beneficence of the project, and the encouragement to believe that the nations will soon learn war no more.

Chancellor Pruyn (Superintendent Weaver in the chair) acknowledged the courteous terms in which Dr. Miles had seen fit to mention his name, and expressed his cordial interest in a movement which seems to have been inaugurated under favorable auspices. It was, however, quite uncertain about his being able to participate in the deliberations of the Congress at the time appointed.

The Convocation then adjourned to Wednesday morning, at nine o'clock.

SECOND DAY.

The session was opened, as usual, with prayer, Rev. Father Dealy, of the College of St. Francis Xavier, officiating.

Chancellor Pruyn extended an invitation to the members of the Convocation to meet him at his residence at nine o'clock this evening: The invitation was duly accepted.

The following order of exercises for the day was adopted, on the recommendation of the Executive Committee:

Order of Exercises.

Wednesday, July 30.

9:00 a. m.—Opening of the Convocation, and Report of the Executive Committee (continued).

9:15 a. m.—The Metric System of Weights and Measures. Discussion of majority and minority reports of the Committee on Coins, Weights and Measures, submitted at the last Convocation and laid over for consideration.

> Professor Charles Davies, LL. D., Fishkill-
> on-the-Hudson.......................
> Regent Robert S. Hale, LL. D., Elizabeth- } *Committee.*
> town.............................
> Professor James B. Thomson, LL. D.,
> New York City.....................

9:30 a. m.—The Moral Element in Teaching—Principal Oscar Atwood, A. M., Plattsburgh High School.

10:15 a. m.—The Study of Latin—Professor Abel G. Hopkins, A. M., Hamilton College.

11:00 a. m.—The Æsthetic Element in the Origin and Use of Language—Professor Charles Chauncy Shackford, A. M., Cornell University.

11:45 a. m.—Greek in our Preparatory Schools—Principal Merrill E. Gates, A. M., Albany Academy.

12:15 p. m.—Discussions on subjects connected with the interests of Education in this State, regularly introduced in writing on or before the first day, and approved by the Executive Committee. The committee recommend that the second day, or so much thereof as may be needed, be devoted to such discussions. Report of President Allen.

12:30 p. m.—Teachers' Scientific Institute—President Jonathan Allen, A. M., Alfred University.

1:15 p. m.—Miscellaneous Business.

1:30 p. m.—Recess.

3:00 p. m.—Art Beginnings—Professor Charles Frederick Hartt, A. M., Cornell University.

4:00 P. M.—The Instruction of Common-School Teachers—Principal Levi D. Miller, A. M., Haverling Union School, Bath.

4:45 P. M.—Influence of an Elementary Instruction in Latin upon the Study of English in Schools—Professor Charles J. Hinkel, Ph. D., Vassar College.

5:25 P. M.—Miscellaneous Business.

5:30 P. M.—Recess.

7:45 P. M.—Of Speculations in Metaphysics—Principal Aaron White, A. M., Canastota Union School.

8:30 P. M.—University Necrology:

Regent John A. Griswold, Troy...........⎫
Chancellor Isaac Ferris, D. D., LL. D., University of City of New York............ ⎬ *Deceased.*
Professor John Torrey, LL. D., Columbia College.......................
Professor Charles W. Cleveland, C. E., Cornell University....................... ⎭

Secretary Samuel B. Woolworth, LL. D., Albany ....⎫
Professor Edward North, L. H. D., Hamilton College .... ⎬ *Committee.*
Professor Daniel S. Martin, A. M., Rutgers Female College .... ⎭

9:00 P. M.—Adjournment, to meet at Chancellor Pruyn's residence, pursuant to invitation.

An invitation to the Convocation to attend the National Teachers' Association at Elmira, next week, was received by telegram from President B. G. Northrop, which was accepted with thanks.

Professor Charles Davies, LL. D., as Chairman of the Committee on Coins, Weights and Measures, made the following report:

The Committee on Coins, Weights and Measures regretted that the want of time prevented the Convocation, at its last session, from acting finally on their supplementary report.

At the session of 1870, the Committee made a full report, which was adopted unanimously by the Convocation; and, although the subject has been much discussed since, there is no evidence that the opinions of the Convocation have been essentially changed.

The Committee, however, is unwilling to ask for a vote of the Convocation in the absence of President Barnard, who is now in Europe, attending the exhibition at Vienna. They feel, however, that the subject, having been before the Convocation for seven consecutive sessions, should now be finally disposed of; hence, they recommend the adoption of the following resolution:

Resolved, That the supplementary report of the Committee on Coins, Weights and Measures, together with the report of the minority, made at the last meeting of this Convocation, be and the same are hereby indefinitely postponed.

The report and resolution were unanimously adopted.

Some discussion followed with reference to an essay upon a new system of coins, weights and measures, submitted by a Mr. Mann, of New York, who is not a member of the Convocation, but no action was taken.

Principal Oscar Atwood, A. M., of the Plattsburgh High School, read a paper on "The Moral Element in Teaching" (Regent Lewis in the chair).

The following is a brief abstract:

Mere intellectual discipline is inadequate to the demands of society. There is something of more importance in the character of every man than the mere amount of knowledge he may possess. What a man does or is inclined to do is of far greater consequence than what he *can* do. Intellect alone never gave society the assurance of a valuable or even a safe citizen. What are our schools doing for the development of the hearts of the children? In all education it may be assumed that that culture which exercises a moulding and formative influence over the affections, the aims, the habits, the motives, must occupy the foremost attention.

Mr. Atwood considered the relation which the teacher holds to the other moral and religious instrumentalities employed for the moral culture of the young.

The recognition of the moral position and responsibility of the teacher is substantially the recognition that culture in its highest sense is for the man, not as an intellectual being simply, but as an immortal soul. Physical, mental and moral culture act as co-working, mutually dependent forces for the elevation of mankind. Religion without education soon sinks to superstition, and education without religion soon loses its impelling motive and its guiding law.

In the organic relation of society, let each agency do its proper work. Let not the school attempt the work of the church nor the church the work of the school, yet let both act in view of the highest development of the youth committed to their charge. There should be not so much the formal religious instruction by an enforced reading of the Scriptures on the part of an unwilling teacher and indifferent pupil, as the calm, steady, powerful example of true, manly, religious character on the part of the teacher—such a character as befits a man aware of his trusts and earnestly alive to his work. The teacher stands, as it were, between the family and the church. He has thus in his keeping the formation of some of the habits most important to the success and happiness of the future man and woman. But beyond these more general habits of life, the general tone of thought, the methods of judging on all the more important questions of life and duty, the language employed, the social habits, the courtesies and graces of life, all these have, in no small degree, been committed to the teacher. If his pupils love him, he stands their ideal of a heroic nature. Long after his lessons are forgotten, he remains in memory a teaching power.

Mr. Atwood closed by urging his fellow-teachers to enter into a full conception of their work, as a part of the great plan which God is carrying forward in order to the complete realization of all the possible excellencies of our humanity.

Professor D. S. Martin thought much more attention is given to extending the departments of our educational institutions than to caring for the moral aspects of the work. In former times, when the schools labored under greater difficulties, the hearts of the teachers were bound up in their work to a greater degree. Prosperity is apt to lead men to partially forget their moral responsibility. This he regarded as an evil to be specially guarded against.

Regent Goodwin spoke of the importance of moral training in our schools, and referred to the tone and sentiment of the paper as in the highest degree praiseworthy.

President S. G. Brown said it occurred to him that in the great enlargement of our educational institutions we are unquestionably losing sight of the moral element, which should not be neglected in any department of education.

Principal Smyth felt that he ought not to let the occasion pass without adding his strong indorsement of the paper just read. Leaving out the religious question, he thought the moral element ought to lie at the very foundation of our educational system. It should be specially attended to in the common schools, as well as in the academies and colleges; and he believed that what this country needs more than anything else at the present day is intelligence and high moral principle.

Vice-Chancellor Benedict said he had long felt that a text-book, inculcating the principles of morality, is a necessity in the schools.

Professor Abel G. Hopkins, A. M., of Hamilton College, read a paper on "The Study of Latin." The speaker took up the subject in a practical light, and considered it in relation to its general aids and advantages. He showed, *first*, its effect upon the character and standing of the educated man. The testimony of great men is in favor of the study of Latin. Rufus Choate and Robert Hall leave on record their indorsement of its value. The speaker also enlarged upon the importance of this subject as related to a proper appreciation of our own literature. A *second* advantage was shown in its relations to practical life. It is here that objections are so often raised against the study of Latin. The speaker endeavored to show that the powers of mind developed by the study of Latin are exactly such as are in constant demand in active life. He also showed that the lawyer, the physician, and the scientist must understand Latin in order properly to preserve the study of their own professions. In closing the essay, he remarked upon the value of Latin as shown in its intimate relations to several of the modern languages of Europe. By simple illustrations from the French and Spanish, he showed that these are but children of the Latin, and that a knowledge of the ancient language gives an easy mastery of the kindred modern tongues.

Professor Wilson, in discussing the paper, said he deemed the study of Latin of great importance in developing the mind. It was a language peculiarly adapted to the youthful period of the world, when it was in use, when words were really made to stand for things. Now we are, as it were, far advanced from childhood to manhood, and language is made to express finer shades of meaning. For this reason, especially, the Latin is particularly well suited to lay the foundation of knowledge in the youthful mind. He was, therefore, an enthusiastic champion of the Latin as a study for youth.

Principal Frost, of Amenia Seminary, said that when the Regents' Academic Examination was first instituted, he had charge of a class in preparation for college. Some of them had never studied English grammar, and none of them had studied it since early boyhood; and yet this class passed the best examination. This was partly because they were better students generally, but, principally, because they turned their knowledge of Latin grammar to the benefit of the English, with no other preparation than two or three meetings, where special terms used in English grammar were explained.

He claimed that a dead language, from that very fact, is better than a living one for the study and teaching of grammar as a system; that the dissatisfaction with and deficiencies in English text-books are owing to this fact, and that the Latin, from its history and experience, is the best of all for grammar uses.

Principal Wiggin remarked that if it was his desire to fit a scholar for the Regents' examination, in the shortest possible time, he would have him study Latin. Nothing else develops the powers of the mind so rapidly.

Professor Cavert said he thought Dr. Wilson mistaken if he thinks the opposition to the study of classics is waning. Public discussion only of the matter has flagged. The opposition is as active as ever. He indorsed fully the value of Latin as a study; but wished to dissent from the proposition that Latin, as such, or that the study of Latin grammar, is of much advantage in the study of English grammar. Grammar grows out of language, and it is because in the study of Latin the pupil has acquired some knowledge of his own language that he the more readily apprehends its grammar. The difficulty that we meet in teaching English grammar arises from teaching our pupils the grammar before we have given them a proper knowledge of the language out of which the grammar grows, and on which it is founded.

Dr. Clarke, of Canandaigua, said: We doubtless could more of us give instances like those alluded to, showing the great value of a knowledge of the Latin in all its scholarly pursuits; but I do not rise to discuss the main topic of this paper, but to allude to one expression in it: " citizenship in the commonwealth of letters." There is, sir, such a citizenship, with its pleasures, its high enjoyments, its duties and its terms of admission. Our language to the great mass of persons is a collection of words conveying in their arrangement some plain idea intended, but to a scholar who has studied the origin and history of the words, as he has gathered them from their original tongue, they not only give the main idea, but each one of them has in itself a wonderful and beautiful history. Now, I do not think it possible for any one to comprehend our language thoroughly without the aids furnished by the original language from which it is drawn.

I hold before you a string of beautiful pearls, from the size of the Kohinoor to the smallest used by glaziers to cut glass; you pronounce them beautiful, and are delighted with them as objects of beauty; but a few of you know the history of these gems—a history running through a period of two thousand years, and involving the history of several of the nations of the earth, and more know something of the great process by which these gems are produced. How differently do those regard these gems! Again, a stranger comes into this assembly; he finds it composed of good-looking men and beautiful women; but he has seen many such bodies, and he has no special interest in it. But point out to him in the assembly the Nestor of American mathematics, the presidents of our leading colleges and other eminent educators of the age, and at once the assembly becomes to him historical, and he regards it with an interest at once new and delightful. So with our language; to one it is but an arrangement of words to convey some idea; to another it is all that and more, for it is an arrangement of gems, each of which has a beautiful and interesting history. An intelligent Christian citizen is the highest result of our Christian civilization. So a noble citizen in this commonwealth of letters is the highest result of the best educational system of any country.

Professor C. C. Shackford, of Cornell University, read a paper on "The Æsthetic Element in the Origin and Use of Language." The following is an abstract:

Language is a work of art rather than an invention. The expression of thought is spontaneous and internal, and not wholly externally induced. It is not a construction of the practical and designing intellect, so much as a work of art, both in its origin and use. It bears all the features of a work of art. It is: 1. An embodiment in material sound of the unseen. 2. An embodiment in sounds which please the ear. 3. It lets us harmoniously into the mysteries of nature. 4. It is not the direct product of pure, scientific thought; but is imaginative, fanciful, sensuous. 5. It is not purely imitative. 6. It is an embodiment of man's ideas of himself and of the universe. The creative element does not operate now in root-making, but in the change, arrangement and modification of words and sentences. The great principle that presides over the struggle for life is æsthetic. The root-makers were poets, and their works were essentially products of art. Their work was genuine play, a free and joyous activity. The sounds were symbols, and the symbolic is the first development of art in other spheres. This creative faculty is still at work, and language is continually making. Changes go on in obedience to principles of euphony, association, accent, metaphor, and in all this the æsthetic element is the most prominent. Language is to be interpreted and understood like a work of art and not a mathematical formula. If this were recognized, it would save many useless disputes. If you wish to see a picture you must get just the right light and distance. So it is with understanding language. The æsthetic element pervades every part of its constitution and all its highest uses.

Principal Merrill E. Gates, A. M., of Albany Academy, read a paper on "Greek in our Preparatory Schools" (Vice-Chancellor Benedict in the chair).

Secretary Woolworth cordially indorsed Prof. Gates' paper, and said he had observed in his own experience the advantages of the course of instruction adopted by Mr. Gates. He could vouch, therefore, for the fact that the paper was no fancy sketch.

President Brown thought that the subjects embraced in the last three papers had been most admirably presented. The practical importance of the study of ancient language had been made deservedly prominent, as also the æsthetic features of the study, and in the last paper we had the benefit of actual experience. One point he thought had been brought out with great clearness, and that is the harmony of knowledge. There is plainly a unity of interest in all the departments of learning.

President Jonathan Allen, A. M., of Alfred University, made a report in behalf of the Committee on subjects connected with the interests of education in this State. The committee made a number of recommendations, among which are important modifications in the Regents' examination, the establishment of teachers' departments in the academies similar to those in the normal schools, the introduction of more effective apparatus in the academies to enable them to keep pace with the discoveries in science, and the acquisition of geological cabinets. Several suggestions were made with the view of increasing the efficiency of the academies and common schools, and the committee closed their report with the following resolutions:

1. *Resolved,* By the University Convocation, that in the continuance of the appropriation for academies and academic departments of union schools, by the Legislature of the State, and in the passage by the Legislature of the supplementary act, which enlarges the scope and the usefulness of academic normal classes, and which requires the academies to respond to the bounty of the State by furnishing free tuition in higher studies, and by admitting pupils from the common schools to the Regents' examinations, and, when successful in such examinations, to a participation in that free higher tuition, we gratefully recognize the reaffirmed policy of the State, permanently to care

for and cherish this important class of our educational institutions, whose prosperity stands vitally related to that of both the common schools to which they are a needed supplement, and the colleges which they supply with students.

2. *Resolved*, That the Regents of the University be requested to establish a second and higher examination, which shall require studies equal in amount to those fixed by this Convocation, in the action of 1866, as the basis for entrance to college.

3. *Resolved*, That the Regents be requested to secure the establishment, on some proper basis, of a permanent teachers' department in those of the academies and union schools whose patronage from students preparing for teachers will warrant it, with such a course of study and methods of training as are demanded for professional teaching.

The first resolution was discussed briefly by Chancellor Pruyn, Principal King and Secretary Woolworth, and was adopted.

After a long discussion, in which Chancellor Pruyn, President Allen, Secretary Woolworth, Principal Flack, Dr. McNaughton, Prof. Wilson, Principal King, Prof. Cavert, Prof. White and others took part, the second resolution was adopted.

The third resolution was laid over for further consideration.

President Allen also read a paper on a Teachers' Scientific Institute, referring to the plans which have been submitted for the inauguration of such an aid to the scientific culture of teachers, warmly advocating the establishing such an institution, and enumerating the salient features which should distinguish it. He urged that the State possesses ample facilities for such a school, and should lose no time in establishing it. He closed by offering the following resolutions:

1. *Resolved*, That the Regents be solicited to carry into effect the exchange of collections, through the medium of the State Museum of Natural History, assisted by the various institutions, according to the recommendations made in the report of the committee to this body, at the session of 1871.

2. *Resolved*, That the Regents of the University be requested to take such measures as may be necessary to secure the establishment of a scientific institute, under the charge of the Regents and the director of the museum, with the special object of giving the scientific teachers of the State a better and more practical knowledge of those branches of science which the geological survey of the State has been engaged in developing; this institute to be inaugurated, if found practicable, at the next meeting of this Convocation.

Chancellor Pruyn called attention to certain inherent difficulties in the way of using the State Cabinet for this purpose, and to the doubt as to what might be the action of the Legislature in regard to it. Appropriations have heretofore been obtained for it with great difficulty, owing to the antagonism which is felt against it as a State institution. He claimed that the matter rests entirely with the academies themselves. He warmly approved of the project, but it was necessary that the principals and trustees should place the matter properly before their representatives.

The hour for recess having arrived, the resolutions on this subject offered by President Allen were laid over for consideration.

Regent Warner offered the following resolutions, which were adopted :

Resolved, That this Convocation tender to Rev. Dr. Miles, of Massachusetts, their earnest sympathy and approval of his efforts, and those of many other philanthropists, for the establishment of an international code of laws looking to the preservation of peace among the great Christian nations of the earth. We heartily thank him for his able address delivered on that subject before this body.

Resolved, That it would gratify this Convocation to be represented at the meeting for consultation on this subject, to be held at Brussels in October next, and that it is our earnest wish that the Hon. John V. L. Pruyn, the Chancellor of the University, who is one of the International Code Committee of this country, attend the proposed Conference.

Recess until three o'clock P. M.

AFTERNOON SESSION—THREE O'CLOCK.

Professor Charles Frederick Hartt, A. M., of Cornell University, read a paper on the subject of "Art Beginnings." He stated that certain abstract art forms, such as frets and meanders, and the ornament known as the Vitruvian scroll, are found the world over, having often doubtless had an independent origin. Prof. Hartt described several ornamental borders from the pottery of the Island of Marajo, Brazil, which are identical with Etruscan forms. This correspondence is the result of the attempt to please the eye by abstract lines. From the constitution of the eye and the inability to see more than one point of an object distinctly at a time, it is necessary to "run the eye over" an object or a line in order to get its full effect. In this way the various parts of the image of the object are brought upon the area of distinct vision. This necessitates the use of the muscles of the eye. Prof. Hartt is inclined to the belief that the pleasure we derive from looking at a straight line results from the perfectly even use of the muscles of the eye in looking over it. While the "running of the eye over" a curve line requires a more complicated use of the muscles of the eye, this gives us greater pleasure, and the more subtle the curvation of the line, the more pleasure it gives us.

In the history of art, straight lines and their combinations were used before curves, and closely coiled spirals and circles before more subtle curves, which shows that the appreciation of the æsthetic effect of lines comes through training.

Prof. Hartt then described the various successive steps taken to the formation of the Greek fret, and showed how this passed by the rounding down of the angles into the Vitruvian scroll. He then pointed out certain accessory ornaments that grew up, in the endeavor to make the Vitruvian border more agreeable by filling in the blank spaces, and he showed how, step by step, with certain changes in the arrangement of the sigmoid lines of the border, these accessory ornaments grew into the so-called honeysuckle figure and similar Greek ornaments, illustrating at the same time his remarks by referring to the decorations of the cornice and walls of the Assembly room. The honeysuckle border developed into the acanthus border, and by a sort of backward growth into the egg and tongue or egg and dart border.

The result of Professor Hartt's studies would show that decorative art begins and develops by the culture of abstract art forms for the simple pleasure afforded the eye, and that savage nations come to appreciate and imitate the beautiful in nature only after preliminary training in abstract lines.

Owing to want of time to discuss the subject at length, the speaker stated briefly that after long and careful research he was able to show that, the world over, among primitive people, woman was the potter, the spinner, the weaver of baskets and mats and their ornaments. To her must be ascribed the origin of the frets and decorations, borders and ornaments used among the Indians of South America to-day, and it is very probable that the first steps in art in the old world were taken by women. Woman to-day is everywhere a decorator, and she it is who loves to cover everything about her with ornament. The results of Professor Hartt's studies in this new field will be given to the world in a volume now nearly ready for the press.

Principal Levi D. Miller, A. M., Principal elect of Haverling Union School, Bath, then read a paper upon "The Instruction of Common-School Teachers." He said that this is one of the problems now before the educators of the State, which many erroneously suppose has been solved by the establishment and support of the costly normal schools. The speaker disclaimed all intention to throw a slur upon these schools or their managers, for he considered their failure more their misfortune than their fault, since they had undertaken an impossible work.

They seek to make teaching a profession. This, so far as the common schools are concerned, is an impossibility. The speaker stated the essentials of a profession as three: First, Steady employment. Second, Good, or fair, remuneration. Third, The prospect of rising in the world; and showed that common-school teaching includes none of these. Men cannot afford to follow the business; women marry at the first opportunity, and even those graduates of normal schools who do not marry do not enter the common schools, for the wages are too low. The figures given show that although the State has spent $1,000,000 upon these normal schools, they have actually furnished less than two per cent of the whole number of teachers. The speaker thought the reason why normal schools have failed, to be precisely the reason they will continue to fail, namely, the impossibility of their work. He thought it evident to thinking men that the common schools must continue to be taught as they have been taught in the past, not by "professionals," but by young men and women in their transition state—that is, before they settle down in life. These are the only ones who can do this work, not only, but the only ones who ought to do it. It is a part of their education. Upon these young men and women, a third of a century hence, are to rest all the responsibilities of the school system and of society itself. A successful school system needs more than good teachers; it needs good trustees, good superintendents, good supporters; it needs parents who know what teaching is, parents who appreciate something of the teacher's work. These young men and women now teaching are to be fathers and mothers, the trustees, the superintendents, the taxpayers of the next generation, and absolutely need this teaching drill to fit them for their work. The best trustees and best supporters of schools to-day, everywhere, are the old teachers. The speaker thought that those men who would turn out these young men and women who are to have the entire management of the next generation, and would put in their places single women, or old maids, who cannot possibly have any direct interest in the next generation, to be enemies of the school system and of society itself, but congratulated his audience upon the fact that their success is an impossibility.

The true way to prepare teachers for the common schools, the speaker thought, was thoroughly to educate these young men and women to the work in the union schools, academies and teachers' institutes, and in the common schools themselves. The system of teachers' classes in academies and union schools he thought a good one, and failures in the past were more due to an inefficient execution of the plan than to the plan itself. In the first place, the amount of money given for doing the work is so small (only about $15,000 a year, or less than is given to one normal school, to 90 or 100 schools, for instructing 1,500 teachers), that they could not afford to give proper time and attention to it. In the second place, the Board of Regents have been so crippled by want of means that they could not give proper supervision to the work, so that inefficiency has often crept into it. Now, the amount of money paid for this work has been increased fifty per cent, and the Regents should employ an officer, if necessary, to see that the work is well done. The impetus given to academic education by the State, the speaker thought, would greatly increase the number of free academical departments, and give a proportional increase in teachers' classes.

These union schools and academies, from ten to twenty in every county, open to all, accessible to all, each one the center of a circle of district schools, would furnish a continual supply of well-qualified teachers; they will, indeed, send out multitudes of good teachers who never join the teachers' class at all.

The speaker illustrated his idea by a reference to Chautauqua county, in which three union schools, Jamestown, Westfield and Forestville, had, during a single year, at a cost to the State of only $600, sent out 191 actual teachers, while the normal school, situated in the same county, in four or five years, at a cost to the State of $100,000, has graduated a far smaller number. As to quality of teachers the union schools do not shrink from the comparison. In addition to the course of present study, which the speaker said must be insisted upon, he spoke of some other things which every instructor of a teachers' class should fasten in the minds of his pupils ; and

First.—That nothing can supply to the teacher the place of thorough, accurate scholarship. A teacher can easily show others what he sees clearly himself. Clear thinkers are clear reasoners. A poor scholar cannot be a good teacher.

Second.—A definite idea of the teacher's work.

Third.—That he is to do honest, faithful work.

Fourth.—That privileges imply obligations.

Fifth.—That authority means superiority, and that the successful teacher always obeys his own laws.

Admission to the teachers' class, the speaker thought, should be conditioned upon the holding of the Regents' certificate, either actually or provisionally. The paper concluded with a recommendation for a more thorough organization of the district schools by the adoption of a code of procedure, and a uniform system of text-books.

Principal King said that, as to examinations of normal classes, he had experienced no inconvenience from not being able to grant by authority of the State licenses to teach to those deserving them ; for he had been accustomed to secure the presence of a school commissioner from his own or neighboring counties, into whose hands he placed the examination of his normal classes, mainly or entirely. After such examinations the commissioner has given his certificates, good of course within his own commissioner's district, *legally*, and, when countersigned by the principal, these certificates have served, through *courtesy*, throughout several counties. When, however, they do not so prove, and a re-examination is required by a commissioner, he has never taken it unkindly. He was so anxious to aid the commissioners in elevating the standard of qualifications for common-school teaching that he would not complain of any number of examinations, but rather would be glad to hold up their hands. It had sometimes occurred to him that the power to grant certificates, after a thorough examination, would be an encouragement to academies ; but he would be quite content to forego all that if only a uniform standard of examination for public-school teachers could be established throughout the State, under the superintendent and the commissioners. Certain qualifications are, indeed, required now. So were certain qualifications required years ago, in order to admit academical students to participate in the literature fund : but the printed questions sent us from Albany have made the number of those participating "small by degrees and beautifully less," and to the great benefit of elementary education, in all the academies. A similar test applied to all the common schools of the State must immediately and powerfully tend to elevate the qualifications of the teachers. Whether this result should come from the office of the

Regents or from that of the Department of Public Instruction, he would hail it gladly.

Principal Flack said that he differed from Principal Miller's paper, which said we might get along without normal schools. He considered them good and essential to educate professional teachers, and we should increase rather than diminish their number. We should not appear, as academic teachers, to oppose them. He opposed the proposal of the Regents granting certificates to teach common or graded schools. The commissioners should control that.

Superintendent Packard, of Saratoga Springs, submitted the following resolution, the consideration of which was deferred until the order of unfinished business to-morrow:

Resolved, That it is the duty of the Board of Regents to secure such legislation as shall enable it to become a licensing power to grant certificates or diplomas of such grades as it shall determine, signed by the Chancellor and Secretary of the Board, such certificates or diplomas to be a license to teach in any of the academic institutions or public schools of the State of New York.

Professor Charles J. Hinkel, Ph. D., of Vassar College, read a paper entitled "Influence of an Elementary Instruction in Latin upon the Study of English in Schools."

The object of Professor Hinkel's paper was to show the beneficial influence of the study of Latin in schools, as an aid and supplement to the study of English. After a brief statement of the constituent elements in a course of English, he first pointed out the advantages which even an elementary instruction in Latin exercises not only upon developing the students' faculties of observation, memory, judgment and generalization, and making them good readers, writers and speakers in their mother tongue, but especially upon fostering and confirming in them a habit of thoroughness highly beneficial to their study of English as well as any other subject. He then gave an analysis of a proper method of studying Latin, by which those advantages may be secured in regard to the pronunciation and delivery, and the translation and explanation of the Latin in all its general features and details.

Recess until 7:45 o'clock.

EVENING SESSION.

Principal Aaron White, A. M., of Canastota Union School, read a paper entitled "Of Speculations in Metaphysics," being a review of an argument upon "The Natural Theology of the Doctrine of the Forces," by Prof. Benjamin N. Martin, D. D., L. H. D., of the University of the City of New York, read before the Convocation in 1871. The chief points in Prof. Martin's paper were stated to be three:

First.—That all the physical forces in nature are in fact but one and the same force, or modification of *one force.*

Second.—That, according to established mathematical law, an infinite force is exerted, either by or in connection with every particle or atom of matter.

Third.—That it is astonishing and utterly incredible that an infinite force should be the endowment of a single atom of matter; therefore, force is not a quality or property of matter.

He infers, therefore, that since we know that mind is an origin of force, we must assume that all force, or the one universal force, originates in mind, the one Infinite Mind, and that thus the doctrine of one universal force in nature conducts us to the knowledge of one God. In reviewing this argument, we examine first the proposition that mind is the only origin of force, and bring against it the common judgment and common language of mankind. To say that the motion of any mass or body of matter is caused by the impulse of mind, is to say that it has a mind, that is, it is alive. For example, a boy may toss a ball. The motion of the boy's body indicates life, and the force acting is the force of mind, but the motion of the ball does not indicate any life in it. It falls to the ground; it is dead. There is nothing clearer to all men than the distinction between the living thing and the dead matter. But Prof. Martin's conclusion obliterates this distinction, and is contrary to the general judgment of mankind. The conclusion is not logical; for, although we allow that a certain force belongs to mind, yet we cannot thence infer that there is no other origin of force.

We now consider Prof. Martin's first point, that " all the forces of nature are one." We refer to the maxim of philosophy, that, " Like causes produce like effects," and argue that since the phenomena of nature, caused by force of some kind, are so various, and often contrary one to the other, therefore we must believe that the causes are also diverse. References are then made to different authorities, to show that the doctrine of only " one force in nature," instead of being established as Prof. Martin appears to claim, is regarded as possible by only a few persons, and certain by none.

Next, the mathematical argument is examined, and it is clearly shown that Prof. Martin has made a great mistake; for the principle from which he reasons will give no such conclusion as he claims. Instead of showing that the force of one particle is infinitely great, it shows that the force of a single particle is infinitely small, even at a distance which may be regarded as infinitely small, or naught. The astonishment of Prof. Martin at what he thought a true conclusion ought to have induced him to suspect an error in reasoning.

Thus it is shown that Prof. Martin's argument fails in its most essential points. But still further, we argue that if his positions were true they would prove conclusions very different from those which are arrived at. If that which all men regard as a property of matter is a property of mind only, we might easily infer that all matter is intelligent, that is, alive; that is, that mind is only a property of matter, and can have no separate existence. We thus run at once to Materialism and Pantheism. Prof. Martin would abhor such results. In conclusion, we say let religion stand upon her own proper foundations of Scripture and true science, and let her not be made responsible for the insane and untenable theories of visionary men, though they be called philosophers.

After the reading of Principal White's paper, Chancellor Pruyn called upon Secretary Woolworth to read an extract from the minutes of the Regents of the University, as follows:

At a meeting of the Regents of the University, held on the 29th inst., it was

Resolved, That in consideration of eminent attainments as teachers, the degree of Doctor of Philosophy be conferred, in open session of the Convocation, on Jonathan Allen, A. M., President of Alfred University, and Alonzo Flack, A. M., Principal of Claverack Academy and Hudson River Institute.

Chancellor Pruyn appointed Presidents Brown and Potter to present President Allen, and Principals Clarke and King to present Principal Flack. The degree was then duly conferred by the Chancellor.

Secretary Woolworth further read from the Regents' proceedings, to the effect that the honorary degree of Doctor of Civil Law had been conferred by the Board upon William Beach Lawrence, LL. D., of Newport, R. I.

Chancellor Pruyn stated that he had notified Mr. Lawrence, by telegraph, of this action, and that Mr. Lawrence had replied, expressing his thanks, and regretting that he could not be present in person on this occasion.

University Necrology being the special order for this evening, Secretary Woolworth, as chairman of the committee, remarked:

On each return of our anniversary we find that death has been doing its work. Since our last meeting John A. Griswold, a member of the Board of Regents, has died. He was greatly distinguished as an energetic and successful business man. His integrity was unimpeached and he was universally respected as a patriot and philanthropist.

Prof. Benj. N. Martin then read a sketch of the life and services of the late Chancellor Ferris, and Prof. D. S. Martin of the character of the late Prof. Torrey of New York city. Principal Clarke read a brief tribute to the memory of Caroline Chesbro. The death of Prof. Charles W. Cleveland, of Cornell University, was also noticed.

The Convocation then adjourned to give opportunity to members to repair to Chancellor Pruyn's residence, pursuant to the invitation given this morning.

THIRD DAY.

THURSDAY—NINE O'CLOCK, A. M.

The Convocation met at nine o'clock, Chancellor Pruyn in the chair. Prayer was offered by Rev. Dr. King.

Professor Harter of the Executive Committee, in behalf of the Chairman, who was detained by illness, reported the following Order of Exercises for this closing session, which was agreed to:

ORDER OF EXERCISES.
Thursday, July 31.

9:00 A. M.—Opening of the Convocation, and final Report of the Executive Committee.

9:15 A. M.—Grammar as a Natural Science—Principal Charles T. R. Smith, A. M., Lansingburgh Academy.

10:15 A. M.—On Education—Professor Patrick F. Dealy, S. J., College of St. Francis Xavier.

11:30 A. M.—Unfinished Business—Discussions on subjects connected with the interests of Education in this State, regularly introduced in writing on or before the first day, and approved by the Executive Committee. Teachers' Scientific Institute—President Jonathan Allen, A. M., Alfred University.

12:30 P. M—Honorary Degrees. Discussion of the subject as presented in the papers submitted by Regent Benedict and Warden Fairbairn, printed in the Regents' Report for 1872, pp. 497–510.

1:30 P. M.—Final Adjournment.

The Committee further reported that this programme disposes of all the business that has come before them. Some of the papers named in the circular have not been read in consequence of the absence of those who were to present them.

(Signed,)   W. D. WILSON,
For the Committee.

Chancellor Pruyn thanked the Convocation for the complimentary resolution adopted yesterday relative to himself as a proposed member of the International Peace Congress, to be held at Brussels in October next. The Chancellor remarked that he doubted whether his engagements would permit him to go abroad this year, but if possible he would do so, for the sake of taking part in the deliberations of that important body, as a representative of this Convocation.

Principal Charles T. R. Smith, A. M., of Lansingburgh Academy, read a paper on "Grammar as a Natural Science (Prof. Davies in the chair).

The science of grammar is to be distinguished from the art of composition, the latter to be studied from beginning to end of school life.

The study of English grammar is very useful, and the "ologies" must not be allowed to crowd it out.

Its principal use is not "to teach us to speak and write the English language correctly;" that is the office of composition, which should be begun long before grammar, and continued long after. The object of education is the development of all the powers. Two of the most important of these are those of classification and generalization. They are of the utmost importance in medicine, law, and non-professional life. They may be developed by the study of the natural sciences, but grammar is by far the most available of the sciences for this purpose, and may be called a natural science not only in this respect, but as a subject-matter. It cultivates the same powers as botany, zoology, geology and physics, and, in the lack of time and apparatus so general, is much better for the purpose. Moreover, the incidental knowledge which it gives is more practical for both purposes. The grammar of Latin and Greek is many-fold better than the English.

Technical grammar should not be studied till the power of abstraction is developed, say at about the fourteenth year, and should occupy more time than any other natural science.

In teaching grammar the instructor should keep in mind the particular faculties which the science is adapted to exercise, and should teach synthetically, and avoid applying the methods of mathematics to a natural science.

Dr. Clark, in discussing the paper, said he thought that to the average scholar grammar is the most difficult of studies. There are certain difficulties to be overcome in acquiring the science which are sorely perplexing. He thought that no scholar should be required to study abstract grammar under the age of fourteen.

Principal Wiggin said: In the remarks of the gentleman who preceded me, we have been reminded of the necessity of gaining the attention of those whom we instruct, and, in part, the methods by which he succeeds in gaining such attention. So far as he has given us a hint as to the ground of his success in this respect, it is admirable. Let us proceed to get a further insight into this subject. Much complaint is made against the text-books in grammar, and much against the subject itself. Practically, the subject of grammar, with me, is not difficult.

Principal King was glad to have English grammar appear on the programme. Such had been his difficulty in securing teachers who were both able and willing to make this a specialty, that he had begun to fear that teaching English grammar was about to take its place among "the lost arts." He had sought in vain at three State Normal schools for two years. Of late Dr. Alden had told him he had a lady graduate who could teach English grammar, and he had engaged her on the spot. What the essayist had said of grammar being readily acquired as an art, he agreed with. He knew of a little girl of ten whose acquaintance with the art of speaking correctly our language was such that an inaccuracy in the speech in others positively gave her pain ; and yet she had never looked into a text-book on this subject.

Most pupils are, on the threshold of this study, demoralized by an overestimate of its difficulties. He had sought to disenchant them of their terror, by assuring them, and convincing them as well, that they knew grammar already—as an art—and knew it better than the wisest of foreigners can after six or eight years of hard study. For example, looking at a table of irregular verbs, he sometimes had remarked, "now all of us who are not idiots have learned these verbs in childhood. We know the whole table, except perhaps a half a dozen or so; let us look for such as we have yet to learn;" and so in twenty minutes the long table is mastered.

The great bulk of the text-book is taken up with what is already known as an art. By dwelling on this, habits of inattention are induced, so that when the pupil comes to the special things which he happens not to know as an art, they escape his notice. It is precisely these specialties, these irregularities and idioms, that are to be sought. As, in spelling, the skillful teacher will not dwell on the plainer words, but, seizing upon that word in a column which is likely to be misspelled, gives it again and again to his class, so the skillful teacher of grammar must make his pupils discern readily and easily what is plain and regular, and then they can go on with advantage to master the idioms of our language.

Principal Curtiss said: With reference to this subject, I must confess that teachers advertise what they never perform. One pretends that he can teach the whole science of grammar in a few weeks, and yet incautiously says he has been seeking for a teacher to teach grammar in his school, from the normal schools. He must have a disrespect for his work, and he must be unwilling that any but himself shall dose students in the manner he uses. The truth is, grammar as a science can be learned only by long, laborious study. The teachers can direct and assist, but it takes experience to master words and sentences so that thoughts can be expressed fully, clearly, appropriately in words. If students will write and rewrite sentences often, they may be able to use words grammatically; otherwise they will never be able to do so. All studies should be pursued in proportion to their usefulness. We have use for the principles of the calculus once in a lifetime, for algebra and geometry once a year, but for grammar every time we wish to express a thought. Therefore it should be studied as an art and science every day of our life.

Professor Patrick F. Dealy, S. J., of the College of St. Francis Xavier, read a paper "On Education." Professor Dealy took the ground that a grave mistake is being made in excluding the religious element from an educational system. There is a Christian view of education and there is an un-Christian one. Everywhere throughout the civilized world education is now the battle-field on which the powers of good and evil are engaged in deadly conflict. It is on Christian education that Christian people fix, under God, their main hope for the future, and it is an irreligious education on which infidelity fixes its main hopes for the future, not under God. No education is worth the name which does not provide for the training of youth in religion and morality, as well as the imparting to them scientific or classical or artistic culture.

Professor J. S. Gould thought that such is the composite nature of our population that it would be impossible to beneficially introduce the religious element into the common-school system. The Catholic would not enjoy the idea of his children being made proselytes to Protestantism, and *vice versa.*

Principal Gates said the central thought of the paper last read—the need of some religious element in instruction, the importance of directing the minds of the young to a knowledge of something beyond this life—met a response in every heart. The last speaker has shown why our common schools cannot undertake such instruction. But the principles laid down by Prof. Dealy are fairly before us. As a Convocation, it is our business to consider new theories of education, and, if old theories are advanced, to look at them in the light of history, "to judge them by their fruits." Are the maxims of this paper new? Pardon me, if I quote: "The tutor must be the faithful auxiliary of the priest; when he is not, he fails." "The masses learn too much—they will not remain humble."

I do not care to ask how the gentleman would select from the masses, in this land, the few whom he would choose for the higher education—whether from an aristocracy of wealth or of descent. Leaving that point, sir, have not the maxims I have quoted a familiar sound? As students of history, have we not seen them tested? Are there not three corners of the earth where they have held their ground, until quite recently, against universal progress? It seems to me there are. And these three lands are Italy, Ireland and Spain! Shall we follow their lead?

Dr. James McNaughton said he thought that very much might be done for moral education, if care be taken in the selection of teachers. Those who are known to be "free thinkers," so called, and such as are not of approved morality, being excluded, and only those who are calculated by example, as well as by precept, to benefit those committed to their charge being chosen, great good to those taught would be the result.

Prof. Albert C. Hale, of Rochester, claimed that a religion that is worth anything must be a practical, vital belief, that rules the thoughts and actions of men. Such a religion cannot be taught in our public schools without militating with the beliefs of many who have just as good a claim to the inculcation of their own exclusive creeds. It would force particular religious tenets upon the hearts and consciences of the young, which would be beyond the proper jurisdiction of the State, and would be contrary to the genius and spirit of the Constitution.

Chancellor Pruyn announced the following committees for the ensuing year :

Executive Committee.

Professor Edward North, L. H. D., Hamilton College.

President Eliphalet N. Potter, D. D., Union University.

President Joseph Alden, D. D., LL. D., State Normal School.

Principal Elisha Curtiss, A. M., Sodus Academy.

Principal Aaron White, A. M., Canastota Union School.

Principal Levi D. Miller, A. M., Haverling Union School, Bath.

Principal Merrill E. Gates, A. M., Albany Academy.

On University Necrology.

Secretary Samuel B. Woolworth, LL. D., Albany.

Professor Edward North, L. H. D., Hamilton College.

Professor Daniel S. Martin, A. M., Rutgers Female College.

On Statistics in Regard to Teachers (under Professor Wilson's Resolution).

Principal Alonzo Flack, Ph. D., Claverack Academy.

Principal John E. Bradley, A. M., Albany High School.

Superintendent David Beattie, A. M., Troy High School.

Principal Noah T. Clarke, Ph. D., Canandaigua Academy.

Principal John W. Chandler, A. M., Elizabethtown Union School.

Deputy State Sup't Edward Danforth, A. M., Albany.

Principal Samuel T. Frost, A. M., Amenia Seminary.

Principal Joseph E. King, D. D., Ph. D., Fort Edward Collegiate Institute.

Principal Samuel G. Love, A. M., Jamestown Union School and Collegiate Institute.

Principal Charles D. McLean, A. M., Brockport Normal School.

Principal Levi D. Miller, A. M., Haverling Union School, Bath.

Principal Winfield S. Smyth, A. M., Central N. Y. Conf. Sem'y, Cazenovia.

Principal James M. Sprague, New Berlin Academy.

Principal Albert B. Watkins, A. M., Hungerford Collegiate Institute, Adams.

Principal Charles J. Wright, A. M., Peekskill Academy.

Under the head of Unfinished Business, the Convocation resumed the consideration of the resolution, submitted by President Allen, recommending the establishment of permanent teachers' departments in some of the academies and union schools. After considerable discussion, the resolution was finally, on motion of Principal Snook, laid upon the table.

The resolution recommending the exchange of collections in Natural History, through the medium of the State Museum, being under consideration, on motion of Vice-Chancellor Benedict ten minutes were allowed to Professor Hall, Director of the State Museum of Natural History, and the subject was further discussed by Principal Gates, Regent Lewis and Assistant Secretary Pratt; after which the resolution was adopted.

The resolution looking to the formation of a teachers' scientific institute was also adopted.

On motion of Principal Curtiss, it was

Resolved, That the committee of fifteen, appointed by the Chancellor last year, to consult the Legislature in reference to the increase of the Literature Fund, be continued, and that the Chancellor have power to fill any vacancies therein.

Regent Lewis offered the following resolution, which was adopted:

Resolved, That the Standing Committee of the Regents on the State Museum of Natural History be requested to prepare and report a plan to be presented at the next annual Convocation, by which the State collections shall be more intimately connected with the educational interests of the State.

On motion of Assistant Secretary Pratt, the thanks of the Convocation were presented to the several railroad and steamboat companies which have generously reduced their rates of fare for the benefit of the members in attendance, viz.:

Hudson River Day Line of Steamers; Champlain Transportation Company; Delaware and Hudson Canal Company, Rensselaer and Saratoga and Albany and Susquehanna Railroad Departments; Erie Railway; New York and Oswego Midland Railroad; Utica and Black River Railroad; Lake Ontario Shore Railroad.

The subject of Honorary Degrees was passed by, after brief remarks by Vice-Chancellor Benedict.

At the request of the Chancellor, the Vice-Chancellor took the chair, and made appropriate remarks on the importance of these meetings of the University Convocation, and their growth in interest and value from year to year; after which, he declared the Convocation adjourned, to meet on Tuesday, July 7, 1874; and the benediction was pronounced by Rev. Dr. Goodwin.

REGISTERED MEMBERS OF THE CONVOCATION.

BOARD OF REGENTS.

JOHN V. L. PRUYN, LL. D., *Chancellor of the University* .. Albany.
ERASTUS C. BENEDICT, LL. D., *Vice-Chancellor* ..... New York city.
JOHN C. ROBINSON, *Lieutenant-Governor* .... Binghamton.
ABRAM B. WEAVER, *Superintendent of Public Instruction* .. Albany.
ROBERT G. RANKIN .... Newburgh.
ELIAS W. LEAVENWORTH, LL. D .... ,.... Syracuse.
Rev. WILLIAM H. GOODWIN D. D., LL. D .... Ovid.
JOHN L. LEWIS .... Penn Yan.
HORATIO G. WARNER, LL. D .... Rochester.
JAMES W. BOOTH .... New York city.
SAMUEL B. WOOLWORTH LL. D., *Secretary* .... Albany.
DANIEL J. PRATT, *Assistant Secretary* .... Albany.

COLLEGES, ETC.

Columbia College—Professor Charles Davies, LL. D.

Union University—President E. N. Potter, D. D.; Prof. William Wells.

Hamilton College—President S. G. Brown, D. D., LL. D.; Professors N. W. Goertner, D. D., and A. G. Hopkins.

University of the City of New York—Professor Benj. N. Martin, D. D., L. H. D.

Alfred University—President Jonathan Allen, Ph. D.

Ingham University—Professor Wm. L. Parsons, D. D.

College of St. Francis Xavier—Professor Patrick F. Dealy, S. J.

Vassar College—Professor Charles J. Hinkel, Ph. D.

Manhattan College—Professor Cornelius M. O'Leary, Ph. D.

Cornell University—Professors Wm. D. Wilson, D. D., LL. D., L. H. D.; Chas. Chauncy Shackford, A. M.; Chas. Fred. Hartt, A. M.; John Stanton Gould.

College of the City of New York—Professor Adolph Werner, M. S.

Rutgers Female College—Professor Daniel S. Martin.

Wittenberg College, Ohio—Trustee Irving Magee, D. D., Albany.

Union University, Dudley Observatory Department—Director George W. Hough.

Union University, Medical College Department, Albany, N. Y.—Professors James McNaughton, M. D., and John V. Lansing, M. D.

New York Medical College and Hospital for Women—Trustee Mrs. D. E. Sackett.

Eclectic Medical College—Professor Joseph R. Buchanan, M. D.

State Board of Medical Examiners—John F. Gray, M. D., LL. D., Chairman, New York city; William S. Searle, M. D.; Horace M. Paine, M. D.

State Normal School, Albany—Miss Kate Stoneman.

State Normal and Training School at Potsdam—Trustee E. A. Merritt; Professor Henry L. Harter.

State Normal and Training School at Genesee—President of Local Board, James Wood.

United States International Code Committee—Secretary James B. Miles, D. D., Boston, Mass.

New York State Teachers' Association—Ex-Presidents James B. Thomson, LL. D., and Edward Danforth.

New York State Library—Librarians Henry A. Homes, LL. D.; S. B. Griswold and George R. Howell.

New York State Museum of Natural History—Director James Hall, LL. D.; Entomologist J. A. Lintner.

Institution for Deaf, Dumb and Blind, Flint, Mich.—Professor George L. Brockett.

ACADEMIES, ETC.

Albany Academy—Principal M. E. Gates, Prof. E. H. Satterlee.

Albany Free Academy—Secretary John O. Cole.

Albany Public Schools—No. 2, Principal L. H. Rockwell; No. 14, Principal J. L. Bothwell; No. 15, Principal L. Cass; No. 20, Principal E. H. Torrey.

Albion Academy—Principal T. F. Chapin.

Alfred University (Acad. Dept.)—Principal J. Allen, Ph. D.

Amenia Seminary—Principal S. T. Frost.

Baldwinsville Free Academy—Principal A. E. Lasher.

Canandaigua Academy—Principal N. T. Clarke.

Canastota Union School (Acad. Dept.)—Principal Aaron White.

Canisteo Academy—Principal Ira Sayles.

Castleton Public School—Principal S. H. Wetherwax.

Central New York Conference Seminary—Principal W. S. Smyth.

Chamberlain Institute—Principal J. T. Edwards.

Claverack Academy and H. R. Institute—Principal Alonzo Flack, Ph. D.; Profs. Wm. McAfee and E. D. Coonley.

Clinton Grammar School (Fem. Dept.) or Houghton Seminary—Principal J. C. Gallup.

Cobleskill Union School (Acad. Dept.)—Principal A. G. Kilmer.

Cortland Academy—Trustee Wm. A. Robinson.

Delaware Literary Institute—Vice-Principal J. W. Chase.

East Greenbush Collegiate Institute—Principal I. G. Ogden.

Egberts High School, Cohoes—Principal O. P. Steves.

Elizabethtown Union School (Acad. Dept.)—Principal J. W. Chandler.

Fairport Union School (Acad. Dept.)—Principal J. B. Hudnutt.

Forestville Free Academy—Ex-Principal L. D. Miller.

Fort Edward Collegiate Institute—Principal J. E. King, D. D., Ph. D.

Friendship Academy—Principal P. Miller.

Glen's Falls Academy—Principal J. S. Cooley.

Green Island Union School—Principal G. H. Quay.

Hartwick Seminary—President H. N. Pohlman, D. D.; Principal James Pitcher.

Haverling Union School (Acad. Dept.)—Principal L. D. Miller.

Hillside Seminary, Norwalk, Conn.—W. J. Cumming.

Homer Union School—Trustee Wm. A. Robinson.

Hudson Academy—President John Stanton Gould; Principal A. Mattice; C. Rockefeller.

Hudson Public Schools—No. 1, Principal D. W. Reid; No. 3, Principal W. C. Wilcox.

Hungerford Collegiate Institute—Principal A. B. Watkins; Mrs. H. N. Butterworth.

Ithaca Academy—Ex-Teacher Emily Bailey.

Jamestown Union School and Collegiate Institute—Principal S. G. Love.

Lowville Academy—Principal G. C. Waterman.

Monticello Academy—Principal F. G. Snook.

Morris Union School—Principal C. J. Majory.

Munro Collegiate Institute—Principal T. K. Wright.

Nassau Academy—Principal A. B. Wiggin.

New Berlin Academy—Principal J. M. Sprague.

New York Conference Seminary—Principal Solomon Sias.

Onondaga Academy—Principal O. W. Sturdevant.

Ovid Union School (Acad. Dept.)—Principal C. H. Crawford.

Owego Free Academy—Trustee Wm. Smyth.

Peekskill Academy—Principals C. J. Wright and R. Donald.

Plattsburgh High School—Principal Oscar Atwood.

Pulaski Academy—Principal S. Duffy.

Rondout Public School—Principal C. M. Ryon.

Salamanca Public School—Principal Danl. A. Sackrider.

Saratoga Springs Union School (Acad. Dept.)—Superintendent L. S. Packard.

Schoharie Union School—Trustee J. W. Smith.

Sodus Academy—Principal E. Curtiss.

South Brooklyn Female Seminary—Principal Wm. N. Reid.

S. S. Seward Institute (Female Dept.)—Principal Mrs. G. W. Seward.

Troy High School—Superintendent David Beattie.

Warsaw Union School (Acad. Dept.)—Principal S. M. Dodge.

Waterford Union School (Acad. Dept.)—Principal A. J. Robb.

Westfield Union School—Trustee Chas. Hathaway.

West Winfield Academy—Principal A. K. Goodier.

Whitehall Union School—Principal C. W. Bardeen.

Whitestown Seminary—Trustee John O'Donnell.

Prof. John J. Anderson, New York city.

Prof. Frederick S. Jewell, Ph. D., Greenbush.

Prof. Michael P. Cavert, Albany.

Prof. Albert C. Hale, Rochester.

C. Harris, Greenbush.

Rev. John James, Albany.

Hattie R. Morrison, Hudson.

Julia S. Hoag, Albany.

Maria L. McMickin, Albany.

Mary E. Burch, New York city.

Wm. H. Whitney, New York city.

Chas. A. O'Reilly, Brooklyn.

INFLUENCE OF THE STUDY OF LATIN UPON THE STUDY OF ENGLISH IN SCHOOLS.

By Professor CHARLES J. HINKEL, PH. D.,

Of Vassar College.

As a certain amount of Latin, generally grammar, Cæsar, and Virgil, is taught in a number of public and private schools, I propose to offer a few remarks on the beneficial influence which even a mere elementary instruction in Latin may, by the help of a suitable method, be made to exercise upon the theoretical and practical study of the English language. After a brief statement of the essential features of a course in English, I shall point out the advantages that may be derived from the instruction in Latin as an aid and supplement to the study of English, and then make some suggestions in regard to the method of teaching Latin, by which those advantages may be secured.

The object of the study of English is the acquisition of a theoretical and practical knowledge and control of the language as the medium for the communication of thoughts. According to the nature of this communication, the leading branches of the study of English are *reading*, *writing*, and *speaking*.

By a careful course of instruction in *reading*, the pupil will learn principally to understand fully what is said in the text, and the form in which it is said. He will further acquire copiousness of expression, control of the language in regard to its syntactical structure, and in addition to this a certain knowledge of literature and of the characteristic features of model composition in prose and poetry.

A course of English *writing*, or composition, proposes to teach him how to select a theme, to collect and arrange the subject-matter, to clothe it in correct and adequate language, and even to acquire to a certain extent the ability and skill of revising and correcting what he has written, and thus to be, as it were, his own critic.

The third and most important part of an English course refers to the use of the language in common conversation and in prepared or extemporaneous speeches, and is designed to lead the scholar not only to speak understandingly, or with the proper tone and emphasis, but also, in particular, to pronounce correctly in point of grammar and of articulation. A proper articulation, too frequently neglected, gives to each letter its full and due sound, sets the organs of speech, lips, teeth, tongue, palate, and throat with ease into action, so as to secure a perfect sound and intonation, and especially avoids the slurring over and dropping of letters and syllables, a habit of indolence which always leads to the dialectic corruption of a language. Grammatical correctness requires the use of exact and pure language, strictly in accordance with the rules of grammar, and free from foreign or uncongenial, obsolete and vulgar modes of expression. The pupil finally is expected to learn how to express himself with clearness, or logical correctness, in language suitable to the subject, and, if not with elegance, at least with refinement.

Now it may be said in relation to these essential parts of a course in English, that the Latin, even if only the rudiments, including select portions of Cæsar and Virgil, are studied, is a most efficient instrument for quickening and advancing the study of the vernacular language. I find the chief argument in favor of this assertion in the fact, that the Latin is a dead and a difficult foreign language of a remarkably fine structure, and as such uncommonly well adapted to be used as a means not only for developing and exercising the faculties of observation, memory, judgment and generalization, but particularly for fostering and confirming in the pupil a general habit of thoroughness which cannot fail to beneficially affect the study of his own language. The English student will realize a thought expressed in his native tongue with much less exertion of the intellectual faculties than if it is communicated through the Latin or any other foreign idiom. Generally speaking, he will easily understand and retain in memory the purport of most of what he reads in English. But for that very reason he is in great and constant danger of being hasty and superficial in his reading. He is apt to overlook many points in regard to form and subject-matter, many details and allusions, many beauties which he would be brought to find out, if he had to overcome difficulties in order to understand the text; if he had to look very closely into the nature and bearing of every word, sentence, and chapter, before he could make out even the general sense of the original. He also will more readily forget what he has read with ease, while he would remember longer, if his mind had been forced to dwell longer upon the text. Lastly, not meeting with any serious difficulties, and perhaps absorbed in the subject of his reading, he is liable to run over the pages without stopping to inquire into the connection of the following with the preceding, and into the purport and general drift of what he reads; in fact, without really knowing what he has read, and, moreover, without noticing or appreciating the formal or stylistic merits or defects of the composition. Again, the English is simpler in structure than the Latin, both in etymology and syntax. For this reason, in reading English, there is not so much room left for exercising the mind by means of eliciting the characteristic meaning of the different forms, constructions, idioms, and of all the finer shades and details in the expression of a thought. In addition to this, the English, as a living tongue, is in a constant process of change, which sometimes makes it difficult to ascertain and to define with certainty, what is or should be considered and followed as the real law of grammar and usage of language.

In all these respects the Latin forms a most valuable aid and supplement to the study of English, for the following reasons. It is, in the first place, a dead language, complete in its structure, not undergoing any more changes of form as the English does, but finished in its organism, a steady object of linguistic study and analysis. And just as anatomy is, for this reason, the most valuable auxiliary science of physiology, because the anatomist can more closely examine into the organs of the dead body of a plant or an animal than the physiologist can into those of the living body, so the study of Latin, the dead language, is the most effective auxiliary of the study of English, or the living tongue.

On the other hand, the Latin is a foreign and a difficult language, remarkable for its abundance of forms and idioms and its harmonious structure, and in etymology and syntax very different from the English. In consequence, everything in Latin is new to the scholar and more or less difficult. He must be very accurate in reading, if he wishes to make out the exact meaning of the author. He will find that often an oversight or mistake in regard to a comma, to a single letter or ending, absolutely prevents him from ascertaining the sense. He must constantly exercise his powers of observation, judgment, and memory, in determining the meaning of the words; in parsing or defining their properties and syntactical relations; in retaining the results of his researches; and, finally, he must reason, in order to comprehend the author and to enter into his way of thinking and of viewing a subject; a way so different from ours. Thus he learns to be thorough in reading; that is, to examine patiently and judiciously what others have said. Accuracy in reading will gradually, and by continued practice in Latin, become with him a confirmed habit, which he will unconsciously transfer to his English reading, and that not only to his reading of English books, but of anything presented to him for reading in practical life, be it a letter, a contract, a report, or any other written document. This general habit of thoroughness, however, will result from the study of Latin only, if the latter is treated by a method which regularly and thoroughly goes through the different steps in reading.

The *first step* in Latin, as in English, is the *pronunciation* and *delivery*. Only the spoken word, well articulated and emphasized, is the complete sign and expression of the idea which it denotes. Therefore, even in Latin, although the different methods of pronouncing it are merely conventional, the first requirement is to pronounce correctly according to some chosen method; the second, to read understandingly; that is, so that prose sentences and verses are not delivered like a number of unconnected words, but with the proper emphasis and in an unconstrained, familiar tone. And because the Latin, as a foreign language, in order to be read well, requires on the part of the pupil greater attention and pains than the native language, the more difficult exercise of reading Latin will greatly benefit his exercises in reading English. He should, accordingly, read aloud every sentence in Cæsar and every verse in Virgil, which he has to translate, bringing out in full force every letter and syllable, and doing full justice to the fine sound and rhythm of the Latin prose sentence and verse. The latter should, of course, always be read metrically and with a harmonious combination of the metrical rhythm and the grammatical pauses. And as reading understandingly pieces of Latin prose and poetry depends upon a complete understanding of the text, it will be extremely useful for the scholars to read aloud some pages of prose or a number of verses, *after* they have been carefully translated and explained, and to make this a regular reading exercise for the whole class.

The *second* step in reading Latin is the *translation*, both oral and written. There is commonly the distinction made between *literal* and *free* translations · the former imitating in English the Latin structure of the sentence as far as it can be done without making it absolutely unintelligible; the latter being a circumlocution reproducing in English more the sense than the words of the Latin sentence. Neither the one nor the other is of real use or value. They are both inaccurate and injurious to the mental discipline of the student. The free translation, instead of bringing out in terse, concise English terms the exact meaning of the Latin text, is generally a weak dilution of the latter, effacing the characteristic features and beauties of the original. The literal translation, on the other hand, is even inferior to the free translation. For while the latter may, at least, give in good English an acceptable periphrase of the contents of a sentence, the so-called literal translations given by students, are generally neither English nor Latin in structure. Both ways of translating, therefore, will alike injure the student's method of studying, by making him superficial and inaccurate; and both will tend to injure his English style, the one making it diffuse, the other, faulty.

An adequate translation must be *idiomatical;* that is, the thought expressed in the Latin idiom, or in the form and structure peculiar to, and characteristic of, the Latin, should be completely and concisely reproduced in form of the corresponding English idiom. Consequently, the scholar must choose for every Latin word that English word or term which precisely expresses the idea which the Latin author wished to convey, and for every member and clause of the Latin sentence, in the collocation and connection of words and clauses, that English structure, connection, and collocation which exactly corresponds to the structure peculiar to the Latin. In this respect he is not only allowed, but often obliged to use two or more words for one in Latin and *vice versa;* to use a sentence where the Latin has, perhaps, a noun with a preposition, a conjunction with a verb, where it has a participial construction; to refer to the end what stands in the beginning of the Latin sentence, etc.; simply because the English in many cases has a different idiom to express what the Latin idiom means. By means of working out such an idiomatical translation, the pupil will accomplish that great object of mental discipline which consists in learning to comprehend and to reproduce completely what another has said; and furthermore, he will vastly contribute to his improvement in speaking and writing well in his mother tongue. And just because this exercise of forming good English sentences is so important, he should compose a written translation of what he reads, at least until he has become so familiar with his author and has acquired such a skill and practice in translating him idiomatically, that an oral translation is sufficient. The greatest orators and rhetoricians, as Demosthenes, Cicero, Quintilian, Lord Chatham, Brougham and others, have laid the greatest stress on the composition of written translations from a foreign language, as a means of learning to speak and to write with fluency and correctness in the vernacular. And with good reason. For in writing a translation, the student has not to carry out at once two tasks, that of inventing thoughts, and of putting them in proper form; but the subject-matter being given to him, his whole power and attention can be directed to the one object of stylistic expression. On that account written translations should form a chief feature even in a course of *English* composition.

The *third* step in the method of studying Latin, is the *explanation* or analysis of the text, the most fruitful exercise. It comprises the following tasks:

First, *parsing* in its usual operations of classifying and defining the words in the sentence, stating their properties, and explaining the construction, collocation and syntactical relations of the words and sentences, together with the rhetorical figures. As all these operations are more complicated in the Latin than in the English, because it is richer in grammatical forms and figures, parsing in Latin will contribute a great deal to the pupil's progress in the knowledge and command of the English idiom.

Next to parsing, and based upon it, comes the *comparison of the Latin with the English idiom and of similar Latin idioms with each other;* as it were, the philosophy of parsing, and at the same time, the foundation of an idiomatical translation. The Latin is in many essential features different from the English idiom, as in the collocation of words, in the number and use of cases, moods and tenses, in the connection of sentences and the extensive use of participial constructions. It also has in many cases to express one and the same idea in different ways of form or construction; which, however, although they may not materially affect the sense in general, are always an evidence of a difference in the conception of the idea, or in the form in which the object is viewed, and consequently of different modifications of the meaning. For instance, in the English sentence, "I read first that oration," the one idea contained in the word *first* may be rendered in Latin by the four forms, of *primus, primam, primum* and *primo;* yet with this distinction, *primus* hanc orationem legi, means "I was the first who read this oration," which is indicated by putting primus in the case of the subject; *primam* hanc orationem legi, "this was the first oration I read," hence primam agrees with the object; *primum* hanc orationem legi, "I read it for the first time or the first thing I did," hence the accusative neuter; and *primo* hanc orationem legi, "I read it in the first place or at first, in the beginning," a relation expressed by the ablative. This example also shows that the Latin sometimes has different forms or endings to express different modifications of a word where the English has but one; and it exhibits, besides, one of those frequent cases in which a so-called literal translation, which would render the four different terms alike by the one word *first*, is out of place, and where the truly literal, that is the idiomatical, translation changes the Latin word into a corresponding English phrase or sentence. The scholars cannot fail to perceive what a fruitful exercise for the mind it is, and how useful for the purpose of analyzing English reading, to examine and to compare similar and different idioms; to ask why is such and such a form, expression or construction used in the Latin text or passage? Are there any similar Latin forms, expressions or constructions, which might be used instead? And if so, what modifications in sense would be introduced by them? What would be in Latin the form or expression of the idea opposite to the one in the text? What is the corresponding form and construction in English? Is it the same as in Latin or different, and if so, why and in what respect?

The final task in the explanation of the Latin text, and the finishing touch in a proper method of reading in general, is that of making a synopsis of what has been read; of pausing at the end of every chapter, if necessary of every sentence, in order to ascertain the full import and bearing of the author's statement, narration or argument, to draw inferences, and even to examine into the nature and value of what he says, and into the form in which he says it; in one word, to view the writing of the Latin author in the light of a historical, scientific or literary document of greater or smaller artistic value. How few students, for instance in reading Cæsar, become aware that already in the first book he reveals to them some of the most important pages of the history of the Helvetians, the French, the Germans, and the Romans! How rarely do they pause to notice the clearness, accuracy and quiet dignity of his narrative; the freshness and simplicity of his style; and his impartial and penetrating observation in regard to characters, situations, customs and manners of people? Therefore I would say to them, do not read on without intermission and reflection, especially if you are not sure of having caught the full purport and bearing of what you have translated; but stop from time to time, above all at the end of chapters and books, to reflect and to reason, to recapitulate, to compare, to criticise; in one word, to make a synopsis. By doing so you will strengthen the highest intellectual faculties, those of criticising and generalizing; you will form a habit of studying which, transferred from your Latin to your English reading, will make of you thorough students and readers, who read carefully, accurately and with critical judgment; you will learn to understand the use of giving, in connection with your English studies, some attention also to the study of Latin; and you will more and more appreciate the writings of Cæsar and Virgil, those two great authors, who, from ancient times to the present day, have been read and studied and valued by the educated classes of all civilized nations.

INSTRUCTION OF COMMON-SCHOOL TEACHERS.

By Principal LEVI D. MILLER, A. M.,

Of the Havering Union School, Bath, Steuben County.

The proper education of common-school teachers is one of the great problems now before the educators of our State. Many have thought this problem solved by the establishment and support of eight costly normal schools; but experience has taught us that such is not the case. After the expenditure of more than a million dollars, these schools, according to the last report of the State Superintendent, have sent into the schools of the State but 553 of the 28,276 teachers, or less than two per cent of the whole number. Many of these, also, are employed in academies, so that to-day it is probable that not to exceed one per cent of the number of common-school teachers are normal graduates.

Now, let it be distinctly understood at the outset that these figures are given and comparisons made, not to throw a slur upon the normal schools, nor upon those having them in charge, but to show that, however good they may be in themselves, they have failed almost entirely to accomplish the object for which they were established, namely, as the law expresses it, "The Education of Teachers for the Common Schools of the State." This failure is probably more their misfortune than their fault, for they have undertaken to do an impracticable, and, in many respects, impossible work; and the reason they have failed is precisely the reason they will continue to fail. They seek to make teaching a profession. This, so far as the common schools are concerned, is an impossibility. The essentials of a profession are, 1st. Steady employment; 2d. Good, or, at least, fair remuneration; and 3d. The prospect of rising in the world. Common school teaching possesses none of these things. From seven to eight months in the year is the time; from $150 to $300 a year the remuneration; and the prospect of rising just—nothing. What persons are ready to take up this business as a "profession?" Certainly not men, for better pay and better prospects call them everywhere else. Women will teach, if at all, only till an offer of marriage is accepted, and so the "professionals" are wanting; and even if they do not marry, normal graduates who are good for anything will not teach in our common schools.

Yet it may be urged that better teachers will command better pay. The matter of pay will be regulated like the price of other labor, by the laws of "demand and supply." With the multiplication of union schools and the increased efforts of the academies, the supply of district-school teachers is likely to exceed the demand. Wages cannot rise materially. So long as one hundred young men or women want to teach, and but fifty or sixty schools are to be taught, wages must, of necessity, tend downward. Nor can the districts afford to pay more. The farmers are taxed enormously already. There is a limit to their ability to pay, and to their disposition also. It is perfectly evident to every thinking man, that the majority of all the district schools in the State must continue to be taught as they have been taught in the past, not by professionals, but by young men and women in what may be called their transition state, that is, before they settle down in life. Nine-tenths of all the district-school teachers, outside of the cities and large towns, are from this class to-day. The normal schools take some of these teachers away from the district schools, but they never return them. The fable of the fox and the sick lion illustrates the relation of the district-school teachers to the normal schools. When asked why he did not visit the lion in his sickness, the fox replied that he noticed the tracks of a great many visitors going into the den, but he never saw any coming out. The State really pays, not for supplying, but for robbing the district schools. The pay of the district-school teachers being so small, and the time for which they are employed so limited, they cannot afford to go far to prepare for their work. Every community must educate its own teachers. These young men and women of whom we spoke are the only ones who *can* do this work not only, but the only ones who *ought* to do it. These terms of teaching are a part, and a vital part, of their education, and upon them, a third of a century hence, is to rest the entire management of our school system. Indeed, we may call it the stepping-stone to all future success. It is almost impossible to read the obituary of any great man, be he lawyer, statesman, scholar or divine, without being informed that in early life he learned self-command, self-reliance and self-respect as a district-school teacher. Who are our best trustees and best supporters of schools throughout our State, but the teachers of twenty, thirty and forty years ago? A successful school system needs more than teachers, it needs good trustees, it needs faithful supporters, it needs parents who know what good schools are, parents who understand and appreciate something of the teacher's work. These old teachers are everywhere among our best and most intelligent citizens. The very foundations of society rest upon them. These men who are clamoring for "professional teachers," who would turn out from the district schools the young men and young women who are to be the fathers and mothers, the trustees, the superintendents, the tax-payers of the next generation, and put in their places persons who, as having no children, have not, and cannot possibly have, any direct interest in the next generation, are the worst possible enemies of our school system not only, but of society itself. Fortunate it is that their success is an impossibility. If, then, as we have seen, the normal schools, which are costing from $150,000 to $200,000 a year, have not supplied and cannot supply "teachers for the common schools of the State," and since they were established for no other purpose, why continue to waste money upon them?

Where, then, shall the work of educating teachers for the common schools be done? We answer, in the union schools, academies and teachers' institutes, and, to some extent, in the common schools themselves. These are found in every part of the State, are accessible to all.

About 1,500 pupils have received instruction in the science of common-school teaching annually in the academies and academic departments of the union schools; but soon, with the impetus recently given by the Legislature to academic education, we expect to see academical departments trebled in every part of the State, and a proportional increase in the number of teachers' classes. This system of teachers' classes, scattered all over the State, is undoubtedly the true one, and if it has come short, in some respects, of meeting the wants of the schools, the fault has not been with the plan, but with the proper execution of the plan. In the first place, the amount of money paid to the academies for doing this work has been so pitifully small, that they could not afford to give proper time and attention to it. Hitherto about $15,000, not so much as is given to one normal school, has been divided among ninety or one hundred academies for instructing 1,500 common-school teachers; and then fault has been found with the academies for want of efficiency. Three union schools in Chautauqua county, Jamestown, Westfield and Forestville, have, within a single year, sent into the common schools of that and adjoining counties, at an expense to the State of only $600, 190 actual teachers, while the normal school located in that county, in four or five years, at an expense to the State of $100,000, has not sent into the common schools nearly so many. If the question of quality of teachers arises, we say visit the schools and see for yourselves.

Another reason for the inefficiency of teachers' classes in many cases has been, that the Regents have been so crippled by want of means that they could not give proper supervision to the work, and the laziness or dishonesty of the principal of a school has thus been enabled to report work well done, which was not done at all, or but imperfectly done. Now, the amount of money paid for instructing teachers has been increased fifty per cent, and the State has a right to expect better work. But the amount is still inadequate. It should be enough to enable a principal of a school, who has a salary of from $1,500 to $2,000 a year, to give his whole teaching time exclusively to the teachers' class, without loss to those who employ him. And in the matter of supervision, the Regents should be enabled to employ a supervising officer, if necessary, who should visit all these teachers' classes, and see that faithful, efficient work is done. It will not do to depend longer upon school commissioners for this supervision, for they are many times incompetent, always over-crowded with their own work, and are generally influenced by political fear of giving offense. An officer, employed by the Regents, would be responsible to the Regents only, and could *afford* to do his duty. This officer could judge of the quality of the classes he might find not only, but of the fitness of a principal of a school for this work. Often the work is committed to young men without any experience, who are wholly incompetent to do it.

Admission to the teachers' classes should be given to none but to those who actually intend to teach, and the educational standard should be the holding of the Regents' certificate, either actually or provisionally. And by provisionally, we mean that these pupils pass the Regents' examination when admitted to it, otherwise they cannot receive the benefit of the State appropriation. We make this exception, because many of those who make our best teachers are young men and women from the country, who have as yet had no opportunity to try the examination. They are strong, healthy, energetic, able and willing to work; they have common sense, talent, and that straightforwardness which the hard culture of poverty produces; they have many times a valuable experience and a pretty good knowledge of books, obtained in the district schools. Yet they have nothing systematic; they know a good deal, but have little order, system or culture; they can do many things, but can do nothing well. Yet three months of drill under a master will make them vastly better teachers than many who already hold the Regents' certificate.

Methods of instructing these classes time forbids us to attempt to give. A whole paper would be required for a single topic. Suffice it to say, that the most thorough instruction in the prescribed branches and practice in teaching, so far as practicable, must be insisted upon. Nor is this all. Every manager of a teachers' class should impress upon the mind of his pupils, among other facts:

1st. That nothing can take the place of thorough, accurate scholarship. Every teacher should know vastly more than he teaches, and should know perfectly all that he attempts to teach. There is not in the world a more pitiable sight than a teacher attempting to explain what he does not understand. Teachers can always show others what they see clearly themselves. But to show what they do not see, "Ay, there's the rub." A poor scholar cannot be a good teacher. Our first business, then, in instructing a teachers' class, is to give to each pupil the most thorough, accurate scholarship. Our schools are cursed with a multitude of incompetent teachers. There has been such a rage of late after "methods," "improved methods," I think they are styled, that the matter of sound scholarship has been very much neglected.

2d. After sound scholarship, he should give his pupils a definite idea of the teacher's work. We often fail here. It is our business to make sound scholars not only, but to show them how to do the same. We utterly fail in our duty to a teachers' class if we do not give to every member of it a clear, definite idea of what he is to do in his school, and how he is to do it. Instructors of teachers often "shoot over." They are full of philosophy, and talk learnedly of imagination, of perception, of beauty, etc., but have little or nothing to say of plain, common-sense arithmetic, grammar and geography, reading, writing and spelling, or how to teach them. Let us be careful to keep down to our work, and instead of firing blank cartridges over our pupils' heads, let us teach them to think clearly, to reason correctly, to analyze carefully, to express themselves clearly and pointedly, to be orderly and systematic, in a word, to do one thing at a time and to do it well.

3d. We should teach our pupils to do honest, faithful work in school, and set them an example. There are, we believe, more failures here from the district school to the college than in anything else. Laziness, shirking, false reports are so easy, and faithful, honest work is so exacting, that we have too much of the former and too little of the latter. A lazy, inefficient, dishonest teacher, teaching a teachers' class, is, as Solomon says of the sluggard, "like smoke to the eyes and vinegar to the teeth." We believe that the teachers of all grades in the State, incompetent as many of them are, are not so incompetent as they are lazy and faithless, and lack far less in learning than they do in moral principle and common honesty. The crying evil of our day, among all classes, is the attempt to get a full day's wages for half a day's work. The idea of value given for value received is little recognized. Men everywhere, teachers as well as others, seem often to forget that every day's labor, every bargain of any kind, should be an equation. But instead the sign of inequality is used and the motto is, "get all you can and give as little as possible." We should teach further, that privileges imply obligations; that free instruction in a teachers' class must be compensated by honest, faithful labor in the schools. We, as a people, are getting too low in our ideas of the sacredness of these implied obligations. Our free-school system, which we esteem our glory, may yet prove our curse. This it certainly will do if it teach our people, as too many already think, that one person has a right to the property of another without a fair consideration. Let us boast of our advanced and improved education as we will, but let us remember that any people are badly educated who have been taught that there is a better way to live than to live honestly, and who have not been taught that he who *gets* more than he gives is a thief and a public plunderer.

The French Commune, with all its devilishness, was but the ripened fruit of seed which is every day sown among us. We may expect all its horrors upon our country at some future day, if we do not, in our systems of education, adhere strictly to the cardinal prinples of justice and honesty.

4th. We should teach our teachers to obey their own rules. The great Ruler of the Universe lays down no law for our guidance which he does not himself obey. The best ruler everywhere is he who obeys the laws which he executes. A teacher is as much bound to obey the laws of the school as are the pupils. He should ask no consideration for himself because he is a teacher. Government in school means superiority, and if this superiority, on the part of the teacher, is not apparent to the pupils no assumption can make it so. None but fools attempt to make the smaller thing pass for the larger, to make a half pound weigh a pound, to make a weak, incompetent, inefficient teacher control scholars vastly his superiors. The teacher who is not morally and intellectually greater than his whole school put together cannot control that school. The sun is king of the solar system, not by assumption nor by the authority of appointment, but because he is, in himself, hundreds of times larger than all his satellites put together. Those men and women whom God made for centers of systems (and surely the teacher is one of them), He has endowed with powers which always command respect and obedience. If, then, we would send out successful teachers, we must send out superior scholars, honest men and women, true, faithful, conscientious, common-sense workers; men and women, the very worth of whose characters will be authority anywhere.

5th. The interest of the instructor of the teachers' class should not cease with the close of the term of his instruction, but should go with the pupils to their work, and he should be their friend in all cases of difficulty. The academy should be the center around which from twenty to a hundred district schools should revolve, and its principal should, in a measure, feel himself responsible, as he certainly is, for the character of each one of these schools. To him the trustees will go directly for their teachers, and he can, if he be competent for his place, thus become a public benefactor. He should be the principal of his own school not only, but indirectly the special guardian of all the district schools into which his pupils go as teachers. He should note every failure, and if it be merely incidental, correct it; if it be radical, advise other employment for that teacher. He should mark every success and reward it by recommendation to larger schools and better pay. This will create emulation and greatly elevate the schools. Say not that this is visionary. It is not. It has been done. It can be done. It must be done.

Here, then, we have a feasible plan for the instruction of common-school teachers. Let the money now wasted upon the fruitless normal schools be used to establish union schools with academic departments, until there shall be from twenty to thirty of these in every county, open to all, accessible to all, each one a center and guardian of a circle of district schools around it, and you have a school system which will reach the people and do them good.

But the best preparation of teachers will fail to make our district schools all that they ought to be without a more systematic organization. The first thing necessary for the accomplishment of this is a Manual of School Organization. The lawyer has his Code of Procedure; the divine his Ritual, or forms of worship, established by long custom; the military officer his work on tactics; the parliamentarian his manual; but the teacher, often young and inexperienced, is left entirely to himself, without compass or guide. Suppose every lawyer practiced law in his own way, every clergyman conducted service according to his own notion, every military officer organized the men under him without any regard to system, or a deliberative body should attempt to do business with no regulations but those made by the chairman, would there not be confusion worse confounded? What the district-school teachers need is such a manual of organization as will make every district school in the State a counterpart of every other school of its kind. Then a teacher, having taught one school, would know exactly how to teach the next one; this would remedy, to some extent, the evil of continual change of teachers. Such a manual, with some discretion left to the teacher, should contain an authoritative order of exercises, which every teacher might adopt and carry out. Every teacher would then know, at the outset, exactly what to do, and he would soon learn how to do it. The work of supervision also would be greatly simplified. The commissioner would know exactly what to expect in every school, so far as organization is concerned, and could judge at a *glance* of its efficiency, and have nearly all his time to give to the *quality* of the *teaching*.

The second thing necessary is a uniform system of text-books. The State assumes the management of the district schools in other respects, and why not in this? The property of the State is taxed to support these schools, and the State, as the protector and guardian of the public property and interests, is bound to secure the greatest amount of good possible with the money thus taken from the people. The State claims to have a system of schools, but what kind of a system is that which has no uniformity of books nor systematic organization? Teachers could accomplish twice as much if the same kinds of books were used in all the schools, and a tax, nearly as burdensome as the school-tax itself, would be saved to the people, because the expense of continually changing books would be avoided. Now the people are the prey of corrupt teachers, book agents, venal school commissioners and publishers, and teachers who would do faithful work are so confused with an endless variety of books that they find it impossible to do so. What kind of a military system would that be which allowed every man to furnish his arms, rifle, shot-gun, musket, carbine or revolver, as he liked? The school-book business is now a great monopoly, enjoyed by a few publishing houses, and books are enormously high. Let the State publish a set of books for the schools, as it furnishes arms for its militia, selling the books at cost. As the Bible Society sends out into the world its millions of cheap Bibles, so let us have an era of cheap and uniform school books.

We, whose business it is to educate teachers in the union schools and academies, say to the Board of Regents and to the Common-School Department, "Give us a manual of district-school organization, or code of procedure for the schools, which shall contain, not the vagaries of some philosophic hobby-rider, nor the theories of the enthusiast, but the sober, common sense and experience of a dozen of our best teachers, and, at the same time, a uniform system of good school books, and we will furnish teachers, thorough, efficient, faithful and true. It is not reasonable to ask more of us.

DIFFERENTIALS AND THE METHOD OF FINDING THEM.

By Professor WILLIAM D. WILSON, D. D., LL. D., L. H. D.,
Of the Cornell University.

It is a common impression that the Calculus is the most difficult and incomprehensible of all subjects. That it is applied to the solution of difficult problems is certain; and it is equally certain that by the use of it we can solve many a problem in science that would be otherwise beyond our powers. But I cannot believe that there is any difficulty in the Calculus itself. I think it as simple and as comprehensible as the multiplication table or the rule of three. And yet there is no introductory exposition of its fundamental principles that seems to me to be quite satisfactory.

Writers on Calculus commonly teach that differentials must be quantities exceedingly small, so small that one of them may be regarded as zero or nothing on one side of an equation and yet treated as something—something that may be divided, or used as a divisor, on the other. Nay, one writer—Robinson—insists that they must be so small that the product of two of them, notwithstanding they are whole numbers, will be, when multiplied together, less than either of them separately. The first of these statements leaves a fundamental matter in uncertainty. The second invests it with a cloud of mystery, and the third deepens the mystery into the intensest gloom.

But it seems to me that none of these statements are necessary; they certainly embarrass the student, discourage many at the outset, and leave others, who have persevered, with the feeling that, although they have learned a good many things, they have really understood nothing.

It is very natural for the student to ask to have these things explained, and to be told precisely how small an increment must be in order that it may be considered a differential.

It is worth remarking that the Calculus—whether we regard it as the method of fluxions with Newton or of infinitesimals with Leibnitz—was the invention of some of the greatest minds the world has ever seen. They were intent on the solution of the problems before them, and the consideration of the foundation of their method seems to have been with them quite a subordinate affair. Such men often fail to see what is obvious to minds vastly inferior to their own. This is my apology for venturing to offer the suggestion contained in the present paper.

I write for those who have studied Calculus, and consequently shall omit much that would otherwise be necessary by way of explanation and illustration. And yet some few preliminary definitions and elementary statements must be made at the outset.

I regard the Calculus, taken in both orders, Differential and Integral, as a method of finding values by means of *rates of variation.*

In Algebra we deal with *constant* quantities. Although x, z, etc., may stand for quantities of unknown value, they are, nevertheless, of the same value, for and throughout the same problem or demonstration.

In Analytical Geometry, on the other hand, the unknown quantities are variable—rather variable and indeterminate than unknown. We give either of them, when there are but two, a value at will, and that fixes or determines the value of the other for the time being. But each so-called unknown quantity may have any value that we may choose to assign it, and it may be conceived as passing successively through an endless number of values in the same equation.

But in the Calculus we deal with the rates of these changes; not with the variables themselves, but with the rates at which they change. This rate of variation we call the differential, and write for the variable x, as the rate, dx.

Now, suppose we have two dependent variables, as x and y, bound together by a natural or physical law. This law we express by a differential equation, and we may have $dx = 2dy$: in which case we know from the equation that if x increases at any given rate, y increases only one-half so fast.

Hence a differential coefficient is any number, whether integral or fractional, by which the rate of variation of one variable must be multiplied in order that it may be equal to the rate of another variable; both variables being dependent, of course, either directly or indirectly, upon each other.

The two variables, when considered as objects in Nature, may be either (1) cause and effect in relation to each other, as, for example, the pressure of the steam in the boiler and the velocity of the driving-wheel; or (2) they may be effects of one and the same cause, as in the case of the hands of a watch: though propelled by the same main-spring, they move with very unequal velocities, or as 12 to 1.

But a rate, in any view of it, is a rate or ratio. It is a fraction, consisting of an amount of change for its numerator, and an amount of time for the denominator, as seven miles in two hours is $\frac{7}{2}=\frac{1}{2}^{x}$.

A differential, therefore, is not an amount or a quantity at all. It is indeed a *number*, and may be used as a factor; but it is not, in itself considered, a quantity. As a factor it must always have a coefficient, which is either unity or $\frac{1}{2}$, or some other number. But, of course, when the coefficient is in either of the forms, 1. or $\frac{1}{2}$, it may be, as it usually is, omitted. But the differential is a rate or fraction by which we can multiply the value or variable as it is ascertained or supposed to be at any one moment and find its value as it will and must be at any other given moment. Thus, the rate of interest is in itself a differential, as seven per cent per annum. If we multiply the sum lent, which is for the moment the sum due, by the rate of interest, we find the increment for a unit of time, one year, and adding that to the sum x, we have the value of x, or the sum due at the end of the year. But the rate is a fraction and not a quantity.

And it is worth while considering that the value of a fraction or rate is quite independent of the value of the numbers by which it is expressed. Thus, one mile a minute, five and one-third rods a second, sixty miles per hour, seven hundred and twenty miles per day of twelve hours, fourteen hundred and forty miles a day of twenty-four hours, ten thousand and eighty miles per week, are all the same, as ratios, or rates of motion, however unlike in form and sound the numbers by which they are expressed. And so long as we use the *value* of the fraction or the ratio only, it makes no difference which of these numbers we use. We can substitute one of them for another at pleasure. But if we reduce the fraction to a form in which the denominator is a unit and then treat the numerator as a whole number, regarding it as a measure of value rather than a rate of variation, the law of its use becomes very different.

In Calculus, however, we deal with the variables in Nature, only, as they are represented by their algebraic symbols, x, y, z, etc. And, in fact, in pure mathematics, we deal with these symbols without regard to the objects which they represent. If, for example, x increases uniformly, we call its differential dx, and regard dx as a single term, not as a term of the second degree, or as the product of d and x.

But in case a variable does not increase (or *decrease*, for it is all the same, so far as the general law is concerned) uniformly, we can compare it with some variable, real or supposed, which does change uniformly, and then, by means of a differential coefficient, express its rate. Thus, $du=xdx$. In this case, if u increases uniformly as the formula indicates, x must increase with an increasing increment. But if we choose to change the equation, we may have $dx=\dfrac{du}{x}$, in which case we have x increasing uniformly, and u with a constantly decreasing increment, that is, it must, in order that it may be always equal to du, be divided by x, which is constantly increasing. Hence, while du is constant, $\dfrac{du}{x}$ grows less and less every moment.

Nor is this all, or, in fact, the most important feature of the case. If we can only once get an algebraic equation between any two or more variables, we can make one of them, as u, what is called the *function*, and *suppose it* to increase uniformly, whether it does so in fact or not, and differentiate u, by writing du. The other variable or variables, if there be more than one, will, if course, be on the other side of the sign of equality, and constitute the other member of the equation. Now, by differentiating this second member, we find by mathematics what must, of necessity, be the rate of variation of the second member, and, if need be, of each one of the variables contained in it. And by consequence, when we find by discovery or experiment what is the *actual* rate of variation of any one of the variables, we can assign to the others, by giving to it its value, the rates they must also have, and thus the Calculus has been found to be a most powerful instrument of discovery.

I proceed, therefore, to exhibit my method of differentiating or finding the differentials for the various possible combinations of variables, according to their commonly recognized classes, algebraic, circular or trigonometrical, and exponential or transcendental.

Suppose now we have the variable x, which increases uniformly, so that $x=1$, $x=2$, $x=3$, $x=4$, etc. These consecutive values constitute a series, with the common difference of one: this common difference is the differential of x, and we write it, for the purpose of Calculus, dx.

But let us see what it means. It means that x increases uniformly at the rate of one unit of increase for each and every consecutive unit of time. The unit of increase may be an inch, a foot, a mile, or any other distance we please. It may be an ounce, a pound, a ton, or any other weight we please, if only the increment be in weight.

So with the time. The time during which x increases one unit of the increment may be a second, a minute, an hour, a day, a year or a century, or millions of them, if we please.

Hence the differential is a rate or ratio. It is an amount of increase, divided by the time of the increase, as one mile per day, three miles an hour, a mile in ten minutes, etc. And we either make the time a unit, or reduce it to one, and then reduce the fractions to a common denominator; make that, by division, if need be, a unit, as seven miles in two hours becomes three miles and a half in one hour, with hour for the unit of time.

Now, suppose again, we have another variable y increasing twice as fast as x in the preceding supposition, and we have a series, 1, 3, 5, 7, 9, etc., with a common difference of two, or $dy=2dx$.

I proceed now to find the differentials, or rates of variation of algebraic quantities.

And first, of the sum and difference of two variables.

Suppose we have x and y and $u=x+y$; what is the differential of u, the function of $x+y$?

Suppose $dx=1$, as in the former case, and $dy=2$, then we have, denoting the successive moments by the letters a, b, c, etc.

$$
\begin{array}{llllll}
& a, & b, & c, & d. \\
x=1, & 2, & 3, & 4, & 5, & \text{etc., successively, and } dx=1. \\
y=1, & 3, & 5, & 7, & 9, & \text{etc.,} \qquad \text{``} \qquad\qquad dy=2. \\
\text{Sums, 2,} & 5, & 8, & 11, & 14. \, \cdot & \qquad \text{``}
\end{array}
$$

Here, we see at once that the differential of the sum, $x+y$, is 3, or the sum of the differentials 1 and 2, or $du=dx+dy$. Or if we subtract one series from the other, term for term, we find in the same way that the differential of the difference of two variables, is the difference of their differentials.

Or if two horses of unequal strength, one of which can raise a weight at the rate of one mile an hour, and the other at the rate of two miles an hour, both pulling together they will raise it at the rate of three miles miles an hour. Or if they pull in opposite directions, they will raise it one mile an hour in the direction of the effort of the strongest horse; we have, therefore, $d(x+y)=dx+dy$ and $d(x-y)=dx-dy$.

Now, in this there is no assumption that the differential is small, or that the amount of time, in which the increment denoted by it takes place, is short. The increase, as already said, may be any amount, and the increment may occur in any length of time.

Now let us try the product of two variables, x and y; we have

$u=xy.$ As before, let a, b, c, etc., denote different moments of time, and we have moments,

$$a, \quad b, \quad c, \quad d.$$
$$x=1, \quad 2, \quad 3, \quad 4, \quad 5, \text{ etc., successively, and } dx=1.$$
$$y=1, \quad 3, \quad 5, \quad 7, \quad 9, \qquad `` \qquad `` \ dy=2.$$
$$\text{Products}=1, \quad 6, \quad 15, \quad 28, \quad 45, \qquad ``$$
$$\text{Differences}=5, \quad 9, \quad 13, \quad 17.$$

We see, on a little inspection, that if we take the differential of one series and multiply it, diagonally across any one of the spaces representing moments of time and denoted by the letters a, b, c, etc., by the value of the differential of the other series, and then reciprocally the differential of the second series diagonally by the value of the variable in the other, and add the products, the amount is equal to the difference for that space.

Thus take the space between 2, 3 in x, 3, 5 in y, and we have twice $2=4$ and once 5, and $4+5=9$. Or, in the other direction, twice $3=6$ and once 3, and $6+3=9$. And so of all the spaces. Hence the differential of the product of two variables is the sum of the product of each variable into the differential of the other, or $du=xdy+ydx$.

Or again: If we take the values of one variable, as x at the beginning and at the end of any moment, as d, for example, add them together and divide the sum by two, we get the average of increase for that moment. If now we treat the values of the other variable for that moment in the same way, and then multiply the average of each variable by the differential of the others and add the sums, we get the same result as before, thus:

$$4+5= \ 9 \text{ divided by } 2=4\tfrac{1}{2}.$$
$$7+9=16 \qquad `` \qquad \text{by } 2=8. \quad \cdot$$
$$\text{Now, } 4\tfrac{1}{2}\times 2=9 \text{ and } 8\times 1=8.$$

And $8+9=17$, which is the increment of the product of the variables for that moment, or the rate is 17 divided by 1.

This last method has the additional advantage, that it may be applied to the case of finding the differential of the product of any number of variables. We have to multiply the differential of each by the product of the average of all the other variables for the same moment, and add these products together; we then have the result as $d(xyz)=xydz+xzdy+zydx$, etc.

Nor is it at all necessary that the variables should increase at any uniform rate. Thus, if we take the sums 1, 6, 15, 28, 45, which, as we have seen, are the product of $x \times y$, when $x=1$, 2, etc., and $y=1$, 3, etc., $dx=1$ and $dy=2$, and take another variable, as z, with a differential $dz=3$, we shall have:

Moments,	*a,*	*b,*	*c,*	*d,*	*etc.*
$z=1$,	4,	7,	10,	13, etc., $dz=3$.	
$xy=1$,	6,	15,	28,	45, etc., $d(xy)=xdy+ydx$.	
Products $=1$,	24,	105,	280,	585.	
Differences $= 23$,	81,	175,	305.		

If, now, we take the moment c, the average for $z=8\frac{1}{2}$, and the average for xy is $21\frac{1}{2}$, $dz=3$, and $d(xy)$ (for that moment) $=13$. Hence we have $(8\frac{1}{2} \times 13)=110\frac{1}{2}+(21\frac{1}{2} \times 3)=64\frac{1}{2}$ and $110\frac{1}{2}+64\frac{1}{2}=175$, which is the increment of $z \times (xy)$ for the moment c.

The result will be the same if we take any other moment.

Or, if instead of 1, 6, 15, etc., we had taken the factors of x and y, of which they are composed, as in the preceding case, and multiplied the three variables, x, y and z together, and treated their averages for the moment c, according to the rule just given, we should have had the same result, derived from the multiplication of three variables instead of two.

It may be said that this is after all only experimental. It is merely a numerical computation, and has not the generality and abstraction of form that mathematicians demand.

Perhaps so. But, then, there is no algebraic method of proving these formulæ, that has yet fallen under my notice, that does not encounter some one or more of the difficulties I mentioned at the beginning of this paper. There is no one of them that I know of that does not involve an absurdity, and that may not be shown to be false by what is known as the indirect method of proof as *reductio ad absurdum.*

But again. We must accept some things that cannot be proved algebraically or by general formula. The multiplication table cannot be *proved* in that way, that I know of. I do not think that any man has ever yet proved algebraically, or by the use of letters, that $3 \times 4=12$. He may say, "let a represent 3 and b 4, and then the product will be ab." So indeed we may call it, and so we may write it. But who shall prove to us that ab is twelve rather than thirteen or eleven?

If, however, we will recur to the first resulting series, 1, 6, 15, 28, 45, etc., and note the differences, 5, 9, 13, 17, etc., we shall see that these differences increase uniformly by 4, and that the second difference, when there are but two factors (it would be the third if there were three, and so on), is a constant; and is, moreover, equal to twice the product of the two differentials, dx and dy.

Now, this is an important fact in regard to the logic of the proof. For it shows that so long as the conditions remain the same, that is, so long as we have the case of two factors to find the differential of their products, the rate of increase or the law of the differential of those products, must remain the same.

If, in the cases before us, $x=y$ and $dx=dy$, then $xdy+ydx$ becomes $2xdx$, which is the differential expression for x^2. Or if we have instead three variables, x, y and z, equal to each other, and their differentials are also respectively equal, we have the differential of a cube, or $d(x^3)=3x^2dx$.

After having found the differential of the product of two variables, it is a much simpler and easier way to find that of three or more algebraically. Thus, for xyz let $s=xy$, then $sz=xyz$, and differentiating sz by the formula for the product of two variables, we have $sdz+zds$. Substituting for s its value, xy, and for ds its value, $xdy+ydx$, and we shall have the result, $xydz+zydx+zxdy$.

Or if we have a fraction, $\frac{x}{y}$, we may make $u=\frac{x}{y}$, clear of fractions, and we have $uy=x$ and $udy+ydu=dx$. For u, substitute its value, and we have $xdy+ydu=dx$, clearing of fractions we have $xdy+y^2du=$ ydx, transposing and dividing, we have $du=\dfrac{ydx-xdy}{y2}$.

In case of a radical, $\sqrt{x}$, we may make $u=\sqrt{x}$, square both sides of the equation and we have $u^2=x$. Differentiating we get $2udu=dx$. Dividing by $2u$ we get $du=\frac{dx}{2u}$. But $u=\sqrt{x}$. Hence $du=\dfrac{dx}{2\sqrt{x}}$, which is the formula for the differential of $\sqrt{x}$.

But with the two formulæ first found by means of series, namely, the differential of the sum of two variables, and that of the product of two, we can find *algebraically* all others, without further reference to series, although such a reference is always possible, and may be used as a means to the desired result.

And in all this there is no assumption that the differential is small, or that it may be treated as nothing on one side of an equation while we use it as something on the other; and there is no need of any such assumption. For the sake of convenience the unit or moment of time should be made the same for all the variables that enter into any one equation. But it may be different for each set of variables between which we may have occasion to make an equation.

5

So, also, the unit of increment may be whatever we choose to have it, only it must be the same for all the variables in any one equation. But it may vary with every equation. It may be an inch, a foot, a yard or a mile. Or, if need be, we can make a unit for the occasion: a unit of five inches, for example, between the inch and the foot, just as the foot itself has been made a unit between the inch and the yard.

I have one more suggestion to make. Take the usual example, $u = x^2$, give x an increment h and find the value of u when x is thus increased, subtract the two equations and divide by h and we have,

$$\frac{u - u^1}{h} = 2x + h.$$

If now we make $h = 1$, the unit of increase, then $2x + h$ is the actual amount of the increase. Thus, suppose $u = 9$, then $x = 3$, and twice $3 + 1$ is 7 and $9 + 7$ is 16, the next value of u; and so on indefinitely.

But again, suppose we make h nothing; x, of course, becomes constant for the time being, and u must be constant also. Hence, neither of them have any actual increase, when h is equal to nothing, or is 0, and $\frac{u - u^1}{h}$ becomes $\frac{0}{0}$.

It is customary to regard the $2x$, that will then remain, as the differential coefficient of the independent variable x. And in doing so, mathematicians are undoubtedly right; the experience of using it for centuries has confirmed that view. But how shall we explain it? When they speak of it as equal to $\frac{0}{0}$, and give us the equation $\frac{0}{0} = 2x$, treating $2x$ as a number, it seems to me that they are darkening counsel by words without knowledge.

What then is $2x$? a quantity? not at all. We have seen that in this case there is no increase to either u or x whatever, so long as h is zero. But $2x$ is the rate or ratio of the rates of the increase of the two variables u and x. It is totally independent of their value and remains a *law* of increase, when they are not increasing at all, as truly and as well as when they do. Take for an illustration the hands of a watch, H and M; the differential equation between them is $dM = 12 dH$, that is, the minute hand moves twelve times as fast as the hour hand. And this ratio of rates is the same when the watch runs so as to keep true time, as when it runs too fast or too slow. Nay, the ratio is founded in the nature and construction of the watch, and is as good and real when the watch is stopped as when it is running. It might even be said to exist independently of the existence of the watch itself, or to have existed as a law or possibility before any watch had been or could have been made.

In the computation of interest we have another good illustration of the same thing. The "rate of interest" is so much per cent, the amount lent is the variable, and may be called s. The unit of increase is a dollar, and the rate is, in this State, seven per cent. This we may indicate by dx. Then sdx is the differential expression for the interest on any sum for *one year*. But if we wish to generalize the formula, and make it applicable to the varying lengths of time for which a sum may remain on interest, we need to add to the expression another factor, t, and we have $tsdx$. And the process of finding the amount of interest on any sum is but the integration of this formula between limits.

I offer one more consideration bearing upon the question, whether differentials are quantities or only rates, as I have proposed to regard them. Suppose we have the equation, $x=f(y)$. Then $dx=df(y)$, in which $df(y)$ is of such a nature that y can have a maximum or a minimum value. At the maximum $df(y)$ becomes nothing, and we have, for that moment, $dx=0$. But the expression, $dx=0$, is absurd. It is true, that one may say, as writers on the Calculus generally, if not always, do, that dx, being only a differential, must be exceedingly, nay, "infinitely" small, and, therefore, we may regard it as nothing. So, indeed, for certain *practical* purposes, we might. But theoretically we may not. For if $dx=0$, we may make dx, however small, unity, and we have $1=0$; then multiplying both members of the equation by 3, we have $3=0$, and then, by combining the equations, $3=1$. Thus any one number may be made to equal any other number, which is both mathematically and logically absurd.

If this is unavoidable, we must put up with it and make the best of it we can. But there is no necessity for the difficulty if we will but regard the differential as a mere rate (the differential co-efficient is indeed a number, while the differential is only a rate). In that case, the interpretation of $dx=df(y)=0$ is, that while x increases uniformly, y increases at a very different rate, and at such a rate that there are moments when it does not increase at all; it is constant, and, therefore, has no *rate of* increase. There is no mystery in this. The thing often occurs, and is always quite intelligible; the cycloid is an example. Suppose a wheel rolls along at a uniform rate on a plane surface, its progress may be represented by dx. But any point in the rim of the wheel will describe a cycloid. Let the distance of this point from the plane be represented by y, and we shall have

$$dx=\frac{ydy}{\sqrt{2ry-y^2}}, \text{—},$$ in which r denotes the radius of the wheel, then $2r=$

maximum value of y and $0=$ minimum value. When the point is at the top of the wheel, y is maximum, and, of course, is not increasing, for the moment, although x continues to increase uniformly as at any other time.

For an illustration, both of the simplification which my method affords, and of the use of small differentials, let us consider the much-discussed case of tangency.

I will not repeat the discussion of this subject as given by any one author. I will trust to your memories for that, and it might be invidious to cite any one. But you will remember that there is much said about a limiting ratio, infinitely small quantities, etc. But to our explanation. So long as the secant line, O E coincides with the line O C the arc, A D C the chord, A C and the tangent, B C are equal. That is, they are each of them equal to zero, and, therefore, equal to each other. But there is neither arc, chord nor tangent. Most writers call them "*infinitely small.*" And certainly they are all of that; for they are simply nothing. But suppose the line E O begins to move, revolving on the point O; it is manifest

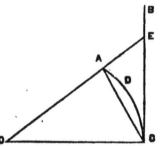

that, as soon as it begins to move, there will begin to be both an arc, C D A a chord, C A and a tangent, C E and so long as the line, O E continues to move they will continue to increase, *but at different rates,* and hence with different differential coefficients, the chord increasing not so fast as the arc, and the tangent somewhat faster. Hence, if we make the arc to increase uniformly, we have for its differential expression dx, x denoting the arc. If now we denote the chord by C and the tangent by T, finding the values of C and T by trigonometry and differentiating by the preceding rules, we have the differentials ordinarily obtained, and that, too, without one word about a differential being small, or, in the words of a distinguished writer, "not a quantity *before it vanishes,* nor *afterwards,* but *when it is vanishing.*"

Or, if we will have the equations in the more usual and useful form, that is, in terms of the coördinates of the point O, we have only to find the analytical equations for these functions, the arc, the chord, the tangent, etc., etc., and then their differentials according to the rules and formulæ already given, and we have the desired result, with as little resort to metaphysical subtleties and incomprehensible quantities as before.

But gentlemen talk of making differentials exceedingly small.! As mathematicians, they can neither make a differential small nor great. Each variable in nature has its differential, its rate of variation, and, *as mathematicians*, we can make it neither greater nor less. We can change the terms of the fraction in which we express it. As I have already said, one mile per minute, five and one-thirds rods per second, and sixty miles per hour, are all of the same value; they express but one and the same rate or differential, howsoever we express it. Man may make small or great, as he chooses, the rate of change in whatever is subject to his control. God can make such changes in the rates of variation in Nature; but as mathematicians we must take the rates as we find them and *express* them—we can't change them—in such terms as best suit our purposes.

But in the case just now under consideration, we can measure the chord of an arc, the arc itself we cannot measure; therefore, if we will express the rate of variation of the arc in units of increment, which are exceedingly small, we may take the length of its chord, which we can measure, for the length an arc, which we cannot, and we get an approximate value for the circumference of the circle in the terms of its radius.

And, in fact, we must always consider the increment as exceedingly small, if we are to use it as a quantity at all, when the differential coefficient contains a variable factor. Otherwise there is no necessity for so regarding it.

It is undoubtedly one of the chief values of the Calculus, that we can thus, by making the values exceedingly small—infinitesimals, as they are called—substitute that of one, whose value is known, or is at least ascertainable, for that of one whose value cannot be otherwise obtained, and possibly cannot be obtained *exactly* at all. In such cases the amount of error diminishes with the decrease in the size of the unit of increase toward zero. But it seems to me much better to reserve the consideration of all such cases until the necessity for using them occurs, and then they can be so explained as to be made perfectly intelligible. The necessity for so regarding the dif ferential is not found in the nature of the differential at all, but it is found in the nature of the cases to which we apply the Calculus.

It has formed no part of my purpose, in preparing and presenting this paper, to criticise any of the accepted methods of finding differentials. If any teacher is satisfied with the one he has been accustomed to use, he will, of course, continue to use it. If not, he is welcome to the one I have now offered.

But I take the more interest in this matter because of the great importance I attach to the Calculus as a means of mental discipline and culture; and this value does not arise at all from its being a difficult study—one that requires great patience, perseverance and continued concentration of thought. It is rather because it puts the mind into a new attitude in regard to all things, and enables the man of thought to see them in a new light and in new relations. I can hardly regard any one as capable of comprehending the highest, the most general and the most comprehensive truths, without the power and the habit of looking at them from the point of view to which the study of the Calculus will, of necessity, carry them.

But I believe that the subject has been very unnecessarily involved in the metaphysical subtleties—not to say absurdities—and that the difficulty of comprehending it, and the consequent disinclination to study it so common in all our schools and colleges, has arisen chiefly from this unnecessary embarrassment. Adopt the explanation I have now given, treat the differential dx as you treat any other factor, and the Calculus may be made as intelligible as the multiplication table. It may be applied to the simplest operations in arithmetic, or in the proof and solution of the simplest problem in geometry—may, in fact, be understood by all persons, and be none the less powerful and wonderful as a means of science in the attainment of its most recondite facts and laws, on that account.

It will also be observed that the formulæ given by my method do not differ at all from those in common use. The only difference is in the explanation given to them and the method of finding and proving them. Nor will this method, so far as I can see, while making them intelligible and bringing them within the easy comprehension of all persons, put the learner in any position of disadvantage in reference to the higher and more difficult questions that he must encounter in his further pursuit of knowledge or in the practical applications of it to the various purposes of life.

THE RELATION OF CHRISTIAN EDUCATORS TO THE MODERN PHASES OF SCIENCE.

By DANIEL S. MARTIN, A. M.,

Professor of Geology and Natural History in Rutgers Female College

GENTLEMEN OF THE CONVOCATION.—In presenting you with a few thoughts in regard to the relation of the Christian educator to the modern problems of science, I must begin by saying that it is with much hesitation that I approach this subject, partly because it may seem, in some respects, a very hackneyed one, and partly from the great importance of the theme, and the consequent difficulty of dealing with it in any adequate manner. I am led to the attempt, however, partly because of that very importance which renders it so hard to treat aright, and partly because, two years ago, in this room and before this body, the gauntlet was openly thrown down to science, and has not yet been formally and fearlessly taken up.

The whole subject seems divisible into three main parts, viz.:

I. The fact of a long and lamentable controversy between Christian and scientific modes of thought.

II. The causes and reasons of this controversy.

III. The methods of its possible removal.

To these three points, Mr. Chancellor and gentlemen, I would, therefore, request your attention.

I. The fact of such controversy.

We are certainly living in one of the most remarkable periods of the history of our world,—one which is marked by such vast, rapid and varied developments of human progress, in its best and noblest forms, as no other age has seen. This great advance, complex and manifold as it is, we are wont well to sum up under the name of CHRISTIAN CIVILIZATION. If we examine it, we shall find it to have in general a twofold aspect, moral and material, and to owe its wonderful character to this fact: it is the expansion of human knowledge, culture, intercourse, and invention, guided and directed by the divine influence of the Christian religion. It is Christianity and civilization, distinct in their nature as heaven and earth, but united in their action on society, that make this world all that it is to-day, and all that it can hope to become in the future.

Between these two great forces, which together are engaged in the improvement and elevation of mankind, one would naturally suppose that there would be the warmest and closest sympathy; that the laborers in each department would look with joy and pride on the achievements of their co-laborers in the other. But such is not the case. To a limited extent, and in occasional instances, we do indeed find such a spirit displayed. But I fear that it is not overstating the facts, to say that the general attitude of science and religion toward each other has been, and still is, one of jealousy, of fear, and of either open or covert opposition.

In every contest which prevails among men, it is generally found that, whatever real and great grounds may exist, much of the estrangement is due to mutual misunderstandings. If these can be removed, the way to peace and harmony is made far easier than it would otherwise have seemed. In this view, let us see if it be not possible to trace some ways in which we, as Christian educators, may help to bring about a better state of feeling in this most unhappy contest between science and religion, in which, from our very position, we must, of necessity, in some degree take part.

Admitting, then, that such a conflict exists, as a great and lamentable fact, we seek to trace for a moment some of its leading causes.

All false and erroneous systems of religion, from their very nature, as founded in and relying upon ignorance, must inevitably hate and oppose the enlightenment of the human mind in almost any direction, as thereby their power is weakened and their downfall shadowed forth. Were our inquiry, therefore, concerned with the conflict between science and religion as it exists in pagan or Mohammedan lands, or even in those Christian countries which cherish any form of superstition, the answer as to the reason of such opposition would be easy and plain enough. But we are looking to the facts as they appear in our own favored country, and in the most advanced and enlightened communities of the globe. Why is it that here such a discord still exists? Why do we find it appearing among ourselves, somewhat as it does in lands overspread with superstition and ignorance?

If we look at the question, it is certainly grave enough to attract our most serious consideration.

Returning again to our former comparison, we see that in every human contest or disagreement, there are almost invariably faults and errors on both sides, which, in some degree, divide the responsibility between the two parties to the strife. So, undoubtedly, will it be found to be here. The errors, the faults, are not confined to either side; and it will be the object of this paper to seek to point out impartially some of these causes.

Here we may as well define our position at once, as standing on the basis of faith in the Christian Scriptures, as embodying the revelation of Himself by the living God and personal Creator of the universe, and containing "all things that pertain unto life and godliness, through the knowledge of God and of Jesus our Lord." We have no desire to discuss this question, or any other, from any different stand-point, and would decline to enter at present into any debate that involves this position. It is to Christian educators, and to such alone, that this discussion is presented.

II. Turning now to the causes of the conflict alluded to, we find that there is one important reason which depends on the fundamental position of the Christian faith. Explain it as we may, the idea of a living, personal God is displeasing to many men, and they seek to avoid it by whatever means can be found. Both philosophy and science afford to such minds an endless series of opportunities for raising questions and difficulties as to the being or the personality of a God; and thus it comes to pass that there is, and has been, a long, active, and irreconcilable conflict between those who accept, and those who dispute, the fact of a Divine existence and control. The former class, of course, includes all religious writers and thinkers; the latter includes many men who have achieved intellectual eminence, not only in science, but in various departments of knowledge. Many of these, however, have been students of nature, and have used their discoveries and reputations in support of atheistic views. Thus, in the minds of many devout men, unacquainted with science, and judging the whole body of scientific thinkers by a part of their number, there has arisen a feeling of alienation and suspicion, which has contributed much to this estrangement.

If we go still deeper, however, and inquire, Why this disposition to exclude the idea of God, which has appeared so strongly in the writings of scientific and philosophical students?—we are unable to explain it, save in the light of that very revelation which such writers reject. Here we are told that the whole race is in some way morally perverted, and alienated from God and all true excellence, while retaining intact its intellectual capacities, and also a large residuum of domestic, social, and public virtue. If this be so, as both history and inward experience attest, it is easy to see why men, even of the highest intellect, do "not like to retain God in their knowledge."

"Professing themselves to be wise, they became fools," and "the fool hath said in his heart, there is no God."

There is little doubt that the disposition thus displayed by many men of science, lies at the root of much of the conflict alluded to. So far and so often as this tendency manifests itself, it cannot but awaken earnest opposition and remonstrance, and result in a feeling of jealousy and suspicion, on the part of believers in the greatest of truths.

But apart from an absolute and intentional advocacy of atheistic ideas, there is on the part of many scientific men a carelessness, or even a hostility, of expression toward religious truth, which awakens deep distrust. Even when this is not the case, there is often a certain kind of nature-worship, a glorification of science as the one and only agency in the advancement of humanity, and an utterly materialistic and secular mode of speech, which cannot but offend and repel many thoughtful minds, who would be ready enough to admit and approve any moderate statement of the claims of science. Professor Huxley, for instance, is a man who stands confessedly among the foremost naturalists of our day; and we honor and admire him, and rejoice in much that he has done. But when he tells us that "objects of sense are more worthy of attention than inferences and imaginations. You cannot see the battle of Thermopylæ take place. What you can see is more worthy of your attention,"—no earnest and thoughtful man can fail to recoil into opposition, both to the logic and to the sentiment. As for the reasoning, what can we see with the material eye? Forms and colors simply, sometimes fixed, sometimes changing. Philosopher, infant, idiot, animal,—all see these same things, and naught else. Cause and consequence, attraction and repulsion, atoms and forces, life and energy, all these are as unseen as the battle of Thermopylæ; and not only so, but they never have been or can be seen, save by the same mind, itself invisible, that conceives alike of nature and of history, of past, present, and future. As to the sentiment, let us weigh carefully all that Professor Huxley has taught us, and that is much, concerning zoölogical classification, and the doctrine of protoplasm, and then compare with it the influence exerted on the minds and hearts of men for over 2,000 years by the tale of the heroic leader and undaunted band, firm in their love and devotion to the laws and honor and freedom of their country, standing calmly to the death in that wild pass in Locris. Humanity is richer and nobler for it to-day, and will be to the end of time. Every truth has its value, and none is to be lightly esteemed;

but all that we have yet learned about protoplasm, or "Man's Place in Nature," is powerless to stir the heart and quicken the spirit and strengthen the hand, as does this ancient record, which is part of the world's best and noblest heritage. Nay, Professor Huxley himself tells us that, ' if he were compelled to choose between absolute materialism and absolute idealism, he should be compelled to accept the latter alternative;' and here the immortal man rises into expression above the mere student of physical science. But this intense secularity, this exclusive looking at the things that are "seen and temporal," repels and prejudices men of earnest moral and spiritual thought. Often it is but a manner of speech that such writers fall into unintentionally, but it is none the less unhappy in its results.

Quite apart from these tendencies that prevail among some men of science, there is a large class of unbelievers and opposers of religion, who have no claim to scientific consideration, and no real care for scientific interests, but who seize upon and magnify every actual or possible ground of difference between natural and scriptural truth, out of mere hostility to the latter. Such persons gain prominence frequently as popular lecturers, newspaper and magazine writers, etc., and create an amount of noise and of mischief totally out of proportion to their own caliber. They pervert and misrepresent science for the sake of assailing religion, and, like the brutal camp-followers of an army, create alienations that react upon the party in whose uniform and name their excesses are committed.

But these are only the more familiar of the many aspects of this subject. It now behooves us to see, on the other hand, if there be not grounds of controversy, less vital and less excusable, on the part of the religious world.

Among the first and most important of these, seems to us to be an underestimation of pure science, and an unfamiliarity with the spirit of scientific investigation. I do not allude here to that sordid view which delights in calling itself by the taking name of "practical," and which would measure the capacities and achievements of the human mind by the standard of cash-books and dividends. The spirit to which I refer is of a nature far more subtle and complex. In part, perhaps, it arises from a certain kind of moral and religious depth of feeling, which, although unhappy and overstrained, is yet an error only, and not a folly or a wrong. Many earnest men, whose hearts are strongly impressed with the moral necessities and responsibilities of our race, and by the fleeting character of all temporal and earthly objects, as compared with the unending life beyond, have been unable to feel much interest in the pursuits of pure science, and have looked upon them as really of but little moment.

There is a great truth in this view, and a great error likewise. We respect the feeling from which it springs, while we regret the tendency that results. To some minds, it may be unavoidable to feel thus, overpowered by the sense of vast and endless issues depending on these few years which their fellow-men around them are hurrying through, careless, hopeless, and Godless. This is especially the case with some Christian ministers, whose hearts not only, but whose hands, are filled and burdened with a work of the greatest and most absorbing responsibility. But all forms of human activity and progress are so bound together that they cannot be separated; and any feeling of this kind would, if logically carried out, condemn the world to ignorance and stagnation.

There is yet another feeling somewhat akin to this last, but far less excusable. I think there is a lingering idea in many minds that there is something a little daring and irreverent in thus pressing into the inmost recesses of life and of nature. This idea, so far as we have it, is a faint echo of classical or other heathenism, of systems in which man was so nearly equal to the gods, that the latter had all the time to keep him at arm's length in order to their own " tenure of office." The universe was, in this state of belief, like some large manufactory, with a high board fence, from which the proprietors, who have pirated, bought, or invented, some improved processes, are forced rigorously to exclude all inquiring visitors, and so fasten up " Positively No Admittance " on every avenue of approach. The lingering remnant of this feeling, which, perhaps, is more wide-spread than would be readily admitted, is fainter now than it has probably ever been in the history of the world before. But it is well that we should note it as one element of our subject. It betrays itself in such common expressions as " daring investigators," or " wresting her secrets from unwilling nature," etc., which have no propriety save where actual hardship or peril is involved. It is the old idea of the jealousy of a miserable tribe of divinities, aroused by the power and energy of man :

> " Audax omnia perpeti
> Gens humana ruit per vetitum nefas.
>
> *   *   *   *
>
> Nil mortalibus ardui est ;
> Cœlum ipsum petimus stultitiâ, neque
> Per nostrum patimur scelus
> Iracunda Jovem ponere fulmina."

How grand is the contrast in the Old Testament Scriptures! "The heaven, even the heavens, are the Lord's, but the earth hath He given to the children of men," and that long-earlier utterance from God himself, giving universal dominion to our race, and issuing the command to subdue the earth. And not only in the Old Testament, but all through the Scriptures, while there is the most positive assertion of the weakness of human wisdom in the sight of God, and of its total inadequacy to help or save men in moral and spiritual relations, there is not a trace of this heathen idea of a divine jealousy of man's attainments in the study of nature. The whole suggestion should be relegated forthwith to the region of omens, witchcraft, and spirit-rappings.

But it is rather to a more general kind of estrangement between the religious and the scientific modes of thought and investigation,—a mutual want of intercourse, appreciation, and understanding,—that we must attribute a great deal of the difficulty. In this respect, the blame is about equally divided between the two sides; and the remedy lies, in part, with whichever will recognize the error Our religious writers and thinkers hold aloof too generally from scientific men. They have not learned, or do not cultivate, a spirit of hearty interest in scientific achievements and inquiries. Looking upon the study of nature as something wholly foreign to their chosen field, a feeling grows up that "the Jews have no dealings with the Samaritans;" and the result is a great and mournful controversy.

If we should yet again recur to our former illustration, we should find it universally recognized that intercourse between nations is usually one of the surest safeguards against war; and that just in proportion as men and communities learn to know each other, visit each others' homes, and look in each others' faces, and feel the common humanity that lives and looks and speaks in each and all, so far does the idea of conflict become painful and abhorrent, and the possibility of peace and of harmony increase.

It is this holding aloof, this separation between our religious and our scientific thinkers, that more than anything else, perhaps, gives rise to this state of discord. Insomuch is this recognized as the prevailing condition of affairs, that any exception to it is regarded as unusual and singular. Scientific men are apt to regard with feelings, and even with expressions, of pleased surprise, a minister who can meet them in anything like free and intelligent converse on questions of recent scientific discovery. It is not, I think, overstating the facts, to say that such cases are really rare. The consequence is, that between the expounders of these two great modes of thought there is little or none of that harmonizing and softening influence, that springs from the friendly comparison of even widely differing views.

Hardly to be separated from this last-mentioned cause, and in great part due to it, is the existence of a vast amount of positive ignorance, on each side, as to the well-known truths and principles of the other. This fact is one of the most conspicuous possible to those who have any real acquaintance with both departments, and yet it seems to be completely unknown or unheeded by the disputants. With what coolness and assumption do scientific writers all the time undertake to extend their reasonings into subjects wholly different in kind from those in which such reasonings are valid! How often are the rules of logic, and the well-known principles of philosophical reasoning, quietly dispensed with, in order to introduce the celebrated "methods of induction" into some new and untried field, wherein experimental or statistical tests are impossible, and induction therefore worthless. On the other hand, what surprising ignorance of familiar facts in recent science may be found "full-high displayed" in many reviews of scientific books and essays attempted in our religious journals. It would be ludicrous, if it were not so melancholy, to witness the treatment received in such quarters by many of the grandest achievements of our day. We no longer hear any question raised as to antipodes, or the motions of the earth ; that is thoroughly past. But there are still to be found men of high intelligence and culture who hesitate about the clearest principles of geology, mock at the glacial era, and set themselves in the face of the whole grand series of conceptions which begin to entitle the modern student to the high name of "*interpres naturæ*," while no less ministering to an intelligent and earnest Christian faith. Two such volumes have been given to the American public within the past year, and they have attracted much attention. One of these, in particular, has been lauded to the skies in at least one leading religious journal; a work with a sounding Latin title, and coolly dedicated to the Supreme Creator, but occupied largely with an onslaught upon the grandest scientific generalization as to the Creator's method which the human mind has attained—the Nebular Theory of the universe. Either not knowing, or not caring to know, that this conception of the philosopher Kant, as well as of the astronomer Laplace, has long since passed into the recognized mental furniture of almost every student of physical science, and is receiving new and cumulative proofs from year to year, the author of this treatise assails it with a tempest of convulsive rhetoric, only comparable to the frantic gong-beating of a "heathen Chinee," under the frightful apprehension of the sun's being swallowed by a dragon. The remedy, in both cases, is equally adapted to the nature and extent of the peril.

But the mischief which such writings are calculated to do is extremely grave. They widen terribly the breach between science and faith, and increase and multiply the difficulties and dangers to be encountered by many minds, in passing from the receptive stage of youth to the reflective stage of independent manhood. It is one of the saddest aspects of modern culture, this hostile position occupied by so many expounders of science and of religion. There are infinite shipwrecks,—shipwrecks of faith, usefulness, and heaven,—that have happened, and will happen, again and again, from this only cause. The fearful words of our Saviour in regard to "offenses," come forcibly to mind in dwelling on this theme; and I can scarce conceive of a higher responsibility resting on a Christian educator, than that of so training the minds that come under his charge that they shall be able to pass safely through these ordeals of intellectual conflict. But no man can lead others in a path that he does not himself know and follow; and hence it becomes every such guide and trainer of youth to look well to his own foundations and methods.

This want of acquaintance with scientific truth on the part of so many Christian writers and teachers,. arises from several causes. Some of these I have already alluded to independently, viz.: (1) the absorbing claims and responsibilities of the ministerial calling, and the overshadowing weight of great moral themes; (2) a lingering half-doubt as to the legitimacy of the spirit of universal investigation; and (3), and most important, a want of sympathy and intercourse with men of scientific pursuits. Among other grounds I would mention the following as of most importance: (1) the want of proper scientific instruction in the course of education; (2) the lack of ready means for keeping pace with the vast and ever-widening progress of scientific research.

The want of proper scientific instruction in youth, is an evil which belongs to the past, but which need not, and, we may hope, will not be felt so much in the future. The men who graduate from our colleges now have generally some fair amount of information in the department of science, and some interest in it; in many cases this interest is very great, and it is only needful to refer for examples to the scientific culture and capacity of many of our most honored and devoted foreign missionaries. But not all our colleges are careful and active in this matter even yet; and in our theological seminaries, where some acquaintance with science should be a matter of most earnest heed, what provision does it receive? We do occasionally hear of a course of lectures before a theological seminary by some gentleman,— perhaps able and eminent in science, perhaps otherwise,—on the "Relations of Science and Religion." The course may be one of great value and importance, as has been the case with some that have been given of late in such connections; but even then, half of those who attend it have never received any such previous training in the rudiments of the subject as would enable them to grasp the real import of the facts and distinctions cited. They hear of the origin of species and varieties, of the principles of structural classification, of the correspondence between the succession of types in time and their advancement in rank, etc., without, perhaps, being able to distinguish between a species and a variety, or having any clear idea of the differences which determine grade in structure, and which, therefore, lie at the basis of classification, and of all our reasonings on the order of rank and the development of life. If the lecturer is able and accomplished, he is above the majority of his hearers; and if such is not his character, he is likely only to do harm, and to occupy himself, and entertain his audience, with rhetorical demolitions of the glacial period, the nebular hypothesis, or the correlation of forces, to say nothing of the doctrine of evolution.

And here I am brought to the mention of two points, which are of vital importance in this whole discussion. These are, our growing system of " elective studies," and the character of our scientific text-books.

(A.) As to the elective system. It has long been, and still is, a great and perplexing question how to make our college education more effective, and to enable it to keep pace with the growth of human knowledge. The advantages of a classical training are unquestionable; but if we attempt to gain the full benefit of them, they occupy an amount of time which leaves little opportunity for the teaching of science, now becoming so highly important. Hence has arisen the anti-classical war, waged so energetically of late years in the name of science (though not largely by men of true scientific eminence), under the plausible title of The New Education.

As the result, we have seen the very wide adoption of a system of compromise, by which students are allowed to choose, in the later years of their course, between scientific study on the one hand and the old curriculum of classical, literary, and, perhaps, philosophical instruction on the other. This seems at first sight very fair and suitable. Every student does as he thinks best in his unfledged wisdom, chooses those studies which fall in with his intended profession, and so everybody is satisfied. Gentlemen of the Convocation, fellow-instructors of youth, let us take warning in time! What will be the result of this system twenty years hence? It needs no prophet to foretell it. These same evils and perils which we have been lamenting to-day, instead of being modified and healed, will be greatly intensified. We shall have a Christian ministry wholly ignorant of science, and a body of scientific men ignorant, not only of classics, so necessary in scientific language, but of the laws and principles of philosophical reasoning. These results may be modified, perhaps, by care and watchfulness on the part of instructors; but a more pernicious and dangerous experiment in our college education it would be hard to devise. Every young man, eagerly looking forward to life, is anxious, of course, to make his college training go as far as it can toward fitting him for his chosen sphere. Inevitably, therefore, the intended naturalist drops philosophy and classics, which are, perhaps, wearisome and dull to him, just as soon as he can, and spends his last year or two in geological excursions and in the chemical laboratory. In like manner, the intended minister thinks he can dispense with scientific studies, and gives himself to Greek, philosophy, and rhetorical practice. Each, perhaps, saves a year and is crippled for a lifetime. That professional one-sidedness, from which arises so much of all this mournful separation and misunderstanding, is fostered and intensified, and a full, broad, liberal scholarship will soon become a thing of the past. It is easy to quote specious maxims about the advantages of concentrating energy on one subject, etc., but these will not do away with the facts. The true work of the college is totally distinct from that of the professional school: it is encyclopædic, not specific; and just so far as we try to combine the two, we shall miserably err. The college lays the broad foundations of general culture, on which the structure of professional scholarship shall be afterward reared; and if it take cognizance at all of the intended career of the student, its aim should rather be to supply and develop those forms of mental training from which his future course will tend by disuse to lead him away.

But, it will be asked, what is to be done? There is not time in the college course for all that it seems indispensable to have taught. I have not space now, nor would it fall, altogether within the scope

· of this essay, to enter upon such a discussion. But almost anything were better than such a perilous separation between professional modes of thought. It is bad enough certainly now, even before the men trained under the elective system have come forward into prominence. There is already plenty of loose logic in the reasoning, and of bad classics in the nomenclature, to be found in our scientific works, and plenty of ignorance of science in our theological and religious writers. Gentlemen of the Convocation, let it be our most earnest aim, in whatever manner and measure we can, to avoid increasing these evils. If the elective system has to be employed, let it be guarded with watchful care. Let a certain amount of scientific training, in principles rather than details, be rigorously insisted on for every man who passes through the college course, *especially* if he looks forward to the ministry; and likewise, let every " scientific course " be required to include the departments of mental philosophy and logic, and I may add, perhaps, of Christian evidences.

(B.) But I pass to the other point of weakness in our scientific instruction, that of text-books. I am sure that my friend, Professor Hartt, will bear me out in all that I may say on this point, and I rejoice that he is with us in this meeting, as representing the department of geology and natural history, in which I should otherwise stand "solitary and alone."

What sort of text-books have we in science? In chemistry and physics we are far better off than in the natural sciences proper; but even in the former the ideal book is very far from being at hand. In geology we have fortunately had Professor Dana's admirable volume for ten years past. But what is the geology of ten years ago, or, one might almost say, of five years ago, to-day? Many doubtful points have been solved, many missing links supplied, and many new and most important additions and modifications have arisen; others are arising from year to year, and almost from month to month. If the teacher is one who can supplement the text-book largely by lectures on these points, very much is gained; this is what every college professor is properly expected to do. But for the multitude of teachers who are not specialists, the men who have the principal work of an academy or seminary on their hands, this is generally impossible. The information of recent discoveries does not reach them; or if it does, it is only in such fragmentary and unreliable forms that they can make no real use of it. In the department of zoölogy the case is ten times worse. With the exception of elaborate works, too large and too expensive to be used by students as text-books, such as Carpenter's Principles of Comparative Physiology, Owen's Anatomy of Vertebrates and of Invertebrates, Herbert Spencer's Principles of Biology, etc., we have no work on philosophical zoölogy that is worth naming. There are some few small text-books in this department; but they are superficial and merely descriptive, not entering at all into the real foundations of the science. One work on the principles of zoölogy, that is still largely in use, was from the first exceedingly weak and defective at many points, and has actually had no revision in more than twenty years that have elapsed since its issue!! What sort of knowledge can be gained from such a text-book to-day?

Here, again, there is an "evil under the sun," which calls for decided remark. I allude to the stereotyping of text-books in science. Such a work can no more be of high value, unless revised from edition to edition, than can the mirror of a solar microscope, unless made to follow the change of position of the sun. But when such a book is issued and puffed and advertised, the object is to "make it pay," and to run it through a number of editions with the least expense and the most profit. Of course, therefore, it is stereotyped; and then no pains are spared to keep it in use as long as possible unaltered, and to hide and palliate every defect that the constant advance of science may reveal or cause. After some years, notes or an appendix will be added, covering so much new matter as can be introduced without involving too great a change in the work, and it is then put forth with new energy. I have particularly in mind a most flagrant case that occurred within a year or two past, in which an eminent publishing house prepared in this way a revised edition of a text-book on chemistry. The book had been a good one in its day, and the reviser was an able and excellent man. But instead of simply announcing these facts, and commending the work on that basis, which would have been perfectly fair, the publishers, in their advertising journal, professedly "devoted to the interests of education," made a violent assault on the new system of chemical nomenclature, on the most flimsy grounds, dissuading teachers from adopting it by all the trivial arguments that could be urged. Their own revised volume, of course, followed the old method; and here was presented the spectacle of a so-called educational paper fighting against the progress and improvement of chemical instruction, in the interest of the publishers' cash-book. Every teacher will recall the bitterness with which some publishers seek to disparage the works of rival houses, and the harshness and grossness which have at times made such publishers' circulars and "journals" worthy competitors with the lowest style of political newspapers.

We need, moreover, a wholly different kind of text-books for the teaching of science. The bane of all of them is the large proportion of detail that is given, and the small amount of principles. Details belong to the professional student; the principles should form part of the liberal education of every man and woman. Details are, of necessity, forgotten; principles can be retained: and if the latter be once mastered and held, any details that may be needed in after life can easily be gained; while no amount of half-remembered particulars will enable a man to grasp at will the general laws of a science; the former are of value only as they illustrate the latter. What is needed in the crowded years of a college course is a class of brief text-books, that shall clearly present the general principles in each department of science. These manuals should never be stereotyped, but should be revised every year or two, perhaps by a committee of professors appointed for the purpose, so as to make the instruction of our colleges and seminaries keep pace with the swift advances of science. They should then be thoroughly studied and recited upon by the class, while all the details which it is desirable or possible to bring in should be given by the professor or teacher in the form of lectures and illustrations. The professional scientific instructor can do this from his own resources; the general teacher, by means of reading and studying for the purpose.

Such manuals, moreover, would serve to supply another want to which allusion was made just now, viz.: that of some ready means by which men in all professions might gain, in brief compass, a trustworthy account of the progress of natural and physical sciences in their several departments.

I would earnestly suggest that the Board of Regents should take some action looking toward such a system, or at least that some committee be appointed among the professors of the State, to consider the possibilities and the means of its adoption. The Board might also require certain standard works in recent science, and the annuals of scientific discovery from year to year, to be placed in the library of every institution reporting to them, or partaking of the Literature Fund of the State.

But I have, perhaps, wandered too far from the immediate theme of this paper, and must pass rapidly on to its conclusion. In speaking of the frequent estrangement or want of sympathy which exists between religious and scientific thinkers, I have traced it largely to a mutual ignorance of each others' real positions and views; and this ignorance, I have sought in turn to trace partly to certain defects in our system of instruction. The mention of these has led to a digression as to the possibility of improvements, hardly germane to the original subject.

One of the last and most important points worthy of especial mention as a cause of difficulty and alienation, is the harsh and captious mode of speech employed by many religious and other critics toward the views of men of science. How freely are such terms as " infidel," " materialist," " unbeliever," etc., applied to men who have really neither made nor intended any unkind allusion to religious men or religious truth, but whose discoveries have led them to the presentation of views which, marking an advance in scientific conceptions, involve, perhaps, some changes in the outward form of conceiving certain Scriptural statements. Instead of calm and fearless inquiry, they are met with stern and positive denunciation. Instead of looking to see what new and valuable expansion of even our Scriptural conceptions may be found, many religious men at once raise the cry of infidelity, and force the unhappy investigator of nature into a position of hostility which he never designed to assume. I myself was never more surprised than on finding the magnificent generalization of the Unity and Convertibility of Material Forces assailed on charges of this kind. Generation after generation this process has gone on, from the time of Galileo till to-day. Astronomy and geology have by this time come nearly through the conflict in triumph. Physics and zoölogy are now in the thick of the fight. The next generation will see them left in possession of the field; but, alas, will the battle be still raging along some farther line, or may we hope for a better day? The best minds in the Christian Church lament this state of things most deeply. It is but a week ago since an honored minister of the Presbyterian body expressed this strong regret and anxiety in a conversation with me, mourning over the unwise and hasty opposition which drives men of science into an unsought attitude of estrangement.

Then, too, apart from direct censure or criticism, there is a slurring, contemptuous mode of speech toward science, frequently indulged in by some writers, which is as unwise as it is unfair. Science is taunted with its frequent changes of views; as if any advancing knowledge must not, of necessity, so alter. Then there is the stock argument of the dissensions and disagreements among the expounders of science, as rendering the whole matter doubtful and trivial; just as though every department of human thought,—history, philosophy, political economy, and last, but not least, religion, evangelical or other,—did not present the same spectacle, of men united in the possession of certain fundamental principles, but differing widely in their application to details. No one complains more frequently, or more justly, of the unfairness of this objection, than do religious teachers when it is urged by unbelievers as an excuse for neglecting the Gospel. But it is equally unfair in the other application, and should never be used by candid thinkers, however convenient it may be in default of any better. It is a sword which cuts only the hand that takes it.

All this is not only unfortunate, but useless; not only useless, but mischievous. Denunciation can always make enemies, but never friends. Some of the ablest writers and thinkers of our day have prejudiced and weakened their happiest efforts by a sharpness of manner that stands in painful contrast to the truth, the dignity, and the real fairness of their matter. Religious critics *must* learn to separate the spiritual truths of the Divine Gospel from the physical conceptions of creation gained from Milton's Paradise Lost. The image of God, still the distinguishing glory of humanity, even in this fallen state, must be recognized as in the spiritual character and not in the bodily frame. Until this is done, at least so far as to allow for the differing conceptions of workers in a different field, the strife must go on unceasingly to the bitter end,—how bitter I dare not say.

But the remedy, gentlemen of the Convocation, lies with the Christian educators of our country. If, along with an earnest spiritual faith, they shall teach caution, patience, and kindliness, a true and broad sympathy with the aims and methods of science, and the charity which "thinketh no evil," we may hope for better things in the days that shall come when our work is past.

But it will be said by some, that "the danger of a wide-spread infidelity is becoming very great. Science threatens to undermine all the foundations of faith. Shall we utter no warning and venture no reproof?" I reply, the greatest danger, by far, is that which arises from these very tendencies on which I have dwelt. The foundations of faith have suffered nothing from the adoption of scientific views which, in times past, were deemed just as dangerous as these which are now so dreaded. The Copernican astronomy, the ages of geology, the nebular hypothesis, have but expanded vastly our conceptions of the Creative power and wisdom, and left the spiritual energy of the Gospel purer than before, because less involved with unrelated physical ideas. Why, then, should the doctrine of the conversion of force, or of the development of species, awaken fears for the Christian faith? It is no new and strange ordeal through which it is called to pass, this eliminating of certain outward forms in which, for a time, it had been clothed. It is an experience which belongs to every age, and is essential to the life and development of the world. Let me not be misunderstood here. I do not speak of the spiritual, but of the physical, elements in our religious ideas. One of the leading American magazines for the coming month sounds this note of alarm in a strenuous article, that seems not only excessive, but undiscriminating as to these very distinctions that are so fundamental.

Such anxieties arise from a want of confidence in the Divine ordering of human progress, and are unworthy of the calm assurance that should be the mark, as it is the privilege, of every Christian believer. It is ours to look forward, and not back, to the Golden Age, to rest in joyful certainty of the coming of an era of wisdom, holiness, and peace. Every past century, through all the storms of history, has contributed to this result; and as believers in the word of God, we may not and cannot fear that His plans or promises shall fail. Our way is plain and our duty is solemn. Let us, as guides and teachers of youth, labor to impress upon their minds and hearts the inward grounds of spiritual confidence. Let us warn them against the timorous and doubting tendencies which go far to create the very conflict which they so much dread. Let us teach them to love and honor the work of science, and to base their faith on better and broader foundations than any that can be shaken by historical or physical discovery. The principles of the Gospel—ruin by nature, atonement by Christ, salvation by faith in Him—are eternal and unchangeable as He from whom they come; but the forms and vehicles in which they are received must change with the changes of human thought and progress. "Let us not, therefore, judge one another any more, but judge this rather, that no man put a stumbling-block, or an occasion to fall, in his brother's way."

It is difficult, however, for men to change conceptions, which are deeply planted in their minds, and associated, however needlessly, with great and cherished truths. The liberal and progressive man of to-day becomes the conservative and the reactionist of to-morrow. Thus it is well and wisely ordered that "the workmen die, but the work goes on." Nay, it must be so, that the work may go on. Let us follow fearlessly the advance of truth, seeking, in all these strifes and collisions, "the things which make for peace;" and when at length we grow into the mental, as into the physical, rigidity of age, and can no longer keep up with the march of thought and knowledge, instead of doubting or despairing as to the result, let us leave the work to abler and stronger laborers, trusting the future of humanity to Him who "fainteth not neither is weary" in all the succession of ages; and let us rejoice that He, who has planned and guided all the laws and all the stages of the world's long epochs of development, will remove us from a sphere wherein our usefulness is ended, to a renewed condition, of power, energy, and purity, in the kingdom of His Son.

THE STUDY OF LATIN.

By Professor ABEL G. HOPKINS, A. M.,

Of Hamilton College.

I may be allowed to express the wish that in presenting a paper at this time I might have offered something which, in its relations to the interest and discussions of this body, should be of a more practical bearing; that I might have had time and opportunity to take up with the suggestion lately made by your secretary to offer some suggestions on the preliminary and preparatory instruction of young men for the study of Latin. And yet I make no apology for offering to you any thought upon a subject of this kind. At a time when discussion is rife, when the different modes of education are being weighed in the balance and some of them found wanting, when utility is arrayed against culture, and science against language, it cannot be without advantage that we should call to mind briefly the aids and advantages which accrue to one from the study of the Latin language. And though the essay which I present be not such as to array you against each other in faction and discussion, and though the thoughts and arguments may be, many of them, familiar, I shall be satisfied with having put them together in form and shape, and with that result which must always flow from the discussion of even old and familiar themes—the awakening of new thought and interest.

There is a blunt old saying, often quoted, that "a fool is never quite a fool unless he knows Latin," and the words are true if understood in their proper satirical application. Nothing is more odious than pedantry, even in a scholar. But when shallowness and superficial training assume the garb of the scholar, and by hackneyed quotations and memorized lines seek to pass among the learned, or, worse still, when they seek to pass off as classical Latin some mongrel compound, wholly innocent of all acquaintance with the grammar, "which would have made Quintilian stare and gasp," the saying is quite apt that "a fool is never quite a fool unless he knows Latin." But the words might equally well and with equal truth assume another and a better form. Equally true is it that a *scholar* is never quite a *scholar* unless he knows Latin. He may be observing, profound, studious, and yet, in culture and finish, in the very consciousness of the man himself, there is always something lacking. There have been scholars who were ignorant of classic lore, there have been profound thinkers and vigorous writers to whom a page of Latin would have been meaningless and strange; and yet if we take the confessions of these very men we shall find that there was something absent from the fullness and roundness of their composition.

What a charm there is which constantly lingers about that age of English society when Horace and Juvenal, Cicero, Livy and Tacitus were brought out from the cells of cloisters to revel in a new life, and to add lustre to the dawning and growing brightness of English learning; when all with eager zeal courted the philosophy and literature of Rome, and social life boasted a rich and varied learning, which for centuries before had been largely the heritage of monks. Then noble men and beautiful women were equally conversant with the authors and poets of the Augustine age. Then Elizabeth, and Lady Jane Gray, and bloody Mary were accomplished Latin scholars, and not only read, but even wrote and conversed in Latin. And from that impulse came that line of English scholars whose pastime and delight it has been to read and to criticise the literature of Rome.

It is my purpose in this sketch merely to point out some of the pleasures and advantages of the study of Latin. One of the most obvious of advantages, though perhaps not the most exalted, is that one may feel himself of the number of educated men. There is a commonwealth of scholars which has all the appliances and organization of civil society. It has its government, its judges, its censors, and citizenship in it gives fame and title. Its privileges are not hereditary. Its ranks are recruited from all classes, and the avenues which lead to its honors are diligence and persevering fidelity. And yet this commonwealth has its passports, its shibboleth, without which foreigners are not naturalized, or, if received at all, are looked upon as adopted citizens with only partial rights and honors. However full and generous may be one's education in other respects, he is always looked upon a little as an alien unless he has a classical training. He does not breathe the same air with them. He may mingle *with* them, but he is not fully of them. They have quenched their thirst at fountains of learning and wisdom which he can never know. They have mingled with great souls and shared in noble deeds and impulses, to which he must ever be a stranger; or, if he knows them at all, he must speak with them through an interpreter or share their thoughts in an imperfect and diluted form. The man of liberal education the world over is the man of classical education. For *education*, if we interpret the word in its best and truest meaning, is not fitting a man specifically to be a banker or artisan or teacher, but it consists in so leading out the powers of the mind and rounding out the whole nature that the man himself shall be complete with a generous culture, and so best fitted for any department of professional or active life which he may choose. Sir Walter Scott, with all the power and witchery of his pen, always lamented his lack of classical knowledge; and if that pen, which has woven Scottish history and legends into tales of such marvelous power, had lent any of its magic to the fields of Roman story, might it not have delineated that history with a thrilling interest surpassing even Bulwer, and investing with a new charm the heroic struggle and dim traditions of 2,000 years ago? What educated man can afford to be without some knowledge of that people whose history is pregnant with teaching and illustration for all time? And by as much as it is better and more thrilling to stand in Rome itself or to tread the field of Marathon than to read the letters of travelers, by so much is it better to know the eloquence of Cicero or the dense and pregnant thoughts of Tacitus in their own words and language than to receive them through the medium of some other tongue. The men of eloquent lips and learned words in the past and in the present have been men who in thought, illustration and diction have drawn largely from the stores of classic learning. It is there that the orator masters his style, there the historian finds his best models, there the poet resorts for imagery. All scholarly men have seated themselves as disciples at the feet of this ancient learning.

And if we read the lives of distinguished men we shall learn something of the value which they have placed upon these sources of intellectual training and of learning. In Rufus Choate's Diary we read substantially as follows: "In my reading of the Odyssey, Thucydides, Tacitus and Juvenal, I need make no change. To my Greek I must add a page a day of Crosby's grammar and the practice of parsing every word in my few lines of Homer. If this, with other studies, is not enough, I will translate a sentence or two from Tacitus." Of Robert Hall, who was, perhaps, the most sonorous and eloquent of English pulpit orators, his biographer tells us: "To the Latin and Greek poets, orators, historians and philosophers, he devoted a part of every day for many years of his life. He studied them as a scholar, but he studied them also as a moralist and philosopher, so that he appreciated their peculiarities and beauties, and carefully improved his style of writing and his tone of thinking by the best models which

they present." And what pleasanter picture have we in all our literature than that of Miles Standish, the Puritan captain, in those turbu-
lent days of our early history, when the profession of the soldier, the
scholar and the Christian went hand in hand?

> "Fixed to the opposite wall was a shelf of books, and among them
> Prominent three, distinguished alike for bulk and for binding,
> Bariffe's Artillery Guide and the Commentaries of Cæsar,
> Out of the Latin translated by Arthur Goldinge of London,
> And, as if guarded by these, between them was standing the Bible.
> Musing a moment before them, Miles Standish paused, as if doubtful
> Which of the three he should choose for his consolation and comfort;
> Whether the wars of the Hebrews, the famous campaign of the Romans,
> Or the artillery practice designed for belligerent Christians.
> Finally, down from its shelf, he dragged the ponderous Roman,
> Seated himself by the window, and opéned the book, and in silence
> Turned o'er the well worn leaves, where thumb-marks thick on the margin,
> Like to the trample of feet, proclaimed that the battle was hottest."

But to say nothing of the fact that, by ignorance of the Latin language, one is debarred from so much that is noble and instructive in
Roman history and literature, how can we read with intelligence and
appreciation much of the literature of our own land? How many
orations and essays have drawn their pointed mottoes and pithy illustrations from Roman authors, and often in their very language?
How could you read the Spectator, the Tatler, the Rambler; how
could you read Goldsmith, or Boswell's Life of Johnson, without
knowing something of the language which is scattered at intervals all
through these works? You can hardly take up an oration delivered
before a body of scholars, or the proceedings of any learned body,
without finding that the speaker or the writer have availed themselves, more or less, of that language with which their own thoughts
were long ago expressed in their richest and most compact form.
Indeed, science, which is so often falsely arrayed against the classics,
goes to the classics for many a text, and draws from that source illustrations and embellishments for many of its truths. Tyndal goes to
Lucretius when he wishes for an apt introduction to a series of scientific essays. Huxley sprinkles Latin phrases through his essays, and
in the midst of a most earnest plea for more scientific culture, pauses
to pronounce a eulogy upon classical training. If we do not believe
in the transmigration of souls, we do believe in the transmigration of
ideas. Those thoughts which lived two thousand years ago, in Roman
form and in Roman garb, have come to life again in our day. The
literature of *our* race is impregnated with them, and he who would
mingle with our educated men and read their works with sympathy

and intelligence, must also know that language and those authors to whom they owe so much.

Another decided advantage in the study of Latin—for it is with the practical rather than the esthetic bearing of this question that I am dealing—is found in practical every-day life. And it is precisely upon this point that an argument is so often raised against classical learning. The lawyer, the merchant, the physician, what are these better, they ask, for the knowledge of a language which is hidden away in musty old books, and which is utterly useless for the intercourse of common life. Such logic as this reminds one of the words of the dull Dutch schoolmaster in the "Vicar of Wakefield." "You see me, young man," he said: "I never learned Greek, and I don't find that I have ever missed it. I have had a doctor's cap and gown without Greek. I have ten thousand florins a year without Greek. I eat heartily without Greek, and, in short, as I don't know Greek, I do not believe there is any good in it." And so, many of the arguments of those who assail the study of Latin would, if reduced to their essence, come nearly to this climax of all arguments: "I do not know Latin, and therefore I do not believe there is any good in it." But let us not deal uncharitably with such arguments. Let us answer with all kindness the reasoning of these eminently practical men, who see no good in anything which does not feed or clothe them, or add to the number of material comforts. Let us be as practical as any one can wish, and let us say, as we truly may, that the arm does strike a better blow; that the artisan does his work with better judgment and accuracy; that the wheelwright, the blacksmith, the farmer, the mason perform their several tasks with greater pleasure, ease and perfection for the study of the Latin language. Let us look at this. What is it in any of the practical industries that makes a superior and trustworthy workman? Is it not the power to reason, compare and judge? And if we were to compare any two courses or plans of education on the basis of their utility and practical results, should not that system be assigned to the first rank which makes the man master of himself and master of his mental powers, whatever his circumstances may be? "If we allow education," to use the language of a famous scientist, "which ought to be directed to the making of men, to be diverted into a process of manufacturing human tools, wonderfully adroit in the exercise of some technical industry, but good for nothing else," does it not woefully fail of its object, and prove false to its name and mission? Now, in the study of Latin or of Greek, the nicest and closest powers of discrimination are brought into active exercise. Comparison is constantly made use of. The judgment is on the alert at every step. Take the analysis of a single sentence for example. It is not a matter of the application of blind and inflexible rules. Language has its laws, to be sure, but there is nice discrimination to be exercised in the application of those laws. A passage from a Latin author is like the disjointed parts of a dissected map, thrown into the hands of the scholar. The sentence is complete, all the parts are there, but how shall they be arranged? Or take the different words of the sentence, and open your lexicon. Each has a score of different meanings, or shades of the same meaning, and whether you will get any sense, or the right sense from the passage, depends on a nice comparison of the relations and possible meanings of subject and object, and verb and predicate.

Between the proper rendering of the first line of the Æneid, and the absurd burlesques which have been made of it, there is a vast difference; but it is *only* the difference between a student who makes no use of his powers of judgment and comparison, and one whose mind is somewhat disciplined in these respects.

Now, are not these the very powers which men need; which men *do* use, and *must* use in the practical affairs of life? The financier who invests his money, well or ill, may trace his success or failure to the discipline or neglect of these faculties. The farmer, to meet with success, must use these powers in the preparation of the soil, and the sowing and ingathering of the seed. The architect, too, must rely largely upon these at every step, from the selection of the material to the completion of his building. We are not placed here to go through life like machines, in obedience to inflexible laws. Reasoning upon the *probabilities* of life forms the basis of nine-tenths of human action.

Rarely, almost never, can we lay down our premises, and then say with absolute certainty, this, and this only, is the course to be taken. It is by comparing one course with another, by balancing the possible, the probable and the expedient that we come to any judgment or decision. And this is precisely the process which every student goes through in analyzing a Latin sentence. By trying the different possible relations of the parts of the sentence, by comparing the varied meanings of the words in their relation to each other, and by comparing the sentence itself with the context, we finally arrive at our judgment of what, on the whole, is the best English equivalent for that sentence.

But let us look a little further into this question, and we shall find that those who plead for shutting out the Latin, or, in general, the classics, from special lines of education, cannot carry out their plan, without being forced to confess their own ignorance, or made mere parrots in the practice of their professions. Shall the lawyer never hear or know the pandects of Justinian? Shall he be ignorant of the laws of the twelve tables, or of the eloquent and subtle arguments of Roman jurists? Shall he not know the source or the meaning of those numberless traditions and maxims which have been handed down through the centuries? Shall he not be able to understand intelligently the terminology of his own profession, and attach no other meaning to the phrases in his law papers than he would to corresponding signs and symbols? If even a slight knowledge of Latin were more general—to use a simple illustration—we should not see, as we so often now do, the little phrase "*cui bono*," which is strictly, in its origin and import, a legal phrase, going the round of the papers, with the implied signification of "what is the good of it," and that, too, singularly enough, used by men who decry the good of classical learning.

And the case of the physician is no better if Latin be excluded. Shall he not know of Celsus and of Galen, who, next to Hippocrates, may be called the fathers of medicine? And as to the common language of his profession, he cannot tell his patient what ails him, without floundering beyond his depth in Greek and Latin. Picture to yourselves such a disciple of the healing art attempting to pronounce upon that disease which to him would be more frightful in its name than in its nature, "the *cerebro-spinal meningitis*." And the scientific man in any department is hardly better off. Zoölogy, paleontology, conchology, all go to the Greek and Latin for their terminology, and, without some knowledge of these languages, the scientist may as well know his bones, his shells or his fossils by numbers or by arbitrary signs. The language of Greece and Rome are the sources from which came largely the frame-work and the setting of science, and to discard or forget these would involve the utter confusion of science, or its reorganization upon an entirely different basis.

But I have failed, as yet, to notice one important advantage in the study of Latin, an advantage, too, which will appeal most strongly to the advocates of what is called scientific education. For *this*, as I understand it, proposes to tolerate, if not to welcome, such languages as the French, German and Spanish. The advantage to which I allude is the intimate relation which a knowledge of the Latin holds to the comparatively easy mastery of other languages. Apart from the value which it has in giving refinement of thought and power of fine analysis and distinction, it has also this important advantage, its relation to several modern languages of Europe.

All language is related more or less closely. And yet the relations of some languages, on account of phonetic and orthographic changes, are very obscure, and can be detected only by the skilled and practiced eye of the philologist. But with the Latin and its allied languages it is not so. Even the eye which is moderately trained can trace the slight changes which in many cases have taken place in the transition from the tongue of Rome to that of Spain, Italy or France. These languages are not only children of the same parent; they are children who have but recently left the maternal roof, and who still, in voice and dress, bear clearly the indications of their parentage. So close and important is this relation, that it is the expressed opinion of some scholars of high standing that a knowledge of Latin will enable a student to acquire *two* or even three modern languages in the same time in which, if ignorant of Latin, he could acquire one. Illustrations of this relation are so common, that almost all will recall some instances. The verb " to be," is nearly the same in all its forms in the Latin, Italian, Spanish, Portuguese and French. The Latin *"caballus"*—a horse—becomes the French *"cheval,"* and the Italian *"cavallo."* The verb *"amo,"* in the Latin, is only the *" aimer "* of the French, and how similar in their conjugations, as, *e. g.*, the first and third persons, *"ego amo"* and *"ille amat"* become in the French *"j'aime"* and *"il aime."* Or, take again the Latin *"senior,"* the comparative of the adjective *"senex,"* and see how naturally this in its growth and changes runs into the French *"seigneur,"* the Italian *"signore,"* and the Spanish *"senor."* A few examples of this kind are enough to illustrate the fact which I have stated. He who has the resources of but one language at his command must live in a comparatively narrow range of thought. To him language is a fossil thing—an instrument made ready for his use—of whose origin or growth he may probably neither know nor care anything. But no one can gain the mastery of another language without beginning to reason and compare, and so the study of philology has already begun. I might prolong this paper, which is already too extended, and show the relations of Latin to our own language; how it lets the light through it, and makes of many a dull word a living picture, so that we see a vivid illustration of the thought. What is our general notion, for instance, of the word conspiracy? What is the loose popular conception of the conspiracy which culminated in the death of Cæsar? Why, that Brutus, and Cassius and Tribonius, and others, in their respective homes, and sometimes by stealthy meetings, were working up their plot. But hold the classical lamp a little nearer, and we see a group of eager, intense, excited men, their heads bending toward a common center, mingling their breath as well as their thoughts, and hatching up some mischief for the State. With such a knowledge we go through life with an illuminated pathway, we speak more intelligently, we use language with better discrimination.

Our country has no firmer patriots, and the youth of our land no warmer friends, than those instructors who put the growing spirit of the age in a way to come in contact with the spirit of liberty, of law and of republican freedom, which comes down to us in the language and literature of Rome. Nor, apart from the consolations of Christianity, can any richer satisfaction be stored away for the leisure hours or declining days of life, than the power to share in those noble thoughts, and to communicate with those great souls which breathe upon us or speak to us from the pages of Cicero, Pliny or Tacitus.

7

A SCIENTIFIC INSTITUTE FOR TEACHERS.

By Jonathan Allen, Ph. D.,
President of Alfred University.

The Legislature of 1865 adopted the following resolution:

Resolved, That the Regents of the University report to the Legislature, at its next session, what means may be necessary, with a plan, for placing the State Cabinet of Natural History in the condition required by the present state of science, to maintain it in full efficiency as a museum of scientific and practical geology and comparative zoölogy; and whether the establishment of a system of free lectures in connection with the cabinet is desirable, and if so, on what general plan the same should be founded.

The secretary of the Regents was instructed to prepare an answer to this resolution. To that end, he obtained the views of several gentlemen actively engaged in scientific pursuits, and their correspondence was published. As a result of this effort, the museum has been largely increased in value and efficiency. It is not our purpose to dwell upon these various plans proposed, only so far as they may be made available to the advancement of scientific instruction in the schools of the State. All these plans propose exchanges, free lectures, professors and students; and no better beginning could be made than by inaugurating the system with such a course of instruction as shall meet the wants of those teachers already engaged in giving instruction in geology, paleontology, and natural history. Every such teacher ought to be practically familiar with all the typical minerals, rocks, fossils, plants and animals, and the best modes of instructing classes in the same. Generally, you will find better teachers in the languages and mathematics than in geology and natural history. This arises not from a want of ability in the teachers themselves, but from the want of proper cabinets and specimens, and skill in their use. Such teachers are compelled to rely largely on text-books. There needs to be organized a kind of scientific State teachers' institute, where the teachers of our public schools and academies, interested in such studies, could spend a few weeks each year, or a longer time for those who wish to enter on more extended studies. There seems to be no insurmountable obstacle in the way of carrying out this enterprise. The scientists of America have been lifted to their feet with enthusiasm over the successful inauguration of the Anderson School of Science, on the island of Penekese, by Professor Agassiz.

Has not the State of New York, in its Museum of Natural History, a nucleus for a practical training school for the teachers of science in our various institutions? The State has expended upon its geological survey and its Museum of Natural History more than $600,000—money well and nobly expended. It is still sustaining these at an annual expense of over $10,000. The benefits to science from these expenditures, and from the labors of the able and skilled scientists employed by the State, cannot well be overestimated. There is no recent geological work in any European language that does not recognize and use the nomenclature first proposed by the geologists of New York. New York is the only one of the States which has established a scientific museum as the result of its geological survey. New York possesses the most complete and unbroken series of the palæozoic rocks known in the world, and for that of the oldest crystalline rocks, and those succeeding to the base of the coal formation, the collection in the museum, with the nomenclature of New York, will always be the standard of reference and authority. If judiciously fostered and used, this museum, with its extensive collections and increasing publications, may be made to perform an important and prominent part in the scientific education of the youth of the State. The great need now is to connect it with our educational system. On the one hand, by such an arrangement, it would be saved by these vital relations with the educational interests of the State from the chances of decay and dissolution, and on the other, it would give these interests new life and vigor. As now situated, the relation of this institution to our educational institutions is analogous to that of the brain to the various ganglia distributed throughout the human body, without the connecting nerves. Supply these nerves, and you have a system complete for the diffusion of intelligence to all parts of our organic system. The museum would be raised from the character of a curiosity shop, where visitors may while away an hour in looking, to that of a genuine instructor of the youth of the State. It is believed that this object can be accomplished with very little, if any, increase of the current expenses of the museum. By a recent act of the Legislature of the State of Illinois, it is required that natural history be made a branch of popular education. Massachusetts requires the museum of comparative zoölogy at Harvard to distribute certain of its duplicate specimens to the normal schools of the State. This State cannot long remain inactive. It has a better equipped museum than any other State for training its students in the knowledge of its own scientific resources. Its doors are already invitingly open. It offers its benefits to the teachers of the State. Will they accept them?

I close by offering the following resolutions:

1. *Resolved*, That the Regents be solicited to carry into effect the exchange of collections, through the medium of the State Museum of Natural History, assisted by the various institutions, according to the recommendations made in the report of the committee to this body, at the session of 1870.

2. *Resolved*, That the Regents of the University be requested to take such measures as may be necessary to secure the establishment of a scientific institute, under the charge of the Regents and the Director of the Museum, with the special object of giving the scientific teachers of the State a better and more practical knowledge of those branches of science which the geological survey of the State has been engaged in developing; this institute to be inaugurated, if found practicable, at the next meeting of this Convocation.

GRAMMAR AS A NATURAL SCIENCE.

By Principal CHARLES T. R. SMITH, A. M.,

Of Lansingburgh Academy.

It is the object of this paper to show the belief of the author in regard to the use, place and relative importance of English Grammar in a course of study, and the methods of teaching appropriate to it.

For these purposes, a distinction is to be made between the science of grammar and the art of composition. It is taken for granted in this discussion, that the latter should be studied in some form from the first year in the primary school to the last of the university course. The power of expressing thought is second in importance only to the power of thinking, and no pains should be spared to develop it. Each pupil should receive exercise not monthly, or semi-monthly, nor even weekly, but daily, in some method of expressing original thoughts; but this is the study of "language," or "composition," or rhetoric, not grammar.

Nevertheless, the study of technical grammar has a useful sphere of its own, and it is feared that there is a tendency to give the branch less attention than it deserves. The growing crowd of "ologies" which are introduced into academies, and into many common schools, seem to supplant it, and it becomes harder year by year to lead pupils to pursue it in academies where the course of study is optional.

"Grammer never'll be no use to me; I ain't goin' to be a preacher nor a lawyer. I guess I'll study 'rithmetic and 'ritin and book-keepin' and phlos'phy, maybe," the young man says who comes in from the country for a winter's "schoolin;" and the town boy's mother thinks her young hopeful "had better not study grammar any more for the present, he finds it so hard, but take up some branch that will be more useful to him," and asks if you have a class in geology. The requirements of the Regents' examination do much to correct this disregard for the study, and it is to be hoped that, under the new distribution of State funds, they will be able to do more; still, teachers must influence their pupils mainly by argument and persuasion.

What, then, is the use of studying grammar? The stereotyped answer comes: "It teaches us to speak and write the language correctly." But does it ? Is it not painfully apparent that the diction of our pupils is determined by early association, and fixed by habit, and is dependent slightly, if at all, upon grammatical acquirements ?

It is true that the long and severe training in the principles of general grammar, which a classical education imposes, generally corrects faulty habits in written language, and often in every-day speech. Not so with grammar, as studied at common schools and academies. The work which these can do in purifying the pupils' vernacular must be mainly done by persistent correction at an age when the laws of syntax are unmeaning jargon and the forms of etymology utterly unintelligible. If grammar is taken up with the idea that a knowledge of the science will undo the habits of years, the learner is doomed to disappointment. This must be done by daily exercise and criticism in the art of composition. What *is* the use of it, then ?

The object of education is the development of all the powers. Two of the most important of these are the powers of classification and generalization. Grammar is the most available branch to develop them.

That the powers of classification and generalization are of great importance, is manifest. The number of facts which address themselves to the human mind is infinite. To gain a knowledge of them separately is impossible. They must be reduced to classes. Classification, then, is the second step in the acquirement of knowledge, and there is no more fruitful source of indistinctness and confusion of thought than improper classifications. A mental process closely allied to classification, and which may for our purposes be called by the same name, is that of determining whether a given fact or phenomenon falls into a previously defined class. Skill in this process is a chief requisite for success in practical life. The *diagnosis* of the physician is an effort to ascertain to what class of diseases the ailment of his patient is to be referred. The lawyer aims to bring the case of his client into a class of cases on which previous decisions have been obtained, and in every occupation the habits of close observation, of attention to nice points of likeness and of difference, necessary for correct classification, are invaluable. No less useful is the power of generalizing. Witness the splendid results of Newton's grand generalization, and, in our own time, the effects upon science and art of the doctrine of the correlation and conservation of forces. These effects appear in the new methods of developing and applying electricity and magnetism, which come under our notice every year and almost every month.

Not a few thinkers have believed that the powers of abstraction, classification and generalization constitute the main difference between the mental nature of man and that of the brutes. Dugald Stewart says of them: "Those powers which enable us to classify objects and to employ signs as instruments for thoughts are, as far as we can judge, peculiar to the human species." It is plain, since these powers are of such great practical value and of such intrinsic nobility, that a system of education ought to make ample provision for cultivating them. The study of botany gives fine opportunities for training the perceptive faculties and for inducing habits of classification. So do zoölogy and mineralogy. Natural philosophy, chemistry and geology, if taught synthetically, afford means for the development of the powers of generalization, and thus we see abundant reason for the study of the natural sciences. But as actually taught, and as in most cases they must be taught, in our high schools and academies, wherein are these sciences superior as means of training to the study of grammar? In fact, for educational purposes, and intrinsically in many respects, it may fairly be maintained that grammar *is* a natural science. What are the characteristics of the natural sciences? In the words of a distinguished teacher of a neighboring State: "All of them consist of facts which must be observed, of classes which must be formed, of inferences which must be drawn, and laws which must be applied." Could a better description of the science of grammar be framed? Of what do orthography and etymology consist, but of "facts which must be observed, and classes which must be formed," and what is the subject-matter of syntax and prosody but "inferences which must be drawn, and laws which must be applied?" When we give the student a list of words like *refer, offer, remit, profit, sin, ruin,* and lead him to observe that the place of the accent determines whether the consonant shall be doubled before an initial vowel in a suffix, and to classify the words accordingly, do we not train him to observe differences and form classes, as truly as when we lead him to assort plants as monocotyledonous or dicotyledonous, or teach him the distinction between artiad and perissad elements?

There is this difference, however, that in the former case he acquires knowledge which he will be almost sure to employ every day of his life, and in the latter, although the process of thought strengthens his mind and develops his love of nature (if disgust at the "hard names" does not overpower every other feeling), his knowledge of the facts will be of little use to him, unless he shall happen to be a professional botanist or chemist. But it is said that the subject-matter of the natural sciences is existence, palpable to the senses, actual, real. Are rocks, and plants, and animals, and forces any more actual and real than the words and idioms of language? Language is a natural growth, a product of various causes, and the study of its uniformities, its anomalies and its laws is as much a natural science as botany, or zoölogy, or geology, or physics.

Most schools lack the means for teaching these sciences objectively and inductively. Herbaria, cabinets, museums and philosophical and chemical apparatus exist only in homœopathic quantity as yet in the academies and union schools of the State. These natural sciences, if taught analytically from a text-book, are of no more value than mathematics for developing the powers of observation, of classification and generalization. In most of the academies a lack of appliances, and still more, a lack of time, prevent teaching them in any other way; but no apparatus is needed for teaching grammar; its specimens we have always with us, its living forms are constantly on our lips, and its cabinets are between the covers of every classic volume.

Besides these considerations, there is this further one, of great importance in this practical age, that for one occasion where we have need to apply the principles of natural history, or physics, or chemistry, there are a hundred where we have use for the principles of grammar in criticising the productions of ourselves or others; for although the *use* of language is almost entirely a matter of habit, yet the criticism of it after it is used, if intelligent, must be scientific.

This discussion has been confined to English grammar; but it is plain that whatever has been said in favor of its study, applies with ten-fold force to the noble tongues of Greece and Rome. Their mechanical construction and precise laws make them far better appliances for training the mental powers of which we have spoken, than our own language.

Educationally, then, the principal uses of grammar are to form habits of close observation, and exercise the powers of classification and generalization, and for these purposes it is to be classed among the natural sciences, and as most available of them all.

At what point of the pupil's progress should it be introduced? It seems to me that the same principles should be observed as with the other natural sciences. There are certain elements of them all, that appeal mainly to the perceptive powers, which may profitably be studied at a very early age. It has long been almost a maxim of education, that childhood is the time for acquiring the art of using language. The organs of speech are flexible and easily habituated to the production of new sounds, and the acquirement of a varied vocabulary is easy and pleasurable. Some of the elementary classifications and distinctions of grammar, e. g., the " parts of speech " may also be acquired, if taught concretely, and are very convenient in teaching composition, the study of which should begin with the child's earliest instruction, and end only with his school life.

Not so with the formal study of grammar. Its chief object, as we have seen it, is to exercise certain mental powers. But those powers cannot be exercised before they exist. Now, if I have observed correctly, the faculty of abstraction, on which these powers depend, is one of the latest to be developed. It has been remarked by some metaphysicians that animals do not possess it at all, and savages manifest it only in a very limited degree, and it is natural that its development in man should be late. Every teacher has experienced the difficulty, if not impossibility, of conveying to a child the idea of an abstract number or of an abstract noun. The child's conceptions are of the concrete and the individual, and his classifications are based upon similarity, not upon general notions. It is my own belief that, as a rule, the power of abstraction is not developed till about the fourteenth year, and that the study of technical grammar should usually be postponed to that age. I deem its importance greater than that of any other of the natural sciences, I had almost said than all of them, and that a proportionate time should be allowed for it in a course of study.

As regards the methods of teaching, they should be at first synthetic, and if the mental process of assigning an individual to a class previously defined, is called by that term, they should be synthetic throughout. To illustrate: if one is teaching the principle of syntax that the subject of the infinitive is in the objective case, he should begin, not by stating the rule and giving examples, but by giving many sentences in which the subject of the infinitive is a personal pronoun, the case of which can be distinguished by its form, leading his pupils to observe the case and generalize for themselves. In this way he will not only train the powers which grammar is adapted to exercise, but he can show them the danger of hasty generalizations, and the difficulty of framing abstract definitions and principles which shall cover all cases, not only in language but in life.

The old-fashioned exercise of parsing, especially when extended to the analysis of sentences, is invaluable in forming habits of close observation and nice distinction. It is difficult to see in what the much vaunted practice of chemical analysis by the pupils, lately introduced into some eastern and western high schools, differs from it as a mental process, or is superior to it as a means of mental training.

In short, in teaching grammar, the instructor should keep in view the particular faculties which the science is adapted to exercise, and not apply the methods of mathematics to a NATURAL SCIENCE.

STATE AID TO ACADEMIC INSTITUTIONS.

REPORT OF THE COMMITTEE OF FIFTEEN ON LEGISLATIVE AID TO THE ACADEMIC INSTITUTIONS OF THE STATE OF NEW YORK.

At the last meeting of this Convocation, the following resolution was adopted:

Resolved, That this Convocation appoint a committee of fifteen to secure, with the co-operation of the Regents, the perpetuity of the legislative aid already obtained, and to perfect and secure the passage of the supplementary law in such a form as shall unite the academic institutions and the common schools of the State in more intimate and mutually helpful relations, to the end of promoting thereby a more thorough training in the common English, as well as the higher branches of education.

Under this resolution, the Chancellor continued the committee of ten of the previous year on "State Aid to Academic Institutions," adding thereto the requisite number to complete the committee. The committee, in pursuance of its appointment, has held two sessions during the year at Albany, one December 26th, 1872, and the other March 6th, 1873. A prolongated and vigorous effort was made on the part of those opposed to the measure to repeal or render nugatory the law of the previous Legislature, but after protracted and earnest discussion in both branches of the Legislature, it was reaffirmed by large majorities and with increased emphasis.

In the discharge of its duties, your committee found it necessary to issue a rejoinder to certain adverse representations. That rejoinder is herewith presented in the form of a supplement to this report.

The supplementary act, which had failed before the previous Legislature, after being amended in several particulars, became a law under the sanction of the last Legislature. The following is a copy of the act, as ultimately passed:

CHAPTER. 642.

AN ACT in relation to academies and academical departments of union schools, and the distribution of public funds.

PASSED May 29, 1873; three-fifths being present.

The People of the State of New York, represented in Senate and Assembly, do enact as follows:

SECTION 1. The sum of one hundred and twenty-five thousand dollars, ordered by chapter five hundred and forty-one of the laws of eighteen hundred and seventy-two, to be levied for each and every year, for the benefit of academies and academical departments of union schools, shall be annually distributed by the regents of the university, for the purposes and in the manner following, that is to say:

§ 2. Three thousand dollars or so much thereof as may be required, in addition to the annual appropriation of three thousand dollars for the same purpose from the literature fund, for the purchase of books and apparatus, to be annually apportioned and paid in the manner now provided by law.

§ 3. Twelve thousand dollars, or so much thereof as may be required in addition to the annual appropriation of eighteen thousand dollars from the United States deposit fund, for the instruction of common-school teachers; the whole sum to be apportioned and paid to the several institutions which may give such instruction as now provided by law, at the rate of fifteen dollars for each scholar instructed in a course prescribed by the said regents, during a term of thirteen weeks, and at the same rate for not less than ten weeks or more than twenty weeks.

§ 4. The said regents shall cause to be admitted to the academic examination, established by them in the academies and academical departments of union schools, any common school, or free school, any scholar from any common school who may apply for such examination bearing the certificate of the principal teacher, or of any trustee of such school, that in his judgment such scholar is qualified to pass the said examination.

§ 5. Free instruction in the classics or the higher branches of English education, or both, shall be given in every academy and academical department of a union school subject to the visitation of the said regents, under such rules and regulations as the said regents may prescribe, to all scholars, in any academy and in any free school, or in any common school, who, on any examination held subsequent to the beginning of the present academic year, shall have received the certificate of academic scholarship issued by the said regents to the extent of twelve dollars, and if the condition of the fund will admit not less than twenty dollars tuition, at such rates of tuition as are usually charged for such scholars in such academies and academical departments respectively, and in case the tuition is free to resident pupils, at the rates charged to non-resident pupils, or at such rates, in all cases, as the said regents may deem reasonable; but such free instruction must be obtained by such scholars within two years from the date of their examination respectively.

§ 6. The said regents may, in their discretion and under such rules as they may adopt, annually apply a sum not exceeding two thousand five hundred dollars, in book or other premiums, for excellence in scholarship and conduct, as shown in the papers and the returns of the academic examination; but the cost of any one premium shall not exceed ten dollars; and the said sum of two thousand five hundred dollars, or such part thereof as may be needed, shall be paid to the said regents out of the amount referred to in the first section of this act, by the treasurer on the warrant of the comptroller.

§ 7. The balance of the said one hundred and twenty-five thousand dollars remaining after the apportionments described in the preceding sections of this act shall have been made, shall be distributed as the literature fund is now by law directed to be distributed, but no money shall be paid to any school under the control of any religious or denominational sect or society.

§ 8. The said regents of the university are hereby authorized to make such just and equitable regulations as they may deem necessary for the purposes of this act.

§ 9. The treasurer shall pay, on the warrant of the comptroller, the several sums to which the said regents may certify any institution to be entitled under the provisions of this act.

§ 10. Every academy shall make up its annual report for its academic year, and shall transmit the same to the regents on or before the first day of September in each year.

§ 11. This act shall take effect immediately.

The report made at the last session of this Convocation, and the rejoinder already referred to, were, of necessity, wholly defensive, being intended to meet the opposition, from various quarters, to our academic institutions. As the remainder of this report, we will turn from these old issues and look toward new ones.

The value of the increased appropriation to the academic institutions of the State cannot well be overestimated. By it the State has declared anew, what it has so frequently declared before, that the academies are an integral and vital part of our educational system. The effect of these enactments will be to give new vigor to these institutions, and, through them, to all our educational interests. They stand so related to all other schools that whatever touches them touches all. The springs of life in our whole educational system will manifest new vitality. The common schools will feel it. The normal schools will feel it. The colleges will feel it. The professional schools will feel it.

But we should not be content with the good already attained. This law has inaugurated the principle of free tuition in academic institutions. This should be the aim and watchword of these institutions, till the principle thus inaugurated has its consummation in free academies throughout the State, for country as well as city and village. To this end it is necessary that the academies so approve themselves to the public in what has already been received, that the State will be ready to grant still larger aid. The academies and their friends have ever been forward in helping on the free-school movement for all the common schools. Of the $10,000,000 thus secured yearly for this end, they have never asked that it be abated or devoted to secondary or higher education, and it would seem that all friends of education could unite in securing free education for all. Let there be a steady, earnest and determined movement on the part of the friends of these institutions, and the object will be accomplished in due time; for it is the opinion of your committee that the people of the State of New York will help well and generously all educational interests. Only show them, by practical demonstration, the great benefits springing from what has already been done, and still larger aid will be cheerfully granted.

It is not so much our purpose, however, to enlarge upon the general benefits of the increased appropriation, as to call the attention of the Convocation to the ways and means devised in the supplemental law for the more efficient and beneficent use of portions of this fund.

I. This law secures a more vital relation between the academies and the common schools:

1st. By providing that "any scholar from any common school who may apply for such examination bearing the certificate of the principal teacher, or of any trustee of such school, that in his judgment such scholar is qualified to pass the said examination," shall be admitted to said examination.

2d. By providing that free instruction in the classics or the higher branches of English education, or both, shall be given in every academy and academical department of a union school subject to the visitation of the Regents, to the amount of not less than twelve, nor more than twenty dollars for each scholar.

This law assumes that these academic, or as they are more familiarly known, Regents' examinations, are a good and valuable thing. That they are, is freely conceded, even warmly maintained by all who have had experimental knowledge of their workings and results. These examinations have come with their imperative demand upon all academies for greater thoroughness in the common branches, and through them it is reaching the common schools. This new law comes in as an aid augmenting this influence.

We doubt not that if all having charge of our public-school interests would, as not a few commissioners have already done, adopt an examination equal in thoroughness and similar in mode for their lowest grade certificates, it would do much to elevate the condition of the schools.

Your committee are, however, of opinion that the time has fully come for an advance movement in the matter of examinations. In order that these examinations accomplish the most good possible, they need to be strengthened and enlarged. This should be done either by adding studies to the present examination, or by instituting a second examination of a higher grade, which shall include other studies essential to be known by every citizen, whatever his pursuits. The latter method is deemed preferable. This examination ought to include studies equivalent in amount to those required for entering the freshman class, either in the classical or the scientific course, as agreed on by this Convocation, with opportunity for elective studies for those who do not desire to pursue a collegiate course.

The Regents are doing a noble and most efficient work for primary education, in the examination already established; but greater achievements await them if they will but press vigorously the advantages already obtained. The examinations now established are giving a new spur to primary education, and the Regents have it in their power, it is believed, to give equal stimulus to higher education.

II. This law appropriates $12,000 additional to the $18,000 heretofore appropriated for the instruction of common-school teachers, thereby providing for more extended and efficient labors in this department. The academies will continue hereafter, as heretofore, largely to train the teachers of their respective localities and thus of the State. The purpose of this provision of the law is to elevate and extend that training. While the smaller academies will be able to continue the present form of the teachers' class with greater efficiency than before, the larger academies may be enabled, under proper arrangements, to organize a permanent teachers' department with its regular professorship; and it is the opinion of your committee that no more valuable service could be rendered, under this appropriation, than for the Regents to perfect some plan whereby all academies, which have a sufficiently large attendance of those preparing for teaching to warrant it, may establish a teachers' department, with courses of training for teachers similar to those now in operation in our normal schools. It is believed all the substantial results of a normal-school training can be secured, with comparatively little additional expense to the State. With one experienced teacher, devoted to the practical methods, the purely educational part can be performed by other teachers in their regular classes; and thus, while the expense to the State would be reduced to a minimum, the advantages to the teacher, by receiving his general education in the society of, and in contact with those seeking a general education, will be greatly enhanced.

III. This supplementary law likewise adds $3,000 to the appropriation heretofore made for philosophical and chemical apparatus. The time has come for a larger application of the term apparatus, either by the interpretation of the Regents, or by special legislation. The needs of science for appliances to illustrate its principles, phenomena, and their various applications to the industries, have very much transcended the limits of the law as now applied. The necessities placed on institutions, created by the growth and widened range of scientific and practical studies, have created in them a want for appliances to facilitate instruction that was comparatively unfelt when the law was first enacted. The science of geology which this State, through its able scientists, has done so much to enrich, extend and illustrate, and the manifold branches of natural history, are comparatively dead sciences in most of our institutions, for want of teachers with practical skill in teaching them and of means for their illustration. The great body of the students in our academic institutions finish their school education with their attendance on them. They go forth as teachers, and as workers in the varied industries of life. These institutions will continue to educate, as they have heretofore done, the great mass of our farmers, artisans and business men who seek any culture above the common school. The value to them of a practical familiarity with the appearance, composition and economical uses of the various soils, ores, minerals, woods, plants and animals; and of a correct knowledge of the characteristics of the various rock formations, with their numerous fossils as found in this State, cannot well be overestimated.

Impressed with this view of the subject, this body appointed a committee to devise some cheap and comprehensive plan to facilitate the organizing of geological cabinets for the schools of the State. Such a plan was mapped out and reported upon at the meeting of 1870. It proposed:

1st. That the several institutions under the visitation of the Regents of the University be invited to make collections of 100 or 200 specimens of a kind that may be found in their respective vicinities.

2d. That these collections of duplicates be sent to the State Museum at Albany, there to be distributed into suites, each of which shall contain a representation of the whole : these cabinets to be carefully labeled, and one returned to each of the institutions participating in the exchange, with a descriptive catalogue particularly stating the locality, name of collector or institution sending, geographical and geological distribution, scientific characters and economical uses.

This committee, in their memorial to the Legislature, well remark that, " scattered as these institutions are over every part of the State, and having within reach of each one of them materials for illustrating, to more or less extent, some feature of mineralogical or other scientific interest, it cannot be doubted that contributions from each one, or from any considerable number of them, would possess extraordinary interest, and that the acquisition of such collections by our academies would do much toward stimulating the youth attending them to those habits of observation and inquiry, and to that love of science which it is the duty of our seminaries to impart, and which becomes to the possessors a source of lasting enjoyment and profitable use." " The State of New York, which has so nobly provided the means of education for every grade of its citizens, by planting and promoting institutions of learning in every section, and by placing the means for acquiring knowledge within the easy reach of all classes, might find it consistent with that liberal policy which has hitherto distinguished its measures, to make a small yearly appropriation toward securing this end." An act was drafted appropriating $2,000 yearly to this object, but it went no further than to be reported to the House from the committee of ways and means, with a recommendation that it be printed as an Assembly document.

The failure to secure this financial aid from the Legislature has prevented, thus far, the carrying out of this very desirable project. The Regents of the University have, by the recent law, at their disposal all the funds, and more, that were asked for in this memorial, and it is believed that no better use can be made of a portion of the same than in carrying out the plan proposed in the report of that committee.

We close this report by recommending the adoption of the following resolutions :

1. *Resolved*, By the University Convocation, that in the continuance of the appropriation for academies and academic departments of union schools by the Legislature of the State, and in the passage by the Legislature of the supplementary act, which enlarges the

scope and the usefulness of academic normal classes, and which required the academies to respond to the bounty of the State by furnishing free tuition in higher studies, and by admitting pupils from the common schools to the Regents' examinations, and, when successful in such examinations, to a participation in that free, higher tuition, we gratefully recognize the reaffirmed policy of the State, permanently to care for and cherish this important class of our educational institutions whose prosperity stands vitally related to that of both the common schools to which they are a needed supplement, and the colleges which they supply with students.

2. *Resolved,* That the Regents of the University be requested to establish a second and higher examination, which shall require studies equal in amount to those fixed by this Convocation in the action of 1866, as the basis for entrance to college.

3. *Resolved,* That the Regents be requested to secure the establishment, on some proper basis, of a permanent Teachers' Department in those of the academies and union schools whose patronage from students preparing for teachers will warrant it, with such a course of study and methods of training as are demanded for professional teaching.

JONATHAN ALLEN, *Ph. D.,*
Principal of Academic Department, and
President of Alfred University.

MAUNSELL VAN RENSSELAER, *D. D.,*
President of Hobart College.

JOSEPH E. KING, *D. D., Ph. D.,*
Principal of Fort Edward Collegiate
Institute.

ALBERT WELLS, *A. M.,*
Principal of Peekskill Academy.

BENJAMIN N. MARTIN, *D. D., L. H. D.,*
Professor in the University of the City
of New York.

JAMES S. GARDNER, *A. M., Ph. D.,*
Principal of Whitestown Seminary.

GILBERT D. MANLEY, *A. M.,*
Principal of Cortland Academy.

ALBERT B. WATKINS, *A. M.,*
Principal of Hungerford Collegiate
Institute.

NOAH T. CLARKE, *A. M., Ph. D.,*
Principal of Canandaigua Academy.

JOHN JONES, *A. M., D. D.*,
        Principal of Geneseo Academy.

GEORGE W. BRIGGS, *A. M.*,
        Principal of Delaware Literary Inst.

SAMUEL G. LOVE, *A. M.*,
        *Principal of Jamestown Union School
        and Collegiate Institute.*

J. DORMAN STEELE, *A. M., Ph. D.*,
        Principal of Elmira Free Academy.

ALONZO FLACK, *A. M.*,
        *Principal of Claverack Academy and
        H. R. Institute,*
                        COMMITTEE.

SUPPLEMENT.

STATE AID TO ACADEMIES AND UNION SCHOOLS.

IN REPLY TO THE ANNUAL REPORT OF THE SUPERINTENDENT OF PUBLIC
INSTRUCTION.

The undersigned, a committee appointed by the University Convocation, a body composed mainly of the officers of the colleges and
academies of the State, to ask of the Legislature an increase of the
funds annually distributed to the academies and academical departments of union schools, in the discharge of that duty prepared a
form of memorial, which was numerously signed by the trustees of
those institutions and others, and submitted to the Legislature of
1872. The memorial asked for an increase of the appropriation,
without indicating the source from which it should come. Not a
remonstrance was presented against it. The Legislature enacted the
following in the general appropriation bill of 1872:

"For the benefit of academies and academical departments of the
union schools, the sum of one hundred and twenty-five thousand dollars, or so much thereof as may be derived from a tax of one-sixteenth
of one mill upon each dollar of the taxable property of the State; the
sum thus arising to be divided as the Literature Fund is now divided,
which is hereby ordered to be levied for each and every year."

This enactment has been strongly denounced in papers which claim
to be the special champions of common-school education, and especially by the Superintendent of Public Instruction, in his annual
report lately made to the Legislature. Objection to the measure
having thus assumed official form, the undersigned feel called upon
to correct inaccuracies of fact, and what they regard as erroneous
arguments upon the subject. In doing this, they will confine themselves to a consideration of the report above referred to. That part
of the report relating to normal schools we pass over, only making
for ourselves and those we represent an unqualified denial of hostility
to these schools operating within their legitimate sphere. The Superintendent objects to this appropriation to the academies: 1. Because
the academies proper are private institutions, outside of the public
school system of the State; 2. Because a large number are sectarian;
3. Because higher education should not be supported by a general

tax. We reply: 1. The Constitution of the State declares that the income of the Literature Fund shall be devoted to the support of academies, and the income of the Common School Fund to the support of common schools. They are thus recognized in the organic law, side by side with the common schools, as a part of the educational system of the State.

The statutes provide for their incorporation, define the powers and duties of their trustees, subject them to the visitation and control of officers duly appointed by the State, and impose the conditions on which they shall be admitted to participate in the public funds. Some of them have been incorporated under special laws, a part of which are in terms declared public laws. Besides creating a fund for their support, the Legislature has made numerous special appropriations to them. This has not been done to private academies, nor to these as private institutions, but to them as a part of the public school system of the State. The Revised Statutes, under the head of "Public Instruction," make the colleges, academies and common schools the public school system of the State. If, therefore, one class of these institutions is public, each of the others is also.

But, says the Superintendent, "a large number of academies have been organized by individuals, stock companies and religious denominations." It is true that individuals associate together and unitedly contribute the funds required by the statute for the establishment of an academy. They then apply to the Regents of the University for a charter, and the statute expressly declares that, on the issuing and recording of this charter, "the funds and property of the academy shall be vested in the trustees named in the charter for the use and benefit of the academy." The individuals lose all title in or control over what they have contributed, so long as it remains an academy. It is public property, to be used only for public education.

There are a few academies which have been established on a basis of capital stock, and this under authority of law. They are, however, prohibited by statute "from making dividends on any portion of their earning while there is any outstanding indebtedness against the said academy or institution." As a matter of fact, no such institution has for years made a dividend to its stockholders, and never has to an extent worthy of notice. We find that in the form of charter under which these academies are incorporated, as well as those on an endowment basis, is the condition that "the property shall never be applied to purposes other than for public academic instruction."

Nearly three and a half millions of dollars are invested in the academic institutions of the State. The great mass, if not all of this property has been contributed and consecrated to the public good, just as truly and much more cheerfully than if raised by tax. It is under State control and used for public education, just as completely as if raised by tax. The contributors have no more control over it, nor realize any more financial benefits from it, than if they had been taxed for the same amount under the provisions of the common-school law. The benefits accruing therefrom go to augment, not the property of the contributors, but public education, and thus the highest well-being of the State. Will the Superintendent name any three and a half millions of dollars raised by tax that is doing more to enlighten and ennoble the public than the above named sum contributed by our public-spirited citizens? Can he do it?

The increased aid secured by the recent legislation will, if perpetuated, greatly increase the amount and efficiency of these voluntary endowments. It is very desirable to cultivate in each citizen all the public spirit possible. Every dollar thus secured relieves taxation, and does the State just as much good as if raised by tax, while every youth educated in such institutions is educated just as much for citizenship and the public good as if educated entirely by means of taxation.

2. The Superintendent says: "It is well known that a large number of academies are institutions of strict sectarian character." The term "sectarian" is largely used, but very little and vaguely defined. It is to be regretted that this course should be pursued in a public document of the character of the Superintendent's report. If the term means, according to our most approved dictionaries, "pertaining to a sect," "peculiar to a sect," "adhering to a sect or religious denomination," and, in its application to academies, adherence to a sect is enforced, or the tenets or doctrines pertaining or peculiar to any sect are taught in them, we say that we do not know of any such academies under the control and patronage of the State. If the Superintendent has some different or occult meaning, by virtue of which he applies the term to those institutions, he was in duty bound to so have stated in his report upon the subject. There are in the State three academies whose trustees are elected by denominational bodies. They are: The Genesee Wesleyan Seminary, Lima, Livingston county; The Central New York Conference Seminary, Cazenovia, Madison county; The Black River Conference Seminary, Antwerp, Jefferson county.

The first two were chartered by the Legislature, with this restriction: "No part of the funds of the corporation hereby created shall ever be applied for the support of theological or other studies than those of literature and the fine arts." The Black River Conference Seminary was chartered under the general law, by the Regents of the University, under the name of the "Antwerp Liberal Literary Institute." The name was changed, and the power of electing the trustees was given to the conference by an act of the Legislature, in 1870. No such restriction as that above quoted is imposed on this seminary. If these can be regarded as sectarian institutions by any proper definition of the term, they are the only ones now sharing in the distribution of the Literature Fund to which that objection can be legitimately made.

The statute expressly provides that "no religious test or qualification shall be required from any trustee, president, principal or other officers of any incorporated college or academy, or as a candidate for admission to any privilege in the same." This charge of sectarianism is without force as applied to the great body if not to all of our academic institutions. Many of these institutions were founded and are sustained by local enterprise or public spirit, no more sectarian, or even religious, than was that which founded or located our normal or any other of our public schools; while most of those institutions which were founded through religious, even denominational enthusiasm, have been devoted to an unsectarian culture. In them, students from all denominations and from no denomination meet upon a perfect equality, find equal rights, privileges and opportunities. These institutions, as a whole, are as free from the taint of sectarian tenets, in their training, as are the normal and other schools. The daily work of all the normal schools, and thanks to the living piety of many of our common-school teachers, of their schools also, is begun by simple religious services, legal enactments and official decisions to the contrary notwithstanding. The same—no more, no less—is done in our academies. Is not a school officer or teacher, coming to his position through denominational impulses, quite as likely to work for the public good as one coming through political machinations? A public officer, though coming into power through politics, if he use his official position, not for party ends but for the public good, is accounted a faithful public servant, worthy of honor; so an institution of learning, coming into existence through denominational inspirations, yet using this existence, not for sectarian ends but for the public weal, should be accounted a public good and worthy of generous support. It is evident that the Superintendent does not clearly discriminate between religious and sectarian. While our academies are unsectarian, yet we admit that to some little degree, in common with the normal and many of the other public schools, they are striving to permeate their culture with broad and high religious sentiments. This, we claim, instead of being a defect or a wrong to be punished, is their crowning glory, for which they are to be upheld and cherished.

3. Upon the subject of aid to academies by taxation the Superintendent quotes from his report of 1870, in which he discusses the question: "Should the academies be made free?" We concede the ability with which he conducts the arguments in that report; but it does not apply to this appropriation which does not propose to make the academies free. It only proposes to encourage higher education by contributing to its support. This the State has always done. This is a policy as fully established as that of the support of common schools. It began in 1790, by making appropriations for academies in land and money often raised by general tax. Loans have been made which were afterward remitted. The proceeds of public lands sold were often applied, half to common schools and half to academies. The Literature Fund was established and confirmed to the academies by the Constitution. A part of the income of the United States Deposit Fund was appropriated to them. Not to speak of the large sums given to the colleges, the higher education of the academies has always been encouraged. But the Superintendent says: "It has never been the policy of the State heretofore to maintain, or in any way to assist, these academies by a general tax." It was not the "policy" of the State so to assist the common schools, until 1851. In this age of progress "policy" changes, generally advances, as it has done in this case; and as it evidently is destined to continue to do, even against the "opinion" of the Superintendent. He says there is nothing in the law to prevent higher studies being taught in the common schools. If this is done, the expense of such teaching will, at least in part, be met from the State tax. Why not, then, let the instruction which the academies furnish be met in the same way?

4. The Superintendent states that aid to academies from the Literature and United States Deposit Fund has amounted, for several years past, to $61,000.

We suppose he makes this as follows:

Annual distribution	$40,000
For books and apparatus	3,000
For instruction of teachers of common schools	18,000
Total	$61,000

Now, the appropriation of $18,000 is for instruction actually given at a rate fixed by law for the instruction of common-school teachers. It is not for the support of the academies, but for the benefit of the common schools. In most instances it costs them all they receive, and in many much more than they receive. The *aid* which they receive from the funds is therefore $43,000, and not $61,000. Again, the Superintendent says the allowance *per capita* has increased from two dollars and forty-eight cents in 1862, and four dollars and sixty-four cents in 1867, to ten dollars and eight cents in 1872, for each academic scholar in attendance. Only $40,000 is distributed *per capita*, and the distribution in 1862 was one dollar and seventy-six cents; in 1867, three dollars and four cents; and in 1872, six dollars and sixty cents. (See Regents' reports for those years.) This increase *per capita* was caused by the severe test of academic scholarship in the Regents' examination, which has been in operation since 1866.

The Superintendent institutes a comparison between the *per capita* apportionment for the last year to academies and common schools, stating that to the latter to be two dollars and eighty-four cents for all who attend the public (common) schools. In a fair comparison, the whole number of scholars who attended the academies would be taken for a divisor, the same as is done in regard to the common schools. The whole number was 31,421. This would have given the *per capita* on $43,000 one dollar and thirty-seven cents, and on $40,000 one dollar and twenty-four cents, instead of ten dollars and eight cents, as he has stated it. Now, while the *distribution* is made on the number of scholars who have passed the Regents' examination, the appropriations are *applied* to the institution, and benefit all the scholars in attendance.

It is deeply to be regretted that a public document which ought, both for the present and all future time, to be authority in fact and in reasoning, should be so full of inaccuracies as we have shown this to be, while the spirit in which it is written is not such as should characterize the head of a department of education for the State, to whom we ought to have been permitted to look for encouragement and support in our efforts to advance the interests of education to which we, no less than himself, have devoted out lives.

It is very evident that these academic institutions must and will continue to exist and thrive in spite of all opposition; and that instead of their influence being deleterious, it will be most salutary and invigorating upon all our educational interests. Assuming thus the continued existence of these institutions founded by private munificence, all the best interests of education demand that the State should supplement this munificence by such aid as shall enable them to become the most efficient possible, furnishing to the youth of the State the very best educational facilities as nearly free as possible. All true culture should be fostered and helped by the State. Thus operating, there is no essential antagonism between them and the free schools proper, and there should be no hostility; but rightly considered they are mutual aids, and both should be treated as co-workers in the great cause of education.

JONATHAN ALLEN, A. M.,
*Principal of Academic Department, and
President of Alfred University.*

JOSEPH E. KING, D. D., Ph. D.,
Principal of Fort Edward Collegiate Inst.

ALBERT WELLS, A. M.,
Principal of Peekskill Academy.

BENJ. N. MARTIN, D. D., L. H. D.,
Prof. in the University of the city of N. Y.

JAMES S. GARDNER, A. M., Ph. D.,
Principal of Whitestown Seminary.

GILBERT B. MANLEY, A. M.,
Principal of Cortland Academy.

M. VAN RENSSELAER, D. D.,
President of Hobart College, Geneva.

J. DORMAN STEELE, Ph. D.,
Principal of Elmira Free Academy.

ALBERT B. WATKINS, A. M.,
Principal of Hungerford Collegiate Inst.

NOAH T. CLARKE, A. M., Ph. D.,
Principal of Canandaigua Academy.

JOHN JONES, A. M., D. D.,
Principal of Genesee Academy.

GEORGE W. BRIGGS, A. M.,
Principal of Delaware Literary Institute.

SAMUEL G. LOVE, A. M.,
*Principal of Jamestown Union School and
Collegiate Institute.*

ALONZO FLACK, A. M.,
Prin. of Claverack Acad. and H. R. Inst.

GREEK IN OUR PREPARATORY SCHOOLS.

BY MERRILL EDWARDS GATES, A. M.,

Principal of Albany Academy.

A prominent Englishman who has carefully watched the career of the men who were educated at Oxford and Cambridge during the first half of this century, writing late in life to an early Oxford friend, makes some suggestive comments in speaking of the college studies of mutual friends. He calls attention to the fact that the university men of that period, who have since become prominent in literature, politics and science, are generally men who were noted in college as especially proficient in the study of Greek. The "honor men" in Greek, almost without exception, have made their mark in life. This is not equally true, he says, of men who have taken honors for scholarship in Latin, the sciences or mathematics.

Greek seemed to be the touchstone for ability. And the truth educed was, *not* that excellence in Greek was the *cause* of subsequent success, but that no other branch of study was so certain to attract and to hold those well-balanced, discriminating yet powerful minds which make themselves felt, by words and deeds, in the life and the history of a generation.

Every teacher of the classics has seen this power of the genius of the Greek language to choose and hold its friends. And yet Greek is commonly spoken of as a study which must be disagreeable at first.

The old proverb concerning bitter shells and sweet kernels has been discarded in every other branch of study; new methods propose to make the whole intellectual diet of the pupil attractive to the mental taste. Yet this old maxim is still quoted of Greek. The difficulties of a strange alphabet are magnified. That ill-starred statistican who first reckoned all the possible forms of a regular Greek verb, and put the result up among the thousands, stands like the angel of the flaming sword, driving away many an eager-eyed young student who would enter the fair garden of Greek literature. The "practical man of business," to whose freely expressed opinion American educators are so often advised to defer, may have come to regard a little *Latin* as in some way useful, because rich in elements of the English language, and may look at the time his boy spends in studying it, as at the worst a tub thrown to that respectable old whale called "classical culture." But the mere mention of Greek, too often calls out anathemas upon the men who would neglect the living present to pry into the musty records of nations long since passed away. The study of Greek is decried as of no "practical" value, and the years spent in it are styled "wasted time." Often the entire future of the boys in our academies turns upon the question "shall I commence Greek," because without the study of Greek a college course is so seldom attempted. And the boy who answers this question affirmatively, and proposes to acquire in college the proverbial "small Latin," as a matter of course allows his anticipations to stop at the "less Greek."

The classical teacher in our academies and high schools, then, has a double responsibility in this matter. His influence with pupils and parents will frequently decide whether the pupil shall begin to study Greek, and so, whether he shall ever look toward a truly liberal education. And where the study has been entered upon, the teacher's ability, method and enthusiasm will decide *how* the boy shall advance. He may drag wearily through his work, with no clear conception of the object to be attained, and no appreciation of the beauty and the capacities of the language he uses. To a student so taught, grammar is only so many disconnected pages, to be memorized by sheer force of will; Xenophon and Cyrus are as lifeless and unreal as are the eternally recurring "Balbus" and "the good citizen" in Latin prose composition; the Anabasis is as weary a waste as any "sea-like expanse of sand, without tree or plant of any kind," which its pages describe; *enteuthen exelaunei*, is a weariness to the flesh; and Homer, if the student ever reaches his verses, is attractive only because the natural boy must take a healthful interest in the narrative of fair hand to hand fighting, and because the heart of even the poorly taught dullard must sometimes thrill responsive to the straightforward, dignified power and the fresh simple beauty of the "Father of Song." But when the teacher does his work wisely and thoroughly, the pupil sees his way from the very first. The inflections that must be committed to memory are analyzed and compared with the Latin the boy has already mastered, perhaps with a glance at early English and Anglo-Saxon. The mutes with their classes, orders and euphonic changes may be indelibly fixed in the pupils mind by the first few strokes of the phonographic alphabet. The "fine print dialects" are not treated as mere arbitrary variations, but in those he discards for the time, no less than in the one he learns, the pupil gets attractive glimpses of the material and intellectual conquests over her sister States achieved by Athens—

> *   *   "the eye of Greece,
> Mother of arts and eloquence."

The pleasure of writing Greek sentences relieves the severe but necessary work of memorizing paradigms. Short, easy questions and answers in Greek, given orally in class, can be made a very attractive form of review. Frequent inflection of nouns, adjectives and verbs, by the class in concert, with the most delicate attention to correct accent, accomplishes much in a few moments, and fosters that absolute Greek accuracy without which no one can come into sympathy with and thoroughly understand and enjoy the language.

And from the first let Greek be taught (as what subject should not be?) with a clear eye to history. Let the historic names the pupil uses in his exercises and meets in his reading, *be* historic to him, from the very first. In a few words, pay to each name of patriot or philosopher, something of his due. Let the brave deed done, the noble thought uttered, ring in the boy's ears and echo in his soul; for Greece has inspired the world, and these deeds and words are the inheritance of the ages.

Make the picturesque Greek life of Xenophon and the orientalism of Cyrus and his host *real* to pupils, by incidents supplied from outside the text, as well as by expanding the suggestive particulars given by the author. While you fix carefully in the pupil's mind, by charts and map-drawing, the relative position of the scenes and places described, fix in his mind, no less carefully, the historic and intellectual significance of the men and events he reads about. In this way, the early lessons in Greek may be made, in truth, a rich seed-time, and the germs of ideas then implanted, and the fields for subsequent thought and investigation then opened to the pupil's view, will help to make his later study, in college and in his own library, fruitful and broad. The boy so trained, sees in his Anabasis the exploits of the daring scouts who showed Alexander the way to his Asiatic conquests,—a new chapter in the history of that struggle between the men and ideas of Europe and those of Asia, which is in progress when Homer's morning-light of history dawns, which fills the pages of so many historians, and which is far from finished in our own day. The inter-Hellenic rivalry between Athens and Sparta becomes a reality to him, as he sees Xenophon exiled from Athens, the guest of Sparta, in his country seat at Scillus, entertaining his old comrades on their way to the Olympic games. Socrates appears upon the scene, in the practical wisdom and ready wit with which his pupil conducts the retreat and harangues the disaffected soldiers. Each step of the simply told narrative becomes instinct with life and interest. And to the pupil so taught, the very phrase " *enteuthen exelaunei stathmon* " becomes a happy omen, as he advances each day a day's march in his knowledge of the language and of the life and history it records.

Something like this, we believe, should be the spirit of elementary instruction in Greek.

For men will no longer look upon the classics as a kind of Eleusinian Mysteries, with a value only to be estimated by the initiated. You all remember the withering sarcasm with which Byron reviews his school course in the classics. That "safe and elegant imbecility of classical learning" which Sydney Smith stigmatized, is not in good repute among Americans. We cannot state too strongly our own faith in the classics properly taught as an educational power. But classical culture, in the proper sense of the term, does not come by simply learning rules and exceptions. An acquaintance with Latin and Greek, is not like the labyrinth-puzzles published in childrens' monthlies, in which the whole interest of the game consists in dodging innumerable lines and corners arranged to entrap you, and the sole advantage derived is finding yourself inside while others are *left out.* In a visit to Rugby, last summer, I was presented with a volume of the examination papers of the school for several years past. The papers on the classics evince a very high degree of accuracy. But the large place still occupied by Latin and Greek verse-making, even in that progressive English school, seems to an American very disproportionate to the importance of the accomplishment. In American schools and colleges, however, the opponents of classical culture cannot point to years spent in acquiring skill in versifying. And it argues ill for either the intelligence or the ingenuousness of such critics, that so many of them fail to distinguish between the English and the American custom, in this respect. Perhaps no one would write down, among *our* characteristic national failings, a tendency to over-laborious and too long continued efforts after true artistic excellence, for its own sake. But when the study of the classics among us is assailed, we say to those who would abolish it: "No, it might not be worth eight or ten years of study to the average American boy, to be able to write Greek and Latin hexameters." But we believe in the careful study of the classics for its intensely practical and truly useful results.

Translation enlarges the boy's vocabulary, and cultivates taste in the use of language. It develops the power to appreciate and express *ideas.* And it has always seemed to me, highly as I value the

" disciplinary " effect of mathematical studies, that the exercise of the reason requisite in translating is much nearer that demanded in business and in actual life, than are the axiomatic demonstrations of pure mathematics. In after-life, the student in our schools will not be met by life-problems or questions in business which can be solved by a ready reference to axioms. In translating a difficult sentence, underlying principles, past experience, the purpose before the author's mind, and the probable drift of the passage as learned from the context,—all these considerations influence the pupil in arriving at the true meaning of the sentence. Are not these problems of translation, with their demand for the combined exercise of memory, logic and " common sense," very like the practical questions of business, the complicated problems of active life ?

We would study the Latin and Greek classics, too, for the history and the ideas they contain. And as they are studied, let the pupil feel that the characters about whom he reads are *human*, belong to the same great race with himself, are governed by the same moral laws and influenced by the same motives and impulses. Let him find, in the demagogues of Athens and Rome, the antetypes of our own Tweeds and Butlers. For it is our sincere belief that faithful instruction in the political history of Rome and Greece, has done and will do much to control the evil tendencies of our own time and land. From such study, boys and young men learn that the words " civil freedom " and " republic " are not a magic spell against corruption and decay. They are reminded that the splendid inheritance of a continent and centuries of the future which America boasts, is not so entailed that our own carelessness and folly may not squander it, and send us, ruined, to speedy oblivion.

We have tried to indicate something of the spirit and the aim with which, as it seems to us, Greek should be taught in our preparatory schools. But we are not among the enthusiasts who believe that any amount of " inspiring power " in the teacher, or any number of attractive " general principles " can do away with the necessity for careful, methodic daily work on the part of the pupil, and systematic preparation on the part of the teacher.

As to the method of instruction, then. Much depends upon the little details of class-room arrangement and the mode of conducting the recitation. The teacher's temperament and characteristics should decide his course in these respects. We have seen too much of the evil effects of slavish attempts at imitation, to offer a " correct method," even if we felt sure we had one to propose.

If the teacher holds his class, makes them use the black-board, secures prompt answers in good English, and does not talk himself, *except when he means to*, experience will settle details. One truth should be constantly borne in mind. The Greek language is pre-eminently accurate. Absolute accuracy in the daily task is the first and last thing to be aimed at. And such accuracy is not at all inconsistent with grace and taste in translation, and a broad, scholarly outlook. The teacher or pupil who cannot attain to the two, however, has no business with the "broad views." Without a clear appreciation of nice distinctions and a thorough mastery of inflections, regular and exceptional, he is no Greek. From the beginning, let the pupil write Greek daily; and let him write always with the accents. To leave the rules for accents until the second year, as is the custom in some of the New England schools, is pernicious in its effect. The pupil feels that he has left a "something unknown" behind him. The thought oppresses him. Instead of feeling himself completely master of the situation, he treads doubtfully.

The injunction, to "make haste slowly," is nowhere more needful than in beginning Greek. The amount of drill which can be profitably expended in writing and reciting proparoxytones and properispomena of the first declension, can hardly be over-estimated. By these exercises alone, the rules of accent as affected by quantity should be thoroughly mastered. With the second declension, let the pupil become perfectly familiar with the principal rules for contraction. The third declension naturally introduces some of the rules for euphonic changes in mutes. Whenever the student meets such a change, let him learn the principle involved. When he reaches verbs, let all the rules of euphony with which he is not already familiar, be thoroughly commited and repeatedly applied. The habit of reviewing orally the written lesson of the day before, I have found an excellent one. Extempore conversational exercises in class, to illustrate the force of pronouns, of the predicate and the attributive adjective, and of the different moods and tenses, give the student greater confidence, and add to the interest of the daily work.

As to grammars, Professor Hadley's development of the verb-forms is undoubtedly the most scientific. His grammar will always be a noble book of reference. It is stored with the fruits of a scholarship so ripe that the world had come to regard its author as one speaking from a wise old age, until death bid us mourn him with a two-fold grief, as a great scholar, and as one who was called from the field where he loved to toil, at the full noon of his manhood. His works will long outlive him.——But for daily recitations in a preparatory school, we have found Goodwin's grammar decidedly the best. It is compact, brief, giving essentials and omitting non-essentials. A bright boy of fifteen may hope to know and apply every page of it with two years' faithful study. It is luminous in arrangement, and matchless in its syntax of the moods. Its etymology, however, may well be supplemented by more careful explanations of euphonic changes, and by such frequent references to their history and laws as make Crosby's the favorite grammar still with many experienced instructors.

There are several excellent books of introductory exercises in Greek prose. Leighton's, Kendrick's, Harkness' or Boise's Lessons may serve the class as a guide in composition. The introduction of prose exercises in beginning Latin and Greek, has wrought a revolution in the method of elementary instruction. And here I wish to pay a tribute to the President of the American Philological Association, Dr. Kendrick, of the University of Rochester. He wrote in 1850, and published in 1851, an "Introductory Book to Greek," followed by an "Ollendorf of the Greek Language," which was the earliest publication of the kind in America, if I am not mistaken. Several later editors have gratefully recognized this book as the suggestion and basis of their Prose Exercises. And you will pardon me if I say that the ideal instruction in Greek which I have tried to describe, seems to me to be well illustrated in the class-room of the man who is notably the foremost Platonist in the land, who has the gift of transporting his classes to the very stage where Æschylus and Sophocles acted, who makes the historic scenes of Thucydides vividly real, and yet who appreciated the importance of accuracy in the elements so fully that he turned aside from the more attractive fields of Greek philosophy and poetry to write the "Introduction" and the "Ollendorf" for beginners.

There are teachers of Latin and Greek who mourn over the fact that their pupils do not enjoy the work. The classical instructor who laments the attractiveness of the sciences and the modern languages because his own department is neglected for them, commonly has himself to blame. We do not advocate the *exclusively* classical education. No man can render fully effective among his fellow-men the power he has gained from the study of Latin and Greek, if he is entirely ignorant of the underlying principles and the main facts of the natural sciences, in this day of their development and glory. We believe in the study of the sciences. But we know that there is a

9

flattering demand for youthful *specialists* in science. The young man who will narrow his vision and concentrate all his powers of investigation upon a few square feet of some one division of science, may hope to know more about that particular subject than does any one else in the world. He may speedily become world-famous, as the best authority upon some such special point as "the parasites of the 'bumble-bee.'"

We do not ridicule such minute investigation. It is the life of the natural sciences. But we do see clearly that the speedy and disproportionate reward of sudden fame paid to such scientific specialism deludes many a young man into preferring to a liberal education a hurried introduction to scientific studies. And we believe that the intelligent teacher of the classics can make his best pupils see this. Without depreciating the results of scientific study, he can make *thoughts* and *ideas* hold their proper ascendency in the minds of his pupils. He has not the brilliant experiments of the physicist with which to attract their attention. But the whole domain of history is his.

Let him increase the student's interest in both branches of study by tracing for him Greek discoveries and advancement in science, and our recent return to early Greek theories in physics. Above all, by wisely-chosen prelections with the class, he may make some of the finest thoughts and most beautiful passages of the classics the early familiar possession of his pupils. He can show them, in Arnold's words, how "all that audacity can dare or subtlety contrive to make the words 'good' and 'evil' change their meaning, was tried in the days of Plato, and by his eloquence and wisdom and faith unshaken, was put to shame."

The teacher of Greek who has never yet translated to a class of eager students, passages from Plato or Sophocles or the historians, who has never seen the look of joyous surprise come over their faces, as the shadowy names of authors become real friends, by the magic sympathy of inspiring thoughts uttered or life-like touches given, has missed a keen joy for himself, and a great source of influence with his classes. Such excursions into Greek literature, introduced sparingly into the routine of careful daily work, will more than compensate the lack of "experiments." And while they add to the pleasure and interest of the pupil's work, they will lead to his more familiar acquaintance with a literature which is supremely rich in itself, while its study links us with the intellectual life of the great minds of all the ages.

THE ANTHROPOLOGICAL PRINCIPLES AND METHODS OF EDUCATION.

By JOSEPH R. BUCHANAN, M. D.,

Professor (elect) in the Eclectic Medical College, N. Y. city.

By those who are acquainted with my labors in establishing a *science of man*, by proving experimentally the functions of the brain, and thereby ascertaining the *anatomy of the soul* (which may be esteemed an eccentric expression to-day), and the correlation of the soul with the body, making manifest the laws of health and development of the normal and the abnormal; in short, the laws of all psychic science, which is at least coextensive and coequal with all physical science, that which I have now to present may be recognized as the practical application of a positive science. To others I would present it, as the result of the experience and investigations of forty years.

As all science, in proportion as it penetrates deeply into nature's mysteries, is the more sure to prevent that startling form of truth which we call a paradox—incredible to the uninitiated (as for example the burning of wood by holding it near a block of ice, or bathing the hands unharmed in melted metal, or the coexistence of free will and necessity), so all successful investigators must, to some extent, tax the faith, the liberality and the courtesy of those to whom they impart their conclusions or discoveries, without the accompaniment of immediate demonstration. Plato says that we should not write and send forth unfamiliar truths which cannot defend themselves, but only those things which need no defense or proof. If I disregard his advice and present propositions which I have not time to prove, I can only say the proof will in time be made ample enough for all. But to philosophic minds attuned to harmony with the divine, truth is always charming, even when coming suddenly as a stranger with no other credentials or proof than her own bright face and graceful movement.

Education aims or should aim to make a perfect or rather a fully developed man; for it can do it, not in one generation—no animal or plant is perfected so speedily—but in a short series. True education is almighty to establish the Kingdom of Heaven over every continent, and realize all the aims of sociology, of religion and philanthropy; but not such education as we have had--the intellectual training of a few faculties of our multiplex nature—which but holds a feeble and unsuccessful struggle with the downward tendencies of man, and often spreads its delusive brilliance over a false civilization —over the wreck of morals, the loss of liberty, the triumph of poverty, disease and crime—which we see in civilized nations, full of pauperism, with no more of happiness or of virtue than a barbarous tribe.

It is the mission of education to put an end to all this. How? By developing man to the full realization of the divine plan of his nature. Then we must ask what is that nature and how is it to be developed? Anthropology alone can satisfactorily answer these questions, for their answer is anthropology, and as an anthropologist I speak. Experience, I know, has given practical but not complete data for answering these questions. The full and final answer must be scientific, and if the science to meet this demand is not in the universities at present, it must be developed from nature and placed there, as the regent of human progress.

Time does not permit even a hasty scientific analysis of man. Human nature has been called a microcosm, but when we study its immensity, it would seem more just to call it a macrocosm. Its infinity of faculties and relations give us our only conception of the divine. To simplify this vast subject by a periscopic view, we must classify in groups; and as the surface of the globe is divided into three climates, the torrid, temperate and frigid, so the elements of human character can be divided into three groups, the animal, moral and intellectual. This grouping is entirely natural, as it corresponds to the occipital, the coronal and the frontal regions of the brain. The occipital, or strictly speaking, occipit-basilar, is in close connection with the apparatus of physical life, and is supplied by the same artery—the vertebral—which supplies the spinal cord. The spinal system is its appendage and under its control, and being supplied with blood from a common source, it is evident that they work together. Hence we may speak of the occipito-basilar region as the seat of animal life, passion and force of character; injuries of this region being accompanied by physiological consequences often dangerous or destructive to life, or to muscular power.

Anteriorly, we have the front lobe, which is commonly recognized as the seat of intelligence. The medical profession is not yet agreed upon the subdivisions of the front lobe for intellectual functions, except as to the organ of language, which has been established by the results of disease. Although I have demonstrated its subdivisions by experiment, and find that they coincide exactly with the clearest *a priori* psychology, as well as with anatomy, it is not necessary to refer to them at present.

The *coronal region* of the brain, which is less necessary to life and has the power of suspending animal life by trance, is antipodal to the animal. When its convolutions expand, they compress and exsanguinate the basilar convolutions. When the basilar convolutions expand, they compress and exsanguinate the coronal. Thus the animal and spiritual elements in man antagonize by a physical as well as moral necessity. The full development of each, with the ascendency of the former, is the proper object of education.

This division corresponds to experience. It is like the classification of Swedenborg—love, will and wisdom; more commonly expressed as intelligence, virtue and force of character or greatness. If we can develop these three, we can accomplish all that is desired to make men wisely intelligent, thoroughly good and practically great.

Can we do this in the university with the aid of the primary school, and make the graduates intelligently wise and as good and as great as their hereditary capacities will permit ? I think we can. At present we aim only to develop the intellect and to repress vicious tendencies. Education, upon the whole, rather enfeebles the character, diminishes the energies that win success, diminishes the practical knowledge which is essential to success, slightly modifies the moral character without giving it any additional strength, fills the mind with knowledge, one-half of which is more ornamental than useful, and gives such a mental discipline that very few of the educated classes have much capacity for original investigation ; very few have the capacity for impartial and unprejudiced reasoning upon practical subjects; very few have the capacity to express their ideas with extemporaneous fluency and eloquence, and none have the ability to support themselves and families without obtaining a great deal of other knowledge which the college does not propose to give.

Young men *fully educated*, should go forth prepared for business, and superior in every business to men who have no collegiate train-ing—worthy citizens—an ornament to any community and a blessing to society.

Believing all this possible, it remains to show how it can be done.

1st. How to develop intellectual power.

2d. How to make good men.

3d. How to make business men and great men.

The second and third divisions of my essay are necessarily excluded to-night by the limitation of time.

To develop man we must remove all hindrances; to develop a tree it must have *room, air and sunshine* and a *mellow soil.* To develop the intellect we must not hinder its development, but give it also room, air, sunshine and a rich soil—and recollect every hour, that intellect like a tree *develops spontaneously,* if you give it opportunity. Every element in man's character which we are to educate, is a spontaneous, irrepressible power, and needs but opportunity which we must furnish.

Every child hungers and thirsts for knowledge as it does for food, and spontaneously learns more in the first five years of its life, than all it ever learns from teachers afterward. It needs no coercion, if we teach it properly; we might as well propose coercion and flogging to make it eat its breakfast, dinner and supper, as to make it satisfy its hunger for knowledge.

It wishes to learn; it is eager and curious; it wishes to see everything and have everything explained; it wishes to observe, and observation is the God-appointed mode of learning everything. The divine wisdom teaches by its works; its visible illustrations; and when we approach to study them, we are opening our minds as docile pupils of the Infinite Being. The universities, in former times, impiously turned aside from the divine path to wisdom, and even the eloquent voice of Lord Bacon could not recall them to the humble and sincere study of truth in nature.

The child is an uncorrupted follower of the Baconian method; the natural method; the divine method; and we must assist these divine impulses to the pursuit of knowledge. He wishes to see everything and we must enable him to see everything possible, and in so doing he will follow us with delight and learn with all the powers of his soul.

I do not mean to say that we can show him everything in the universe; but whatever we cannot show him we can tell him, and he will be eager to hear these explanations. We can show him plants and flowers; show him where to find them; show him their minute structure, by the microscope and by drawings, and tell him of the movements of their juices.

We can take him out to gather stones and gather health on the hill side at the same time; show him how they lie and how they came there; show him maps of the situations you cannot visit; show him how to break them, how to examine them with the microscope, and how to ascertain their composition by analysis; show him maps and models of geological strata and tell their geological history; show him the models of animal life that preceded man; tell the story of the earth's wonderful history; and he will be an engrossed listener with every faculty of his mind in bounding vigor, observing, recollecting, understanding and reasoning, trying to master the theme. But if in the rich copiousness of the strange facts, he becomes engrossed in mere observation and recollection, and does not ask any questions for explanation, the teacher must ask him if he understands the how and the why, and give him time to reason as well as to learn. If he accepts the fact of snows on mountain tops and fires down in the earth, without asking *why* one must be cold and the other hot, ask him to explain it, and lead him into the *rationale* with an active curiosity.

In the study of the sciences properly conducted, the *highest reasoning power* is as active as mere observation and memory. Reason should never halt for a moment, but question and answer should be in constant play. At first the teacher will ask most of the questions, for children are so little encouraged to think or reason, they will not at first be expert; but if the teacher does his duty, the children will become the questioners, and keep him busy to systematize and direct their curiosity.

It is the pre-eminent advantage of the sciences, rightly taught, that they develop the whole mind (which term I cannot limit to physical science), as nothing else can. Could we fully comprehend creation, our minds would approximate the Divine, and every portion that we do comprehend brings into our souls a divine influx and increases our mental stature. What an expansion of the soul it gives when we fully comprehend any one of the great mysteries of nature. When the science of the soul and its correlations with the body are fully comprehended, that science alone will make philosophers.

These methods apply to all the sciences. The chemical student should begin with familiar bodies; simple experiments and philosophic explanations to accompany the experiments. The same course of question and answer, experiments and illustrations when necessary by drawings and models, should be applied to all the sciences; and the teacher who rightly conducts the business of question and answer until his pupils know how to ask every question that belongs to the proper investigation of any subject, will have developed them into original investigators, original reasoners, who will make their mark in after life. This is the mental discipline that is worth all other kinds.

But this is not all. When a boy has learned, for example, the phenomena of heat—and by boy I mean a lad eight or ten years of age—and I would say, judging from my own experience, that an *average boy* ought to have a pretty good idea of the outlines of chemistry, natural philosophy, geology and botany, by the time he is ten or eleven years old—not their most recondite details and principles, but a good practical knowledge.

When a boy has learned the phenomena and laws of heat, he should, after having expressed his ideas fully in answer to questions, give a short lecture on them. Each day, as anything has been learned, pupils should be required to stand up and *tell all they have learned* in the lesson on any particular subject, making it the point of honor to give the most perfect and clearest recapitulation. After such practice, require them, at the close of a lesson, to stand up and *relate the whole* of what they have learned in that lesson in their own way, assisted by any notes they may have made. After such daily practice let each pupil take a subject, prepare his experiments, and lecture with the assistance of a few notes. Thus they will all become gradually fluent and clear extemporaneous lecturers; and after fluency and precision are thus acquired, they will take up the practice of oratory by declamation and by extemporaneous speaking. I have witnessed the success of this method. It is just forty years since a little boy about three feet high, who had been thus trained, stood up before the Kentucky legislature at Frankfort, and gave a lecture on Chemistry. I regret that his able and enthusiastic teacher, the Rev. Benj. O. Peers (subsequently President of Transylvania University), did not live longer for the benefit of humanity.

The school of science, thus conducted, should become also the school of philosophy and of eloquence, by training the pupils to philosophic investigation and lucid systematic expression. All that the pupil knows of natural philosophy, chemistry, geology, botany, physiology and hygiene, he should be ready to recall and clearly present when he leaves the school. And as the value of intellectual education may be measured by the amount of knowledge and mental power that remains with the pupil, there is no comparison between such a method of teaching and the method of reading a large amount, recollecting enough to answer a few questions and being unable to reproduce this knowledge with readiness, clearness and force. It is not the amount of rain which floods a tract of land which determines its productive capacity, but the amount that is retained in the soil and absorbed by the plants. How many enormous readers fail to show any superiority in society, and how many have traveled in Europe whose conversation gives no indication of knowledge or improvement acquired by foreign travel?

This method of teaching should be applied to everything—to natural philosophy and physiology, geography, history, mathematics and the practical arts.

There are four principles for all intellectual teaching.

1st. Show everything that can be shown to the eye, because in most persons the memory of the eye is the only good memory that they have; and the impressions on the eye wake up the whole mind to clear and vigorous action.

2d. Impart everything that cannot be imparted to the eye, by the voice of the living teacher, and make no more use of books than is necessary as an assistance.

3d. Require every important idea that is obtained to be reproduced by the pupil, in his own language and method, with clearness, system and force; and at the end of each week require him to bind up the sheaves of his harvest, by narrating in a formal lecture all that he has learned.

4th. Compel him to understand thoroughly everything, and to reason independently about everything by critical questioning, allowing him to pass over no phrase or statement without clearly understanding and critically appreciating it; and toward the end of his pupilage give him subjects of investigation, with the library and the laboratory and all nature, to hunt up his answer as an original investigator.

This is the natural system of teaching, which will secure the earnest attention and interest of the pupil. From infancy onward he is eager to learn, unless his ardor is repressed by difficulty and discouragement. Spread a feast of knowledge and he *will not be kept away.* No other punishment will be required than to suspend him from school and keep him away from the delights of companionship and of interesting knowledge.

The teacher who cannot spread this attractive feast—who cannot present the ocular illustrations that make a proposition clear and interesting—who cannot talk so that his pupils are eager to listen to him, was not designed by nature for the profession of teaching, or his capacities have been injured by imitating bad examples. Any young

man of fair capacity can be made such a teacher; and only one who
has been so taught is already prepared to teach.

Therefore, the compulsory law of education should be, not that
every parent should be compelled to send his child to school, but that
no parent should be allowed to compel his child to stay away, for
when education is as it should be, no teacher should have a pupil who
did not come by voluntary attraction. In other words, no child should
be *sent* to school, forced into repulsive mental studying, required to sit
under task-masters and tyrants, and feel himself a slave, deadening
his moral nature by learning to hate his intellectual benefactor.
'Twere better to have no schools at all than such, and trust to mothers,
to social intercourse, newspapers and spontaneous reading for intelligence.

Unless the pupil loves his teacher, he is demoralized, hardened in
heart, and to that extent prepared to be a future tyrant in his family.
You may educate a man without love, you may educate love out of
him, but if you do, you are preparing him to be a demon, and it were
better he had never known any such education.

In the *oral system* of education, the teacher and the pupil are
friends, as naturally as mother and son. Instead of conspiring to
ridicule, or to bar out their teacher, they would be his body-guard in
danger, and the upholders of his rights at all times. When a new
pupil from the school of slavery and birch comes into such an institution, example would at once reform him; but if of the incorrigible
sort, his comrades would soon expel the devil of his animality, and
teach him to act like a gentleman.

But the transcendent merit of the *oral system* is, that it deals in
living knowledge instead of the mere corpse. The idea that comes
from the utterance of the living teacher, is a *living* idea — clothed in
the spiritual strength of the living teacher — for it comes in his voice,
freighted with all his strength of will, his power of thought, his social
sympathy and his enthusiasm. All this it pours into the receptive
soul of the pupil. As cords finely strung respond to kindred vibrations, so does soul respond to soul. With the vicious we become
corrupt, or at least angry and miserable. With the good we become
good, or at least happy, serene and receptive of all good—we inhale
the moral atmosphere around us. But the cord wakes no Æolian
response until its vibrations reach its analogue, and the teacher
elicits the glow of sentiment and subtlety of thought, with power,
only when his own soul is poured forth in his voice. The voice
carries with it the soul-power, to pour it into another soul, and as the

south wind brings warmth to call out the violets from the cold earth, so does the teacher's voice, rightly modulated, carry life and beauty into the soul of the pupil. Every idea carried by the voice is a living idea, not the dead form of abstract thought which comes from symbols on the dead page of a book, but a live thought in the frame-work of will and courage, kindness and grace with which it was associated in the mind where it originated. The sentiment is not in the words, but in the invisible soul-power that goes with them and is felt, and goes into the soul of the pupil to become a permanent portion of his spiritual life.

Hence the pupil of the true oral teacher is growing in character as well as in thought. He is assimilating to his teacher, absorbing his soul-power, and thus maintaining the integrity of his own powers, as they all grow in harmony; while the student of the dead book assimilates to its lifeless nature, becomes languid, spiritless, timid, sensitive, dreamy and unfit for active life. With the latent capacity of a giant, years of book study reduce him to a timid weakling, for exclusive devotion to books must make a man, to some extent, as lifeless as they are, which is expressed by the term book-worm.

Oral teaching, ocular teaching and Socratic teaching will do all that is possible for the intellect, and if we had no other illustration, our experience in medical schools is conclusive on this subject. In the medical schools we have no time to trifle or to study ornament, or ask what is best for mental discipline. When two hundred young men sit before us, demanding to be qualified as promptly as possible for the business of life, qualified to stand in the breach and repel the assaults on human life from hidden foes, we must be stern utilitarians, for every hour that is lost in gathering the roses of literature, may be the loss of a human life. We are like an army rushing to battle that must finish its campaign in four months, and *we do it.* Every winter we make more than a twelvemonth's march across ten kingdoms of science, and if the campaign is not successful, the results are disastrous to society. I believe it is generally successful, and our experience proves that four months of oral teaching are more than equivalent to twelve months of study.

But I may be asked, can this system of teaching be applied to reading, writing, grammar, languages, oratory, political economy, mechanical science, engineering and technology generally? It surely can, but time will permit only a glance at the methods.

Reading and writing should be taught together. The first lesson should be writing and reading together, but should not be given until after some months of teaching, by showing familiar objects, flowers, plants, animals, machines and geometric forms, and learning their names and uses, and practicing on the blackboard in drawing simple forms.

Then let them all commence drawing some letters and calling their real names, such as *a, o, e,* writing them large on the blackboard. Let them have a friendly competition as to which can make the best letter immediately under the copy, one at a time, then altogether, with examinations and criticism on the performance, and laughter at blunders. Then let them write a consonant, say the letter *l.* Let them all pronounce it by its true sound — *l-l-l* — and all write it; then write and pronounce it in combination with the vowels, as *a-l.* These exercises can be immensely varied. By learning the true powers of the letters, and reading their own writing, they would become simultaneously good writers and good readers, and would find these exercises really interesting, for children love to draw and scribble, and these exercises should be interspersed with the drawing of familiar objects, faces, instructive and ludicrous pictures. The exercise should be continued no longer than it is interesting, alternating with lessons on objects, and with *singing.*

I have just seen a statement of the report of Mr. Harris, superintendent of the schools of St. Louis, in which this method of teaching reading has been carried out, not only with good success and satisfaction, but, it is said, with so much advantage as to save *one whole year of time* to the primary schools.

Grammar, I would teach practically, almost without books, by repeating before them all possible blunders, inaccuracies and inelegancies of speech, to have them correct the error, as "I is very sick," "Look at them boys," "I ain't got none," "You hadn't ought to," giving the reasons fully for every correction. Those reasons would be the practical science, thoroughly mastered and acquired without memorizing a single rule. Instead of cramming their minds principally with abstract rules, which they do not always apply to correcting their own speech, the speech itself would be rectified, and the reason associated with the correct mode of expression, all being done quickly, pleasantly, and with interest, occupying so little time that grammar would be not a laborious study but an incidental diversion in the progress of other studies. The final exercise would be in miscellaneous reading from books, newspapers or compositions, introducing slight errors ingeniously, to see if they could escape detection by the pupils.

Languages I would teach in the same practical way, almost without books at first, but frequently using the blackboard. I would repeat simple words and phrases in the language, and have the class repeat the same together, or practice on them one at a time. Familiar salutations, "*bon jour*," "*bon soir*," and short phrases, "*donnez moi*," etc., with the names of the books, desks and familiar objects in the room, would give their first vocabulary. Writing on the blackboard familiar sentences to be repeated by all, and a requirement that all conversation should be in the language studied, would soon make it familiar as their own vernacular. Books with interlinear translations would presently prove very useful, and I have seen nothing to compare with the interlinear books of Perrin's fables for the French and the London university series for the classics, which I first saw forty years ago.

The grammar of foreign languages should be taught like the grammar of our own, *in the concrete,* not in the abstract; first teach the spoken language, then point out its rules and their violations, thus you have the rule in the concrete before you abstract it; that is the easy, natural method. To make the abstract rule, and then get a language to fill it up, or support it, is like building a house from the steeple downward.

To apply this inductive method to lingual studies, by getting the language first and the rules afterward, is as great an improvement as the application of the Baconian system of induction to the study of science.

Truth in the concrete, as God presents it to us in nature, is always interesting. Let us always present science in the visible concrete, and blend it with the soul-power of the teacher.

History is a theme which the teacher should make as fascinating as a novel, and which may be brilliantly illustrated by drawings, models, engravings and stereoptic views, which bring before us the ruins of cities, the rivers and mountains, the columns, the halls, the castles, the armor and the faces of the illustrious dead. Geography is even more capable of being made a fascinating story. Novels are the most attractive and engrossing literature that we have, but they are not equal to geography rightly taught. With proper maps and drawings, and stereoptic views, which every academy should have, the pupil should be led along through all the striking and memorable scenes of other lands, with comments on the great events that have occurred, and on the living population, their domestic life and condition, their palaces and hovels, their manufactories, mines and all forms of industry, their morals and manners, their government and wealth, giving all and indeed far more than the traveler could realize in a journey in the same region.

There can be no place of entertainment to compare with a proper school, no place like it for intellectual and moral progress. Place it in a grove on a green hill with all the necessary apparatus, and eloquent teachers, and the songs of the young, and it will carry our young humanity into an Eden, the spirit of which they will bring out into the great world.

If the State will not help to establish this Eden, will not furnish the apparatus it requires, the State deserves to be indicted, and we should draw up the indictment. If the system which I have sketched, but not developed, will not make much better educated young men by the age of sixteen than we have been accustomed to graduate from universities at the age of twenty-two, I am utterly mistaken in the dictates of science and of experience, the science of man, and the experience of the best teachers of many countries.

But *to make a good man* is a greater performance than to make an intellectual man. Its greater difficulty is conceded, for while a thousand universities have attempted the former with some degree of success, none attempt the latter.

Plato debated whether virtue could be taught like knowledge, and from the earliest age to the present day the opinion has prevailed that it could not, and that though knowledge and intellectual discipline might be imparted, character could not be essentially changed.

But *if virtue be worth more than intelligence,* an efficient system of moral development by education would be worth more than all the world has yet achieved in intellectual education; and that such a system is strictly practicable, I am prepared to show in a convincing manner, and I have already received the cordial approbation of the enlightened thinkers to whom the system has been made known.

BEGINNINGS OF ART, OR EVOLUTION IN ORNAMENT.

By Ch. Fred. Hartt, A. M.,

Professor of Geology in Cornell University.

On my two expeditions to the Amazonas, in 1870 and 1871, there was obtained from a burial mound on the Island of Marajó or Johannes, a lot of ancient pottery, consisting of burial urns, idols, utensils of various kinds, personal ornaments, etc., many of which were richly ornamented with grecques and scrolls and borders of a very high order of development. The resemblance borne by some of these ornaments to Old-World classic forms was very striking, and certain borders were, even in their accessories, identical with similar ornaments in Etruscan art. It has already been pointed out by Owen Jones that the so-called Greek fret has a very wide distribution, occurring not only in Egyptian and Greek art, but in that of India and China, while in the New World it was cultivated widely in both Americas. The distribution of these simple ornamental forms among widely separated savage tribes renders it extremely unlikely that they should have all been derived from a common source, and their independent origin is all the more probable since it has been conclusively shown that identical myths, religious ideas, manners and customs, found in different parts of the earth, have often orginated independently of one another. It is quite easy to understand how pottery might be invented by two different tribes, but how is it possible that the same series of ornamental forms should arise among several independent and disconnected peoples? To the solution of this question I have addressed myself, and in this paper I propose to give, in a very condensed form, some of the more important results of my studies.

Purely æsthetic decorative art has had its origin in the attempt to please the eye by lines and colors, just as music has originated in the attempt to please the ear by a rythmic series of sounds. Imitative decorative art appeals to the understanding; it is a song with words, but merely æsthetic ornament is visible music without words, and it is to this latter division of ornament that I shall principally invite your attention.

Color and form in ornament are so very different in their functions that they must be considered apart. Of the two, form is the more important element, and in the following discussion color will be left out of consideration.

The secret of the pleasant effect produced upon us by beautiful lines is, I believe, to be found in the structure of the eye itself, and I shall attempt to show that a line is beautiful, not because of any inherent quality of its own, but, primarily, because of the pleasure we take in making the requisite muscular movements necessary to run over it with the eye, though, through education, we may afterward come to recognize, at a glance, a form that has once given us pleasure; just as in music, the first few notes of an *aria*, in an overture, may be sufficient to recall the general effect of the complete composition.

When I look out of my window at a landscape, the image of a very large tract falls upon my retina. I see at once a multitude of houses, and the infinitude of objects that go to make up the picture, and apparently I see everything distinctly, but this is really far from being the case. If I look suddenly out at a landscape that I never saw before, and fix my gaze upon a church spire for a few moments, the image of the landscape falls immovably upon the retina; but if I now suddenly withdraw and try to sketch my landscape, or write a description of what I have seen, I shall find myself totally unable to reproduce it. I have only an indistinct impression of the church spire and perhaps of a few prominent objects in the immediate vicinity. I have *seen* the landscape but I have not *observed* it. Now let me return, paper in hand, to sketch the same landscape. I do not fix my eye immovably upon one point, but I deliberately run it over the leading lines of the view, and I then trace lines upon the paper that produce the same effect upon my eye as those in nature have done. My sketch will at best be imperfect, but its accuracy will be in proportion to the care with which I have examined the outlines in the landscape. In observing an object we do not then look fixedly at it, but we run the eye over it. Let us see what this means.

The whole retina is not equally sensitive to light, and the whole of a visual image is not distinctly perceived at once. Directly in the back part of the eye is a little spot, about a line in diameter, called the yellow spot of Sœmmering, and to this distinct vision is limited, for we see distinctly only that part of an image that falls within it. It is even doubtful whether we see at one time distinctly, or in other words, can *observe* more than a point in that image. Look at the middle of this page : you really see clearly only the point directly before your eye. The rest is indistinct. To observe a word on another part of the page, you must move the eye so that its image may fall on the yellow spot. So in reading, you run the eye over the words, or, by moving the eye, cause their images to fall successively upon the yellow spot, and, for convenience, the words are arranged in straight, horizontal lines. The eye-ball, otherwise immovable, may be rotated in its socket by the action of muscles, of which, in each eye, there are four principal ones, arranged in pairs, as in the follow-

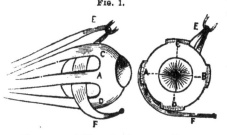

Fig. 1.

ing diagram : When *A* con-tracts, the pupil is turned in the direction B A. The pair B A then cause the eye to rotate from side to side, while the pair C D move it up and down. By combining two contiguous muscles, as, for instance, A and C, we may move the eye obliquely in any direction. Of the oblique muscles represented in the diagram I will not here speak, as they are apparently not so important in observation as those just described. If I look at the middle of a straight, hori-

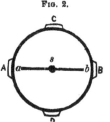

Fig. 2.

zontal line, my head being held erect, the image of that line (*a b*, Fig. 2) will lie on the retina directly between the muscles A B, the central point falling in the middle of the yellow spot *s*. In running my eye over that line, I use the mus-cles A B in such a way as to draw the image through the yellow spot, and if, in doing so, I use these muscles with perfect regularity, I say the line is straight. Perpendicular and horizontal straight lines are the most easy to examine, because their images fall directly between two opposing muscles. An oblique line is hard to examine, and we shall find ourselves instinctively turning the head so as to bring it in the plane of rotation of one or the other set of muscles. In following a curved line with the eye, it will be observed that two muscles are used together, one contracting more rapidly than the other. A curve is therefore more difficult to observe, or run the eye over, than a straight line, and the difficulty increases with the subtleness of the curvature. The æsthetic effect of curves is appreciated only after long training. Their beauty is primarily due to the pleasure we take in making the muscular movements necessary to follow them, and this pleasure is strictly akin to that which we feel in tracing them with the hand, either upon paper or simply in gesture. Pleasure-giving, graceful, muscular movements are always in curves, and their grace depends upon the subtleness of the curve.

If decorative art has had a beginning and an evolution, we should expect to find a progress from straight lines to circles and spirals and ellipses, while more subtle curves, such as we find in nature, would come in later, and this is the case, not only in the art-history of nations, but also in that of individuals, for the child must be educated not only to make, but to appreciate and enjoy beautiful lines.

Man, the world over, seeks to give pleasure to the eye. He is not satisfied that an object should be useful to him; it must be at the same time beautiful; and indeed he is usually quite as anxious that it should look well, as that it should minister to his comfort. It is not enough that clothing should be warm; its lines must be graceful, and it must be covered, more or less, with ornament. A house of logs would hold a congregation and supply all the facilities for public worship, but that is not enough. It must be a palace, and its walls must be enriched with beautiful forms. It is verily surprising to see what an important element ornament is in life. Is it then wonderful that man, everywhere striving to please the eye by lines, should occasionally invent independently similar ornamental forms, or that decorative art should, in its beginning, evolve in the same direction in different countries?

The class of ornaments which I have studied with the greatest care and at the same time with the greatest success, is that to which the so-called "Greek fret" and "honeysuckle ornament" belong, and I now propose to discuss the question of the origin and evolution of these decorative forms, premising that other classes of ornaments may be studied in exactly the same way.

If a single straight line is pleasant to the eye, two parallel straight lines are still more so; for, in running the eye over one of the lines, we have a sort of accompaniment produced by the indistinctly seen second line, or, in looking along an imaginary line between the two, we get the indistinct effect of both; but it must be observed that the lines must neither be too near together, nor too far apart, else the effect of the parallelism is either impaired or entirely destroyed. The whole surface of an object, as, for instance, of a vase, may be orna-mented by a great number of parallel lines, and this is often the case in primitive or rude art; but, with culture, comes the tendency to draw more or less narrow bands of lines following the most important lines of the object.

A further step is to make two parallel lines more agreeable to the eye by filling in the space between them with lines drawn in various directions, and in this way the frets have originated. By drawing equidistant parallel lines directly across between two parallel lines, as in Fig. 3, we make a series. This, as it exists in the drawing, is a series in *space*, but as it grows up under the hand, or as it is examined by the eye, is a series in *time*, and in looking from A to B, an effect is produced upon the eye analogous to that produced upon the ear by the repetition of the same musical note, with the same interval. If lines be drawn only part way across, from both sides alternately, as in Fig. 4, we have a sort of rhythm produced. If the lines all reach the center, they may be, and often are, even in very savage art, connected together by twos, as in Fig. 5. This produces a series of units, each one of which is pleasant to examine with the eye. This is the simplest form of the fret. If the lines are drawn not quite to the center, they may be connected by oblique lines, as in Fig. 6, A, and lines drawn past the center may be connected in the same way, as in C, but neither of the resulting units is very agreeable to the eye, and such attempts are characteristic either of a rude stage of art, or of the work of a bungler. When the lines are not drawn to the center, they may be joined as in B, and this form of fret was much cultivated in America, but it is objectionable, apparently on account of the obliquity of the units, and is vastly inferior to the fret Fig. 7, A, where lines drawn past the middle are united in a similar way. This last is the true Greek fret, though it occurs also in American aboriginal art. This fret may be made more or less involved, as in Fig. 7, but the simple forms are the more pleasing.

I have observed that in Brazil, and elsewhere in America, the artist took care to separate the units in this fret from one another, either by drawing lines between them, as in Fig. 8, A, or by placing them in cartouches, B. The addition of the line in A enhances the beauty of the series by breaking

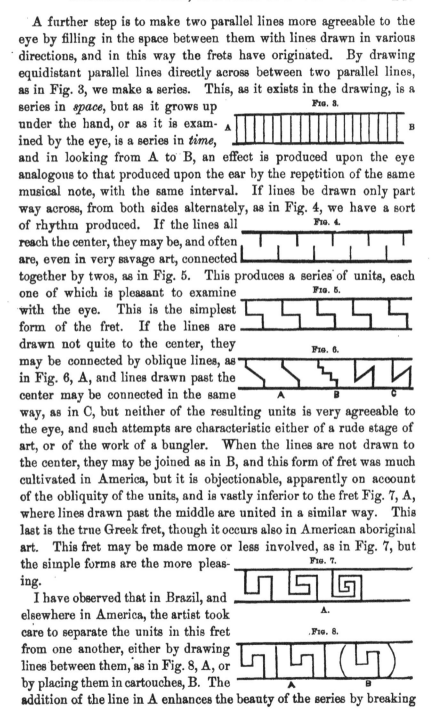

Fig. 3.

Fig. 4.

Fig. 5.

Fig. 6.

Fig. 7.

A.

Fig. 8.

up the monotony and introducing a pleasant alternation. The attempt to separate the units resulted, however, in bringing about their firm union; for some one observed that by obliterating the dot-ted spaces in Fig. 9, the whole series could be drawn without lifting the hand: hence arose the current fret, Fig. 10. Examples of the modification of ornaments by obliteration of parts in this way are common not only in aboriginal but also in classic and modern art.

Fig. 9.

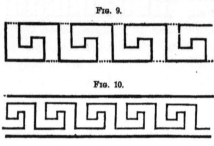

Fig. 10.

The bounding lines, Fig. 10, were afterward added, and they greatly heighten the beauty of the border. The current fret is not only pleasant to run the eye over, but it is pleasant to trace with the hand. Current frets may of course be more or less involved.

Unless care is taken in drawing a current fret, one is apt to round off the angles, and in running the eye over this ornament, there is a tendency not to follow lines down to the angles, but to switch off from one line to another, cutting off the corners. It was soon found that frets drawn, probably at first unintentionally, with rounded corners, were pleasant to examine with the eye, and after-ward they were purposely rounded down, giving rise to the beautiful

Fig. 11.

linked scrolls, Fig. 11. At first, the most important part of this ornamental border was the scroll, and the connecting line was treated, so to speak, as a mere hair-line; but, by and by, the eye began to take more and more pleasure in

Fig. 12.

following this connecting line, and it came finally to be cultivated, to the neglect of the scrolls, giving rise to the form Fig. 12.

Some have claimed that this last ornament was originally emblem-atic of water. This was certainly not the case, and it never came to mean water until after the ornament, having fully grown, was recog-nized as resembling the curling waves of the sea. In Etruscan art we frequently find a series of little dolphins gracefully leaping over the crests, or fishes are drawn in below. Here, undoubtedly, the ornament was treated as representing water or the sea. A host of beautiful borders grew up by combining two or more series of these scrolls and shading the spaces in various ways, but I have not time to speak of them here.

With the culture of the sigmoid curves and the neglect of the spirals, much vacant space is left which will look better if filled in with ornament.

In Brazil I have found little triangles drawn in these spaces, as in Fig. 13, while exactly the same border is found in Etruscan art.

It will be observed that the sides of the little triangles are approximately parallel to the parts of the sigmoids and bounding lines to which they are adjacent, thus producing a pleasant effect on the eye. The next step in the

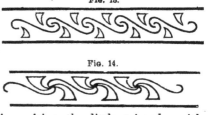

Fig. 13.

Fig. 14.

evolution of this border consists in uniting the little triangles with the sigmoids, as in Fig. 14, and this form I have observed on a Peruvian vase.

With progress in culture comes the love of variety and change. Savage music, savage art, everything in fact in savage life, is monotonous. Savages love repetition, and a border is at first drawn with all the frets running in the same direction, but in course of time it is found that a change of direction relieves the eye, and the series comes to be broken up into bars, alternating in direction. This is observable not only in the classic Greek frets, but also in similar ornaments in America. In the intervals a square figure is often introduced, and this, both in Greek and South American art, sometimes contains a cross or a quatrefoil. Similar breaks were often introduced into the scroll border, in which case the bars were separated by a figure, Fig. 15, A, shaped more or less like a cross section of a biconcave lens.

·Fig. 15.

A.

In Old World decorative art the great step was taken when the sigmoids were taken apart and alternately reversed, as in Fig. 16. This gave an opportunity for the growth between the sigmoids, of accessory ornaments which developed into an infini-

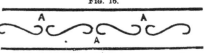

Fig. 16.

A   A

A

tude of beautiful forms in Egyptian and Greek art. It will be observed that in this series the little volutions, Fig. 16, A, A, A, are turned alternately up and down. The accessory ornament corresponding to Fig. 15, A, has, therefore, a broad base upon which to expand on one side and a narrow one on the other. These accessory ornaments may be developed both above and below the sigmoids, but in this case

FIG. 17.

a double series is formed, and a single one is more effective. In Greek art they were principally culti- vated on the upper side, giving rise to a single series of alternately broad and narrow figures supported on a line of sigmoids as in Fig. 17. I would, therefore, claim that the

FIG. 18.

upright, so-called honey- suckle ornament or An- themium was developed from the accessory orna- ment A, Fig. 15, while the oblique honey-suckle ornament, Fig. 18, appears to have been developed from the little triangles, Fig. 13.

In the Greek honey-suckle ornament the lines are not only subtle and beautiful, but they flow from one another and from the parent stems tangentially, according to a recognized and readily explainable law in decorative art. For, just as gestures that flow tangentially from one another are more agreeable to the muscles of the arm, so lines tangential to one another are more pleasant for the eye to follow than those that start abruptly from one another.

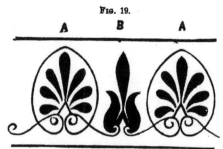

FIG. 19.

A   B   A

The beautiful bounding line to the figure A, Fig. 19, appears to have been added after the attention had been attracted to the elegant outlines of the Anthemium. When the fig- ures A A were drawn close together, but little space was left for the narrow figure B, which was therefore compressed as in Fig. 17. As the ornaments A and B were cultivated, the sigmoids were neglected, and, in course of time, they dropped out entirely from some of the borders, leaving, however, at the base of the ornament, two little volutes, which are turned in a direction opposed to that of the generating volutes. These little basal volutes are most remarkably persistent, and serve to aid us in determining the origin of many decorative forms, that have changed to such an extent, that their relation to the Anthemium would otherwise not have been suspected. Time will not allow me to trace out at great length the line of evolution of this series of ornaments, and I can only allude to the Acanthus border as its richest and most luxuriant outgrowth. This is a matter of history and I do not need to discuss it here.

Decorative art has grown up in the constant attempt to please the eye by more beautiful forms, and through the survival of the most beautiful or the fittest to please; for pure, well-constructed forms are persistent, while those that are abnormal, bizarre or not adapted to the eye, die out. We still, to-day, use straight lines and frets, and a host of beautiful forms, many of which, doubtless, have come down to us from an immense antiquity. They are normally beautiful and we shall always need them. These, I may add, are also the forms which we shall find most widely distributed over the earth.

The connection between the manufacture of pottery and the evolution of ornament, is exceedingly close; and some of the most beautiful ornamental borders, etc., have originated on pottery, the soft, easily-scratched clay offering an excellent surface for drawing upon. In savage America the manufacture of pottery falls to the lot of women. It is a branch of cooking, and having the charge of domestic affairs, she makes the vessels in which to prepare her food. But she not only makes the pottery, she also ornaments it. Elsewhere, as among certain tribes in Africa, among the Papuans and the Figís, woman is the ceramic artist. Llewellyn Jewett thinks that the Celtic burial urns were made and ornamented by women. But, the world over, woman, among savage tribes, not only makes pottery but she spins and weaves, and makes and decorates clothes. She is in fact the primitive decorative artist. Even in civilized life she still loves to cover with beautiful purely æsthetic forms everything her hand touches, and it is through her influence more than to that of man that decorative art flourishes to-day. I do not know whether her greater susceptibility to the influence of decorative art forms springs from an inherent difference in herself, or whether, what is more probable, it is owing to the wants of an entirely different life from that which man leads.

Ornament is something so necessary to civilized life, so universally necessary, that like music and the other fine arts, it merits serious and intelligent study. A song is evanescent, but a good ornament is a joy forever. To-day, in our craving we cover everything about us with a motley mixture of classic and detestably rude forms, and half the educated really do not know how to distinguish a good ornament from a bad one. Ornamental art will never take its proper rank and be fully appreciated until it is, in the first place, systematically studied; and in the second place, intelligently and widely taught.

OF SPECULATIONS IN METAPHYSICS.

By Aaron White, A. M.,

Principal of the Canastota Union School.

Review of an argument upon "The Natural Theology of the Doctrine of the Forces," by Prof. Benj. N. Martin, D. D., L. H. D., of the University of the City of New York, read before the University Convocation in 1871.

The first part of this essay consists of a presentation of certain "New Views" of the physical forces in nature; especially of light, heat, electricity, magnetism, chemical affinity and universal gravitation. Their several relations to each other are examined at some length, and an attempt is made to show that, although their phenomena are diverse and often contrary to each other, yet these forces are only various manifestations of one force,—one universal force.

Next, gravity being assumed as the representative of all forces, an argument is made, based upon the Newtonian law of gravitation, from which the author concludes that the force exerted by a single particle of matter, or in connection with a single particle of matter, is infinitely great, or rather is an infinitely great force multiplied by infinity,—an infinite of the second order.

Next, he shows that force never can be conceived except as the attribute of some substance. He then argues that this astonishing force, expressed by an infinity of the second order, cannot be the endowment of the atom of matter, and asks: "What then, is the seat of this infinite force?" In answering this question he inquires, "What is our conception of force; and what is the origin of this conception?" He shows that this idea of force, as a cause of motion, arises in the mind naturally from the consciousness of its own action and experience. Force is therefore known to us only as an attribute of mind; as therefore we have no knowledge of any other origin of force, except the mind, we ought to conclude that the one comprehensive force of the universe, is the attribute of an intellectual and spiritual being. Thus the study of nature conducts us to the knowledge of God.

In reviewing this article, our purpose is not, by any means, to deny the conclusion. If we are sincere, the study of nature may conduct us to the knowledge of God. That conclusion is fully admitted; it accords with our feelings, it affords us great comfort and hope, and a high motive for study. But, believing that the argument is unsound, and that, if its points were admitted, it might rather prove a far different conclusion, we have undertaken to examine it.

To begin then by examining the author's most important position, that "force is an attribute of mind, and cannot be an attribute or quality of matter."

We have here two propositions, first, that "force is an attribute of mind," and second, that "it cannot be an attribute or quality of matter."

As to the first, that "force is an attribute of mind," we have no occasion to disagree with the author.

His account of the history and origin of the idea seems to be true.

It arises, in our minds, from the consciousness of our own mental action, from the voluntary movement of our bodies, and from the experience of resistance overcome.

We cannot deny that a certain force belongs to the mind, but are we therefore authorized to *affirm* that there *can be* no *other origin* of force?

The author says, that since the only origin of force, of which we have *experience*, is mind, therefore, we are to assume a similar origin for all the forces of nature, or as he will have it, for the one universal force of nature. He says that the burden of proof must be upon those who deny his general conclusion. It seems to me very bad logic to assert that, because mind is one origin of force, therefore, there can be no other; but since he requires proof on the negative, let us appeal to the common judgment and common language of man.

Let a million of men, a fair per centage of them being philosophers, observe a ball tossed from the hand; the ball rises then falls to the ground. Will not every one of that million at once recognize the voluntary movement of the person, and admit the agency of mind, and at the same time recognize the fall of the ball as a consequence of its weight or gravity? One is alive, the other, dead.

There is no judgment upon which all men are more sure to agree than this, that the one body is alive and the other not alive. Yet that judgment is based upon the observed motion, and the motion is the effect of force; force in one case, a quality of mind; in the other a quality of dead matter. The movement of an animal's body, indicates the action of will and the quick work of intelligence, passion and judgment, but the motions produced by gravitation have not in them these signs. We say then, that the common judgment of mankind, observing this irreconcilable difference of effects, will not allow the identity of the causes.

The author wished to confine our reasoning to the narrow limits of our own experience, and judging by that experience, we would say, that if the motion of dead matter is due to the impulse of a mind, then a living mind must exist in that dead matter; therefore, that dead matter is not dead but alive and we begin to see that our admissions have led us into gross absurdity. But if we still cling to our argument, and admit no absurdity, we must say that all *matter* is in fact, *alive;* that every property of matter is, in fact, a manifestation of *mind* and *intelligence.* And, having gone so far, must we not also admit the converse of this, and say that mind itself, is only a property or a combination of properties of matter? And therefore again, that mind can have no separate existence, and must perish with the body? And still further, that God is only nature, in our minds personified, but really having no personal existence? Is not this simply materialism and Pantheism?

It is evident that the logic of this argument is not good, and it seems to me that one grand error was, claiming that, since we have had personal experience in ourselves of only one origin of force, therefore, we are are to presume that there is no other.

We turn now to the first material point in the essay, which is, that " there is only one force in nature." Not intending here to debate this point in full, upon its own merits, we will, however, say, that it is our conviction, after careful study, that the proposition can never be demonstrated by human reasoning, for the reason that its proofs, if it is true, transcend the powers of the human mind.

It has long been a maxim, and has been considered an *axiom* of philosophy, that "like causes produce like effects." Destroy this axiom and our systems of philosophy all perish at once. How then can we contemplate all the varied phenomena of motion; motions under the law of gravity, motions caused by what we call electricity or magnetism, or heat, or what we term chemical force, explosion of gases or gunpowder, or motions of all kinds of animals of various orders; I say, how can we believe that all these various and contrary effects, are chargeable to one and the same physical cause? It is true that some persons have thought of such a thing as possible, but if our actual knowledge must be bounded by the limits of experiment, our efforts to sustain this proposition must be forever futile.

Prof. Martin claims for this proposition high authority; but I think he claims more than those to whose authority he defers, claim for themselves.

I depend for information here, chiefly upon a volume of essays upon the "Correlation and Conservation of Forces," edited by Prof. E. L. Youmans, and published by Appleton & Co. Let us therefore examine briefly what is the great doctrine under the name "Correlation." Prof. Grove, in his introductory chapter, says: "The position which I seek to establish in this essay is, that the various affections of matter which constitute the main object of experimental physics, viz., heat, light, electricity, magnetism, chemical affinity and motion, are all *correlative*, or have a reciprocal dependence; that neither, taken abstractly, can be said to be the essential cause of the other, but that either may produce or be convertible into any of the others." Again, in his concluding chapter this passage occurs: "Even should the mind ever be led to dismiss the idea of various forces, and regard them as the exertion of *one force*, or resolve them definitely into motion, still it could never avoid the use of different conventional terms for the different modes of action of this one pervading force." Please to notice the expression. "Even should the mind ever be led to dismiss the idea of various forces." This expression shows that Prof. Grove has not yet dismissed the idea of "various forces." In the list of correlated forces above given by Prof. Grove, gravitation was not included. He remarks concerning it in another place: "To my mind, gravitation would only produce other force when the motion caused by it ceases. In no other sense can I conceive a relation between gravitation and the other forces; and, with all diffidence, I cannot agree with those who seek a more mysterious link." I think that these quotations fully show that Prof. Grove, while trying to prove the relationship or correlation of certain forces, does not try to prove their identity; nor does he believe that such identity can be proven. He also admits the existence of various other forces not included in his discussion.

The principle of conservation is thus defined by Prof. Faraday: "Force can neither be created nor destroyed." He says, also, near the close of his article on Conservation: "Those who admit the possibility of the common origin of all physical forces," etc.; and again, "Those who admit separate forces inter-unchangeable," etc. These expressions do not show that any of those to whom he refers, calling them "high and piercing intellects, which move within the exalted regions of science," regard the *unity* of forces as proven, but only that some of them admit the possibility that all forces *may have* a common origin, while others deny even that possibility.

If we call the alchemist *visionary*, because he believed that one kind of matter might be changed to another, much more may we call him visionary who believes that there is but one kind of matter; and it seems to me that he is no less visionary, who believes that there is only one kind of .force in nature, than he who believes that there is only one kind of substance in which force can manifest itself. But Prof. Martin claims, for his first important proposition, that " the forces of nature are all one," or, as he expresses it again, "all forces in this vast scheme are manifestations of one." Thus we see that the fundamental proposition of the essay which we are reviewing stands upon a very uncertain foundation, being utterly incredible to the common mind, and hardly admitted as possible, by the most visionary philosophers.

We come now to the second strong point in the essay, that "an infinite force is exerted in connection with every particle of matter." To prove this point he assumes that "all the forces of nature are one," that "gravity may be considered as the representative of that one force;" then admitting the law that the force of gravity, between masses of matter, varies inversely as the square of the distance, he finds that, the distance being diminished, the force is rapidly increased, and therefore, when the distance becomes infinitely small, the force becomes infinitely great; and more than this, for should the force vary inversely as the distance only, then the distance becoming infinitely small, the force becomes infinitely great; but since it varies inversely as the *square* of the distance, the final expression for the force between two particles, in actual contact, is infinity multiplied by infinity, or an infinity of the *second order*. This result, he thinks, is "truly astonishing." He is evidently trying to realize the magnitude of this wonderful conclusion. What! The weight of a single atom of matter greater than the weight of the whole earth!! Greater than the weight of all the planets put together!!! Greater than the weight of all the planets,—sun, moon and stars included, and repeated more times than any man can count!!!! *Impossible!* and yet *True!* He says, "This result is truly astonishing." It is. But it seems equally astonishing that so *absurd* a result should not have awakened a suspicion that some fallacy had crept into the reasoning.

When the grand ocean steamer, having safely crossed the tumultu ous deep, defiant of tempest and billow, drawing near to an unknown continent, in darkness and silence, suddenly strikes the rock-bound coast, she goes quickly to the bottom. What then does the wise commander do? Will he still insist that he has not lost his course? Will he dash himself again upon the same rock, *with* or *without* a vessel? Will he not rather swim for his life? And, if so be that he can once more touch dry land, perhaps he will be content to walk upon his own feet, like another mortal.

But Prof. Martin finds no obstacle in this astonishing absurdity. He puts aside all objections; he presses right on, and uses this absurd conclusion to sustain another absurdity—that gravity cannot be, as we had supposed, a property of matter.

The beginning of his argument was good. He details the particulars of certain experiments made with equal spheres of lead suspended by fine cords, which experiments, when carefully conducted, proved that a certain appreciable force of attraction was exerted between the two; small, but still a certain finite quantity. He then supposes the distance between their centers to diminish continually to nothing; and not regarding, at all, the necessary variation of the mass of matter, in order to find the force between two atoms, nor the fact that two spheres cannot approach each other any nearer than so as to bring their surfaces into contact, he has made a very serious mistake. Still further, after this mistake had been pointed out to him, he still insists, in a note printed with his essay, that it is not a mistake. He even suggests that the centers of gravity will not be *precisely* at the *centers* of the two *spheres*, and may even *move out* to the SURFACES. Thus, while basing his argument upon the law of universal gravitation, as enunciated by Sir Isaac Newton, he *stultifies* the law itself by his apologetic note.

To prevent all misunderstanding, I have quoted, from the English edition of Newton's Principia, one proposition which is exactly applicable to this experiment: " If to the several points of a given sphere there tend equal centripetal forces, decreasing in a duplicate ratio of the distances from the points, I say, that another similar sphere will be attracted by it, with a force reciprocally proportional to the square of the distance of the centers." Newton said nothing about the centers moving out toward the surfaces.

Let us begin again from the same experiment with the two spheres of lead. When placed at a certain short distance from each other, their mutual attractive force was a small finite quantity. Suppose that the diameters of the two spheres were exactly twelve inches each, and their densities uniform throughout. Let the spheres move toward each other till the surfaces are in contact; so far, in the experiment, the attractive force has been constantly increasing, but it is still very small, for the distance between the centers is twelve inches. If the distance between the centers be still further diminished, the diameters must also be diminished, hence the volume is diminished, and, the density remaining constant, the mass or quantity of matter is also diminished. Let the centers approximate each other, while the surfaces remain in contact; the diameters diminishing equally toward zero. The distance between the centers will be always equal to the diameter of either sphere. The mass will now vary as the cube of the diameter. But the attractive force varies directly as the mass, and inversely as the square of the distance between the centers; that is, varies as the cube of the diameter divided by the square of the diameter; that is, as the diameter. Now, remembering that when each diameter was twelve inches, the attractive force was a small, finite quantity, we see that when each diameter becomes *infinitely small*, so that either globe may be regarded as an atom of matter, the attractive force also becomes *infinitely small*.

$$g \propto \frac{D^3}{D^2} \propto D$$

When D becomes *very small*, g also becomes very small. This conclusion shows the truth as to the force of a single atom of matter; a conclusion very different from that of Prof. Martin, and not revolting to reason.

Let us briefly recapitulate. The first assumption, that all the forces in nature may be regarded and treated as one, stands upon a very loose foundation; being admitted as possible by only a few, and by none, as we suppose, being regarded as established. Yet, to one who denies this position, the argument has but little significance.

The second point, that, according to the well-established law of universal gravitation, an infinite force multiplied by infinity belongs to each minute atom of matter, is a total failure; yet, if this were true, it would not establish the conclusion which the author seeks to draw from it, that "force is not an attribute of matter."

The third great point was, that since mind is able to exert a certain limited force, therefore all force is an attribute of mind and not of matter. To this we reply, the conclusion cannot be inferred from the premise, and is opposed by the universal judgment and language of mankind, for it obliterates the clear distinction between *animate* and *inanimate* nature.

A right principle is not strengthened by a false argument. If the positions of this essay could be sustained, we should be bound to accept its legitimate conclusions, although they might be Pantheism, Materialism, or any other absurdity; but, since the argument is plainly fallacious, we can afford to disregard it.

I think we may properly say, in conclusion, let religion rest upon its own foundations of Scripture and true science, but let it not become responsible for *insane* and *untenable* theories.

INFLUENCE OF JOHN STUART MILL ON MODERN EDUCATION.

By Professor Cornelius M. O'Leary, A. M., M. D., Ph. D.,
of Manhattan College.

Among the many thinkers whose intellectual activity has stamped the present century with its characteristic spirit, John Stuart Mill stands pre-eminent. Fearless and independent of thought, he proved himself a worthy successor, in those respects, to Hobbes, Locke and Hartley, whom he far outstripped in the many-sided character of his speculations. Indeed, the variety and diversity of the themes he has handled, no less than his quickness of discernment, keenness of perception and depth of penetration, availed to assign him the position of favorite thinker of his day. The time has passed when the philosopher of repute might conduct his inquiries in a given direction regardless of parallel lines of speculation ; when the psychologist, for instance, might confine himself to the bare phenomena of consciousness, without regard to the steadily increasing data of physiology, or the theologian disdain to notice the labors of a Lyell or an Agassiz. The fact that Mr. Mill could turn the light of a rare intellect on the widely contrasted questions of Woman's Rights, Scholastic Logic, Civil Liberty, the Philosophy of Sensation, and the long train of questions affecting human happiness, and deftly gather the sinuous threads which interweave those diverging themes, specially fitted him to exert a powerful influence on the intellectual workings of his day. Hence, the authority of his opinions weighs as much in the United States and the continent of Europe as within the insular confines of his native land. Indeed, his advanced position on the two great questions of the day, viz., Representative Government and Woman's Rights, has especially enhanced among us the interest felt in his speculations, and wonderfully increased his influence over youthful thought in America. A master of that didactic style which seeks to give light from smoke, he knew how to present the subtlest thought in the clearest light, and give exceptional vigor to his utterances, by stripping them of all unneeded verbiage, and spurning the fictitious aids of ornament. Uniformly dispassionate, and soaring above the prejudices of creed and country, he imparted the same spirit to his writings, the most attractive charm, perhaps, they possess. He assails his adversaries with no rude blows, but his piercing thrust swiftly enters where a loosened rivet discloses a flaw in the armor. Tied to no system, sincere of heart, candid and impartial, of deep and varied erudition, possessing rare power of analysis, he brought to his allotted task those qualities of mind and heart best calculated to obtain for him a ready, attentive and most numerous audience. It is no wonder, therefore, that his name has become a household word in the land, and that his books are found in the hands of every educated person. But if his influence is great, it matters much in proportion to determine whether it is salutary and conducive to the growth of sound principles among us. For this reason I have thought it not amiss to devote a few moments to the consideration of those aspects of his doctrines which are most constantly viewed, and are most fruitful of results, good or otherwise.

Mr. Mill's system of logic first drew attention to the keen subtlety of his mind, and stamped him at once as a profound and original thinker. As a teacher of logic he has rendered incalculable service to the Aristotelian system of dialectics, by strengthening its fundamental principles and reviving mental processes which had fallen into desuetude through lack of appreciation and a proper intelligence of their scope. As a striking and instructive example of this return to long neglected formulæ, the restored use of connotation cannot fail to impress us. The words *meaning* and *signification*, so often employed as synonymous with connotation, define either the thing denoted or the attribute connoted, and give rise to consequent confusion. But if we keep in view the function of connotation, which is to denote a subject and imply an attribute, the mind grasps the concrete and the abstract at the same moment, and perceives an essential distinction in the first step towards the process of generalization. To determine, for instance, the truth of the proposition "Slavery is inhuman," we first establish the connotation of the word inhuman, which is done by stating that whatever is opposed to the mandates of humanity is inhuman, and thus exclude the usual concomitant ideas of cruelty, hatred, etc., which would encumber the simple connotation. I have dwelt on this revival of an old process, as it indicates on the part of Mr. Mill a just appreciation of the elder logicians, which, however, I regret to say, did not extend itself to the once favored but now much abused syllogistic reasoning of Aristotle. In his haste to establish induction as the only real process of reasoning, Mr. Mill has overlooked the valid claims of the syllogism. It is true of a syllogism that nothing can occur in the conclusion which is not contained in the premises — *nihil potest esse in conclusione nisi prius fuerit in præmissis* — whereupon two main objections are raised against it as a ratiocinative process. In the first place, the conclusion, it is urged, is but a repetition of what was already said, and contains no new assertion. The conclusion indeed contains no new assertion, but states explicitly what was implied in the premises, and thus brings before consciousness a latent feature of the general proposition which contained it. In this manner Archbishop Whately meets the first objection. The second, more formidable, maintains that we are not warranted in believing a general truth before we see all that it contains, *i. e.*, before we develop it syllogistically. In reply, I contend that the admission of a general principle does not imply that we see all it essentially involves; the finite character of the human mind precludes this. It is enough that the mind seize the generic properties of the subject of a general proposition, and apprehend that portion of the extension of the attribute corresponding to the subject. In the proposition "All animals are mortal," provided the mind sufficiently understands the signs and characters of animality, and the connotated term mortal, it can be said to understand the general truth thus expressed without the consciousness of the implied truth that certain unknown animals are mortal. The objection proceeds on the assumption that human knowledge is adequate and exhaustive, whereas rather it resembles the Koh-i-noor diamond whose facettes flash singly on the vision. It takes for granted that no argument is sound which does not proceed from the known to the unknown, but if we substitute the words "from the better known to the less known," terms which will describe the relation of the mind to most phases of human knowledge, we will readily perceive the weakness of Mr. Mill's position. It is of the nature of the mind that it acquire knowledge gradually; truth comes not in sudden floods of revelation, but enters the mind as the gentle dews of night settle on the fields. The sum of our knowledge is made up of thrums and threads, a patch-work more or less skillfully joined together. The light falls on it unequally, and not till we direct the steady ray of our intellect on the mazy loom, can we follow out each clue to the end. Even then perplexities and doubts assail us; what we once deemed clear is now obscure, the evidence of yesterday is dimmed to-day, and the lamp of reason so often flickers, that with many doubt prevails, and they turn from its guidance as from the light of an *ignis fatuus*. How then can it be said that the mind must have an adequate knowledge of a generic truth before it develops it syllogistically, if our advance in knowledge is thus gradual and unsteadily progressive? Surely this advance is best subserved by that instrument which represents the mind's progressive change from the better to the less known. The syllogism is thus constantly invoked, enters into every phase of our intellectual life, and the effort to asperse its utility bespeaks an imperfect appreciation of the part it plays in the development of truth. The substitution of induction for the discursive argument of the schools has proved a failure, in so far as every argument exhibiting the essential feature of induction is an implied syllogism. The inductive method merely suppresses the general proposition usually occupying the position of major in the syllogism, and presents the form of an enthymeme. As a readier and more effective organon for the discovery of truth, this argument possesses decided advantages over the syllogism, which is cumbersome and unwieldy. But as a test of the truth of a given inference, the syllogism is indispensable. Even Mill himself partially admits this when he describes the syllogism as a valuable precautionary test and security for avoiding errors in the process of proving. It is, therefore, highly illogical, while subordinating the syllogism to the readier and more direct method of induction, to misview its legitimate function and to detract from the signal service it has rendered in establishing many important truths. I have thus insisted on the claim of the syllogism to be considered an instrument for the discovery as well as for the manifestation of truth, it having become the vogue, since the publication of Mill's Logic in 1843, to view the syllogism as a paralogical argument which led the schoolmen into an endless series of errors. Though few writers on the abstruse science of logic have avoided errors of language so completely as Mr. Mill, and have consequently not so admirably succeeded in conveying to the minds of their readers the just sense of their idea, he has nevertheless allowed himself to be entrapped into a glaring misuse of a simple word in connection with one of his most popular works. In his "Subjection of Women," Mr. Mill enounces the opinion that the State and society have withheld her long coveted rights from woman, and that those social and legal barriers once removed, she would speedily wield the scepter in those realms over which he considers her fittest to rule. Mr. Mill takes for granted that whatever is withheld by the State in matters appertaining to its jurisdiction is a right withheld, and that the removal of an undue legal restriction is all that is required to justify the immediate exercise of the so-called right. In this Mr. Mill helps to perpetuate an old and widely prevalent error. A right, inherent or acquired, is the power bestowed by competent authority to perform certain acts under prescribed conditions, any one of which lacking, the right ceases. Accepting this definition, which embodies the idea of right entertained by writers on morals and jurisprudence, let us examine how far Mr. Mill's notion accords with it. He demands that the arena of politics be opened to woman, that her counsels be heard in the senate, and her influence be felt in the cabinet. The State is appealed to as the giver of those privileges, and its sanction being accorded to woman's tentative in this new field of action, the question is settled and other considerations are deemed secondary. If, indeed, the State law were the *ultima ratio*, the conclusion would be fair and logical; but there are so many side issues to the question, looking for solution to other tributaries, that the acceptance of the so-called right would be, to say the least, rash, till it has been determined whether the exercise of it harmonizes or conflicts with other duties and obligations. I do not intend to discuss the vexed question of woman's rights, not even to venture an opinion; but testing the word rights, as used in this connection, by the definition above given, I maintain that the distinction must be observed between privileges which the law is competent to bestow, and the freedom to perform certain actions with which it does not interfere; its active permission in the one case being a warranty of right, and its passiveness on the other being nothing more than an acknowledged want of jurisdiction. If then the law were to proclaim its neutrality touching the social and political barriers which separate the sexes, it would still remain to be considered whether woman's exercise of that freedom, which the prohibitory action of the law had hitherto withheld, is consistent with her position of wife and mother. Mr. Mill, therefore, overlooks the real *status* of the question in viewing the so-called rights of woman with reference to the law which, justly or unjustly, interferes with their exercise, and most men would consider the question far from being satisfactorily disposed of, were the law, even in despite of the most serious inconveniences, to grant the whole catalogue of rights, for the reason that they are called rights, till the higher law which governs human actions had been invoked, and they were found to harmonize with its requirements. I do not say that Mr. Mill has not discussed the relations between woman's rights and her natural condition, but his endeavors to pre-empt them from all other liens, by making the law as competent to grant as to withhold them, still leaves the burden of proof on his side, and weakens his noble advocacy of woman's cause.

In his examination of Sir William Hamilton's Philosophy, Mr.

Mill has exhibited another strange departure from the real meaning of an important word, substituting therefor a purely accidental verbal signification ; and I refer to the instance particularly, as it has a more important bearing on his metaphysical tenets than even the misuse of the word rights on his sociological doctrines.   Influenced by the sensism of Locke, who, true to the old Palmare of Aristotle, " *Nihil potest esse in intellectu quodnon prius fuerit in sensu,*" sought the source of all our ideas in the senses, Mr. Mill endeavors to measure the infinite by the sensible finite, and consequently rejected the *ens infinitum* of the schools as a senseless abstraction.   The negative prefix was fatal to him.   Instead of accepting the scholastic definition of the phrase, he analyzed it for himself, and resolved it into the twofold negative *in*, priv., and *finis*, limit, *i. e.*, negation.   And, he asks, how can two negatives give rise to a positive ?   However, by way of inconsistency, he admits a qualified infinite, such as infi-wisdom, infinite goodness, but an absolute infinite he absolutely repudiates.   This mistake of Mr. Mill, as that of his predecessor, Locke, springs from their idea that the finite precedes the infinite in the order of human knowledge.   If, indeed, we admit that the idea of the infinite is reached by the removal of those limits which mark the finite, the former necessarily becomes a mere abstraction, for the removal of limits by the mind is simply substituting the indefinite for the finite; we merely hide the limits from view.   But if we accept the definition of infinite given by the scholastic philosophers, we avoid all ambiguity of language, and obtain a clear idea of what is meant.   The infinite, say they, is that which is so great that nothing greater can exist, or be conceived to exist.   These words convey a clear and definite idea to the mind, and it can be shown accordingly that such an infinite is no mere abstraction, but necessarily precedes the idea of the finite.   Upon analysis we find that our first underlying idea is of being, being without respection, without modification. Before we can conceive the mode, we must have an idea of a subject in which alone the mode can find an objective abiding place.   To what is this idea of being, pure and simple, equivalent ?   Is it not to the infinite being, possessing the *tò esse* in its plenitude, the recipient of all modes without number or restriction.   Such is the notion of infinite being taught in the schools whence the celebrated Gioberti elaborated his system of ontologism.   If we annex mode to this being we limit it, and thus it will be seen that instead of bridging the chasm which separates the finite from the infinite by proceeding from the former to the latter, the true logical process is from the latter to the former. Our first idea is of unmodified being that is infinite; this subsequently viewed with reference to a mode becomes modified being, that is, finite. As the supposed intuitive knowledge of God hinges on this definition, an intuition which gives us no mere impersonal abstraction, such as the God of Mr. Mill, but a God possessing personal attributes in an infinite degree, the God, in a word, of Christianity, it will be seen how pregnant with mischievous consequences is Mr. Mill's qualification of infinite being as a senseless abstraction.

And yet it was of that being Mr. Mill uttered those memorable words: "And if such a being can sentence me to hell for not so calling him, to hell I will go." The habit of thought acquired by long and close study of Scotch philosophy, had rendered Mr. Mill's mind incapable of admitting any truth which did not have its tap-root in consciousness. His whole scheme of psychology rests on the data of consciousness, and all mental processes are nothing more than transformed sensations. Our knowledge of the external world is nothing but a series of sensations, between which and the objects exciting them there is no necessary link, so that if we could assign any other possible cause, internal or external, for their existence besides the material, then, there is nothing in Mr. Mill's philosophy to prevent us. What his views are on the normal condition of man, may be gathered from his known acceptance of Comte's theory; views to which I had the distinguished honor of inviting your attention last year. Much has been said and written of Mr. Mill's principles of utilitarianism, and as the subject is interesting and practical, I will venture to express an opinion thereon. Mr. Mill takes a far wider view of utilitarianism than those who restrict it to the merely useful in life. With him it is the subordination of virtue to happiness, and the substitution of prospective happiness as an incentive to practice virtue; for all other motives and consideration he tells us, in substance, to be happy and we will be virtuous, and not as the old saw has it, " Be virtuous and you will be happy." The pursuit of happiness is natural to man, so that he must propose to himself in all his actions an increase of happiness as the only sufficient motive to act. All human actions, therefore, look to an increase of happiness, and from the varied character of these may be inferred the varying views entertained by men of that happiness they necessarily pursue. If that is in every instance a virtue which prompts men to augment their happiness, it occurs to me that the barriers between vice and virtue fall to the ground, since there is nothing left but virtue. It is true indeed that Mr. Mill regards only that as true happiness, which is so regarded by all virtuous and intelligent men; but the term is relative, after all, for what happiness, for instance, would the illiterate man experience in being shut up all day in a library? while the same confinement would be a source of keen happiness to the studious and intelligent man. And so, all through the diverse conditions of human life, scarcely any two men take the same view of happiness. If then virtue must be subordinated to happiness, happiness being a relative term, so must virtue, and relative in the same way. Does, then, Mr. Mill mean that the savage, who enjoys a rare satisfaction in dancing around his writhing victim at the stake, performs a virtuous action, and all the higher in the scale of virtue as his satisfaction is more intense? If this does not follow from his utilitarian doctrines, then I do not profess to understand them. Of course, our author refines his ideas, so that practically he confines the operation of his principle to those cases where happiness is born of true virtue; but the restriction is arbitrary, and so long as the dictum has sanction of his pen (alas! it is too late to withdraw it), that we should practice virtue for happiness' sake, and not strive to procure happiness by virtue, so long must he be logically responsible for the consequences I have pointed out. Happily there is a limit to censure as there is to praise, and the few remaining words I have to say of the great English philosopher will be words of eulogy. Mill was an earnest friend of the human race; he constantly yearned to break the fetters of the last bondsman, and to lift the vassal from his degradation to the highest dignity of manhood. His love for his kind could brook no curtailment of rights, and it is no wonder that in battling for an ideal freedom, he often overstepped the bounds which the conservative voice of the world had pronounced impossible. His unselfish nature sought to share with the weaker sex the privileges of his own, and his noble plea for the restitution of their rights to women, echoes the eloquence of earnestness and loftiness of purpose : without any guide but his wonderful intellect, a spurner of authority and tradition, he broke adrift from the beliefs of men and hewed a pathway for himself. He perceived many sublime truths, dimly fell into many errors his contemporaries could not correct, and with his virtues and his faults he has passed to that tribunal which can alone determine a reward for the one and a penalty for the other.

[*Continued from Convocation Proceedings for* 1868, 1869 *and* 1872.]
ANNALS OF PUBLIC EDUCATION IN THE STATE OF NEW YORK.*

By DANIEL J. PRATT, A. M.,
Assistant Secretary of the Regents of the University.

THE FOUNDING OF KING'S (AFTERWARD COLUMBIA) COLLEGE.

The records of Trinity Church, in New York city, state that in 1703, "the Rector and Wardens were directed to wait upon Lord Cornbury, the Governor, to Know what part of the *King's Farme,* then vested in Trinity Church, had been intended for the college which he designed to have built." [1]

We have previously quoted from the proceedings of the Society for the Propagation of the Gospel, etc., for the year 1704, a statement that "there are also Proposals going on for Building a College on the Queens new Farm by subscription"; and have shown that Mr. Malcolm's school of 1732-9, "for teaching Latin, Greek and Mathematicks," may be regarded as the "germ of Columbia College." [2]

In 1725, Dr. George Berkeley (afterwards Bishop), published in London "A Proposal for the better supplying of Churches in our Foreign Plantations, and for converting the Savage Americans to Christianity, by a college to be Erected on the Summer Islands, otherwise called the Isles of Bermuda." [3]

A more eligible site was subsequently sought, and it has been claimed that, had the scheme gone into effect, New York would probably have been selected. Moreover, Bishop Berkeley afterwards became a friend and adviser of the first President of King's College. These incidents are our warrant for referring in this connection to an otherwise foreign and abortive scheme, and for quoting the following curious paragraphs concerning it:

*   *   *   *

* Entered according to act of Congress, in the year 1871, by DANIEL J. PRATT, in the office of the Librarian of Congress, at Washington.

[1] Moore's Hist. Sketch of Col. Coll., p. 6.

[2] *Annals of Public Education,* etc., as revised and separately printed in 1872, pp. 86, 124, 125.

[3] Berkeley's Works, ii, 281.

Why *Bermuda* was chosen for the place of the college will best appear from the Dean's own words. In speaking of the choice of a *situation,* he says, "It should be in a good air; in a place where provisions are cheap and plenty; where an intercourse might easily be kept up with all parts of America and the islands; in a place of security, not exposed to the insults of pirates, savages or other enemies; where there is no great trade which might tempt the readers or fellows of the college to become merchants, to the neglect of their proper business; where there are neither riches nor luxury to divert, or lessen their application, or to make them uneasy and dissatisfied with a homely frugal subsistence; lastly, where the inhabitants, if such a place may be found, are noted for innocence and simplicity of manners."[1] All these advantages, he imagined, were to be found in the islands of *Bermuda,* in a more considerable degree than in any other place in the *British American* dominions.

The scheme, for some time, met with all the encouragement that was due to so benevolent a proposal. The King granted a charter, appointing Dr. BERKELEY the first President of the intended college.   *   *   *   *

The monies arising from the sale of lands in *St. Christopher's,* that were ceded to the British crown by the treaty of *Utrecht,* amounted to eighty thousand pounds; and Queen ANNE designed that sum as a fund for the support of four *American* Bishops. But that design failing by her death, Dr. BERKELEY, by dint of application and address, notwithstanding Sir ROBERT WALPOLE's opposition, procured a parliamentary grant of twenty thousand pounds of that money, for the establishment of his college.

*   *   He came immediately [1729] to *Rhode Island,* with a view of settling a correspondence there, for supplying his college with such provisions as might be wanted from the northern colonies. But soon after his arrival he was convinced that he had been greatly misinformed with regard to the state of *Bermuda,* and that the establishment of a college there would not answer his purpose. He then wrote to his friends in *England,* requesting them to get the patent altered for some place on the *American* continent, which would, probably, have been *New York;* and to obtain the payment of the sum that had been granted him.

Accordingly, Bishop GIBSON applied to Sir ROBERT WALPOLE, then at the head of the Treasury, in his behalf; but the answer was unfavourable. With regard to the request for the payment of the money, Sir ROBERT replied: "If you put the question to me as a Minister, I must and can assure you that the money shall most undoubtedly be paid, as soon as suits with public convenience; but if you ask me as a friend, whether Dean BERKELEY should continue in *America,* expecting the payment of twenty thousand pounds, I advise him, by all means, to return home to *Europe,* and to give up his present expectations." The Dean, being informed of this conversation by his good friend the Bishop, and fully convinced that his whole plan was defeated, resolved to return to *England;* and accord-

[1] Berkeley's Works, ii, 284.

ingly he embarked at *Boston*, in September, 1731. Not long after the whole eighty thousand pounds above-mentioned was given to the Princess ANNE, on her marriage with the Prince of *Orange*.[1]

The foregoing paragraphs constitute the meagre extant record'of what was said and done with reference to a college for the province during the first one hundred and twenty years from the organization of the colonial government, viz., from 1626 to 1746. Meanwhile, Harvard College had become a century, and Yale almost a half-century old, though the Massachusetts colony was scarcely older, and Connecticut was much younger than New York. This backwardness on the part of our ancestors has placed them in unfavorable contrast with their eastern neighbors. By way of explanation and apology, it has been urged that the other colonies named were founded mainly in the interests of religion and learning, but New York rather as a commercial enterprise; also, that the former were each homogeneous as to population and character, and would, therefore, act promptly and efficiently in matters relating to the welfare of society; while New York, by reason of her several nationalities, was too heterogeneous, as well as too much absorbed in material pursuits, to become the early patron of liberal learning. At length the disadvantage became apparent to our own people, and both business shrewdness and jealous self respect were stimulated to supply this educational need. The condition of the colony, in this respect, is forcibly set forth by one of our early and prominent historians, who, referring to Yale College, has said:

* * The inhabitants of New Haven (to whose honour be it mentioned) raised a large sum to begin the institution within five or six years from the date of their Indian purchase of that town, then called Quinipiáck. It was from this seminary that many of the western churches in New York and New Jersey were afterwards furnished with their English clergymen. Mr. Smith,[2] who was a tutor and declined the rectors's chair in Yale College, vacant by the removal of Dr. Cutler, was the first lay character of it belonging to the colony of New York. Their numbers multiplied some years afterwards, and especially when, at his instance, Mr. Philip Livingston, the second propietor of the manor of that name, encouraged that academy by sending several of his sons to it for their education.

To the disgrace of our first planters, who beyond comparison surpassed their eastern neighbours in opulence, Mr. Delancey, a graduate of the university of Cambridge, and Mr. Smith, were, for many years, the

---

[1] Chandler's Life of Samuel Johnson, D. D., First President of King's College, pp. 50-54.

[2] This seems to be one William Smith (not the historian) who graduated in 1719 became tutor in 1722, and died in 1769.

only academics in this province, except such as were in holy orders; and so late as the period we are now examining [1746], the author did not recollect above thirteen more,[1] the youngest of whom had his bachelor's degree at the age of seventeen, but two months before the passing of the above law [for raising money by lottery], the first towards erecting a college in this colony, though at the distance of above one hundred and twenty years after its discovery and the settlement of the capital by Dutch progenitors from Amsterdam.[2] * *

As to the actual inception of King's College, the records of legislation in its behalf are the first, and, for some years, almost the only sources of information:

[IN GENERAL ASSEMBLY.]

Die Jovis, 3 ho. P. M. Oct. 23, 1746.

* * * *

Ordered, That a Bill be brought in, for raising the Sum of, *Two Thousand, Two Hundred and Fifty Pounds,* by a publick Lottery for this Colony, for the Advancement of Learning, and towards the founding of a College within the same; and that Mr. *Cruger*[3] and Capt. *Richards,*[4] prepare and bring in the same.

* * * *

Die Veneris, 9 ho. A. M., Oct. 24, 1746.

* * * *

Mr. *Cruger* (according to Order) presented to the House, a Bill, entitled, *An* Act, *for raising the Sum of,* Two Thousand, Two Hundred and Fifty Pounds, *by a publick Lottery for this Colony, for the Advancement of Learning, and towards the founding a College within the same;* which was read the first Time, and ordered a second Reading.

* * * *

Die Sabatii, 9 ho. A. M. Oct. 25, 1746.

The Bill, entitled, *An* Act [etc., as above]; was read a second Time, and committed to a Committee of the whole House.

* * * *

Die Martis, 3 ho. P. M. Oct. 28, 1746.

Mr. *Cruger,* from the Committee, to whom was refered, the Bill, entitled, *An* Act [etc., as above]; reported, That the Committee had

---

[1] The persons alluded to, were: Messrs. Peter Van Brugh Livingston, John Livingston, Philip Livingston, William Nicoll, Benjamin Nicoll, Hendrick Hansen, William Peartree Smith, Caleb Smith, Benjamin Woolsey, William Smith, jun, John McEvers, John Van Horne.

[2] Smith's Hist. of N. Y. (Hist. Soc. ed., 1829) ii, 118, 383.

[3] Henry Cruger, of New York.   [4] Paul Richards, of New York.

gone through the Bill, made several Amendments, and added a Clause thereto; which they had directed him to report to the House; and he read the Report in his Place, and afterwards delivered the Bill, with the Amendments, and Clause, in at the Table; where the same was again read, and agreed to by the House.

Ordered, That the Bill, with the Amendments, and Clause, be ingrossed.

*　　　　*　　　　*　　　　*

Die Mercurij, 3 ho. *P. M. Oct.* 29, 1746.

*　　　　*　　　　*　　　　*

The ingrossed Bill, entitled, *An* Act [etc., as above]; was read the third Time.

Resolved, That the Bill do pass.

Ordered, That Mr. *Cruger*, and Capt. *Stillwell*,[1] do carry the Bill to the Council, and desire their Concurrence.

*　　　　*　　　　*　　　　*

[IN COUNCIL.]

Wednesday, the 29th *day of October*, 1746.

*　　　　*　　　　*　　　　*

PRESENT, *The Hono*ble CADWALLADER COLDEN, Esqr., Speaker,
ARCHIBALD KENNEDY,
JAMES DE LANCEY,
DANIEL HORSMANDEN,
JOHN MOORE, Esqrs.

*　　　　*　　　　*　　　　*

A Message from the General Assembly by Mr Cruger & Capt Stilwell with a Bill Entituled, " An Act ".[etc., as above] Desiring the concurrence of the Council thereto.

Ordered, That the said Bills [the above with two others] be now read

Then the said three Bills were read the first time and

Ordered a second Reading

*　　　　*　　　　*　　　　*

Tuesday, the fourth day of November, 1746.　*P. M.*

*　　　　*　　　　*　　　　*

PRESENT—*The Hono*ble PHILIP LIVINGSTON, Esqr, Speaker,
ARCHIBALD KENNEDY,
PHILIP COURTLANDT,
DANIEL HORSMANDEN,
JOHN MOORE, Esqrs.

*　　　　*　　　　*　　　　*

Then the said three Bills were read the second [time] and *Ordered* to be committed.

*　　　　*　　　　*　　　　*

[1] Richard Stillwell, of Richmond Co.

Saturday, the Eighth day of November, 1746.

* * * *

PRESENT—[as on the 29th day of October, and]
    PHILIP COURTLANDT, and
    STEPHEN BAYARD, Esq^{rs}.

* * * *

The Council Resolved themselves into a Committee to consider of the following Bills, vizt

* * * *

The Bill entituled, " An Act " [etc., as above]

* * * *

The Committee having duely weighed & considered of the said four Bills and being ready to make their Report thereon

The Speaker resumed the Chair

Ordered, That the said Report be made immediately

Then the Hono^{ble} Daniel Horsmanden Esqr Chairman of the said Committee in his place Reported that the Committee had gone through the said four Bills and had directed him to report them without amendment

Which Report on the Question being put was agreed to & approved of and the Bills severally

Ordered a third Read^g

Then the said four Bills were read the third time and

On the Question being severally put

Resolved, that the said Bills do pass

Ordered, that the Hono^{ble} Daniel Horsmanden Esqr do acq^t the General Assembly that the Council have passed the said four Bills without amendment

* * * *

[IN GENERAL ASSEMBLY.]

Die Lunæ, 3 *ho. P. M. Nov.* 10, 1746.

* * * *

A Message from the Council, by the honourable *Daniel Horsmanden,* Esq ; acquainting this House, That the Council have passed the following Bills without Amendment, viz.

The Bill, entitled, *An* Act [etc., as above].

Die Sabatii, 9 *ho. A. M. Dec.* 6, 1746

*   * His Excellency was pleased to give his Assent to thirteen Bills, passed this Session, the Titles whereof are, *viz.*

* * * *

9. *An* Act, *for raising the Sum of,* [etc., as above].

* * * *

An Act for Raising the Sum of Two Thousand Two Hundred and Fifty Pounds by a Public Lottery, for this Colony for the Advancement of Learning & Towards the Founding a Colledge within the same. Passed December 6, 1746.

In as much as it will greatly Tend to the Wellfare & Reputation of the Colony That a Proper & Ample Foundation be Laid for the Regular Education of Youth, & as so good & Laudable a design must readily excite the Inhabitants of this Colony to become Adventurers in a Lottery of which the Profits shall be Employed for the founding a Colledge for that Purpose.

Be it enacted by his Excellency the Governour, the council and the General Assembly, and it is hereby enacted by the Authority of the Same, That a Lottery be Erected within this Colony, and that for & towards the Raising the Sum of Two Thousand Two Hundred & Fifty Pounds, it shall & may be Lawfull, For any Person or Persons, Natives or Foreigners, bodies Politick or Corporate, To contribute by Paying at or before the respective Times by this act Limited in that behalf, to any Person or Persons hereinafter to be appointed for that purpose, The sum of one Pound Ten Shillings or Divers entire Sums of one pound Ten Shillings upon this act, and that every contributer or Adventurer, For every such sum of one pound Ten Shillings which he she or they shall so advance, Shall be Interested in Such Lott or Share of & in the said Lottery Established by this act, as is hereinafter Directed & appointed, and the Same Entire Sums of one Pound Ten Shillings Each, are hereby appointed to be paid unto such Person or Persons as aforesaid on or before the first Day of June next.

And be it further Enacted by the Authority aforesaid That Peter Vallete and Peter Van Brugh Livingston shall be managers for Preparing & Delivering out Tickets Receiving of money for the said Tickets, & to oversee the Drawing of Lotts, and to order do & Perform such other matters & Things as are hereafter in & by this act Directed & appointed by such managers to be done & Performed, and That such managers, shall meet Together from time to time, at some Public Place as to them shall seem most convenient for the execution of the Powers & Trust in Them Reposed by this act, and that the said managers, Shall cause Books to be prepared in which every Leaf shall be Divided or Distinguished into Three columns and upon the Innermost of the said three columns, there shall be printed Ten Thousand Tickets numbered, one, Two, Three and so onwards in Arithmetical Progression where the common excess is to be one, until they arrive to and for the number of Ten Thousand, and upon the middle column in every of the said Books shall be Printed Ten Thousand Tickets of the same Breath & form, and numbered in like manner, And in the extream column of the said Books there shall be Printed a Third Rank or Series of Tickets of the same number with those of the other two columns, which Tickets shall Severally be of an oblong Figure, and in the said Books shall be Joined with oblique Lines, Flourishes or Devices, in such manner as the said Managers shall think most safe & convenient, and that every Ticket in the

Extream or third columns of the said Books shall have Printed thereupon, besides the number, The following words viz. "The Possessor
of this Ticket if drawn a Prize shall be Entituled to the Prize so
Drawn, subject to such Deduction as is Directed by an Act of this
colony in that behalf

And it is further Enacted by the Authority aforesaid, That the
said Managers, shall carefully examine all the said Books, withthe
Tickets therein, and that the same be contrived, numbered & made
according to the True Intent & meaning of this Act, and all and
Every such Manager Respectively is and are hereby Directed &
Required upon his or their Receiving of every or any Entire Sum of
one Pound Ten Shillings in full Payment for a Ticket, From any
Person or Persons contributing or Adventuring as aforesaid To cut
out of said Book or Books, through the said oblique Lines, Flourishes
or Devices, indentwise a Ticket of the Tickets in the said Extream
Columns which one of the said Managers shall sign with his own
name, and he or they shall Permit the contributer or Adventurer [if
it be Desired] to write his or her name or Mark on the two corresponding Tickets in the same Book and at the same time the said
Managers, or one of Them shall Deliver to the said contributer or
Adventurer the Ticket so cut off, which He She or They are to keep
& use for the better ascertaining & securing the Interest, which he
she or They, his, her, or their Executors, Administrators, or Assigns
shall or may have in the said Lottery for the monies so by him her or
Them contributed or Adventured, until the said adventure by the
Drawing the Lots, and the Payment of such Tickets as shall be Fortunate shall be fully Determined.

And be it further Enacted, That the said Managers at a Meeting as
aforesaid shall cause all the Tickets of the middle columns in the
books. To be cut indentwise through the said oblique Lines, Flourishes or Devices and carefully rolled up as much alike as may be &
made fast with Thread, and in the Presence of such contributors or
Adventurers as will be there present, cause all the said Tickets which
are to be Rolled up & made fast as aforesaid to be put into a Box to
be Prepared for that Purpose, and to be marked with the letter (A)
which is presently to be put in another strong Box & to be Locked
up with two Different Locks & Keys, to be kept by as many managers and Sealed with their Seals, until the said Tickets are to be
Drawn as is hereinafter mentioned and that the Tickets in the first
or Innermost Columns of the said Books shall remain still in the
Books, for Discovering any mistake or Fraud if any such should happen to be committed contrary to the true Intent & meaning of this
act.

And be it further Enacted by the same Authority, That the Managers before mentioned, shall cause to be Prepared other Books in
which Every Leaf shall be Divided or Distinguished in two columns,
and upon the Innermost of these two columns there shall be Printed
Ten Thousand Tickets and upon the outermost of the said two columns there shall be Printed Ten Thousand all which shall be of
Equal Length & Breath as near as may be, which Two columns in

the said Books shall be Joined with some Flourishes or Devices through which the outermost Tickets may be cut of Indentwise, and that One Thousand Six Hundred & Sixty Five Tickets part of those to be contained in the outermost Columns of the Books Last mentioned shall be called the Fortunate Tickets to which Benefits shall belong as hereinafter Mentioned, and the said Managers shall cause the said Fortunate Tickets to be written upon or otherwise Expressed, as well in Figures as in words at Length in manner following, That is to say, upon, one of Them, Five Hundred Pounds, upon one of them Three Hundred Pounds upon one other of them Two Hundred Pounds, upon Ten of them Severally one Hundred Pounds, upon Thirty of them Severally Fifty Pounds, Upon Forty of Them Severally Twenty five Pounds upon Fifty nine of them Severally Fifteen Pounds, upon four Hundred of them severally Ten Pounds, and upon one Thousand one Hundred & Twenty Three of them Severally Five Pounds, which sums so to be written or otherwise Expressed upon the said Fortunate Tickets will Amount in the whole to the sum of Fifteen Thousand Pounds, which is the Produce of Ten Thousand Tickets, according to the Valuation of one Pound Ten Shillings for each Ticket as before Mentioned.

And be it further Enacted by the Authority aforesaid, That the Managers before mentioned, shall cause all the said Tickets contained in the outermost column of the Last mentioned Books, in the Pesence of such contributors or Adventurers as will then be there Present To be cut out Indentwise, Through the said Flourishes or Devices & carefully Rolled up as near as may be alike & fastened with Thread, and put into another Box to be Prepared for that Purpose, and to be marked with the Letter [B] which box shall presently be put into another strong Box & Locked up & Sealed in the manner as Box Letter'd (A) until these Tickets shall also be Drawn in the manner & form hereafter mentioned, and that no money shall be received from any contributor or Adventurer, towards this Adventure as aforesaid after the first Day of June next, and that the whole Business of Roleing up & cutting off and Putting in the said Boxes the said Tickets & locking up & sealing the said Boxes, shall be Performed by the said Managers, on or before the first Day of June next. And to the End every Person concerned, may be well assured That the counter Part of the same Number with his or her Tickets is put into the Box marked with the Letter (A) from whence the same may be Drawn & that other matters are done as hereby Directed, some Public Notification in Print shall be given of the Precise time or times of Cutting the said Tickets & putting them into the Boxes, To the End that such Adventurers as shall be minded to See the same done may be Present at the doing thereof.

And be it further Enacted by the Authority aforesaid, That on or before the said first Day of June next, The said Managers Shall Cause the said Several Boxes, with all the Tickets therein, To be brought into the City Hall of the city of New York by nine of the clock in the Forenoon of the same Day, and shall then & there attend the Service in order for Drawing, with Two clerks, with Books prepared for that

Purpose, To Enter down all the Fortunate Tickets, and the said Managers being Prepared for Drawing, shall cause the two Boxes containing the said Tickets, To be severally taken out of the other two Boxes in which they shall have been Locked up, and the Tickets or Lots in the Respective Innermost Boxes, being in the Presence of the said Managers and of such Adventurers as will be there Present for the Satisfaction of Themselves, well shaken & mingled in Each Box distinctly, & some one Indifferent & fitt Person to be appointed & Directed by the Managers, shall take out & Draw one Ticket from the Box, where the said Numbred Tickets shall be as aforesaid Put, and one other Indifferent & fit Person to be appointed & Directed in the like manner; shall Immediately Draw a Ticket or Lot from the Box where the one Thousand six Hundred & Sixty Five Fortunate & Eight Thousand Three Hundred & Thirty five blank Tickets, shall be Promiscuously put as aforesaid & Immediately both the Tickets so drawn, shall be opened and The number as well of the Fortunate as the blank Tickets, shall be named a Loud, and if the Ticket Taken or Drawn from the Box containing the Fortunate & Blank Lots, shall appear to be Blank, then the numbred Ticket so Drawn, with the said Blank at the same time Drawn, shall be wrote upon Blank, and shall both be put on one File, and if the Tickets so Drawn or taken out of the Box containing the Fortunate & Blank Lots shall appear to be one of the Fortunate Tickets then the sum written upon such Fortunate Ticket [whatever it may be] shall be entered by the Clerks so appointed, into the Books prepared for that Purpose, Together with the Number coming up with the said Fortunate Ticket, and one of the said Managers shall set their Name as witness to Every such Entry, and the said Fortunate & numbered Tickets so Drawn together, shall be put upon another file, and so the said Drawing of the Tickets shall continue, by taking one Ticket at a Time out of Each Box, and with opening naming aloud & Fileing the Same, and by Entering the Fortunate Lots insuch method, as is before Mentioned, Until the whole Number of Tickets, shall be completely Drawn, And if the same cannot be Performed in one Days time the said Managers Shall cause the Boxes to be Locked up & Sealed, in the manner as aforesaid, and adjourn til the next Day, and so from Day to Day & Every Day [except Sundays] and then open the same & Proceed as above, till the said whole Number of Tickets shall be compleatly Drawn as aforesaid.

And to the End that the Adventurers may have all Possible Satisfaction in the Due Regular & Just management of the said Lottery Be it enacted by the Authority aforesaid, That the Mayor, Recorder, Aldermen & Commonalty of the City of New York, may & are hereby Impowered to appoint Every Day during the whole course of the Lottery, two or more of their body to Inspect all & Every Transaction of the said Lottery hereby Directed and Required, and that each county in the Colony may & are hereby Impowered If They see cause to Depute two Justices of the Peace, or other Reputable Freeholders or Inhabitants For the aforesaid Inspection with Proper Certificates of their being so Deputed, From the next or any subsequent General Session of the Peace, and the said Managers are hereby Directed &. Required to Admit Them, and the said Members of the said Corporation to the aforesaid Inspection accordingly.

And to the End the Fortunate may know, whether absent or Present to what Degree they have been so, and that Speedy Payment may be made upon the Fortunate Tickets to the Persons Entitled thereto Be it Enacted by the authority aforesaid, That during the course of the Drawing the said Managers are here by Required, weekly to give Publick notice, in the New York Post Boy of the numbers of the Tickets drawn Blank and also of the numbers of the Tickets drawn against the Fortunate Lots, and the Sums written on the same and as soon as the drawing is over, shall pay the said sums to such persons, who shall Produce Tickets with the Numbers Drawn against such Fortunate Lots, They the said Manager first Deducting Fifteen per cent out of the said Fortunate Lots & to be applyed as hereafter is Directed

And be it further enacted by the Authority aforesaid, That if any Person or Persons shall Forge or Counterfeit any Ticket or Tickets to be made forth on this act, or Alter any of the numbers thereof or bring any Forged or counterfeited Ticket, or any Ticket whereof the Number is Altered, knowing the same to be such, to the said Managers or either of them for the Time being, To the Intent to Defraud the Colony, or any Contributer or adventurer or the Executors, Administrators or Assigns of any Contributer or Adventurer upon this Act, That then Every such Person or Persons [being thereof Convicted in Due Form of Law] shall be adjudged a Fellon, and shall suffer Death, as in Cases of Fellony, without Benefit of Clergy, and the said Managers or Either of Them are hereby Authorized Required & Impowered to Cause any Person or Persons bringing such Altered Forged or Counterfeited Ticket or Tickets as aforesaid to be apprehended and to Commit Him, Her or Them to his Majisties Goal of the City of New York, to be Proceeded against for the said Fellony according to Law—

And be it enacted by the Authority aforesaid, That every of the Managers hereby appointed for Putting this Act in Execution before his Acting in such commission Shall take the oath following that is to say, I, A, B, do swear That I will Faithfully Execute the Trust Reposed in me and That I will not use any Indirect Art or means, or permit or Direct any Person to use any Indirect Art or means to obtain a Prize or Fortunate Lot for myself or any Person whatsoever, and that I will do the utmost of my Endeavours to prevent any undue or sinister Practice to be done by any Person whatsoever and that I will to the best of my Judgment declare to whom any Prize Lot or Ticket of Right does belong according to the true Intent of the act of Gouvernour council & general Assembly Passed in the Twentyth year of his Majisties Reign in that behalf, which oath shall be administered by one of the Justices of the Supream Court of this Colony.

Provided always and be it enacted by the Authority aforesaid that the managers hereby appointed, before they take the oath Prescribed by this act or Perform or Execute any thing therein contained shall first Enter into the following Recognizances to our Sovereign Lord the King, his Heirs & Successors, That is to Say, Each of them before one of the Justices of the Supreme court, in the sum of Four Thousand Pounds with two sufficient securities Each in half that sum Conditioned that they shall & will well & Truely, each for his Part Execute the Trust Reposed in Them by this act & well & Truely observe do & Perform all the Directions thereby Required to be done & Performed by Them, according to the True Intent & meaning thereof, which several Recognizances, are to be delivered to the Treasurer, by the Justice before whom the same shall be so taken [having first caused the same to be Recorded in the Minutes of the Supreme Court] in order to be Lodged in the Treasury.

And be it further Enacted by the Authority aforesaid, That the several Deductions of Fifteen per cent, upon the whole number of Fortunate Tickets shall be paid into the Hands of the Treasurer of this Colony by the Managers hereof, out of which there shall be allowed in Case the Lottery shall be actually Drawn, The following sums viz. "To Each of the said Managers the sum of one Hundred & Twenty Five Pounds, To each of the Two Clerks six shillings per diem For every Day They shall be actually employed in the said Drawing To Each of the Two Persons who shall Draw the Tickets Three shillings per Diem, for Every Day they shall be so Employed, and all Reasonable Charges, For Printing Books, Tickets & advertisements & such other Incidents as may necessarily be required in the said Lottery, and the monies ariseing from the said several Deductions of Fifteen pr cent, upon the whole number of Fortunate Tickets, The aforesaid charges of Management being first Deducted, shall be paid into the hands of the Treasurer, To be and Remain in the Treasury, To & for the Purpose of Founding a Colledge for the Education of Youth and to & for no other Purpose whatsoever in such Manner as shall be hereafter Directed by Act or Acts of the Governour Council & Generel Assembly.

And That the Purpose of Founding the said Colledge may not be obstructed by any other application of the moneys to arise from the Profits of the said Lottery Be it enacted by the authority aforesaid That Each & Every Representative in General Assembly, For the Time being, who shall hereafter in General Assembly, move or consent to the applying or appropriating the said money to any other Purpose whatever Than the Founding the Colledge aforesaid shall be and hereby is Declared & made forever Incapable of Sitting & voting in this or any Future General Assembly, and new Writts shall Issue accordingly.

And be it further Enacted by the same authority, That no Fee or Gratuity whatsoever shall or may be Demanded or taken of any Person or Persons, contributer or Adventurer to the Lottery aforesaid by any Manager or Managers, or any other officer or officers appointed by this Act, For any thing that shall be done Pursuant to this act upon Pain That any officer or Person offending by taking any Fee or Gratuity contrary to this act, shall Forfeit the sum of Fifty

Pounds to the Party grieved, To be Recovered with full Cost in any of his Majisties Courts of Record within this Colony.

And be it Enacted by the Authority aforesaid, That in case all the said Ten Thousand Tickets, shall not be sold & Disposed of before the said first Day of June next, That then the Money That has been Received for any Ticket or Tickets by virtue of this act, shall be by the said Managers Repaid to the Person or Persons of whom the same shall have been Received, his her or their Executors, Administrators or Assigns, He, She or They first Producing the several Tickets for which such Repayment, shall be Required, and the Lottery hereby Erected & made, shall from thence forth become void, any thing in this Act contained to the contrary hereof notwithstanding, and in such case the Treasurer aforesaid shall pay out of any money then in the Treasury (except such as shall be appointed for the annual support of Government) The several Incidents before mentioned, upon proper certificates signed by the said Managers, and Receipts thereon, shall be good Vouchers to him for the Payment thereof, For the amount of which the General Assembly shall & will Provide ways & means to Repay & Replace the same.

Provided and be it Enacted, That in case the said Ten Thousand Tickets aforesaid, be sold and disposed of in the manner aforesaid before the first day of June next, That then the Managers shall proceed to the Drawing the Lots in manner aforesaid, first giving Publick Notice there of in the New York Post Boy at Least Fourteen Days before the Drawing the same, any thing in this act to the contrary notwithstanding

And be it further enacted by the Authority aforesaid, That if either of the before mentioned Managers shall happen to Die Remove out of this Colony or Refuse to Act, according to the several and Respective Powers & Authorities hereby Directed & Required, It shall & may be Lawfull to and for the Governour or commander in Chief for the time being by and with the advice & consent of his Majisties Council to nominate & appoint some other fit Person or Persons to be Manager or Managers in the place & stead of the Manager or Managers so dying Removing or Refusing to Act as aforesaid any thing herein contained to the contrary notwithstanding Provided that the Person or Persons who may be so appointed shall be obliged to take the Like oath, Enter into the Like Recognizance & Sureties as is herein Directed to be done by the Managers named in this act and be in all Respects as subject to observe & Perform the several Directions of this Act, as if he or They had been named or appointed in it.[1]

[1] MS. Laws, in office of Secretary of State.

NEW YORK, *Jan* 5, 1746, 7.

By a Law passed the last Sessions, a Publick Lottery is directed, to consist of 10,000 Tickets, at 30s. each, 1665 of which to be fortunate, viz.

Number of prizes.	Value of each.	Total value.
1 of..........................	£500	£500
1 of..........................	300	300
1 of..........................	200	200
10 of..........................	100	1000
30 of..........................	50	1500
40 of..........................	25	1000
59 of.	15	885
400 of..........................	10	4000
1123 of..........................	5	5615

1665 Prizes, }
8335 Blanks, } 10,000 Tickets at 30s. makes............. £15,000

15 per Cent. to be deducted from the Prizes. The Profits will be employed towards founding a College within this Colony, for the regular Education of Youth; And as such a laudable Design will greatly, tend to the Welfare and Reputation of this Colony; it is expected the Inhabitants will readily be excited to become Adventurers. Publick Notice will be given of the Precise Time for putting the Tickets into the Boxes, that such Adventurers as shall be minded to see the same don, may be present at the doing thereof. The Drawing to commence on or before the first Day of June next, at the City-Hall, of New York, under the Inspection of the Corporation, who are impowered to appoint two or more of their Body to inspect all and every Transaction of the said Lottery; and two Justices of the Peace, or other reputable Free-holders or Inhabitants of every County in this Colony, if they see Cause to depute the same at their next or any subsequent general Sessions of the Peace. Notice will be given in the *New - York Post Boy* fourteen Days before the Drawing. The Managers are sworn faithfully to execute the Trust reposed in them, and have given Security for the faithful Discharge of the Same. As the late Lottery has given general Satisfaction, the same Care will be taken, and the same Regulations observed in this, with respect to the Tickets, the Drawing, Keeping the Books, and other Particulars, as near as possible. The Blanks as well as Prizes will be published weekly in the *New - York Post Boy*. Such as forge or counterfeit any Ticket, or alter the Number, and are thereof convicted, by the said Act are to suffer Death as in Cases of Felony. The Money will be paid to the Possessors of the Benefit Tickets as soon as the Drawing is finished.

Tickets are to be had at the Dwelling-houses of Messrs. Peter Vallette and Peter Van Brugh Livingston, who are appointed Managers.[1]

The results of the first lottery in aid of Columbia College are

[1] New-York Weekly Post Boy, Numb. 207,² Jan. 5, 1746-7.

given in full in *Parker's Gazette.* Nos. 229, 230, 231 and 232 contain ten pages of figures. The last sheet, issued as a supplement to No. 234, is missing from the New York Historical Society file. The highest prize, £500, was drawn by ticket No. 3306, on the 12th day of June, 1747. The printer in a note states: "*The highest Prize drawn we hear proves the Property of the Honourable* JOSEPH MURRAY, *Esq. of this City.*"

The following is the announcement in No. 229, above referred to :

In Pursuance of a Law of this Colony entitled, An Act for raising the Sum of £2250, by a publick Lottery for this Colony, for the Advancement of Learning, and towards founding a College within the same ; *passed in the 20th Year of his Majesty's Reign ; the Managers of the said Lottery met at the* City-Hall *in* New-York, *on Monday last, with* two Clerks, *for the Drawing the same, and in the Presence of two of the Members of the Corporation of this City, proceeded therein as follows,* viz.

Monday,	June 1, Numb.	5144, 299, 2478, Blanks.
Tuesday,	June 2.	9254, Blank.
Wednesday,	3,	2454, Blank,
Thursday,	4,	3314, Blank,
Friday,	5,	5517, Blank,
Saturday,	6,	495, Blank.

The Drawing so few for the Week past, is occasioned by there being yet a small Number of the Tickets unsold ; which, however, some Gentlemen have engaged to take off, in case they shall not be purchased within a limitted Time, so that an Opportunity still remains for any Person to be supplied with Tickets until Wednesday Morning next, when the Drawing as fast as possible will certainly go on, and no more be sold after that Time.[1]

[IN GENERAL ASSEMBLY.]

Die Martis, 3 ho. P. M. May 19, 1747.

*   *   *   *

Mr. Cruger moved for Leave to bring in a Bill, for prolonging the Time of drawing the publick Lottery, till the first of *September* next. *Ordered,* That Leave be given to bring in a Bill accordingly.

*   *   *   *

Die Martis, May 26, 1747.

*   *   *   *

Mr. *Cruger* (according to Leave) presented to the House, a Bill, entitled, An Act, *to prolong the Time limited for drawing the Lottery, appointed in and by an Act, entitled,* An Act, *for raising the Sum of,* Two Thousand, two Hundred, and Fifty Pounds, *by a publick Lottery for this Colony, for the Advancement of Learning,*

[1] New-York Revived Weekly Gazette in the Post-Boy, Numb 229³, June 8, 1747.

and towards the founding a College within the same; which was read the first Time, and ordered a second Reading.

*   *   *   *

Nothing further relative to this bill appears in the Journal of the General Assembly, and the drawing seems to have occurred at the time appointed by the above statute.

Die Veneris, 9 *ho. A. M. August* 21, 1747.

*   *   *   *

Ordered, That a Bill be brought in for raising the Sum of, *Two Thousand, Two Hundred, and Fifty Pounds,* by a publick Lottery, for a further provision towards founding a College, for the Advancement of Learning within this Colony, and that Mr. *Cruger,* and Capt. *Richards,* prepare and bring in the same.

*   *   *   *

Die Sabatii, 9 *ho. A. M. August* 22, 1747.

Mr. *Cruger* (according to Order) presented to the House, a Bill, entitled, *An* Act, *for raising the Sum of,* Two Thousand, Two Hundred, and Fifty Pounds, [etc., as above]; which was read the first Time, and ordered a second Reading.

*   *   *   *

Die Martis, 9 *ho. A. M. August* 25, 1747.

The Bill entitled, *An* Act, [etc., as above]; was read a second Time, and committed to a Committee of the whole House.

*   *   *   *

Die Mercurij, 9 *ho. A. M. Sept.* 2, 1747.

*   *   *   *

Ordered, That the Managers of the late Lottery, do, by *Tuesday* next, lay before this House, an Account upon Oath, of the Charge of the Management thereof; and an Account of what Monies they have paid into the Treasury, in pursuance of the Act for that Purpose.

Ordered, That the Clerk of this House, serve the aforesaid Commissioners [for certain military purposes] and the Managers of the said Lottery, with copies of these Orders forthwith.

*   *   *   *

Die Jovis, 3 *ho. P. M. Sept.* 10, 1747.

*   *   *   *

The House being informed that Messieurs *Vallette,* and *Vanbrugh Livingston,* Managers of the late Lottery, attended at the Door, they were called in, and presented to the House (according to Order), their Accounts, sworn to, and then withdrew.

And the Titles thereof being read,

Ordered, That Captain *Richards,* Mr. *Clarkson,* and Mr. *Cruger,* be a Committee to examine the said Accounts, and make Report thereof to the House.

*   *   *   *

We do not find any subsequent record as to this Report.

Die Mercurij, 3 ho. P. M. Oct. 7, 1747.

*   *   *   *

Ordered, That a Bill be brought in for raising the Sum of, [etc., as under date of August 21]; and that Mr. *Cruger,* and Col. *Lott,* prepare and bring in the same.

*   *   *   *

Die Jovis, 9 ho. A. M. Oct. 8, 1747.

*   *   *   *

Mr. *Cruger* (according to Order) presented to the House, a Bill, entitled [as indicated above]; which was read the first Time, and ordered a second Reading.

*   *   *   *

Die Veneris, 3 ho. P. M. Oct. 9, 1747.

*   *   *   *

The Bill, entitled, [as indicated above]; was read a second Time, and committed to a Committee of the whole House.

*   *   *   *

The above bill failed to become a law during the session which ended November 25, 1747. A similar bill was introduced and passed, in an amended form, during the next session. Meanwhile, *private* Lotteries were prohibited by an act, which recognizes the immoral tendency of a free lottery system, entitled:

An ACT *to prevent private Lotteries within this Colony.*

Pass'd the 25th of November, 1747.

WHEREAS several persons, of late, have set on Foot, and opened private Lotteries within this Colony; which being under no Restrictions by Law, are attended with pernicious Consequences to the Publick, by encouraging Numbers of labouring People to assemble together at Taverns, where such Lotteries are usually set on foot and drawn: For Remedy whereof;

I. BE IT ENACTED by his Excellency the Governor, the Council, and the General Assembly, and it is hereby Enacted by the Authority of the same, That if any Person or Persons whatsoever, shall, after the Publication of this Act, presume to open, set on foot, or draw any private Lottery whatsoever, under whatsoever Name, Title or Denomination, the same may pass; he, she or they, shall respectively forfeit and pay double the sum of which such Lottery shall consist; to be recovered by any Person or Persons who will sue for the same, in any Court of Record within this Colony; one Half of which Forfeiture to be paid to the Treasurer of this Colony, for and towards the Support of this Government, and the other Half to the Person that shall sue for the same as aforesaid.[1]

*   *   *   *

Die Martis, 9 ho. A. M. Feb. 23, 1747–8.

*   *   *   *

Mr. *Cruger,* moved for Leave to bring in a Bill, for raising the Sum of, *Two Thousand, Two Hundred and Fifty Pounds,* by a publick Lottery, for a further Provision towards founding a College, for the Advancement of Learning within this Colony.

Ordered, That Leave be given to bring in a Bill accordingly.

*   *   *   *

Die Mercurij, 9 ho. A. M. Feb. 24, 1747–8.

*   *   *   *

Mr. *Cruger* (according to leave) presented to the House, a Bill, entitled, [as above]; which was read the first Time, and ordered a second Reading.

*   *   *   *

Die Jovis, 9 ho. A. M. Feb. 25, 1747–8.

*   *   *   *

The Bill, entitled, [as above]; was read a second Time, and committed to a Committee of the whole House.

*   *   *   *

Die Veneris, 3 ho. P. M. Feb. 26, 1747–8.

*   *   *   *

Mr. *Cruger,* from the Committee of the whole House, to whom was refered, the Bill, entitled, [as above]; reported, That the Committee had gone through the Bill, altered the Title, and made several Amendments to the Body of the said Bill, which they had directed him to report to the House; and he read the Report in his Place, and afterwards delivered the Bill, with the Amendments, in at the Table, where the same were again read, and agreed to by the House.

Ordered, That the Bill, with the Amendments, be ingrossed.

*   *   *   *

Die Veneris, 9 ho. A. M. March 4, 1747–8.

The ingrossed Bill, entitled [as amended], *An* Act, *for raising the sum of,* One Thousand, Eight Hundred Pounds, *by a publick Lot-*

---

[1] Livingston and Smith's Laws of N. Y., i, 405.

tery, for a further Provision towards founding a College for the Advancement of Learning, within this Colony; was read the third Time.

Resolved, That the Bill do pass.

Ordered, That Mr. *Verplank,* and Mr. *Nicoll,* do carry the Bill to the Council, and desire their Concurrence.

* * * *

[IN COUNCIL.]

Tuesday the 8th *day of March,* 1747.

The Council met according to adjournment

PRESENT— *The Honble* PHILIP LIVINGSTON, Esqr, Speaker,
ARCHIBALD KENNEDY,
JAMES DE LANCEY,
PHILIP CORTLANDT,
JOHN MOORE,
JOHN RUTHERFORD, Esq^rs.

The Speaker assumed the Chair

A Message from the General Assembly by Mr Nicoll & Mr Verplank with a Bill Entituled, "An Act for raising the sum of £1800 "by a publick Lottery for a further provision towards founding a "Colledge for the advancement of Learning within this Colony" desiring the concurrence of the Council thereto

Ordered, that the said Bill be now read

Then the said Bill was read the first time and

Ordered a second reading

* * * *

Wednesday the 9th *day of March,* 1747.

* * * *

Ordered, that the Bill Entituled [as above] be now read the second time and

Ordered to be committed

* * * *

Saturday the 19th *day of March,* 1747

* * * *

The Council resolved it self into a Committee to consider of the Bill Entituled [as above]

The Committee having duly weighed and considered of the said Bill and being ready to make their report thereon

The Speaker resumed the Chair

Ordered, that the said Report be made imediately

Then the Honble John Moore Esqr Chairman of the said Committee in his place Reported that the Committee had gone through the said Bill and had directed him to report the same without any amendment

Which Report on the Question being put was agreed to and approved of and

Ordered, that the said Bill be read the third time

*   *   *   *

Friday, the 25th *day of March,* 1748.

*   *   *   *

Ordered, that the Bill Entituled [as above] be now Read the third time

Then the said Bill was Read the third time and

On the Question being put

Resolved, that the said Bill do pass

Ordered, that the Hon[ble] John Moore Esq[r] do Acquaint the General Assembly that the Council have passed the said Bill without any Amendment

*   *   *   *

[In General Assembly.]

Die Mercurij, 9 *ho. A. M. March* 30, 1748.

*   *   *   *

A Message from the Council, by the honourable *John Moore,* Esq; acquainting this House, that the Council have passed the Bill, entitled, [as above]; without any Amendment.

*   *   *   *

Die Sabatii, 9 *ho. A. M. April* 9, 1748.

*   *   *   *

A Message from his Excellency [Governor Clinton], by Mr. *Banyar,* Deputy Secretary.

Mr. Speaker, his Excellency requires the immediate Attendance of this House, at the Council-Chamber, at Fort-George, *in this City* [New York].

The Speaker left the Chair, and with the House, attended accordingly; and being returned, he resumed the Chair, and reported to the House, that his Excellency had, in the Presence of the Council, and the Members of this House, given his assent to eleven Bills, passed this Session; the Titles Whereof are, *viz.*

*   *   *   *

An Act, *for raising the Sum of* One Thousand, Eight Hundred Pounds, [etc., as above].

An ACT *for raising the Sum of* One Thousand Eight Hundred Pounds, *by a publick Lottery, for a further Provision towards founding a College for the Advancement of Learning within this Colony.*

Pass'd the 8th of April, 1748.[1]

The body of the above act being an almost verbatim copy of that enacted December 6, 1746, already recited, except as to dates and the amount to be raised, need not be reproduced.

The following criticism on the act is alike applicable to the preceding one for raising £2,250:

*   *   *   *

" An Act for raising the sum of £1800 by a Lottery "
On this Act Mr Lamb observes, that, although the money thereby to be raised, is directed to remain in the hands of the Treasurer, to and for the purpose of founding a College and to no other use whatever, a very extraordinary clause immediately follows, enacting, that, if any member should thereafter move for applying the said money to any other purpose, he should be incapable of sitting in that or any future Assembly, Mr Clinton likewise complains, that by this Act Commiss^rs were nominated for that trust without his being consulted.[2]

*   *   *   *

An Act to revive an act Entituled an act for raising the sum of Eighteen Hundred Pounds by a Publick Lottery for a Further Provision towards founding a college for the Advancement of Learning within this colony with an Addition thereto.

[Passed October 28, 1748.]

Whereas an act passed the ninth Day of April Last Entitled an act for raising the Sum of Eighteen Hundred Pounds by a Publick Lottery for a further Provision towards founding a college for the advancement of Learning within this colony, did for want of a Sufficient Number of contributors expire the first Day of September last, by which means the Managers appointed in the said Act cannot proceed to the drawing the Lottery thereby Erected, For Remedy whereof, Be it enacted by his Excellency the Governour, Council & General Assembly, & it is hereby enacted by the Authority of the Same, That the said act Entituled an act for raising the Sum of Eighteen Hundred Pounds by a Publick Lottery for a further Provision towards founding a college for the Advancement of Learning within this colony, Shall be and hereby is revived and every clause Matter & Thing therein contained Enacted to be & remain of full Force & Virtue to all Intents Constructions and Purposes whatsoever except so much thereof as Shall be alter'd by this Act. And Be it further Enacted by the Authority aforesaid that instead of the first Day of September Last as was directed by the aforesaid Act, the Drawing of the said Lottery shall begin on the fourteenth Day of

[1] Livingston and Smith's Laws of N. Y., i, 406.   [2] N. Y. Col. Doc., vi, 685.

November next, or sooner if full, And all the matters whatsoever directed by the above mentioned Act to be done, & Performed by the first Day of September Last, if done on or before the Fourteenth day of November next, Shall be good & Valid to all intents constructions & Purposes whatsoever, anything in the said Act to the contrary notwithstanding.

And be it further enacted by the Authority aforesaid in order to answer the good Purposes intended by the Act aforesaid. That in case the whole Number of Tickets should not be sold by the said fourteenth Day of November next in such case the Managers shall cause all the Tickets of the outermost collumns which shall then remain undisposed of to contributers or adventurers to be delivered into the hands of the Treasurer of this Colony for the time being, to be by him retained & kept as cash received from the said Managers, to be contributed & Adventured by the Publick towards the filling up of the said Lottery at the risque and for the benefit of this colony, and shall be signed with the name of one of the Managers, and the corresponding Tickets in the same books shall be wrote upon thus (Colony of New York) which Tickets so delivered into the hands of the said Treasurer shall by him be kept for the better Ascertaining & securing the Interest which this colony shall or may have in the said Lottery, for the Tickets so contributed or Adventured until the adventure by the Drawing of the Lots and the Payment of such Tickets as shall be Fortunate be fully determined.

Fort George in the City of New York
   the 28th day of October 1748

I assent to this Bill Enacting
   the Same and Order
   it to be Enrolled,
              G CLINTON

City of New York Die Mercurii ye 19th of October 1748.

In the Twenty Second year of his Ma tys reign General Assembly for the colony of New York. This bill having been read three Times Resolved this bill do Pass.

                  DAVID JONES Speaker

(Endorsed) Die Mercurii ye 19th of Octor 1748
   This bill being Passed
               Ordered
That Mr Nicol & Mr Cruger do carry this bill to the council and desire their concurrence.

Council chamber New York, 20th Octor 1748. This bill was then read the first Time & Ordered a second Reading
   Oct 24, Read the second Time & Ordered to be Committed.
   Oct 25, Reported without Amendment and Read the third Time & Passed

                  Gw BANYAR[1]

           [1] MS. Laws, in Office of Sec'y of State.

An ACT *for vesting in Trustees, the Sum of* Three Thousand Four Hundred and Forty-three Pounds, Eighteen Shillings, *raised by Way of Lottery, for erecting a College within this Colony.*

Pass'd the 25th of November, 1751.

WHEREAS the Sum of *Three Thousand Four Hundred and Forty-three Pounds, Eighteen Shillings,* has been raised within this colony, by Way of Lottery, for erecting a College for the Education of Youth, within the same; which Sum being not conceived sufficient, without further Addition, to answer the said End of erecting, compleating and establishing a College for the Advancement of useful Learning, it is conceived necessary, that Trustees be appointed, as well for the setting at Interest the said Sum of *Three Thousand Four Hundred and Forty-three Pounds, Eighteen Shillings,* already raised for the said Purpose, as for receiving the contributions and Donations of such Persons as may be charitably disposed, to be Benefactors and Encouragers of so laudable an Undertaking:

I. BE IT THEREFORE ENACTED *by his Excellency the Governor, the Council and the General Assembly, and it is hereby Enacted by the Authority of the same,* That the eldest Councellor residing in this Colony, the Speaker of the General Assembly, and the Judges of the Supreme Court, the Mayor of the city of *New-York,* and the Treasurer of this Colony, for the Time being, together with *James Livingston,* Esq; Mr. *Benjamin Nicoll,* and Mr. *William Livingston,* or the Survivor or Survivors of them, the said *James Livingston, Benjamin Nicoll,* and *William Livingston,* shall be, and hereby are appointed Trustees for managing the said Sum of *Three Thousand Four Hundred and Forty-three Pounds, Eighteen Shillings,* and for managing any other Sum or Sums of Money, Lands, Goods, or Chattels, which may be contributed or given, by any Person or Persons whatsoever; to be imployed for the said Use and Purpose, of erecting, compleating, and establishing a College, for the Advancement of Learning, within this Colony: All which said Sum and Sums of Money, they, the said Trustees, and the major Part of them, and of the Survivors of them, shall be, and hereby are impowered, required, and directed, to put out at Interest, yearly, and every Year, together with the Interest arising thereon, until the same shall be employed for the Use and Purpose of erecting and establishing a College for the Advancement of Learning, within this Colony, in such Manner as shall, by some Act or Acts hereafter to be passed for that Purpose, be directed.

II. AND BE IT FURTHER ENACTED *by the Authority aforesaid,* That if any Lands, Tenements, or Hereditaments, shall be given by any Person or Persons whatsoever, towards founding the said College, the aforesaid Trustees, and the major Part of them, and of the Survivors of them, shall be, and hereby are enabled, to let the same to farm, to the best Advantage, for advancing the said Undertaking, rendering the Rent to the Treasurer of this colony, for the Time being, for the Use and Purpose aforesaid.

III. AND BE IT FURTHER ENACTED *by the Authority aforesaid,* That the Treasurer of this Colony shall, and he is hereby required and directed, to pay to the Borrowers, such Sum and Sums of the Money aforesaid, from Time to Time, as shall be specified in the Securities by them to be given, with the Consent of the major Part of the Trustees aforesaid, or of the Survivors of them; which Securities shall be, in the Names of two or more of the Trustees aforesaid consenting, with Conditions for the Payment of the Money and Interest there-from arising, to the Treasurer of this Colony, for the Time being, for the Use and Purpose aforesaid: And such Securities, given as aforesaid, shall be to the said Treasurer, good Vouchers and Discharges for the Sums paid thereon by him, and therein mentioned.

IV. AND BE IT FUTHER ENACTED *by the Authority aforesaid,* That the aforesaid Trustees shall be, and hereby are enabled, to receive Proposals from any of the Cities or Counties within this Colony, which shall be desirous of having the said College erected within their said Cities or Counties, touching the placing or fixing the same therein, respectively; and the said Trustees, and every of them, shall be, and hereby are required, to render a just and true Account on Oath, of all their Proceedings in the Premisses, to the Governor, Council, and General Assembly, when by them, or any of them, thereunto required.[1]

* * Of these trustees, ten in number, two belonged to the Dutch Reformed Church, one was a Presbyterian, but seven were members of the Church of England, and some of these seven were also vestrymen of Trinity Church. These circumstances—the known sentiments of this large majority of the trustees—their well understood, and very natural desire, that the proposed college should be connected with their church—might sufficiently account for the offer made to them by Trinity Church, not long after their appointment, "of any reasonable quantity of the Church farm, * * for erectting, and use of a college;" * * however, * * it may not unreasonably be inferred, that the then recent grant of the King's Farm to that corporation, had been made with a view to the advancement of learning as well as of religion; that some condition to that effect had been at least implied, on occasion of that grant.

If such were the case, the present offer from the church was but the carrying out, after a lapse of fifty years, of this original design. * * The jealous apprehensions entertained of any, the smallest, approach to a church-establishment within the province, caused violent opposition to the plan, as soon as it became known, of obtaining a royal charter for the college. This determined opposition to the plan of the Trustees, was maintained chiefly by one of their number, the only Presbyterian at their Board, Mr. William Livingston; a gentleman, by his birth, his connexions and his position in society; by his superior education, his industry and talents as a lawyer, already eminent; and afterwards, in the various high stations which he filled, greatly distinguished for patriotic devotion to his country. A declared enemy of all church establishments, he, in this matter of the college, was actuated by conscientious, probably, but mistaken views of the

---

[1] Livingston and Smith, i, 450.

design and tendency of the incorporation which he so zealously endeavored to defeat. With this view, he commenced on the 22d of March, 1753, in *The Independent Reflector*, a paper published under his direction, his " Remarks on our intended College." After considering, first, the great importance of the institution, he goes on, in subsequent numbers, to discuss the proper mode of its establishment, which he insists should be, not by *Charter*, but by *Act of Assembly*: in which case it was taken for granted, that the plan of the institution would be more consistent with the views of those who professed themselves advocates "for constituting a college on a basis the most catholic, generous and free."[1]

*   *   *   *

It seems proper to add to the above statement by President Moore, that this Mr. Livingston was a grandson of Robert Livingston, who came to this country from Scotland about the year 1675; the father of Philip, Robert and Gilbert, the first of whom had two distinguished sons: Philip, one of the signers of the Declaration of Independence, and William, the subject of this notice. The latter graduated at Yale College in 1741, and was for some fourteen years governor of New Jersey, which office he held at the close of his life in 1790. He was a delegate from that State to the Convention of 1787, for framing the federal constitution. One of the standard editions of the Colonial Laws of New York (Livingston and Smith's) perpetuates his name in connection with that of Mr. William Smith, from whose History we have already quoted. Chancellor Robert R. Livingston was a son of Robert, and hence second cousin of William.

Mr. Livingston's acknowledged prominence among the opponents of certain views and measures which finally prevailed in the establishment of the College, seem to entitle his controversial writings to a place among the Educational annals of the period under consideration; and for this reason we copy verbatim and entire the articles in the *Independent Reflector* relating to the College. Each article filled, with slight exception, a number of the paper (or rather *tract*), which, though in newspaper form, was not a *news*paper in the ordinary sense of the term. The papers are subscribed "Z.," "A.," "B.," "A. & Z.," and "Academicus"; all which seem to indicate various authors, although the articles themselves are characterized by an apparent unity of style.

[1] Moore's Hist. Sketch, pp. 8–10.

13

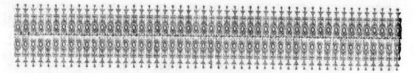

THE
INDEPENDENT REFLECTOR.

NUMBER XVII.

Thursday, March 23, 1753.

Remarks on our intended COLLEGE.

*Nullum non posse majus meliusve Reipublicæ afferre munus,
Quam docendo et erudiendo Juventutem.*　　　　　CICERO.

THE Design of erecting a College in this Province, is a Matter of such grand and general Importance, that I have frequently made it the Topic of my serious Meditation. Nor can I better employ my Time than by devoting a Course of Papers to so interesting a Subject. A Subject of universal Concernment, and in a peculiar Manner involving in it, the Happiness and Well-being of our Posterity!

THE most convenient Situation for fixing the Fabric, tho' obvious on the least Reflection, has been made Matter of laborious Enquiry, as well as afforded a copious Fund for private Conversation. That the College ought to be plac'd in or near this City, appears evident from numberless Arguments, that naturally occur to the most superficial Thinker. But while we have been amusing ourselves with disputations concerning the Situation of the Building we have been strangely indolent about its Constitution and Government, in Comparison of which, the other is a Trifle that scarce deserves Attention. To expatiate on the Advantages of Learning in general, or a liberal Education in particular, would be equally impossible and useless. Impossible from the narrow Limits of my Paper: And useless, because no Arguments that can be urged, are capable of rendering the Assertion more evident, than the irresistible Demonstrations of Experience.

THAT the College ought therefore to be situated near our Metropolis, and that it will be productive, if properly regulated, of unspeakable Benefit to this Province, I shall lay down as two *postulata* not to be questioned.

BEFORE we engage in any Undertaking, common Prudence requires us maturely to consider the End we propose, and the means most conducive to its Attainment.

To imagine that our Legislature, by raising the present Fund for the College, intended barely to have our Children instructed in *Greek* and *Latin*, or the Art of making Exercises and Verses, or disputing in Mood and Figure, were a Supposition absurd and defamatory. For these Branches of Literature, however useful as preparatory to real and substantial Knowledge, are in themselves perfectly idle and insignificant. The true Use of Education, is to qualify Men for the different Employments of Life, to which it may please God to call them. 'Tis to improve their Hearts and Understandings, to infuse a public Spirit and Love of their Country; to inspire them with the Principles of Honour and Probity; with a fervent Zeal for Liberty, and a diffusive Benevolence for Mankind; and in a Word, to make them the more extensively serviceable to the Common-Wealth. Hence the Education of Youth hath been the peculiar Care of all the wise Legislators of Antiquity, who thought it impossible to aggrandize the State, without imbuing the Minds of its Members with Virtue and Knowledge. Nay, so sensible of this fundamental Maxim in Policy, were PLATO, ARISTOTLE, and LYCURGUS, and in short all the ancient Politicians who have delivered their Sentiments on Government, that they make the Education of Youth, the principal and most essential Duty of the Magistrate. And, indeed, whatever literary Acquirement cannot be reduced to Practice, or exerted to the Benefit of Mankind, may perhaps procure its Possessor the Name of a Scholar, but is in Reality no more than a specious Kind of Ignorance. This, therefore, I will venture to lay down for a capital Maxim, that unless the Education we propose, be calculated to render our Youth better Members of Society, and useful to the Public in Proportion to its Expence, we had better be without it. As the natural Consequence of this Proposition, it follows, that the Plan of Education the most conducive to that End is to be chosen, and whatever has a Tendency to obstruct or impede it, ought carefully to be avoided.

THE Nature, End and Design of such Seminaries, is to teach the Students particular Arts and Sciences, for the Conduct of Life, and to render them useful Members of the Community. "*Science* in Pro-"priety of Language signifies, a clear and certain Knowledge of "anything, founded on self-evident Principles or Demonstration: "Tho' in a mere particular and imperfect Sense, it is used for a Sys-"tem of any Branch of Knowledge, comprehending its Doctrine, "Reason and Theory, without an immediate Application thereof to "any Uses or Offices of Life." This twofold Definition of the Word *Science*, I may probably have Occasion to make use of hereafter.

THE vast Influence of any Education upon the Lives and Actions of Men, and thence by a kind of political Expansion, on the whole Community, is verified by constant Experience. Nay, it discriminates Man from Man, more than by Nature he is differenced from the Brutes: And beyond all doubt much greater was the Disparity between the renowned Mr. LOCKE, and a common Hottentot, than between the latter and some of the most sagacious of the irrational Kingdom. But the Influence of a Collegiate Education, must spread a wider Circle proportionate to the Number of the Students, and their greater Progress in Knowledge.

THE Consequences of a liberal Education will soon be visible throughout the whole Province. They will appear on the Bench, at the Bar, in the Pulpit, and in the Senate, and unavoidably affect our civil and religious Principles. Let us adduce, a few Arguments from Reason, Experience and History.

A YOUTHFUL Mind is susceptible of almost any Impression. Like the ductile Wax, it receives the Image of the Seal without the least Resistance. "What is learned at that tender Age, says QUINTILIAN, is "easily imprinted on the Mind, and leaves deep Marks behind it, "which are not easily to be effaced. As in the Case of a new Vessel, "which long preserves a Tincture of the first Liquor poured into it : "And like Wool which can never recover its primitive Whiteness "after it has once been dyed ; and the Misfortune is, that bad Habits "last longer than good Ones." The Poet HORACE, to whom it must have been very natural to draw Similes from Liquor, makes use of the same comparison.

Quo semel est imbuta recens, servabit odorem
Testa diu.—

What season'd first the Vessel, keeps the Taste.   CREECH.

THE Principles or Doctrines implanted in the Minds of Youth, grow up and gather Strength with them. In Time they take deep Root, pass from the Memory and Understanding to the Heart, and at length become a second Nature, which it is almost impossible to change. While the Mind is tender and flexible, it may be moulded and managed at Pleasure : But when once the Impressions are by Practice and Habit, as it were incorporated with the intellectual Substance, they are obliterated with the greatest Difficulty. *Frangas enim citius quam corrigas, quae in pravum induerunt,* said an Author, alike celebrated for his Skill in Rhetoric, and his Knowledge of Mankind.

FROM these Premisses, the natural Inference is, that we cannot be too cautious in forming the human Mind, so capable of good, and so passive to evil Impressions.

THERE is no Place where we receive a greater Variety of Impressions, than at Colleges. Nor do any Instructions sink so deep in the Mind as those that are there received. The Reason is, because they are not barely imprinted by the Preceptor, as at inferior Schools ; but perpetually confirmed and invigorated by the Suscipients themselves. Tho' * Academies are generally Scenes of endless Disputations, they are seldom Places of candid Inquiry. The Students not only receive the Dogmata of their Teachers with an implicit Faith, but are also constantly studying how to support them against every Objection. The System of the College is generally taken for true, and the sole Business is to defend it. Freedom of Thought rarely penetrates those contracted mansions of systematical Learning. But to teach the establish'd notions, and maintain certain Hypotheses, *hic Labor hoc opus est.* Every Deviation from the beaten Tract is a kind of literary Heresy ; and if the Professor be given to Excommunication, can scarce escape an Anathema. Hence that dogmatical Turn and Impa-

---

* Note, *That for the greater variety of Language, I shall use the Words* Academy, College, *and* University, *as synonimous Terms; tho', in strict Propriety, they are far from being equipollent Expressions.*

tience of Contradiction, so observable in the Generality of Academies. To this is also to be referred, those voluminous Compositions, and that learned Lumber of gloomy Pedants, which has so long infested and corrupted the World. In a Word, all those visionary Whims, idle Speculations, fairy Dreams, and party Distinctions, which contract and imbitter the Mind, and have so often turn'd the World topsy-turvy.

I MENTION not this to disparage an academical Education, from which I hope I have myself received some Benefit, especially after having worn off some of its rough corners, by a freer Conversation with Mankind. The Purpose for which I urge it, is to shew the narrow Turn usually prevailing at Colleges, and the absolute Necessity of teaching Nothing that will afterwards require the melancholy Retrogradation of being unlearned.

·FROM this Susceptibility of tender Minds, and the extreme Difficulty of erasing original Impressions, it is easy to conceive, that whatever Principles are imbibed at a College, will run thro' a Man's whole future Conduct, and affect the Society of which he is a Member, in Proportion to his Sphere of Activity; especially if it be considered, that even after we arrive to Years of Maturity, instead of entering upon the difficult and disagreeable Work of examining the Principles we have formerly entertained, we rather exert ourselves in searching for Arguments to maintain and support them.

THO' I have sufficiently shewn the prodigious Influence of a College upon the Community, from the Nature and Reason of the Thing, it may not be improper, for its farther Corroboration, to draw some Proofs from Experience and History.

AT *Harvard* College in the *Massachusetts-Bay*, and at *Yale* College in *Connecticut*, the Presbyterian Profession is in some sort established. It is in these Colonies the commendable Practice of all who can afford it, to give their Sons an Education at their respective Seminaries of Learning. While they are in the Course of their Education, they are sure to be instructed in the Arts of maintaining the Religion of the College, which is always that of their immediate Instructors; and of combating the Principles of all other Christians whatever. When the young Gentlemen, have run thro' the Course of their Education, they enter into the Ministry, or some Offices of the Government, and acting in them under the Influence of the Doctrines espoused in the Morning of Life, the Spirit of the College is transfused thro' the Colony, and tinctures the Genius and Policy of the public Administration, from the Governor down to the Constable. Hence the Episcopalians cannot acquire an equal Strength among them, till some new Regulations, in Matters of Religion, prevail in their Colleges, which perpetually produce Adversaries to the hierarchical System. Nor is it to be question'd, that the Universities in *North* and *South-Britain*, greatly support the different Professions that are establish'd in their respective Divisions.

SENSIBLE of the vast Influence which the Positions and Principles of Colleges have upon the public, was that politic Prince King HENRY the Eighth. No sooner had he determined to repudiate his Queen, thro' his Love for ANNE BOLEYN, than, the better to justify his Divorce, or rather to guard himself against the popular Resentment, by the Advice of CRANMER, the State of his Case was laid before all the Universities, who, agreeable to his Wishes, determined his marriage with CATHERINE, to be repugnant to the divine Law, and therefore invalid.

IN the Reign of King JAMES II. of arbitrary and papistical Memory, a Project jesuitically artful, was concerted to poison the Nation, by filling the Universities with popish and popishly-affected Tutors; and but for our glorious Deliverance, by the immortal WILLIAM, the Scheme had been sufficient, in Process of Time, to have introduc'd and establish'd, the sanguinary and antichristian church of *Rome*.

SINCE then, the extensive Influence of a College so manifestly appears, it is of the last Importance, that ours be so constituted, that the Fountain being pure, the Streams (to use the Language of Scripture) may make glad the City of our GOD.

Z.

I HOPE my Correspondents will not be displeased, at seeing the Publication of their Letters thus long deferred, after assuring them, that tho' they have, contrary to my Inclination, been unavoidably postponed, they will by no means be forgotten; but receive due Honour, as soon as possible, after I have finished my Remarks on the College; which, for its great Importance, will probably engross four or five of my succeeding Numbers.

New-York: *Printed by J. Parker, at the New Printing-Office in* Beaver-Street, *by whom Letters to the Author are carefully delivered.*

NUMBER XVIII.

THURSDAY, MARCH 29, 1753.

A Continuation of the same Subject.

Tros Rutulusve fuat, nullo discrimine habebo.   VIRG.

I HAVE in my last Paper shewn, from Reason, Experience and History, the vast Influence of a College, upon the civil and religious Principles of the Community in which it is erected and supported. I shall now proceed to offer a few Arguments, which I submit to the Consideration of my Countrymen, to evince the Necessity and Importance of constituting *our* College upon a Basis the most catholic, generous and free.

IT is in the first Place observable, that unless its Constitution and Government, be such as will admit Persons of all protestant Denominations, upon a perfect Parity as to Privileges, it will itself be greatly prejudiced, and prove a Nursery of Animosity, Dissention and Disorder. The sincere Men of all Sects, imagine their own Profession, on the whole, more eligible and scriptural than any other. It is therefore very natural to suppose, they will exert themselves to weaken and diminish all other Divisions, the better to strengthen and inlarge their own. To this Cause must in a great Measure be ascribed, that Heat and Opposition, which animate the Breasts of many Men of religious Distinctions, whose intemperate and misapplied Zeal, is the only Blemish that can be thrown upon their characters. Should our College, therefore, unhappily thro' our own bad Policy, fall into the Hands of any one religious Sect in the Province: Should that Sect, which is more than probable, establish its religion in the College, shew favour to its votaries, and cast Contempt upon others; 'tis easy to foresee, that Christians of all other Denominations amongst us, instead of encouraging its Prosperity, will, from the same Principles, rather conspire to oppose and oppress it. Besides *English* and *Dutch* Presbyterians, which perhaps exceed all our other religious Professions put together, we have Episcopalians, Anabaptists, Lutherans, Quakers, and a growing church of Moravians, all equally zealous for their discriminating Tenets: Whichsoever of these has the sole Government of the college, will kindle the Jealousy of the Rest, not only against the Persuasion so preferred, but the College itself. Nor can any Thing less be expected, than a general Discontent and Tumult; which, affecting all Ranks of People, will naturally tend to Disturb the Tranquility and Peace of the Province.

In such a State of Things, we must not expect the Children of any, but of that Sect which prevails in the Academy will ever be sent to it: For should they, the established Tenets must either be implicitly received, or a perpetual religious War necessarily maintained. Instead of the liberal Arts and Sciences, and such Attainments as would best qualify the Students to be useful and ornamental to their Country, Party Cavils and Disputes about Trifles, will afford Topics of Argumentation to their incredible Disadvantage, by a fruitless Consumption of Time. Such Gentlemen, therefore, who can afford it, will give their Sons an Education abroad, or at some of the neighboring Academies, where equally imbibing a Zeal for their own Principles, and furnished with the Arts of defending them, an incessant Opposition to all others, on their Return, will be the unavoidable Consequence. Not to mention, that Youth may become strongly attached to the Places at which they are educated. At this season of Life they receive the deepest Impressions: And, for the Sake of a Wife or a Friend, and a thousand other Reasons that cannot now be enumerated, a Gentleman may turn his Back upon the Place of his Birth, and take up his Residence where the Morning of Life has been agreeably passed. Hence, besides the Expence of such Education prejudicial to us, we may frequently lose the Hopes of our Country, lose perhaps a Man every Way qualified to defend its Interests, and advance its Glory.

Others, and many such there may be, who not able to support the Expence of an Education abroad, but could easily afford it at Home, thro' a Spirit of Opposition to the predominant Party, will rather determine to give their Children no Education at all. From all which it follows, that a College under the sole Influence of a Party, for want of suitable Encouragement, being but indifferently stocked with Pupils, will scarce arrive to the Usefulness of a *Schola illustris*, which being inferior to a College is, I hope, much short of what is intended by Ours.

ANOTHER Argument against so pernicious a Scheme is, that it will be dangerous to Society. The extensive Influence of such a Seminary, I have already shewn in my last Paper. And have we not reason to fear the worst Effects of it, where none but the Principles of one Persuasion are taught, and all others depressed and discountenanced? Where, instead of Reason and Argument, of which the Minds of the Youths are not capable, they are early imbued with the Doctrines of a Party, inforced by the Authority of a Professor's Chair, and the combining Aids of the President, and all the other Officers of the College? That religious Worship should be constantly maintained there, I am so far from opposing, that I strongly recommend it, and do not believe any such Kind of Society, can be kept under a regular and due Discipline without it. But instructing the Youth in any particular Systems of Divinity, or recommending and establishing any single Method of Worship or Church Government, I am convinced would be both useless and hurtful. Useless, because not one in a Hundred of the Pupils is capable of making a just Examination, and reasonable Choice. Hurtful, because receiving Impressions blindly on Authority, will corrupt their Understandings, and fetter them with Prejudices which may everlastingly prevent a judicious Freedom of Thought, and infect them all their Lives, with a contracted turn of mind.

A PARTY-COLLEGE, in less than half a Century, will put a new Face upon the Religion, and in consequence thereof affect the Politics of the Country. Let us suppose what may, if the College should be entirely managed by one Sect, probably be supposed. Would not all possible Care be bestowed in tincturing the Minds of the Students with the Doctrines and Sentiments of that Sect? Would not the Students of the College, after the course of their Education, exclusive of any others, fill all the Offices of the Government? Is it not highly reasonable to think, that in the Execution of those Offices, the Spirit of the College would have a most prevailing Influence, especially as that Party would perpetually receive new Strength, become more fashionable and numerous? Can it be imagined that all other Christians would continue peaceable under, and unenvious of, the Power of that Church which was rising to so exalted a Preheminence above them? Would they not on the Contrary, like all other Parties, reflect upon, reluct at, and vilify such an odious Ascendancy? Would not the Church which had that Ascendancy be thereby irritated to repeated Acts of Domination, and stretch their ecclesiastical Rule to unwarantable and unreasonable lengths? Whatever others may in their Lethargy and Supineness think of the Project of a Party-College, I am convinced, that under the Management of any particular Persuasion, it will necessarily prove destructive to the civil and religious Rights of the People: And should any future House of Representatives become generally infected with the Maxims of the College, nothing less can be expected than an Establishment of one Denomination above all others, who may, perhaps, at the good Pleasure of their Superiors, be most graciously favoured with a bare Liberty of Conscience, while they faithfully continue their annual Contributions, their Tythes and their Peter-Pence.

A Third Argument against suffering the College to fall into the Hands of a Party, may be deduced from the Design of its Erection, and Support by the Public.

The Legislature to whom it ows its Origin, and under whose Care the Affair has hitherto been conducted, could never have intended it as an Engine to be exercised for the Purposes of a Party. Such an Insinuation, would be false and scandalous. It would therefore be the Height of Insolence in any to pervert it to such mean, partial and little Designs. No, it was set on Foot, and I hope it will be constituted for general Use, for the public Benefit, for the Education of all who can afford such Education: And to suppose it intended for any other less public-spirited Uses, is ungratefully to reflect upon all who have hitherto, had any Agency in an Undertaking so glorious to the Province, so necessary, so important and beneficial.

At present, it is only in Embrio, yet the Money hitherto collected is public Money; and till it is able to support itself, the Aids given to it will be public Aids When the Community is taxed, it ought to be for the Defence, or Emolument of the Whole: Can it, therefore, be supposed, that all shall contribute for the Uses, the ignominious Uses of a few? Nay, what is worse to that which will be prejudicial to a vast Majority? Shall the whole Province be made to support what will raise and spread desperate Feuds, Discontent and ill-Blood thro' the greatest Part of the Province? Shall the Government of the College be delivered out of the Hands of the Public to a Party! They who wish it, are Enemies to their Country: They who ask it, have, besides this *Anti-Patriotism*, a Degree of Impudence, Arrogance, and Assurance unparallel'd. And all such as are active in so iniquitous a Scheme, deserve to be stigmatized with Marks of everlasting Ignominy and Disgrace. Let it, therefore, ever remain where it is, I mean under the Power of the Legislature: The Influence, whether good or bad, we shall all of us feel, and are, therefore, all interested in it. It is, for that Reason, highly fit, that the People should always share in the Power to inlarge or restrain it. That Power they will have by their Representatives in Assembly; and no man who is a Friend to Liberty, his country and Religion, will ever rejoice to see it wrested from them.

It is farther to be remarked, that a public Academy is, or ought to be a mere civil Institution, and cannot with any tolerable Propriety be monopolized by any religious Sect. The Design of such Seminaries, hath been sufficiently shown in my last Paper, to be entirely political, and calculated for the Benefit of Society, as a Society, without any Intention to teach Religion, which is the Province of the Pulpit: Tho' it must, at the same Time, be confessed, that a judicious choice of our Principles, chiefly depends on a free Education.

AGAIN, the Instruction of our Youth, is not the only Advantage we ought to propose by our College. If it be properly regulated and conducted, we may expect a considerable Number of Students from the neighbouring Colonies, which must, necessarily, prove a great Accessation to our Wealth and Emolument. For such is our Capacity of endowing an Academy; that if it be founded on the Plan of a general Toleration, it must, naturally, eclipse any other on the Continent, and draw many Pupils from those Provinces, the Constitution of whose Colleges, is partial and contracted: From *New-England* where the *Presbyterians* are the prevailing Party, we shall, undoubtedly, be furnished with great Numbers, who, averse to the Sect in vogue among them, will, unquestionably, prefer the free Constitution, for which I argue, to that of their Colleges in which they cannot enjoy an equal Latitude, not to mention that such an Increase by foreign Students, will vastly augment the Grandeur of our Academy.

ADD to all this, that in a new Country as ours, it is inconsistent with good Policy, to give any religious Profession the Ascendency over others. The rising Prosperity of *Pennsylvania*, is the Admiration of the continent; and tho' disagreeing from them, I should always, for political Reasons, exclude *Papists* from the common and equal Benefits of Society: Yet I leave it to the Reflections of my judicious Readers, whether the impartial Aspect of their Laws upon all Professions, has not, in a great Degree, conduced to their vast Importation of religious Refugees, to their Strength and their Riches: And whether a like Liberty among us, to all Protestants whatsoever, without any Marks of Distinction, would not be more commendable, advantageous and politic.

A.

*   *   *   *

The Letter from Portius, containing a Scheme for endowing the College, is also come to Hand, and shall not fail of being duly honour'd.

NUMBER XIX.

THURSDAY, APRIL 5, 1753.

The same Subject continued.

—— *Timeo Danaos dona ferentes.*   VIRG.

AS nothing would be more fruitless than to excite the Apprehensions, or raise the Hopes of my Readers, by a Prospect of remediless Evils, or unattainable Blessings, I consider my former Papers upon this Subject, only as a Prelude to what is yet to come. It would be of little Use to have shewn the fatal consequences of an Academy founded in Bigotry, and reared by Party-Spirit; or the glorious

Advantages of a College, whose Basis is Liberty, and where the Muses flourish with entire Freedom; without investigating the Means by which the one may be crushed in Embrio, and the other raised and supported with Ease and Security. In all Societies, as in the human Frame, inbred Disorders are chiefly incurable, as being Part of the Constitution, and inseparable from it, while, on the contrary, when the Rage of Infirmities is resisted by a sound Complexion of Body, they are less inherent, and consequently more medicable. For this Reason, it must necessarily be esteemed of the utmost Importance, that the Plan upon which we intend to form our Nursery of Learning, be concerted with the most prudent Deliberation; it being that alone upon which its future Grandeur must evidently depend.

To delineate a compleat Scheme for so great a Work, is beyond the Stretch of my Abilities: And to imagine that these Imperfect Attempts, will be of any other Use than as a Spur to greater Inventions, is a Piece of Vanity with which the *Reflector* scorns to be thought chargeable. But should they prove useful to his Country, either by inspiring others to communicate something more perfect, or inciting our Legislature to a serious consideration of this Subject, I shall think the general Design of these Papers sufficiently answered.

In pointing out a Plan for the College, I shall first shew what it ought not to be, in order that what it should be, may appear with greater Certainty.

As Corporations and Companies are generally founded on Royal Grants, it is without Doubt supposed by many, that our College must be constituted by Charter from his Majesty, to certain Persons, as Trustees, to whose Government and Direction it will be submitted. Nor does the Impropriety of such a Plan strike the unattentive Vulgar, tho' to a considerate Mind it appears big with mighty Evils.

> *Nec quæ circumstant te deinde pericula cernis*
> *Demens*   Virg.

It is necessary to the well-being of every Society, that it be not only established upon an ample and free Bottom; but also secured from Invasion, and its Constitution guarded against Abuses and Perversion. These are Points of which I beg Leave to think my Readers fully convinced. Nor can they wonder at the Novelty of my Scheme, when an University, hatched by the Heat of Sectaries, and cherished in the contracted Bosom of furious Zeal, shall be shewn to be the natural consequence of a Charter Government.

But to consider an Academy founded on a Royal Grant in the most favourable Light, Prudence will conpel our Disapprobation of so precarious a Plan. The Mutability of its Nature will incline every reasonable Man, to prefer to it that Kind of Government, which is both productive of the richest Blessings, and renders its Advantages the more precious, by their superiour Stability. A Charter can at best present us with a Prospect of what we are scarce sure of enjoying a Day. For every Charter of Incorporation, as it generally includes a Number of Privileges subject to certain express or implied Conditions, may, in particular, be annulled, either on a Prosecution in the

Court of *Kings-Bench* by *Quo warranto* or by *Scire Facias* in Chancery, or by *Surrender.* Nor does it require a great Abuse of Privilege to determine its Fate by the two first Means, while mere Caprice, or some thing worse, may at any Time work its Dissolution by the latter. I believe my Countrymen, have too high a Sense of the Advantages of Learning, to risk the College upon so unsettled a Basis; and would blast a Project so ineffective of its true End, to make Room for a Scheme by which the Object of Public Attention may be fixed on a Bottom more firm and durable. How would it damp the sanguine Prospects, of the fervent Patriot; disappoint the honest Well-wisher of his Country; and blacken the Hopes of every Lover of the Muses into Dispair, should an inconsiderable Mistep subvert so noble a design! Yet, to these fatal Evils would a Charter be exposed: Should the Trustees exceed their Authority, however inconsiderably it might affect the Interest of the College, their acting contrary to the express Letter, would *ipso facto* avoid it. Or should they, either thro' Ignorance, Inattention or Surprize, extend their Power in the least beyond those Limits, which the Law would prescribe upon a Construction of the Charter, a Repeal might be obtained by Suit at Common Law, or in Equity. And perhaps such might be the Circumstances of Things, as to render a new Incorporation at that Juncture, utterly impracticable. Besides, upon its Dissolution all the Lands given to it, are absolutely lost. The Law annexes such a Condition to every Grant to a Body politic: They revert to the Donor. Nor is there much Reason to expect a charitable Reconveyance from the Reversioner.

BUT if this may possibly be the Case, should even the Scheme of the Instruction of our Youth continue unperverted by the Directors of our Academy, what Abuses of Trust might they commit, what Attacks upon the Liberty and Happiness of this Province might they make, without Correction or Controul, should they be influenced by sinister Views? While the Fountain continues pure and unpolluted, the Stream of Justice may flow through its Channels clear and undisturbed. But should arbitary Power hereafter prevail, and the tyrannical Arts of JAMES return to distress the Nation, the Oppression and Avarice of a future Governor, may countenance the iniquitous Practices of the Trustees, or destroy the Charter by improving the Opportunity of some little Error in their conduct; and having seized the Franchise, dispose of it by a new Grant to the fittest Instruments of unjust and imperious Rule, and then adieu to all Remedy against them: For were they prosecuted by his Magesty's Attorney General in the *King's-Bench* a *Noli prosequi* would effectually secure them from Danger; while the Authority of a Governor rendered a Suit in Equity entirely useless. Thus would the Cause of Learning, the Rights and Privileges of the College, our public Liberty and Happiness, become a Prey to the base Designs and united Interest of the Governor and Trustees, in Spite of the most vigorous Efforts of the whole Province: Nor could a happy Intervention to the general Calamity, be expected from the other Branches of the Legislature, while his Majesty's Representative would give a hearty Negative to every salutary Bill, the Council and Assembly should think proper to pass. I say, his Majesty's Representative; for tho' our gracious Sovereign can delegate his executive Authority, he cannot transfer his Royal Virtues; and more than once has this Province beheld a Vicegerent of the Best of Princes, imitate the Actions of the Worst. Reflections of this Kind will pronounce it a Truth most glaringly evident, that whatever Care may be taken in the Construction of a Charter to give our College an extensive Bottom, to endow it with the richest Privileges, and secure them by the most prudent Methods, it may still become the Spoil of Tyranny and Avarice, the Seat of slavish, bigotted and persecuting Doctrines, the Scourge and Inquisition of the Land. And far better would it be for us to rest contented with the less considerable Blessings we enjoy, without a College, than to aim at greater, by building it upon the sandy Foundation of a Charter-Government.

But after all, it may be urged, that should the College be founded on a Royal Grant, it might still be raised upon as unexceptionable a Basis, and as munificently endowed with Privileges as upon any other Footing. This is not in the least to be doubted. That a specious Charter will be drawn, and exhibited to public View, I sincerely believe: A Trick of that kind will unquestionably be made Use of, to amuse the unattentive Eye, and allure the unwary Mind into an easy Compliance. But it will be only *latet Anguis in Herba*, and when a copious Fund is once obtained, a Surrender of the Charter may make Way for a new One, which tho' sufficiently glaring, to detect the Cheat, will only leave us Room to repent of our Credulity. This is beyond Dispute, a sufficient Reason with some, for establishing the College by Charter, tho', in my humble Opinion, it is one of the strongest Arguments that can be urged against it. We should be careful, lest, by furnishing the Trustees with a Fund, to render themselves independent of us, we may be reduced to the Necessity of being dependent upon them. If the Public must furnish the Sums by which the College is to be supported, Prudence declares it necessary, that they should be certain to what Uses the Monies will be applied; lest instead of being burdened with Taxes to advance our Interest, we should absurdly impoverish ourselves, only to precipitate our Ruin. In short, as long as a Charter may be surrendered, we are in Danger of a new One, which perhaps will not be much to our liking: And, as this Kind of Government will be always subject to Innovations, it will be an incontestible Proof of our Wisdom to reject it for a better.

It has in my last two Papers been shewn, what an extensive and commding Influence the Seat of Learning will have over the whole Province, by diffusing its Dogmata and Principles thro' every Office of Church and State. What Use will be made of such unlimited Advantages, may be easily guessed. The civil and religious Principles of the Trustees, will become universally established, Liberty and Happiness be driven without our Borders, and in their Room erected the Banners of spiritual and temporal Bondage. My Readers may, perhaps, regard such Reflections as the mere Sallies of a roving

Fancy; tho', at the same Time, nothing in Nature can be more real. For should the Trustees be prompted by Ambition, to stretch their Authority to unreasonable Lengths, as undoubtedly they would, were they under no Kind of Restraint, the Consequence is very evident. Their principal care would be to chuse such Persons to instruct our Youth, as would be the fittest Instruments to extend their Power by positive and dogmatical Precepts. Besides which, it would be their mutual Interest to pursue one Scheme. Their Power would become formidable by being united: As on the contrary, a Dissention would impede its Progress. Blind Obedience and Servility in Church and State, are the only natural Means to establish unlimited Sway. Doctrines of this Cast would be publicly taught and inculcated. Our Youth, inured to Oppression from their Infancy, would afterwards vigorously exert themselves in their several Offices, to poison the whole Community with slavish Opinions, and one universal Establishment become the fatal Portion of this now happy and opulent Province. Thus far the Trustees will be at Liberty to extend their Influence without controul, as long as their Charter subsists: And thus far they would undoubtedly extend it. For whoever, after being conscious of the uncertain Nature and dismal Consequences of a Charter College, still desires to see it thus established, and willingly becomes a Trustee, betrays a strong Passion for Tyranny and Oppression: Did he wish the Welfare of his Country, he would abhor a Scheme that may probably prove so detrimental to it; especially when a better may be concerted. It would therefore be highly imprudent to trust any Set of Men with the care of the Academy, who were willing to accept it under a Charter.

If it be urged, that the Reasons above advanced, to prove the Danger and Mutability of a charter Government, militate strongly against the Consequences I have deduced from them, let it be considered, that it will be in the Power of one Person only, to encourage or oppose the Trustees in the Abuse of their Authority. This Point, I think, is sufficiently evinced. Time may, perhaps, furnish the Trustees with an Opportunity of corrupting him with Largesses; or the change of Affairs, make it his Duty to encourage the most slavish Doctrines and Impositions. Where then will be our Remedy, or how shall we obtain the Repeal of a Charter abused and perverted? Be it ever so uncertain in its Nature, it will still be in the Power of a Governor, to secure it against the Attacks of Law and Justice: Or, to render us more compleatly miserable, he may grant a new One, better guarded against any Danger from that Quarter. In the present Situation of Things, we have, indeed, no Reason to fear it. But as they may possibly assume a different Face hereafter, let us at least be armed in a Matter of so great Consequence, against the Incertainty of future Events.

But after all it cannot be expected, that a Charter should at once be so compleatly formed, as to answer all the valuable Purposes intended by it. Inventions are never brought to sudden Perfection; but receive their principal Advantages from Time and Experience, by a slow Progression. The human Mind is too contracted to comprehend in one View, all the Emergencies of Futurity ; or provide for and guard against, distant Contingencies. To whomsoever, therefore, the Draft of a Charter shall be committed Experience will prove it defective, and the Vicissitude of Things make continual Alterations necessary. Nor can they be made without a prodigious Expence to the Public, since, as often as they are expedient, a new Charter will be the only Means to effect it.

I Hope my Readers are by this Time convinced, that a Charter College will prove inefficacious to answer the true End of the Encouragement of Learning ; and that general Utility can never be expected from a Scheme so precarious and liable to abuse. I shall in my next Paper exhibit another Plan for the Erection of our College, which if improved, will answer all the valuable Ends that can be expected from a Charter, and at much less Expence : While it will also effectually secure all those Rights and Privileges which are necessary to render the Increase of true Literature more vigorous and uninterrupted.

B.

Number XX.

THURSDAY, APRIL 12, 1753.

A farther Prosecution of the same Subject.

Si vincimus omnia nobis tuta erunt, Commeatus abunde municipia atque Coloniæ patebunt ; sin metu cesserimus, eadem illa adversa fient.   Sal.

I HAVE in my last Paper endeavoured to explode the Scheme of erecting our College by Charter, as a Means wholly inadequate to the End proposed. Many of my Readers are doubtless convinced, how justly it lies open to the Objections I have raised against it ; and therefore expect, that something more effectual be proposed in its Stead : While others that remain unsatisfied, may, perhaps, find their Doubts removed, by perusing the Plan I shall lay before them.

But I would first establish it as a Truth, that Societies have an indisputable Right to direct the Education of their youthful Members. If we trace the Wisdom of Providence in the Harmony of the Creation ; the mutual Dependence of human Nature, renders it demonstrably certain, that Man was not designed solely for his own Happiness, but also to promote the Felicity of his Fellow-Creatures. To this Bond of Nature, civil Government has joined an additional Obligation. Every Person born within the Verge of Society, immediately becomes a Subject of that Community in which he first breathes the vital Element ; and is so far a Part of the political Whole, that the Rules of Justice inhibit those Actions which, tho' tending to his own Advantage, are injurious to the Public Weal. If therefore, it belongs to any to inspect the Education of Youth, it is the proper Business of the Public, with whose Happiness their future Conduct in Life is inseparably connected, and by whose Laws their relative Actions will be governed.

SENSIBLE of this was the *Spartan* Law-giver, who claimed the Education of the *Lacedemonian* Youth, as the unalienable Right of the Commonwealth. It was dangerous in his Opinion, to suffer the incautious Minds of those who were born Members of Society, to imbibe any Principles but those of universal Benevolence, and an unextinguishable Love for the Community of which they were Subjects. For this Reason, Children were withdrawn from the Authority of their Parents, who might otherwise warp their immature Judgments in Favour of Prejudices and Errors obtruded on thim by Dint of Authority: ut if this was considered as a prudent Step to guard the Liberty and Happiness of that Republic; methinks it will not be unadvisable, for our Legislature, who have it in their Power, to secure us against the Designs of any Sect or Party of Men, that may aim at the sole Government of the College. If there the youthful Soul is to be ingrafted with blind Precepts, contracted Opinions, inexplicable Mysteries, and incurable Prejudices, let it be constituted by Charter: But if from thence we expect to fill our public Posts with Persons of Wisdom and Understanding, worthy of their Offices, and capable of accomplishing the Ends of their Institution, let it not be made the Portion of a Party, or private Set of Men, but let it merit the Protection of the Public. The only true Design of its Erection, is to capacitate the Inhabitants of this Province, for advancing their private and public Happiness; of which the Legislature are the lawful Guardians: To them, therefore, does the Care of our future Seminary of Learning properly and only belong.

INSTEAD of a Charter, I would propose, that the College be founded and incorporated by Act of Assembly, and that not only because it ought to be under the Inspection of the civil Authority; but also, because such a Constitution will be more permanent, better endowed, less liable to Abuse, and more capable of answering its true End.

IT is unreasonable to suppose, that an University raised by private Contribution in this Province, should arrive at any considerable Degree of Grandeur or Utility: The Expence attending the first Erection, and continual Support of so great a Work, requires the united Aid of the Public. Should it once be made an Affair of universal Concern, they will, no Doubt, generously contribute by Taxes, and every other Means towards its Endowment, and furnish it by a provincial Charge, with whatever shall be necessary to render it of general Advantage. But altho' our Assembly have already raised a considerable Fund for that Purpose, who can imagine they will ever part with or dispose of it to any other Uses, than such as they shall think proper and direct. If the College be erected at the Charge of the Province, it ought doubtless to be incorporated by Act of Assembly; by which Means the whole Legislature will have, as they ought to have, the Disposition of the Fund raised for this Purpose: The Community will then have it in their Power to call those to an Account into whose Hands the public Monies shall be deposited for that particular Use: And thus the Sums though necessary for the Improvement of Learning, will be honestly expended in the Service for which they are designed; or should they be embezzled, it might easily be detected, and publicly punished : Besides, no particular Set of Men can claim a Right to dispose of the provincial Taxes, but those impowered by the Community ; and therefore, if the Colony must bear the Expence of the College, surely the Legislature will claim the Superintendency of it. But if after all, it should be thought proper to incorporate it by Charter, it is to be hoped, they will reserve the public Money for some other Use, rather than bestow it on a College, the Conduct of whose Trustees would be wholly out of the Reach of their Power.

A FURTHER Argument in Favour of being incorporated by Act of Assembly, may be deduced from the End of its Institution. It is designed to derive continual Blessings to the Community ; to improve those public Virtues that never fail to make a People great and happy ; to cherish a noble Ardour for Liberty ; to stand a perpetual Barrier against Tyranny and Oppression. The Advantages flowing rom the Rise and Improvement of Literature, are not to be confined to a Set of Men: They are to extend their chearful Influence thro' Society in general, — thro' the whole Province ; and therefore, ought to be the peculiar Care of the united Body of the Legislature. The Assembly have been hitherto wisely jealous of the Liberties of their Constituents: Nor can they, methinks, ever be persuaded, to cede their Authority in a Matter so manifestly important to our universal Welfare, or submit the Guidance of our Academy to the Hands of a few. On the contrary, we are all so greatly interested in its Success, as to render it an Object worthy of their most diligent Attention,— worthy of their immediate Patronage. Should a Number of private Persons have the Impudence to demand of our Legislature, the Right of giving Law to the whole Community ; or even should they ask the smaller Privilege, of passing one private Act, would it not be deem'd the Height of Effrontery? In what Light then ought the Conduct of those to be considered, who, in claiming the Government of our University, ask no less considerable a Boon, than absolute universal Dominion.

To a matter of such general, such momentous concern, our Rulers can never too particularly apply their Thoughts, since under their Protection alone Learning must flourish, and the Sciences be improved : It may indeed be urged, that the Nature of their Employment forbids them to spend their Time in the Inspection of Schools, or directing the Education of Youth: But are the Rise of Arts, the Improvement of Husbandry, the Increase of Trade, the Advancement of Knowledge in Law, Physic, Morality, Policy, and the Rules of Justice and civil Government, Subjects beneath the Attention of our Legislature? In these are comprehended all our public and private Happiness ; these are consequences of the Education of our Youth, and for the Growth and Perfection of these, is our college designed.

ANOTHER Reason that strongly evinces the Necessity of an Act of Assembly, for the Incorporation of our intended Academy, is, that by this means that Spirit of Freedom, which I have in my former Papers, shewn to be necessary to the Increase of Learning, and its consequential Advantages, may be rendered impregnable to all Attacks. While the Government of the College is in the Hands of the People, or their Guardians, its Design cannot be perverted. As we all value our Liberty and Happiness, we shall all naturally encourage those Means by which our Liberty and Happiness will necessarily be improved: And as we never can be supposed wilfully to barter our Freedom and Felicity, for Slavery and Misery, we shall certainly crush the Growth of those Principles, upon which the latter are built, by cultivating and encouraging their Opposites. Our College therefore, if it be incorporated by Act of Assembly, instead of opening a Door to universal Bigotry and Establishment in Church, and Tyranny and Oppression in the State, will secure us in the Enjoyment of our respective Privileges both civil and religious. For as we are split into so great a variety of Opinions and Professions; had each Individual his Share in the Government of the Academy, the Jealousy of all Parties combating each other, would inevitably produce a perfect Freedom for each particular Party.

SHOULD the College be founded upon an Act of Assembly, the Legislature would have it in their Power, to inspect the Conduct of its Governors, to divest those of Authority who abused it, and appoint in their Stead, Friends to the Cause of Learning, and the general Welfare of the Province. Against this, no Bribes, no Solicitations would be effectual: No Sect or Denomination plead an Exemption: But as Parties are subject to their Authority; so would they all feel its equal Influence in this Particular. Hence should the Trustees pursue any Steps but those that lead to public Emolument, their Fate would be certain, their Doom inevitable: Every Officer in the college being under the narrow Aspect and Scrutiny of the civil Authority, would be continually subject to the wholesome Alternative, either of performing his Duty, with the utmost Exactness, or giving up his Post to a Person of superior Integrity. By this Means, the Prevalence of Doctrines destructive of the Privileges of human Nature, would effectually be discouraged, Principles of public Virtue inculcated, and every Thing promoted that bears the Stamp of general Utility.

BUT what remarkably sets an Act of Assembly in a Light far superior to a Charter, is, that we may thereby effectually counterplot every Scheme that can possibly be concerted, for the Advancement of any particular Sect above the rest. A Charter may, as I have shewn in my last Paper, be so unexceptionably formed, as to incur the Disapprobation of no Denomination whatever, but unexceptionable as it may be we cannot be sure of its Duration. A Second may succeed, which, perhaps, would be disapproved of by all but one Party. On the contrary, we are certain that an Act of Assembly must be unexceptionable to all; since Nothing can be inserted in it, but what any one may except against; and, as we are represented in the Assembly by Gentlemen of various Persuasions, there is the highest Probability, that every Clause tending to abridge the Liberty of any particular Sect, would by some or other of our Representatives be strongly opposed. And this will still be the Case, however repeatedly Innovations may be attempted by subsequents Acts.

ANOTHER Advantage accruing to the College itself, and consequently to the Community in general, is that larger Donations may be expected, should it be incorporated by Act of Assembly, than by Charter. Every generous Contributor, would undoubtedly be willing to have some Security for the Disposition of his Gratuity, consistent with the Design of his Donative. Nor is it improbable, that the most bounteous Person would refuse to bestow a Largess, without being convinced of the Honesty and Propriety of its Application. Under a Charter no Security to this Purpose can possibly be expected. This is sufficiently evinced by my last Paper. Besides which, if a Charter be obtained, it will without Doubt, be immediately or eventually in favour of one particular Party;. the Consequence of which will be plainly this, that the other Sects amongst us, being a vast Majority, instead of contributing to the Support of our Academy by private Donations, will endeavour to discourage each other from it. But should our University be established by Act of Assembly, as every Individual would bear a Part in its Government, so should we all be more strongly induced, by private Gifts, to increase its Endowments.

ADD to all this, that should the Persons intrusted with the immediate Care of our Nursery of Learning, commit any Error in their Conduct, the Act of Assembly would not be void, but in as full Force as if the Error had not been committed. And should they designedly transgress the Bounds of their Authority, the Act might be so constructed, as to disqualify them for holding their Offices, and subject them to the severest Penalties; to be recovered by his Majesty, or the Party aggrieved, or by both. It is also to be remarked, that should the Act of Incorporation be at any Time infringed, and the Liberty of the Students invaded, their Redress would be more easily obtained in a Court of Law.

To this Scheme it may be objected, that the Creating a Body-Politic by Act of Legislation, without a previous Charter, is unprecedented, and an Infringement of the Prerogative of the Crown, and may possibly for those Reasons be damned by the King, who cannot repeal a Charter; and farther, that every End that can be proposed by Act only, may be obtained by a Charter-Incorporation; and an Act posterior, confirming it, and enlarging and regulating the Powers of the Body. In Answer to which, let it be considered, that it is not only the King's Prerogative, to grant a Charter, but also to grant it upon certain Terms; a Non-Compliance with which, will cause its repeal; and from thence arises the Precariousness of a Charter. Should an Act be passed in Consequence of a Charter, it must be either to prevent its Precariousness, or to add new Privileges to those granted by it. If the former should be the Reason for passing an Act, it would militate against the Royal Prerogative, as well as an Act to incorporate the College; and therefore would, in all Probability, meet with the same Fate, and by that Means the Charter would stand alone. If the Act should be only in Aid of the Charter, it would still leave it in as uncertain a State, as without an Act. So that in either Case the College would be exposed to those Inconveniencies, which, in my last Paper I have shewn to be the natural Consequences of a Charter Government: Besides which, should the College be established by a Charter, the Public will lose most of those Advantages, which I shall in my next Paper propose, as some of the substantial Parts of an Act of Assembly.

MANY other convincing Arguments might be urged with Success, in favour of an Act of Assembly for the Incorporation of our intended College, would the Bounds of this Paper admit their Insertion. Those I have had Room to enforce, are, I am convinced, sufficiently striking, to engage the Assent of every candid and unprejudiced Thinker. To the Wisdom of our Legislature, these Hints will be perfectly useless: Nor do I aim at any Thing more upon so important a Subject, than barely to open the Eyes of some of my less impartial Readers; and testify, how entirely the true Interest of this Province commands the most ardent and sincere Wishes of the *Independent Reflector.*

B.

To the Gentlemen who favoured me with their Sentiments on the Subject of the College, in two Letters signed B C. *and* A Friend, *I return my profoundest Thanks.*

NUMBER XXI.

THURSDAY, APRIL 19, 1753.

Remarks on the COLLEGE *continued.*

—— *Si quid Novisti rectius istis,*
Candidus imperti: si non, his utere mecum.   HOR.

THAT a College may be a Blessing or a Curse to the Community, according to its Constitution and Government, I think appears sufficiently evident from my former Papers. That incorporating it by an Act of Assembly, will be the best Means of securing the first, and avoiding the last, is in my Opinion, equally clear and incontestible. On a Subject of such general Importance; a Subject that concerns our Liberty and our Privileges, civil and religious; a Subject that will affect the Prosperity of our Country, and particularly involves in it, the Happiness and Misery of our Posterity, it would have been unpardonable in a Writer, whose Services are entirely devoted to the Public, to have passed it over in Silence, or handle it with Indifference and Langour. No, it deserves my most deliberate Attention, and fervent Activity; and calls for the Assistance of every Man who loves Liberty and the Province. Fully sensible of its unspeakable Importance, I shall now proceed to point out those Things which in my Judgment, are necessary to be inserted in the incorporating Act, for the Advancement of the true Interest of the College, and rendering it really useful to the Province. Such Things as will effectually prevent its being prejudicial to the Public, and guard us against all the Mischiefs we so justly apprehend, should it ever unhappily fall into the Hands of a Party.

FIRST: That all the Trustees be nominated, appointed, and incorporated by the Act, and that whenever an Avoidance among them shall happen, the same be reported by the Corporation to the next Sessions of Assembly, and such Vacancy supplied by Legislative Act. That they hold their Offices only at the good Pleasure of the Governor, Council and General Assembly : And that no Person of any Protestant Denomination be, on Account of his religious Persuasion, disqualified for sustaining any Office in the College.

IN Consequence of this Article we shall have the highest Security, that none will be dignified with that important and honourable Office, but such as are really qualified for executing it, agreeable to the true Design of its Institution. Should either Branch, or any two Branches of the Legislature, propose and elect a Candidate obnoxious to the Third, the Negative of the latter is sufficient to prevent his Admission. The three Branches concurring in every Election, no Party can be disobliged, and when we consider the Characters of the Electors, all Possibility of Bribery and Corruption, seems to be *intirely excluded*.

SECONDLY: That the President of the College be elected and deprived by a Majority of the Trustees, and all the Inferior Officers by a Majority of the Trustees with the President ; and that the Election and Deprivation of the President, be always reported by the Trustees, to the next Session of Assembly, and be absolutely void, unless the Acts of the Trustees in this Matter, be then confirmed by the Legislature.

BY this Means the President, who will have the supreme Superintendency of the Education of our Youth, will be kept in a continual and ultimate Dependence upon the Public ; and the Wisdom of the Province being his only Support, he will have a much greater Security, in the upright Discharge of his Duty, than if he depended solely on the Trustees, who are likely to oust him of his Office and Livelihood thro' Caprice or Corruption. That Station being therefore more stable, will at the same Time be more valuable ; and for this Reason we have the stronger Hopes of filling the President's Chair with a Man of Worth and Erudition, upon whose good Qualifications and Conduct, the Success and Improvement of the Students, will eminently depend.

THIRDLY: That a Majority of the President and Trustees, have Power to make By-Laws not repugnant to the Act of Incorporation, and the Law of the Land : That all such By-Laws be reported to the House of Representatives at their next succeeding Session, *in hæc Verba*, under the Seal of the College, and the Hands of the President and five Trustees ; and that if they are not reported, or being reported are not confirmed, they shall be absolutely void.

HENCE it is easy to conceive, that as on the one Hand there will be a great Security against the arbitrary and illegal Rule of the President and Trustees ; so on the other, the immediate Governors of the

College will have all proper Authority to make such salutary Rules as shall be necessary to advance the Progress of Literature, and support a Decorum and Police in the Academy,—as well as maintain the Dignity and Weight which the Superiors of it ought undoubtedly to be enabled to preserve over their Pupils.

FOURTHLY: That the Act of Incorporation contain as many Rules and Directions for the Government of the College as can be foreseen to be necessary.

As all our Danger will arise from the Mis-Rule of the President and Trustees; so all our Safety consists in the Guardianship of the Legislature. Besides, the Advantage herefore, of being by this Article secured from arbitrary Domination in the College; the Business of the Trustees and President will be less, and they with their Subordinates, more at Leisure to concert the Advancement of the College.

THE FIFTH Article I propose is, that no religious Profession in particular be established in the College, but that both Officers and Scholars be at perfect Liberty to attend any Protestant Church at their Pleasure respectively: And that the corporation be absolutely inhibited the making of any By-Laws relating to Religion, except such as compel them to attend Divine Service at some Church or other, every Sabbath, as they shall be able, lest so invaluable a Liberty be abused and *made a cloak for Licenciousness.*

To this most important Head, I should think proper to subjoin,

SIXTHLY: That the whole College be every Morning and Evening convened to attend public Prayers, to be performed by the President, or in his Absence, by either of the Fellows; and that such Forms be prescribed and adhered to as all Protestants can freely join in.

BESIDES the fitness and indisputable Duty of supporting the Worship of God in the College; obliging the Students to attend it twice every Day, will have a strong Tendency to preserve a due Decorum, Good Manners and Vertue amongst them, without which the College will sink into Profaness and Disrepute. They will be thereby forced from the Bed of Sloth, and being brought before their Superiors, may be kept from Scenes of Wickedness and Debauchery, which they might otherwise run into, as hereby their Absence from the College will be better detected.

WITH respect to the Prayers, tho' I confess there are excellent Forms composed to our Hands, it would rather conduce to the Interest of our Academy, if, instead of those, new Ones were collected, which might easily be done from a Variety of approved Books of Devotion among all Sects; and perhaps it may be thought better to frame them as near as possible in the Language of Scripture. The general Form need be but few. Occasional Parts may be made to be inserted when necessary; as in cases of Sickness, Death, &c. in the College, or under general Calamities, as War, Pestilence, Drought, Floods, &c. and the like as to Thanksgivings. Many of the Forms of Prayer contained in the English Liturgy, are in themselves unexceptionably good; but as establishing and imposing the Use of those, or of any other Protestant Communion, would be a discriminating Badge, it is liable to Objections, and will occasion a general Dissatisfaction. As the Introduction of them, therefore, will prejudice the College, it is a sufficient Reason against it. It will be a Matter of no small Difficulty to bring the greatest Part of the Province, to the Approbation of praying at any Time by Forms; but since they are in this Case absolutely expedient, our Affection for the Prosperity of this important Undertaking, should incline us, while we give some Offence in one Article, to remove it by a Compensation in another of less Consequence to the College.

SEVENTHLY: That Divinity be no Part of the public Exercises of the College, I mean, that it be not taught as a Science: That the Corporation be inhibited from electing a Divinity Professor; and that the Degrees to be conferred, be only in the Arts, Physic, and the Civil Law.

YOUTH at a College, as I have remarked in a former Paper, are incapable of making a judicious Choice in this Matter; for this Reason the Office of a theological Professor will be useless: Besides, Principles obtruded upon their tender Minds, by the Authority of a Professor's Chair, may be dangerous. But a main Reason in support of this Clause, is the Disgust which will necessarily be given to all Parties that differ in their Professions from that of the Doctor. The Candidate for the Ministry will hereby in his Divinity Studies, whenever he is fit for them, be left to the Choice and Direction of his Parents or Guardians. Besides, as most of the Students will be designed for other Imployments in Life, the Time spent in the Study of Divinity, may be thought useless and unnecessary, and therefore give Umbrage to many. Nor will their whole Course of Time at the College, be more than sufficient for accomplishing themselves in the Arts and Sciences, whether they are designed for the Pulpit, or any other learned Profession. And it may justly be doubted, whether a Youth of good Parts, who has made any particular Proficiency in the Elements, or general Branches of Knowlege (his Instruction in which is the true and proper Business of a collegiate Education) would not be able to qualify himself for the Pulpit, by a Study of the Scriptures, and the best Divinity Books in the College Library, as well without as with the Aid of a Professor; especially if it be enacted,

EIGHTHLY: That the Officers and Collegians have an unrestrained Access to all Books in the Library, and that free Conversation upon polemical and controverted Points in Divinity, be not discountenanced; whilst all public Disputations upon the various Tenets of different Professions of Protestants, be absolutely forbidden.

NINTHLY: That the Trustees, President, and all inferior Officers, not only take and subscribe the Oaths and Declaration appointed by Statute, but be also bound by solemn Oath, in their respective Stations, to fulfil their respective Trusts, and preserve inviolate the Rights of the Scholars, according to the fundamental Rules contained in the Act. And that an Action at Law be given and well secured to every inferior Officer and Student, to be brought by himself, or his *Guardian*, or *prochein Amy*, according to his Age, for every Injury against his legal Right so to be established.

AND in as much as artful Intrigues may hereafter be contrived to the Prejudice of the College, and a Junto be inleagued to destroy its free Constitution, it may perhaps be thought highly expedient, that the Act contain a Clause

TENTHLY: That all future Laws, contrary to the Liberty and Fundamentals of this Act, shall be construed to be absolutely void, unless it refers to the Part thus to be altered, and expressly repeals it; and that no Act relating to the College, shall hereafter pass the House of Representatives, but with the Consent of the Majority of the whole House; I mean all the Members of Assembly in the Province.

NOR would it be amiss to prescribe,

ELEVENTHLY: That as all Contests among the inferior Officers of the College, should be finally determined by the Majority of the Members of the Corporation, so the latter should be determined in all their Disputes, by a Committee of the whole House of Representatives, or the major Part of them.

THESE are the Articles which in my Opinion, should be incorporated in the Act for the Establishment of the College; and without which we have the highest Reason to think, the Advantages it will produce, will at best fall short of the Expence it will create, and perhaps prove a perpetual Spring of public Misery — *A Cage*, as the Scripture speaks, *of every unclean Bird* — The Nursery of Bigotry and Superstition — An Engine of Persecution, Slavery and Oppression — A Fountain whose putrid and infectious Streams will overflow the Land, and poison all our Enjoyments. Far be it from me to imagine I have pointed out every Thing requisite to the Preservation of Liberty, and the Promotion of the Interest of the College; I only suggest such Heads as occur. Beyond all doubt my Scheme is still imperfect. Should our Legislature themselves enter upon this momentous Affair, the Example of a British House of Commons, in Matters of great Importance, might be worthy their Imitation. I mean, that the Bill be printed and published several Months before it passes the House. The Advantage I would propose from this Step is, that while it only exists as a Bill, the Objections against it would be offered with Freedom, because they may be made with Impunity. The general Sense of the People will be the better known, and the Act accommodated to the Judgment and Esteem of all Parties in the Province.

A.

Number XXII.

THURSDAY, APRIL 26, 1753.

The same Subject continued and concluded in,

An Address to the Inhabitants of the Province.

> *If we retain the Glory of our Ancestors,*
> *Whose Ashes will rise up against our Dulness,*
> *Shake off our Tameness, and give Way to Courage;*
> *We need not doubt, inspir'd with a just Rage,*
> *To break the Neck of those, that would yoke ours.*
>
> Tatham's distracted State.

Flectere si nequeo superos, Acheronta movebo. Virg.

My Dear Countrymen,

IN a Series of Papers, I have presented to your View the Inconveniences that must necessarily result from making the Rule of the College, the *Monopoly* of any single Denomination. I have considered it in a Variety of Lights, and explor'd it's numerous Evils. To prevent them in the most effectual Manner, I have concerted a Plan, the Heads of which have been offered to your serious Consideration. Throughout the whole, I have given my Thoughts with the Freedom and Independence suitable to the Dignity of the Subject, and the Character of an impartial Writer. Upon my Representation of the Matter, nor Awe, nor Hope, hath had any Influence. But urg'd by the Love of Liberty, and a disinterested Concern for your, and your Posterity's Happiness, I have disclos'd the Importance,—the prodigious importance of the present Question.

Far be it from me, to terrify you with imaginary Dangers, or to wish the Obstruction of any Measure conducive to the public Good. Did I not foresee,—was I not morally certain of the most ruinous Consequences, from a Mismanagement of the Affair, I should not address you with so much Emotion and Fervor: But when I perceive the impending Evil; when every Man of Knowledge and Impartiality entertains the same Apprehension; I cannot, I will not conceal my Sentiments. In such a Case, no Vehemence is excessive, no Zeal too ardent. The Alarm given is not confined to Particulars. No, the Effects I presage are dreaded far and wide as a general Calamity. Would to God our Terror was merely panic! but it is founded on the unerring Testimony of History, of Reason, and universal Experience.

Nor fancy I aim at warping your Judgment by the Illusion of Oratory, or the Fascination of Eloquence. If in the Sequel, I appear rather to declaim than prove, or seem to prefer the Flowers of Rhetoric to the Strength of Argument, it is because, by the clearest Demonstration, I have already evinc'd the Necessity of frustrating so injurious a Step. My Assertions have not been unsupported by Evidence, nor have I levell'd at your Passions, till I had convinced your Reason. After this, you will pardon a more animated Address, intended to warm the Imagination and excite your Activity.

Of Prejudice and Partiality, I renounce the Charge; having alike argued against all Sects whatever, as I am in reality perfectly neutral and indifferent. For the Sincerity of my Intentions, I lay my Hand upon my Heart, and appeal to the enlighten'd Tribunal of Heaven.

ARISE, therefore, and baffle the Machinations of your and their Country's Foes. Every Man of Vertue, every man of Honour, will join you in defeating so iniquitous a Design. To overthrow it, nothing is wanting but your own Resolution. For great is the Authority, exalted the Dignity, and powerful the Majesty of the People. And shall you the avow'd Enemies of Usurpation and Tyranny,—shall you, the Descendants of *Britain*, born in a Land of Light, and rear'd in the Bosom of Liberty,—shall you commence Cowards at a Time when Reason calls so loud for your Magnanimity? I know you scorn such an injurious Aspersion. I know you disdain the Thoughts of so opprobrious a Servility; and what is more, I am confident the Moment you exert a becoming Fortitude, they will be sham'd out of their Insolence. They will blush at a Crime they cannot accomplish, and desist from Measures they find unsuccessful. Some of you, perhaps, imagine all Opposition unavailable. Banish so groundless a Fear. Truth is Omnipotent, and Reason must be finally victorious. Up and try. Be Men, and make the Experiment. This is your Duty, your bounden, your indispensable Duty. Ages remote, and Mortals yet unborn, will bless your generous Efforts; and revere the friendly Hand that diverted the meditated Ruin, as the Saviour of his Country.

THE Love of LIBERTY is natural to our Species, and an Affection for POSTERITY, interwoven with the human Frame. Inflamed with this *Love*, and animated by this Affection, oppose a Scheme so detrimental to your Privileges so fatal to your Progeny. Perhaps you conceive the Business is done. What! do you take it for granted that so it must be! Do you not think yourselves free? Our Laws, our Assemblies, the Guardianship of our Mother Country, the mildest and the best of KINGS, do they not convince you that hitherto you know not what is Servitude? And will you trifle with an inestimable Jewel? Will you dance on a Precipice, and lay your Hand on a Cockatrice's Den? Unresisting will you yield, and resign without a Struggle? Will you not even venture at a Skirmish, to bequeath to your Posterity the priceless Treasure yourselves enjoy? Doubtless you resent the Insinuation. Courage then my Brethren: Reason is for us, that Reason whose awful Empire is spurn'd by your Adversaries; for such are those whoever they be, that aspire to a Superiority above their fellow Subjects. Whence then should proceed your remissness in a Concern so momentous? Whence so tame a Submission, so ignominious a Compliance? Thou GENIUS OF LIBERTY dispensing unnumber'd Blessings! Thou SPIRIT OF PATRIOTISM ever watchful for the public Good! Do ye inspire us with Unanimity in so interesting a Cause, and we will assert our Rights against the most powerful Invasion!

YOU, Gentlemen of the CHURCH OF ENGLAND, cannot but condemn the unaccountable Assurance of whatever Persuasion, presumes to rob you of an *equal* Share in the Government of what *equally* belongs to all. With what Indignation and Scorn, must you, the most numerous and richest Congregation in this City, regard so insolent an Attempt! You who have the same Discipline, and the same Worship with the Mother Church of the Nation, and whose fundamental Articles are embrac'd by all Protestant Christendom,— what Colour of Reason can be offered to deny you your just Proportion in the Management of the College? Methinks a due Respect for the national Church, nay common Decency and good Manners, are sufficient to check the presumptuous Attempt, and redden the Claimant with a guilty Blush. Resent, therefore, so shameless a Pretence, so audacious an Incroachment.

NOR can you Gentlemen of the DUTCH CHURCH, retrospect the Zeal of your Ancestors in stipulating for the Enjoyment of their religious Privileges, at the Surrender of the Province, without a becoming Ardor for the same Model of public Worship which they were so anxious in preserving to you in its primitive Purity. Or higher still, to trace the Renown of your Progenitors, recollect their Stand, their glorious and ever memorable Stand against the Yoke of Thraldom, and all the Horrors of ecclesiastic Villainy, its inseparable Concomitants. For their inviolable Attachment to pure unadulterated Protestantism, and the inestimable Blessings of Freedom civil and sacred, History will resound their deathless Praises; and adorned with the precious Memorials of their heroic and insuppressible Struggles against Imposition and Despotism, will shine with eternal and undecaying Splendor. Impell'd by their illustrious Example, disdain the Thoughts of a servile Acquiescence in the usurp'd Dominion of others, who will inevitably swallow up and absorb your Churches, and efface even the Memory of your having once formed so considerable a Distinction. Pity Methinks it would be and highly to be deplor'd, that you should, by your own Folly, gradually crumble into Ruin, and at length sink into total and irrecoverable Oblivion.

REMEMBER Gentlemen of the English PRESBYTERIAN Church, remember with a sacred Jealousy, the countless Sufferings of your pious Predecessors, for Liberty of Conscience, and the Right of private Judgment. What Afflictions did they not endure, what fiery Trials did they not encounter, before they found in this remote Corner of the Earth, that Sanctuary and Requiem which their native Soil inhumanly deny'd them? And will you endanger that dear-bought Toleration for which they retired into voluntary Banishment, for which they agoniz'd, and for which they bled? What drove your Ancestors to this Country, then a dreary Waste and a barren Desart? What forced them from the Land of their Fathers, the much-lov'd Region where first they drew the vital Air? What compell'd them to open to themselvs a passage into these more fortunate Climes? Was it not the Rage of Persecution and a lawless Intolerance? Did they not seek an Asylum among the Huts of Savages more hospitable, more humaniz'd than their merciless Oppressors? Could Oceans stop or Tempests retard their Flight, when Freedom was attack'd and Conscience was the Question? And will you entail on your Posterity that Bondage, to escape which they brav'd the raging Deep, and penetrated the howling Wilderness!

YOU, my FRIENDS, in Derision called QUAKERS, have always approv'd yourselves Lovers of civil and religious Liberty; and of universal Benevolence to Mankind. And tho' you have been misrepresented as averse to human Learning, I am confident, convinced as you are of the Advantages of useful Literature, by the Writings of your renown'd *Apologist*, and other celebrated Authors of your Persuasion, you would generously contribute to the Support of a College founded on a free and catholic Bottom. But to give your Substance to the Bearing of Bigotry, or the tutoring Youth in the *enticing Words of Man's Vanity*, I know to be repugnant to your candid, your rational, your manly Way of thinking. Since the first Appearance of the *Friends*, thro' what Persecutions have they not waded? With what Difficulties have they not conflicted, e'er they could procure the unmolested Enjoyment of their Religion? This I mention not to spur you to revenge the Indignities offered to your Brethren, who being now beyond the Reach of Opposition and Violence, you, I am sure will scorn to remember their Tribulations with an unchristian Resentment. But to make their inhuman Treatment a Watch-Tower against the like Insults on your Descendants, is but wise, prudent and rational. At present, as ever you ought, you enjoy a righteous Toleration. But how long you will be able to boast the same Immunity, when the Fountain of Learning is directed, and all the Offices of the Province engrossed by one Sect, God only knows, and yours it is to stand on your Guard.

EQUALLY tremendous will be the Consequences to you, Gentlemen of the FRENCH, of the MORAVIAN, of the LUTHERAN, and of the ANABAPTIST Congregations, tho' the Limits of my Paper deny me the Honour of a particular Application to your respective Churches.

HAVING thus, *My Country-Men*, accosted you as distinct Denominations of Christians, I shall again address you as Men, and reasonable Beings.

CONSIDER, *Gentlemen*, the apparent Iniquity, the monstrous Unreasonableness of the Claim I am opposing. Are we not all Members of the same Community? Have we not an equal Right? Are we not alike to contribute to the Support of the College? Whence then the Pretensions of one in Preference to the Rest? Does not every Persuasion produce Men of Worth and Virtue, conspicuous for Sense, and renown'd for Probity? Why then should one be exalted and the other debased? One preferr'd and the rest rejected? Bating the Lust of domineering, no Sect can pretend any Motive for monopolizing the whole? Let them produce their Title, and we will submit. Or do they think us so pusillanimous that we dare not resist? What! are we to be choak'd without attempting to struggle for Breath? One would, indeed, imagine the *Business was done*, and that with a Witness. One would fancy he already beheld *Slavery* triumphant, and *Bigotry* swaying her enormous, her despotic Sceptre. But you, I trust, will asswage their Malice, and confound their Devices. You, I hope, will consider the least Infraction of your Liberties, as a Prelude to greater Encroachments. Such always was, and such ever will be the Case. Recede, therefore, not an Inch from your indisputable

Rights. On the contrary declare your Thoughts freely, nor loiter a Moment in an Affair of such unspeakable Consequence. You have been told it,—Posterity will feel it. Indolence, Indolence has been the Source of irretrievable Ruin. Langour and Timidity, when the public is concerned, are the Origin of Evils mighty and innumerable. Why then in the Name of Heaven, should you behold the Infringement, supine and inanimate? Why should you too late deplore your Irresolution, and with fruitless Lamentation bewail your astonishing, your destructive Credulity? No; defeat the Scheme before it is carried into Execution: Countermine it e'er it proves irreversible. Away with so pestilent a Project: Suffer it no longer to haunt the Province, but stigmatize it with the indelible Brands of the most scandalous Infamy. Alas, when shall we see the glorious Flame of PATRIOTISM lighted up, and blazing out with inextinguishable Lustre? When shall we have *One Interest*, and that Interest be the *common Good*.

To assert your Rights, doth your Resolution fail you? To resist the Domination of one Sect over the Rest, are you destitute of Courage? Tamely will you submit, and yield without a Contest? Come then, and by Imagination's Aid, penetrate into Futurity. Behold your Offspring train'd in Superstition, and bred to holy Bondage. Behold the Province over-run with Priest-Craft, and every Office usurp'd by the ruling Party!

PAUSE, therefore, and consider. Revolve the Consequences in a dispassionate Mind: Weigh them in the Scale of Reason, in the Ballance of cool deliberate Reflection. By the numberless Blessings of LIBERTY, heavenly-born;—by the uncontroulable Dictates of CONSCIENCE, the Vicegerent of GOD;—by the Horrors of PERSECUTION, conceived in Hell, and nurs'd at *Rome;*—and by the awful Name of REASON, the Glory of the human Race; I conjure you to pluck out this Thorn, which is incessantly stinging and goading the Bosom of every Man of Integrity and Candour!

NEXT to the most patriot KING that ever grac'd a Throne, and the wisest Laws that ever bless'd a People, an equal TOLERATION of Conscience, is justly deem'd the Basis of the public Liberty of this Country. And will not this Foundation be undermined? Will it not be threatned with a total Subversion, should one Party obtain the sole Management of the Education of our Youth? Is it not clear as the Sun in his Meridian Splendor, that this Equality — this precious and never-to-be-surrender'd Equality, will be destroy'd, and the Scale preponderate in Favour of the Strongest? And are we silent and motionless, to behold the Abolition of those invaluable Bulwarks of our Prosperity and Repose? Is not the Man, — the Man do I call him? Is not the Miscreant, who refuses to repel their Destruction, an Accomplice in the Crime? Does he not agree to sacrifice that which, next to the Protection of our Mother Country, constitutes our Security, our Happiness, and our Glory? He is beyond Question chargeable with this aggravated Guilt.— Let us, therefore, strive to have the College founded on an ample, a generous, an universal Plan. Let not the Seat of Literature, the

Abode of the Muses, and the Nurse of Science; be transform'd into a cloister of Bigots, an Habitation of Superstition, a Nursery of ghostly Tyranny, a School of rabbinical Jargon. The Legislature alone should have the Direction of so important an Establishment. In their Hands it is safer, incomparably safer, than in those of a Party, who will instantly discover a Thirst for Dominion, and lord it over the Rest.

Come on then, *My Country-Men,* and awake out of your Lethargy! Start, O start, from your Trance! By the inconquerable Spirit of the ancient Britons; — by the Genius of that Constitution which abhors every Species of Vassalage; — by the unutterable Miseries of Priest-Craft, reducing Nations and Empires to Beggary and Bondage; — by the august Title of Englishmen, ever impatient of lawless tyrannic Rule; — by the grand Prerogatives of Human Nature, the lovely Image of the infinite Deity; — and what is more than all, by that Liberty *wherewith* Christ *has set you free*; — I exhort, I beseech, I obtest, I implore you, to expostulate the Case with your Representatives, and testify your Abhorrence of so perillous, so detestable a Plot. In Imitation of the Practice of your Brethren in *England,* when an Affair of Moment is on the Carpet, petition your respective Members to take it into their serious Consideration. Acquaint them with your Sentiments of the Matter, and I doubt not, they will remove the Cause of your Disquiet, by an Interposition necessary to the public Prosperity, and eventual of their own immortal Honour.

Z.

---

*T*HE *Reflector's Sentiments, relating to the religious Worship of the College, having been objected to under pretence, that no Prayer can be calculated to please all Parties, he intends, in some future Paper, to exhibit a Form, against which no Protestant of the most scrupulous Conscience can except.*

Number XXIX.

THURSDAY, JUNE 14, 1753.

*　　　　　*　　　　　*　　　　　*

To the Independent Reflector.

SIR,

AMONG the many Objections raised by the Enemies of civil and religious Liberty, against your Sentiments on our future 'College, there is one which for its peculiar Malignity, deserves, in 'my Opinion, the severest Animadversions. It has often been 'advanced by Persons equally unacquainted with your Subject and 'Design, that instead or delineating a just Plan for so noble a 'Structure, you have endeavoured, by raising the Heat of Parties, to 'prevent our having any College at all. This Assertion contains a 'double Charge, either Part of which were it true, would be suffi- 'cient to blast the growing Reputation of your weekly Reflections.

' For my Part, I have considered your Papers with the Impartiality
' becoming a Friend of public Vertue, and cannot discover the least
' Marks of an Attempt to raise Animosities among your Fellow
' Creatures. You have indeed animated the various Sects among us,
' to guard against the Encroachments of each other, which to me
' appears to be the most natural Means for suppressing the Growth of
' party Zeal: For the Heat of Sectaries consists not in a mutual
' Watchfulness, by which they severally keep themselves in a State of
' Independence; but on the Contrary is the natural Offspring of a
' persecuting Spirit in the prevailing Persuasion, and the just Resent-
' ment of the injured and oppressed. Where all Men enjoy an equal
' Freedom in Profession and Practice, there can be no Room for the
' Exertion of so uncharitable a Fervour; and nothing but unwarrant-
' able Encroachments can be productive of Heat and Opposition. In
' endeavouring, therefore, to support the Freedom of each particular
' Sect, you have evidently aimed at the Repose and Tranquility of the
' Whole.

' But after all, had You arrouzed the Spirit of Party among the
' People of this Province, is there not sufficient Reason to warrant
' such a Conduct, tho' so loudly exclaimed against? Does not one
' Persuasion openly and avowedly claim the Management of an Affair,
' with which the Happiness of all Sects is most intimatedly connec-
' ted? And will not so daring an Encroachment justify the utmost
' Rage of the Parties insulted? While any Denomination continues
' so insolent a Claim, it becomes a public Writer industriously to rake
' up the Sparks of Party, and fan the Fire of Opposition till it
' mounts into an universal Blaze.

' The second part of the Charge is, that you aim at having no Col-
' lege. And for this Assertion, whoever candidly reads your Papers,
' will own there is not the least Foundation. You have convinced
' the World that you are sensible of the vast advantages of a Public
' Academy, and would willingly have it secure against the Attacks of
' every Denomination, that it might continue an inexhaustible Fund
' of universal Happiness, to latest Posterity. It is true you have
' declared, that you would prefer our present illiterate State, to all
' the Benefits we can possibly purchase by raising a College at the
' Expence of our Liberty: And this, doubtless, is what they mean by
' your aiming at having no College at all. Nor can they be persuaded,
' that rough uncultivated Liberty, is infinitely preferable to the most
' polished and ornamented Servitude.

I am your Humble Servant,

B   ACADEMICUS.

Rye, 18th *May,* 1753.

[For typographical convenience, we have transposed the next preceding and
succeeding articles from their original order.]

NUMBER XXVII.

THURSDAY, MAY 31, 1753.

A Prayer.

AMONGST numberless other Absurdities, it hath often been asserted by those for a partial College, that no prayer could possibly be formed, but what would be rejected by all other Denominations, on Account of the Party by whom it was composed. I shall therefore lay before the Reader, a Prayer wholly collected from the Scriptures, except the Passages in Italics;[1] against which, I presume, no Christian of any Persuasion can object, without at the same Time manifesting his Irreverence for the sacred Oracles.

*   *   *   *

[This Prayer being very long, we copy only the last third of it (omitting the marginal references of the original to books, chapters and verses), which will sufficiently illustrate its character and scope :]

*   •   *   *   *

WISDOM is better than Rubies, Length of Days are in her Right Hand, and in her Left Hand Riches and Honour: Her Ways are Ways of Pleasantness, and all her Paths are Peace. Let the Knowledge of Wisdom be sweet unto our Souls, as is the Honey-Comb unto the Taste. Let us perceive the Words of Understanding, and cry after Knowledge. Doth not Wisdom cry, and Understanding put forth her Voice? She crieth at our Gates, at the Entry of *this House*, at the coming in at the Doors unto us doth she call, unto us lifteth she her Voice. Let us therefore hear Instruction, be wise and refuse it not: Watching daily at Wisdom's Gates, and waiting at the Posts of her Door: For whoso loveth Instruction, loveth Knowledge.

UNTO thee, O God, do we give Thanks, unto thee do we give Thanks. We will praise the Lord for it is good, it is pleasant, and Praise is comely for the Upright. It is a good Thing to give Thanks unto the Lord, and to sing Praises unto thy Name, O Most High! To show forth thy loving Kindness in the Morning, and thy Faithfulness every Night. We bless thee, that when the Fulness of Time was come, thou didst send forth thy Son made of a Woman, made under the Law, to redeem them that were under the Law, that we might receive the Adoption of Sons. That we have an Advocate with the Father, even Jesus Christ the Righteous. That he is set on the Right Hand of the Throne of the Majesty in the Heavens, Angels and Authorities, and Powers being made subject to him. *That he hath* sent us another Comforter to abide with us forever, even the Spirit of Truth. The Lord is good, his Mercy is everlasting, and his Truth endureth to all Generations.

LET thy Salvation and thy Righteousness be openly shewed in the Sight of the Heathen, and let all the Ends of the Earth see the Sal-

---

[1] The compiler does not adhere to this rule in the use of the words "*Levi*" "*Amen*," and "*Our Father who art in Heaven.*"

vation of our God. Let the Word of the Lord have free Course, and let it be glorified. Save thy People, O Lord, and bless thy Heritage: Feed them also, and lift them up forever. Bring thy Seed from the East, and gather them from the West: Say to the North give up, and to the South keep not back. Bring thy Sons from afar, and thy Daughters from the Ends of the Earth. From the rising of the Sun to the going down of the same; let thy Name be great among the Gentiles, and the Earth be full of the Knowledge of the Lord, as the Waters cover the Sea. Grace be with all them that love the Lord Jesus Christ with Sincerity. Give King *George* thy Judgments, O God, and thy Righteousness, that he may judge the Poor of the People, save the Children of the Needy, and break in Pieces the Oppressor. Let him redeem their Souls from Deceit and Violence, and let their Blood be precious in his Sight. Let his Throne be established in Righteousness, and upheld with Mercy. Make him exceeding glad with thy Countenance. Through the tender Mercy of the most High, let him not be moved. Cloath his Enemies with Shame, but upon himself let the Crown flourish. Grant him length of Days, and let his Glory be great in thy Salvation. *Bless his Royal Highness* George *Prince of Wales, the Princess Dowager of Wales, the Duke, the Princesses, and all the Royal Family.* May thy loving Kindness be before their Eyes, and may they walk in thy Truth. Smile *on our Governor.* May he walk in Uprightness: And may his Ways please the Lord. Teach our Senators Wisdom. Let our Rulers be able Men, such as fear God, Men of Truth, hating Covetousness. That Justice may run down as a River, and Righteousness as a mighty Stream. Peace be within our Borders, and Prosperity within our Palaces. Make our Officers Peace, and our Exactors Righteousness. Let Violence never be heard in our Gates; Wasting or Distruction in our Borders: Let our Walls be called Salvation, and our Gates Praise. In the Name of our Lord Jesus Christ, let there be no Divisions among us, but that we may be perfectly joined together in the same Mind and in the same Judgment. Purify the Sons of *Levi;* purge them as Gold and Silver, that they may offer unto the Lord an Offering in Righteousness. Let the Servants of the Lord be gentle to all Men, apt to teach — patient — Examples to the Believers, in Word, in Conversation, in Charity, in Spirit, in Truth, in Purity.

LET *us know above all Things,* that the Fear of the Lord is the Beginning of Wisdom, and the Knowledge of the Holy is Understanding. Let us love our Enemies, bless them that curse us, do good to them that hate us, and pray for them that despitefully use us, and persecute us. Father forgive them, for they know not what they do. Now to the King eternal, immortal, invisible, the only wise God, be Glory and Majesty, Dominion and Power, both now and ever, *Amen. Our Father who art in Heaven,* &c.

IN like Manner occasional Parts may be composed, adapted to the Morning, and Evening, Sabbath, Sickness, Death, War, Famine, Fasting, Thanksgiving, &c.

A. & Z.

15

NUMBER L.

THURSDAY, NOVEMBER 8, 1753.

The Advantages of Education, with the Necessity of instituting Grammar Schools for the Instruction of Youth, preparatory to their Admission into our intended COLLEGE.

> *My* SPIRIT *pours a Vigour thro' the Soul,*
> *Th' unfetter'd Thought with Energy inspires,*
> *Invincible in Arts, in the bright Field*
> *Of laurel'd Science, as in that of Arms.*
>
> THOM. Lib.

TO enumerate all the Advantages accruing to a Country, from a due Attention to the Encouragement of the Means of Education, is impossible. The happy Streams issuing from that inexhaustable Source, are numberless and unceasing. Knowledge among a People makes them free, enterprising and dauntless ; but Ignorance enslaves, emasculates and depresses them. When Men know their Rights, they will at all Hazards defend them, as well against the insidious Designs of domestic Politicians, as the undisguised Attacks of a foreign Enemy : But while the Mind remains involved in its native Obscurity, it becomes pliable, abject, dastardly and tame : It swallows the grossest Absurdities, submits to the vilest Impositions, and follows wherever its is led. In short, irrefragable Arguments in favour of Knowledge, may be drawn from the Consideration of its Nature. But it is sufficient barely to observe its Effects. He must be a Stranger to History and the World, who has not observed, that the prosperity, Happiness, Grandeur, and even the Strength of a People, have always been the Consequences of the Improvement and Cultivation of their Minds. And indeed, where this has been in any considerable Degree neglected, triumphant Ignorance hath open'd its Sluices, and the Country been overflowed with Tyranny, Barbarism, ecclesiastical Domination, Superstition, Enthusiasm, corrupt Manners, and an irresistible confederate Host of Evils, to its utter Ruin and Destruction. While *Egypt* was the School of the Ancients, her martial, was not inferior to her literary, Glory. The successful Defence of the Greeks, against the powerful Invasion of *Persia*, is to be imputed, rather to their Art than to any other Cause. And when *Rome* had compleated the conquest of the World, she triumphed over it as much in Science as in Power and military Valour.

BUT as necessary and advantageous as the Education of Youth is to a Country, it has often been remarked, that of all the Provinces on the Continent, not one has been so culpably inattentive to this important Article as ours. I wish it was in my Power, to disprove the truth of the Observation. We are not only surpassed by several of our Neighbours, who have long since erected Colleges for publick Instruction, but by all others, even in common Schools; of which I have heard it lamented, that we have scarce ever had a good One in the Province. It is true, we had a Law which declared in its Preamble, that the Youth of this Province, were not inferior in their

Geniusses to those of any other Country: But against this it is to be observed, ·that the Law is long since expired, and probably our natural Ingenuity abated, and even tho' this was not our Case, I can by no Means agree, that the natural Fertility of our Geniusses, is a sufficient Reason for the total Neglect of their Cultivation. ·

It is with joy I observe the present Disposition of our Legislature, to remove the Scandal of our former Indolence, about the Means of Education, in the Measures we are pursuing for the Establishment of a College. That important Design must flourish under the Care of the Public. Our Province is growing and opulent, and we are able to endow an University in the most splendid Manner, without any Burden upon the People. Scarce any Thing at present but the Nature of its Constitution demands the Study of the several Branches of the Legislature. And that alone is a Subject worthy their utmost Vigilance and Attention. A College in a new Country, and especially in a Province of such scanty Limits as ours, will necessarily make a vast Alteration in our Affairs and Condition, civil and religious. It will, more or less, influence every Individual amongst us, and diffuse its Spirit thro' all Ranks, Parties and Denominations. If it be established upon a generous and catholic Foundation, agreeable to the true Nature and End of a Seminary for the Instruction of Youth in useful Knowledge, we and our Posterity will have Reason to bless its Founders, and long will it continue the Fountain of Felicity to the Province. But should it unhappily be made the Engine of a Party in Church or State — should it be constituted with any Badge of religious Discrimination of Preference, we have no Reason either to believe or wish its Prosperity. Such an impure Source must necessarily poison us with its infected Streams, endanger our precious Liberties, discourage our Growth, and be obstructive to the public Emolument. But this Matter I have fully considered in some of my former Papers on the College. The laudable Generosity which our Assembly have already exhibited in their Sentiments relating to its Constitution, have procured them the most general Applause, and inspired the People with a Confidence that they will faithfully guard their Privileges sacred and political.

Whoever has been at a College, is not ignorant, that the Youth at their Initiation, must be considerably instructed in the Latin and Greek Tongues; their first exercises there, consisting in reading the principal Authors that have written in those Languages. Hence it is plain, that good Grammar Schools, are absolutely necessary in a Course of Education, to the Growth and Prosperity of our College, where, instead of studying the Rudiments of those Languages, after only one Year's Exercise in them, the Youth enter upon sublimer Employments in Logic, Philosophy, Ethics, &c. in which it is impossible for School Boys, thro' the Immaturity of their Judgments, to make any valuable Proficiency. At the same Time, therefore, that we institute a College, we should by no Means neglect the Encouragement of Schools, without which it will be thin and unprosperous. To what Purpose shall we rear a vast and costly Edifice, and raise an expensive Fund for the Support of Instructors, but for the Benefit of the

Students? And to supply the latter without good Schools throughout the Province, will be impossible, unless the College itself be made one, which will be a Scheme both unexampled and absurd.

WITH Submission therefore, to my Superiors, I would propose, that an Act be passed for building and establishing two Grammar Schools in every County, and enabling the Inhabitants, annually to elect Guardians over them, and impowering the Assessors to raise Fifty Pounds per Annum, as a County Charge, for the Support of each Master, to be nominated and paid by those Guardians.

THIS Step is, in my Opinion, not only feasible, but free from all the Objections which lie against a Grammar School Education in the College, and will, besides, be attended with very good Consequences.

FIRST: Two Schools in a County will probably, for many years, be more than sufficient for the Instruction of the Children to be sent from it to the College, and both of them may be raised at a very inconsiderable Sum. In the Colonies to the Eastward, they are built upon the Commons, contain but one Room, are tight and warm, and not more costly nor larger than a common Log Cottage. The Master suits himself with a Lodging in the Village, and so do his Pupils generally at a very cheap rate. The Masters among them are such as have been graduated at their Colleges, and for want of Estates, stoop to this Employment, till they have more fully prosecuted their Studies; and having but just finish'd their collegiate Education, are perhaps better fitted for that Business, than Persons of riper Years, who have worn off their academical Learning, and are determined upon some particular Office or Occupation. I make no doubt therefore, but that it will be easy to supply our Schools with Preceptors, at Fifty Pounds per Annum each, since there are many such in those Colonies who are glad to take up with a more inconsiderable Sum. But as it seems agreed to fix the College in this City, the Salaries of the same Officers, if Grammar Schools be supported in the College, must be vastly augmented, because their additional Expences in Diet and Dress, must be very much enhanced; and perhaps it will be no easy Matter to provide a Fund for the College, sufficient to sustain the continual Charge of so many Masters.

SECONDLY: Supporting the Youth at those Schools in the Country, will be but a Trifle compared with the prodigious Expence of maintaining them in the City, which probably will prevent many from bestowing upon their Children a publick Education.

THIRDLY: It is worth Consideration, that as Boys at a very early Age may be fit for the Grammar School, the Tenderness or Weakness of Parents, may raise Objections against sending them to *New-York*, at the proper Time, for their Study of the Tongues; and in Consequence thereof, to their utter Ruin, prevent their ever passing thro' the College who might otherwise be constantly kept, during their Infancy, at a Country School, under the Care of their Parents, till they were in Age, and Capacity, prepared for entering the College. And, indeed, I cannot help thinking, but that this Objection alone would prove fatal to the Scheme of supporting Grammar

Schools in the College; for where one Man would agree to put a Lad of Ten or Twelve Years of Age to School, Fifty or a Hundred Miles from him, many, rather than submit to it, would refuse giving their Children any Education at all, especially if it be also considered how susceptible tender Minds are of all Impressions, whether Good or Evil, and how necessary it is in forming their Morals, that they should be kept under the Eye of their Parents.

FOURTHLY: It is not to be supposed that, let a Boy's Genius be never so promising, he can be well-fitted for his Entrance into the College, in less than four Years. Nor will he thence carry off much Knowledge, unless he continues his Studies there, at least four Years more. So that, if he is sent to the College for his Attainment of the Tongues, his Absence from Home, and Residence in the City, will take up eight Years, where the Expence of his Tuition, extraordinary Dress and Diet, will perhaps exceed his Father's Purse, and for that unsurmountable Objection, prevent his ever having the Means of an Education; when, if one Half of that Time was spent at no Charge for Tuition, and a very trifling Expence for his Board and Dress in the Country, his Talents might be cultivated to the Advantage of himself and the Public.

FIFTHLY: At these Country-Schools it will be in the Power of those Parents to have their Children taught Latin and Greek, who are neither able nor inclined to give them an academical Education, from which they will be deterred by the Expence of maintaining them four Years in *New - York*. Nor, tho' they should not intend them so ample an Education as they would receive in the College, would it in many Cases be improper to let them pass thro' the Grammar Schools. I have known many Men, without any other Assistances in Education than what they received at such Schools, make a very agreeable and useful Appearance in Life: And it is, perhaps, principally to be ascribed to the Number and Cheapness of those little Country Seminaries, that the *Scotch*, in the Article of Literature, support the Reputation of exceeding in general, any other Nation in the World. Besides the Advantage of acquiring a Knowledge of those Languages sufficient to read and examine the Writings of the Ancients, the shortest Course that can be recommended for the Attainment of any considerable Accuracy in the Knowledge even of our own Language, is by a tolerable Acquaintance with the Latin and Greek Tongues. Whoever understands those Languages, and English, will find the latter vastly augmented and inriched by Derivatives from the former, The Technical Terms, or Words of Art, are deduced almost intirely from those Fountains, as well as many others of Use, even in common Conversation. It would be an endless Piece of Work to be indebted to our Dictionaries (which by the Way are seldom to be depended upon, often unsatisfactory, and defective) for the Meaning of Words; which must always be the Case, when we are ignorant of the Languages from whence they are derived. Besides, Boys in the Study of the Languages, are imployed in a Manner best suited to their Capacities. Plain Rules of Morality and History are generally the Subjects of the Books put into their

Hands. Whatever they are designed for, there can be no Danger of an Excess in their Studies of these Things, and their Progress in them principally depends upon the Memory, a Faculty of the Mind which is generally exercised the first of any others in Youth. In a Course of Grammar School Learning, they are enured to Books and Attention, in a Manner the most easy and natural. Their Capacities gradually opened—their Curiosities raised—Their Powers strengthened—their Views extended, and their Minds familiarized to Inquiry: All which must be necessary and advantageous to them in any Employment in Life, even tho' they do not enter upon collegiate Exercises in a more deep and abstruse Course of Studies. It is Dr. Swift who says, "*The Books read at School are full of Incitements to Virtue, and Discouragements from Vice, drawn from the wisest Reasons, the strongest Motives, and the most influencing Examples. The very Maxims set up to direct modern Education, are enough to destroy all the Seeds of Knowledge, Honour, Wisdom and Virtue among us. The current Opinion prevails, that the Study of Greek and Latin is Loss of Time.*"

Sixthly: It may be observed, that few, if any, of the Pupils in the Grammar School to be erected in the College, will be of an Age to admit of their living within its Walls. Their tender Years will render it necessary for them to board at private Houses in the City, for the Advantage of Nurses to exercise over them a Mother's Care, which will prevent the Masters from that narrow Inspection into their Conduct from which they cannot so well be exempted at a School in the Country, and at the same Time weaken the Support of a suitable Government in the College, where, unless the strictest Regimen is observed, the wildest Confusion and Disorder will take Place, to the absolute Ruin of the Students.

I only add, that no Instance can be assigned that Grammar-School-Learning was ever a Part of the Instruction in any College or University; and I conceive, for the Reasons before offered, it would be very improper for us to begin such an unprecedented Institution. The Encouragement of County Schools, will supply our College with Students, in a Manner best suited to our Circumstances; and if we neglect them, I think one may venture to predict, that the Academy will never rise to any Considerable Fame, nor answer the general Expectations of the Province.

A.

NUMBER LI.

THURSDAY, NOVEMBER 15, 1753.

WHEN I consider, either the favourable Sentiments which the Author of the following Letter is pleased to entertain of some of my Reflections, or the Importance of the Subject he has chosen, and the masterly Manner in which he handles it, I think it would be an Injury, both to the Public and myself, to refuse it a Place in the REFLECTOR.

To the INDEPENDENT REFLECTOR.

Philadelphia, October 21, 1753.

SIR,

' THO' we are unknown to each other, and my Residence is out
' the Province, for which your Papers are more particularly
' calculated, I cannot restrain my Acknowledgments to an Author
' who inspired with an amiable Disinterestedness, so industriously
' aims at the Advancement of the Honour and Happiness not only of
' his own Country, but of universal Mankind. I heartily approve of
' your Papers in general ; but of those on the Subject of the College,
' I have the highest Opinion. The Method you therein pursued is
' strictly accurate, and the Scheme you proposed for its Constitution
' and Government, judicious and wholesome. I do not remember to
' have heard any Man, who has impartially considered it, advance any
' material Objection against it. Nor do I believe, from what I know
' of the State of your Province, that a more advantageous Scheme
' can possibly be recommended to a People split into such a Diversity
' of religious Opinions. Yours not only obviates the Jealousy of
' each, but effectually secures all in the lasting Enjoyment of their
' Liberties. And in this View of your Sentiments on that important
' Subject, it has been Matter of Surprize to many Gentlemen among
' us, who heartily desire to see Learning prevail in the Plantations,
' that, after the Plan you have drawn up and proposed, the Affair of
' the College should have so tardy a Progress. These Colonies have
' hitherto been too much despised by some British Politicians, whose
' Indifference has often exposed us to sundry political Disadvantages.
' The best Means for raising a Sense of our Importance, and in Con-
' sequence of it, an Attention to our provincial Interests, is, in my
' opinion, to encourage the Education of Youth in all our Prov-
' inces. The Importation of Foreigners, and our own Growth, will,
' indeed, people our Country. Our Lands may be cultivated, and our
' Commerce enlarged; but our Reputation, and even our Strength,
' will principally depend upon able Councillors, sensible Representa-
' tives, and Officers of Judgment and Penetration. But, how shall
' we preserve those Rights of which we are ignorant? How intro-
' duce Measures necessary for our general Prosperity, but with great
' Art and Address? Tho' we are entitled to all the Rights of English-
' men, we have not an equal Security with those of our Fellow Sub-

'jects, who enjoy the Happiness of living under the immediate
'Protection of our gracious Sovereign.   The Infancy of our Country,
'necessarily exposes us to many Defects which are not to be found in
'a State grown perfect and compact by Time and Experience.   Our
'political Frame must attain its full Maturity by Steps gradual and
'slow.   Nor shall we ever behold this happy Period, 'till we apply
'our Thoughts to the Consideration of our Condition, Interest and
'Relations.   There are doubtless some Instances of Persons of that
'Turn among us: A few will, however, but little avail us: Their
'Influence will be no wider than their Sphere.   Such a Spirit must
'become general, before the Advantages will be so; and of all the
'Methods we can pursue, there is none so likely to enkindle and
'diffuse it, as the Encouragement of Education, thereby furnishing
'our Colonies with Men of Sense and Literature, with enterprizing
'Heads, and Hearts inflamed with Patriot-Fire.

'I ASSURE you, *Sir*, I am deeply affected with the Indifference
'which prevails among some of you in the important Undertaking
'of erecting a College; and I think the Opposition to your Scheme,
'as it retards that useful Design, a Shame to your Adversaries.
'Such a *Seminary* would not only be advantageous to your Province,
'in the View I have before considered it, but would attach to it many
'of our Youth.   Our Academy is only intended to teach the lower
'Kinds of Knowledge; and, indeed, in that Respect, will, undoubt-
'edly, be of admirable Service.   But if the College of *New-York*, is
'established upon the free Bottom you proposed, by which all the
'Students, of whatever Protestant Denomination, will be received
'upon, and admitted to a perfect Parity of Privileges, it cannot but
'prosper, and invite Pupils from all our Colonies, as it will, in
'Reality, be preferable to the public Seminaries of all of them, each
'savouring more or less of religious Party.   Nor has the Catholicism
'of your plan been less happy in obviating the Objections which the
'Gentlemen of the *West-Indies*, have hitherto raised against most
'of our Northern Colleges.

'THE Contention about introducing the *English* Liturgy, tho' I
'profess myself a Churchman, has, in my Opinion, had more Regard
'paid to it, than ought to be allowed to any Thing that impedes so
'good a Design.   You, indeed, have insisted, that no Form used by
'any Church in your Province should be introduced, lest a Discrimi-
'nation of one Sect enkindle the Jealousy of the Rest, to the Preju-
'dice of the College.   I concur with you in Opinion, if a Form could
'be agreed upon free from the Objection: But you'll admit it a great
'Pity, that such a trifling Dispute, should retard so glorious and
'beneficial an Undertaking.   The Form of Prayer you Proposed as
'a Model, tho' ingenious, will, I believe, never be consented to,
'because I do not suppose your Assembly will ever think proper to
'give themselves the Trouble of preparing a Set of Forms.   In
'Favour of the Liturgy of the Church of *England* it is urged, that
'the Nation has approved it; but it must be confessed, that tho' it is
'very well suited to the State of a Church, it will require a consider-
'able Alteration, to adapt it to the State of such a Seminary: The

'Forms of the *Dutch* and *French* Protestant Churches are as good,
'and will require less Alteration and Addition; and if it should not
'be thought proper to introduce them, rather the Contention about
'Forms should impede that noble Design, the Prayers, I think,
'should be left to the Discretion of the President, with the Trustees,
'to whom it should be committed, to draw up a Formulary, to be
'laid before your Legislature for their Approbation and Establish-
'ment.

'THESE, Sir, are my Sentiments of the Matter, and upon your
'Promise to correct them, you have Leave to give them a Place in
'your Paper. I hope, at your next Session, something difinitive will
'be done in this Affair. May God inspire your Legislature with a
'generous Regard to the Liberties of their Countrymen, and assist
'them in establishing the College upon such a Foundation, as that it
'may continue a perpetual Blessing to your Province, and of great
'Utility to Mankind.

I am, &c."

A.

The Independent Reflector, the organ of Mr. Livingston's opposition to the college, ceased with its 52d number, on the 22d of November, 1753; the printer, Parker, refusing to go on with it. In the
month of January following, Mr. Livingston reprinted the whole,
with a long preface; and bearing on its title page " Printed until
tyrannically suppressed in 1753."

Contemporary with this *Independent Reflector*, but of less note,
were several publications relating to the college controversy, and
turning upon the same points that Mr. Livingston professed to have
in view.[1]

---

*An Act further to continue the duty of Excise and the Currency of
the Bills of Credit emitted thereon, for the purposes in the former
act and herein mentioned.*

[Passed July 4, 1753.]

Whereas, by an act of the Governor Council and General Assembly entituled, " an act for laying an excise on all strong liquors retailed
in this Colony," passed the twelfth year of her late Majesty Queen
Anne, there was granted to and for the use in the said act particularly
mentioned, a duty of excise on all strong liquors retailed in this
colony for the term of twenty years, to determine on the first day of
November, in the year one thousand seven hundred and thirty four,
which by several subsequent acts has been prolonged to the year one
thousand seven hundred and fifty-seven:—

And whereas, it has been the intention of the legislature for several
years past, to establish a seminary within this colony, for the educa-

---

[1] Moore's Hist. Sketch, p. 11.

tion of youth in the liberal arts and sciences, and as at present, no other means can be devised, than by a further continuance of the aforesaid act, and the bills of credit issued thereupon, and his Excellency the Governor having been pleased to approve the intentions of the General Assembly to proceed upon that good design at this session, as signified by their votes at their last meeting; — The General Assembly therefore pray it may be enacted and,

Be it Enacted   *   *   That the before mentioned act, entituled, [as above] * * be, remain and continue of full force and virtue, to all intents, constructions and purposes whatsoever, until the first day of November, which will be in the year of our Lord one thousand seven hundred and sixty seven.

And be it further enacted   *   *   That the Treasurer of this colony for the time being, is hereby enabled and directed, to pay unto the trustees mentioned and appointed in and by an act passed in the twenty fifth year of his present majesty's reign entituled, "An act for vesting in Trustees the sum of three thousand four hundred and forty three pounds eighteen shillings, raised by way of lottery, for erecting a college within this colony, out of the moneys arising by the duty of excise, the annual sum of five hundred pounds, for and during the term of seven years, to commence from and after the first day of January now next ensuing, to be by them apportioned and distributed in salaries for the chief master or head of the seminary, by whatever denomination he may be hereafter called, and for such and so many other masters and officers, uses and purposes, concerning the establishment of the said seminary, as the said trustees shall from time to time in their discretions think needfull: always provided, that the whole charge and expence of the same, do not exceed the above sum of five hundred pounds a year, any thing in the acts aforesaid to the contrary notwithstanding.

And be it further enacted   *   *   That the said Trustees, shall be and are hereby impowered to apportion and appoint the quantum of the salary's of the several masters and officers of the seminary hereby intended to be established, and to direct the payment thereof by quarterly or half yearly payments, as they in their discretion shall think most fitting and convenient.

And be it further enacted   *   *   That the Trustees aforesaid, shall ascertain the rates which each student or scholar shall annually pay, for his or her education at the said seminary, for all of which sums they shall account with the governor or commander in chief for the time being, the council or the General Assembly when by them or any of them thereunto required, and which said sums shall be applied to and for such use or uses as shall be directed by an act or acts hereafter to be passed.[1]

   *   *   *   *

[The continuation of these *Annals of the founding of King's College*, etc., may be expected in future issues of the Convocation Proceedings.]

---

[1] MS. Laws, in office of Secretary of State.

UNIVERSITY NECROLOGY.

CHANCELLOR ISAAC FERRIS, D. D., LL. D.

By Professor Benj. N. Martin, D. D., L. H. D.

Isaac Ferris was born in the city of New York, on the 13th of October, 1799. He belonged to a family which was honorably distinguished in the Revolution, by the zeal and devotion of its members in the cause of their country. Living, as they did, in that troubled district of the State which lay outside of the city, and between the lines of the opposing armies, they shared the passionate impulse of the time, which divided that community between the two conflicting parties; and attaching themselves to the national side, every male member of the family took up arms in defence of his country.

He was a bright and intelligent lad, and early imbibed, — in great part through his mother's influence, — a taste for study and a desire to obtain an education. The fact that he had to obtain it by his own exertions was due, not, as has been imagined, to the poverty of the family, but to a certain distrust on the part of his father, Mr. John Ferris, of the influence of higher education. In this feeling he was not alone. In the social habits and the moral sentiments at that time prevalent among the cultivated class, there was much that involved temptation, and tended to subvert the simplicity of morals and the appreciation of industry. The father had seen so many proofs of the reality of this danger that he was little disposed to encourage the wishes of his son; and therefore, though he liberally supplied the boy with pocket-money, he declined to assume the costs of his education. This decision of his father threw upon the youth the burden of his own support, for he was too deeply impressed with the value of intellectual culture to be willing to abandon the hope of it. He saved his pocket-money, therefore, for books; and exchanging the pair of skates which his father allowed him, for a Latin grammar, he began to achieve his education. By the aid of a somewhat distinguished teacher, who was one of his relatives, he obtained the moderate culture which was all that was then requisite for entrance upon the college course; and in 1811, when he was about thirteen, became a member of Columbia College, from which institution he graduated, with the first honors, in 1815.

The remainder of his course was fraught with similar difficulties, under all of which, however, he enjoyed the sympathy and countenance of his mother. Thus encouraged, he devoted himself to the ministry of the Gospel, and in due time had worked his way through the Theological Seminary, from which he came forth a preacher of righteousness, in 1820.

His first settlement in the ministry was in New Brunswick, N. J., where he remained for some three years, when he resigned his post and took charge of the Middle Dutch Church, in the city of Albany. In this position he continued for twelve years—down to 1836. He then removed to the city of New York, and became pastor of the Market-street church, where he remained till 1852. While there, he was invited to become the head of the University of the city of New York, in which position the later years of his active life were spent.

His ministerial career has been so fully and appreciatively described that I do not propose to enlarge upon it. Next, however, to his ministerial work, was his sympathy and appreciation of education; and it is to this aspect of his life that I propose to refer particularly.

During his early ministry he became much interested in the work of the Albany Female Academy, of which he was an earnest friend and supporter. It was by means of his connection with this institution that he was enabled, on his subsequent removal to New York, to contribute so largely to the cause of female education in that city. While pastor of the Market-street church there, he became deeply sensible of the want of proper facilities for female instruction. Under the sense of this want he became one of the founders, perhaps the principal founder, of the Rutgers Female Institute, which was designed as an instrument of high culture for ladies. It may interest some of the friends of the Albany Female Academy to know that that institution is particularly referred to in the articles of association of the Rutgers Institute, as one of the model institutions after which the new one was to be framed.

This Institute became distinguished among the city seminaries for the excellence of its methods, the judiciousness of its administration and the great prosperity which for many years attended its efforts to diffuse a higher culture among ladies. His success in the management of this institution suggested his name for the chancellorship of the University of the city of New York. After that post became vacant by the withdrawal of Chancellor Frelinghuysen, Dr. Ferris was elected to succeed him, in 1853.

The University was at that time greatly in need of a responsible head, in whom the public could confide. The means of the institution were of the smallest; and of the fund for the payment of its debt of $75,000, only half was subscribed. Dr. Ferris speedily took hold of the arrested work, and by his assiduous exertions the remaining half was subscribed, the whole collected, and the institution relieved permanently of the embarrassment of debt.

Other efforts were then undertaken for the repair of its building and the refurnishing of apparatus; and soon its first productive subscription was obtained, amounting to some $60,000. The great advance in prices which soon after began to prevail, speedily rendered these means as inadequate as its scantier ones had been before, and new funds were obtained for the new exigencies. Before the close of Chancellor Ferris' connection with the University, the sum of $170,000 had been contributed to its productive funds, and some noticeable though not great expansion had been given to its curriculum of studies.

As an educator, Dr. Ferris was distinguished by a genuine and warm sense of the importance of the work. At every period of his life he appreciated its worth; in every place in which he dwelt he gave attention to its improvement. The educational institutions of every community of which he was a member were the better for his presence among them. Education, too, in every branch and department, was an object of his care. The Albany Female Academy engaged his regard while he labored in that city; and the same regard was afterwards given to the Rutgers Institute in New York. When this institution was subsequently chartered as a female college, he expressed a very warm interest in its prosperity. In the University, he was, of course, conspicuous.

During nearly the whole period of his residence in the city he was the president of the New York Sunday School Union, and he vindicated the propriety of his election to that position by the constancy of his interest in the enterprise.

During many years he was in the habit of visiting the Sunday schools when in session, and his benignant countenance became familiar to thousands upon thousands of our city children, as that of one who felt the most cordial interest in their welfare. Over children and youth his influence was of that happy kind which mingles dignity with gentleness. His appeals to the moral feeling and to the home affections of his pupils were his constant and ready means of direction and control, and they will long be remembered with grateful regard by many whose early years were passed under his guidance.

As an instructor, he was not remarkable for brilliancy or originality. He aimed rather at accuracy and thoroughness. He sought to make the student familiar with the distinctions drawn and the principles inculcated in the text book. For this purpose he spared no pains to exhibit them. He was wont to prepare with much care and patience analyses of the subject-matter, and these he placed frequently upon the blackboard, and thus succeeded in exhibiting to the eye the important relations of the author's ideas. By this means he was enabled to impart an acquaintance with certain fundamental ideas, and a knowledge of their relations to each other, which often gave a happy familiarity with the subject.

But his work is done, and his career, full of honor and usefulness, is ended. Under the pressure of advancing years he resigned his position in the University in 1870, and withdrew from the severer labors of a life, every year of which had been full of activity and exertion for the best and noblest objects for which a good man can live. He retired to a quiet home in one of the villages that are springing up around the expanding metropolis, which had been both his birthplace and the principal scene of his labors; and, still surrounded with the friends who loved and the pupils who venerated him, he breathed his life peacefully away on Monday evening, June 16th, of the present year; and passed to the presence and communion of the Saviour, whose service on earth had been his chief labor and his great joy.

PROFESSOR JOHN TORREY, LL. D.

By Professor DANIEL S. MARTIN, A. M.

Among the names that stand high in the history of science in the United States, few have been better known or more truly respected than that of John Torrey. He was one who seemed to connect all the rapidly increasing scientific development of the present day in our country, with the interesting epoch of its early beginnings. He had commenced the pursuit of botany, when a boy, in the first decade of this century; he had kept pace with all its vast progress and expansion, and down to the latest weeks of his active, useful and stainless life, he retained, undiminished, the interest of his youth, and continued to enlarge the attainments of his manhood. It is not often that such a one is taken from among us, for men of this character are few—and, alas, it will not be long before all who were the leaders of American science in its early days, will be gathered to their fathers. It is fitting, then, that we should pause for a little while, and consider some of the circumstances and some of the elements of character which have made so eminent and so honored, him whom we, both as students ourselves and as instructors of others, are called to remember and to mourn.

Eulogies upon the character and work of the departed are common, and there is about them always a suspicion of exaggeration, which tends to weaken their real power; yet it is a natural impulse of the human mind and heart, belonging to every age and nation and finding utterance in every variety of human speech. But like all universal sentiments of our nature, it gains, under the light of Christianity, a higher meaning and a nobler aim; and it is in these aspects that we, as Christian educators, should consider the life and labors of Professor Torrey. Not merely should we celebrate his services to science, his devotion to his professional duties, or the honor and trust that he received; but we should look at once deeper and higher, and learn for our own profit also, the foundation and the crown of all this high excellence, in the Gospel of the grace of God.

The details of this notice have been gathered, in large measure, from the two excellent obituaries of Dr. Torrey that have appeared in the "Cap and Gown," of Columbia College, by his friend and colleague, Professor Henry Drisler, and in the "American Journal of Science and Arts," by his pupil and co-laborer in botany, Dr. Asa Gray.

Dr. John Torrey was born in the city of New York, in 1796, and his associations and interests through life were largely connected with the place of his birth. He came of honorable Revolutionary stock, his grandfather having been quartermaster, his uncle major, and his father ensign, in one of the light infantry regiments called "Congress's Own," raised in the city of New York. The regiment was at the battle of White Plains, and Dr. Torrey's father was in the rearguard in the retreat from that place; and having served with honor through the war and attained the rank of captain, he entered New York again upon Evacuation Day—the anniversary of which is still so much observed in that city. Among the many honors which Dr. Torrey received, the only one which he dwelt upon with the feeling of pride, was his membership in the New York section of the Order of the Cincinnati, to which he had thus a threefold right.

It was given to Dr. Torrey to serve his generation and his country in calmer and more peaceful times, but he was enabled to do it no less truly and faithfully than these honored ancestors. He lived nearly to fourscore years, but "his eye was not dimmed nor his natural force abated," and in all that long life no stain or shadow was suffered to fall on its simple uprightness and purity.

He was not a college graduate, having studied, prior to his professional course, only in the schools of New York and Boston. Choosing the medical profession—perhaps in consequence of his early developed taste for botany and chemistry—he entered the College of Physicians and Surgeons, the subsequent union of which with Columbia College gave him much close relation with that institution in his later life. His scientific fame begins to date from this period. In 1817, while still a student of medicine, he had already become one of the founders of the New York Lyceum of Natural History, a society whose subsequent work forms no small part of the record of scientific development in America. By the close of the same year, he had prepared and presented to the Lyceum, his first botanical work, a "Catalogue of all the Plants Growing Spontaneously within Thirty Miles of New York." This list enumerated 1,300 species, of which but 450 had been recorded by the few previous observers.

The next work in the same department was a more ambitious effort—no less than a classification of the flora of the northern and middle sections of the United States. Of this, only the first volume appeared—New York, 1824—the same year in which he was appointed to the professorship of chemistry in the Military Academy at West Point. This office he held until 1827, when he was elected professor of chemistry and botany in his Alma Mater, the College of Physicians and Surgeons. In 1826, he printed a compendium of the previously named work, and then, for reasons affecting the principles on which he had begun his labors, he abandoned the further prosecution of the task, and commenced anew. He had set out by adopting the artificial or sexual system of Linnæus, but being satisfied that the natural system, which had been for some years followed in France, and had been introduced into England and Scotland by Brown, Lindley, Hooker, and others, was preferable, he prepared the way for his future labors by introducing to the students of the science at home, "Lindley's Introduction to the Natural System of Botany." This work was printed in 1831, and Dr. Torrey subjoined to it an appendix of the North American genera of plants, arranged according to the same system, in which he had the honor of being the pioneer in this country.

Long before this, Dr. Torrey's name and labors had become well known, and his services to botany recognized by distinguished writers on the science abroad, and by foreign societies. He was early made a member of the Physiological Society of Lund, Sweden, of the Wernerian Society of Edinburgh, and of several others. Through his correspondence with earnest men engaged in similar pursuits, he was enabled to enlarge his own knowledge of the science and to increase his collections. He thus came more thoroughly prepared to the great work, which, in conjunction with his pupil, Dr. Asa Gray (then professor in the University of Michigan), he, after years of preparation presented to the public, and through which his name will be permanently associated with the history of botanical science on this continent. This great work, "A Flora of North America, containing abridged descriptions of all the known indigenous and naturalized plants growing north of Mexico, arranged according to the natural system," was published at New York, 1838–40, two volumes, 8vo.

From an early period in Dr. Torrey's scientific career, he had become the fortunate recipient of a large and constantly increasing amount of most interesting material, in the plants that were collected by explorers and by expeditions throughout various portions of our vast western territory, as well as in regions lying beyond our national boundaries, both north and south. Nor did this influx of material, for study ever cease to come to him, as long as his life was spared, and down to its very close.

Dr. Torrey's contributions to botanical science were not confined to these more elaborate productions; in various periodicals and journals of learned societies, he published many papers, which would form, if collected, several volumes, besides reports of the various land explorations of the United States government. His last extensive contribution to his favorite science was the botanical portion of the Natural History of the State of New York, in two volumes 4to, 1863, comprising full descriptions of all the indigenous and naturalized plants hitherto discovered in the State. He had been chosen State botanist upon the organization of the survey in 1836, and he discharged the onerous work of preparing the New York flora in a manner which no other State has at all equaled. In this undertaking he has become immortal in connection with the teachers and educators of New York, who all have access to, and most of whom are familiar with these two noble and beautiful volumes—the fruit of so much labor by a distinguished citizen of the State and lover of the science.

Dr. Torrey had, meanwhile, been elected to the chair of chemistry in the College of New Jersey, at Princeton. With his professorship in the city, and his labors in connection with the State survey, he was now busily engaged—all too much so for the prosecution of much important work in botanical discovery, which he would have been only too glad to carry out. As it was he accomplished a great amount of research, by assiduous devotion to study, occupying the evenings of his busy days with his herbarium and his library. This habit he maintained up to the closing years of his life, and in it we have the secret of the high attainment which he not only reached but maintained.

When the United States Assay Office was first established at New York, Dr. Torrey was selected by the secretary of the treasury as its proper head. This office, however, he resolutely declined, unwilling to assume the responsibility of the care of treasure. A less lucrative and more laborious position, that of chemist to the assay office, he accepted; and only laid down its exacting duties when his last daily reports were signed, upon the day of his death.

The character of Dr. Torrey, as a man, was one of which those who knew him best speak in terms of warmest interest and respect. A transparent kindliness, an exact faithfulness, a conscientious care; these were his leading traits. His was a bright and beautiful old age, rich with the memories of a long and active life, busy to the last with cheerful labors and studies, in a peaceful home, among his children, close to the college with which so much of his life had been identified, and surrounded by the collections and the library that he had gathered for so many years. To young men, especially to those interested in science, he was exceedingly cordial and helpful. No wonder that he was able to say, as he did about a year before his death, on returning from a visit to Florida, where some of his friends playfully spoke of his having gone to seek the far-famed Fountain of Youth, "Give me the Fountain of Old Age; the longer I live the more I enjoy life." No finer passage, as was remarked by one of his scientific friends, in an obituary notice, can be found in the De Senectute.

Though so prominently known as a botanist and also as a chemist, Dr. Torrey retained a strong interest in his original profession as a physician. He held that calling in very high esteem, and strove to impress upon the young medical men who passed under his instruction, his own lofty ideal of professional honor and dignity. In his service to the government in his latest years, the same high-mindedness marked him; and in a time so painfully abundant in breaches of trust and honor, he has left a record that is a bright example of purity.

It is a matter of peculiar interest as well as of peculiar delicacy to refer to the inward life, the religious character, of men who, like Dr. Torrey, shrank from any idea of high personal attainment; but "the memory of the just is blessed;" and for those who are still laboring in this world, amid many discouragements and fears, the example and influence of such a life are too precious to be hid.

Dr. Torrey was not only a man of high culture and high honor in the profession of medicine, not only a distinguished professor in several of our oldest colleges, not only one of the leading botanists of the United States, during a long and active life—he was also a humble, believing Christian. In the funeral discourse of his pastor, Dr. Thomas S. Hastings, this aspect of his character appeared in some highly interesting forms. He was a man of very deep humility and of a retiring spirit, which shrank from outward show or human applause; and could he have had the ordering of his own funeral service, he would have requested that no eulogies be passed upon his character, but that the only theme should be that of the grace of God. The sincerity and depth of his religious interest proved itself by the fact, not generally known, that he was wont to give private religious counsel to his students and to young men who were associated with him, and to pray for the young physicians who had gone forth from his instruction, and for his employes in the assay office. In all the questions, so perplexing to many, that arise between science and faith, he held a cheerful and unshaken confidence, both as to his own personal views and the ultimate issue for the world. Dr. Asa Gray, his early pupil, his eminent co-laborer and his sorrowful memorialist, in speaking of this point, says, "In this respect, as well as in the simplicity of his character, he much resembled Faraday." Would that all our scientific professors were such as he!

He received during his life, much honorable distinction among American scholars. Having given two articles on mineralogy to the first volume of Silliman's Journal, during the years that passed since he thus appeared before the world of science, he was twice president of the New York Lyceum, and once of the American Association for the Advancement of Science; besides being a member of the American Academy, and one of the incorporators of the National Academy at Washington. American science and scholarship, and the colleges of the State of New York, have lost a great and honored name; but in his high example and pure influence, " he, being dead, yet speaketh."

PROFESSOR WILLIAM C. CLEVELAND, C. E.

By Professor WILLIAM C. RUSSEL, A. M.

Professor William Charles Cleveland was born in Baltimore, July 5, 1839. His father was a schoolmaster of unusual attainments and great thoroughness, in that city, but in 1844, removed to Cambridge, Mass., and died when his son was about twelve years of age. The boy inherited from him only his love of science, conscientious accuracy and industry, and high tone of character. He attended the high school of the town, and was fitted by private instruction for the Lawrence Scientific School. There he spent seven years, graduating in 1862 with the highest honors, and afterwards assisting as instructor. When the war broke out, he offered his services to the government, and was employed as inspector of iron-clads. When peace was restored, he opened an office in Boston, as civil engineer, but in 1868 relinquished active business and became professor of civil engineering at Cornell University. Into his new duties he brought not only uncommon attainments but a high standard of excellence. He was a thorough mathematician and accomplished draughtsman, and he expected from his pupils equal thoroughness. He labored with them most faithfully, demonstrating at the blackboard, often for two hours without intermission, superintending their draughting, hearing recitations and explaining special difficulties to the very limit of his strength. He was often at his study table until two o'clock in the morning, and was obliged to begin the work of the next day exhausted. He was repeatedly warned that his persistence in this course must be fatal, but he always replied that he had undertaken to make his department equal to any in the United States, and he should never cease in the endeavor from any personal consideration. This unfortunate mistake could have but one result; he generously and recklessly but unwisely staked his life, and lost it. His strength was exhausted, his stamina used up. On the 9th of January, 1873, he caught cold, and in a week, under an acute attack of pneumonia, died at the age of thirty-three years and a half, leaving his widow and a little daughter unprovided for. He was a man of remarkable variety of accomplishments; painted landscapes in oil with great success, was a violinist, sculptured in clay, and was a botanist and geologist of thorough research. His bust of President Elliot, of Harvard University, in possession of James Russel Lowell, is full of genius. His lectures on geology made a deep impression on his hearers; and his collection of fossils was purchased, after his death, by the Agassiz Museum, at Harvard.

His accomplishments in art and science, however, were the smallest part of him. He was an earnest, conscientious, faithful man, devoted above all things to the truth, in word and deed; humble in appreciating himself; simple and childlike in his affections, and thoughtless of his interest where others were concerned. In the effort to do more than he had strength to do, anxious to elevate the standard of proficiency in his department, thoughtful only of securing thorough and excellent work, he sacrificed himself in the career of usefulness; not wisely, not profitably even for others, but most unselfishly and generously. Whom the gods love die young.

Milton Keynes UK
Ingram Content Group UK Ltd.
UKHW010027300124
436936UK00003B/67

9 783368 851132